About the Authors

Sharon Kendrick started storytelling at the age of eleven and has never stopped. She likes to write fast-paced, feel-good romances with heroes who are so sexy they'll make your toes curl! She lives in the beautiful city of Winchester – where she can see the cathedral from her window (when standing on tip-toes!). She has two children, Celia and Patrick and her passions include music, books, cooking and eating – and drifting into daydreams while working out new plots.

Twenty-four years ago, *USA Today* bestselling author **Judy Duarte** couldn't shake the dream of creating a story of her own. That dream became a reality in 2002, when Mills & Boon released the first of over sixty books. Judy's stories have touched the hearts of readers around the world. A two-time *RITA* finalist, Judy's books won two Maggies and a National Reader's Choice Award. You can contact her at judyduarte.com

Brenda Harlen is a multi-award winning author for Mills & Boon who has written over twenty-five books for the company.

Secrets Under the Mistletoe

SHARON KENDRICK

JUDY DUARTE

BRENDA HARLEN

MILLS & BOON

First Published in Great Britain 2025
by Mills & Boon, an imprint of HarperCollins*Publishers* Ltd
1 London Bridge Street, London, SE1 9GF

www.harpercollins.co.uk

HarperCollins*Publishers*
Macken House, 39/40 Mayor Street Upper,
Dublin 1, D01 C9W8, Ireland

ISBN: 978-0-263-41915-3

FSC www.fsc.org MIX Paper | Supporting responsible forestry FSC™ C007454

This book contains FSC™ certified paper and other controlled sources to ensure responsible forest management.

For more information visit: www.harpercollins.co.uk/green

Printed and Bound in the UK using 100% Renewable Electricity at CPI Group (UK) Ltd, Croydon, CR0 4YY

CHRISTMAS IN DA CONTI'S BED

SHARON KENDRICK

This book lovingly acknowledges the feisty and wonderful McCormick women – and most especially Joan and Eileen.

CHAPTER ONE

NICCOLÒ DA CONTI hated marriage, Christmas and love—but most of all he hated it when people didn't do what he wanted them to.

An unfamiliar feeling of frustration made him bite back a graphic expletive as he paced the floor of the vast New York hotel suite. Outside, skyscrapers and stars glittered against the deepening indigo sky, though not nearly as brightly as the Christmas lights which were already adorning the city.

But Niccolò was oblivious to the party atmosphere, or even to the onset of this most hated time of year. All he could think about was his only sister and wondering why she was being so damned *disobedient.*

'I do not want,' he said, sucking in a ragged breath in an attempt to control his rapidly spiralling temper, 'some tacky topless model acting as your bridesmaid. I have worked long and hard to establish a degree of respectability in your life, Michela. Do you understand what I'm saying? It cannot be allowed to happen, and what is more—I will not allow it to happen.'

From the other side of the glitzy New York hotel penthouse suite, Michela's expression remained unchanged as she looked at him.

'But you can't stop me from having her, Niccolò,' she said stubbornly. 'I'm the bride and it's my decision. That's the thing.'

'You think so?' His mouth hardened and he felt another hot flicker of rage. 'I could refuse to pay for this wedding for a start.'

'But the man I'm marrying is rich enough to carry the cost of the marriage if you decide to take such drastic action.' Michela hesitated. 'Though I'm sure you wouldn't want the world to know that Niccolò da Conti had refused to finance his only sister's wedding, just because he doesn't approve of her choice of bridesmaid. Wouldn't that be a step too far in the modern world—even for a man as old-fashioned as you?'

Niccolò flexed and then relaxed his fingers, wishing there were a nearby punch-bag on which he could vent his mounting frustrations. The world usually ran according to his wishes and he was not used to having them questioned. Bad enough that Alekto Sarantos was acting like some kind of prima donna…without having to cope with the bombshell that Alannah Collins was here.

His mouth tightened with anger as he thought about his sister and the sacrifices he had made. For too long he had fought to keep their tiny family unit intact and he was not prepared to relinquish control over her just yet. Because old habits died hard. He had faced shame and tragedy and had seen them off. He had protected Michela as much as was within his power to do so, and now she was about to enter into marriage, which would see her secure for life. His careful vetting of would-be suitors had paid dividends and she was about to marry into one of the most powerful Italian-American families in New York. She would have the sanctity he had always wished for her and nothing would be allowed to tarnish the occasion. Nothing and no one.

Especially not Alannah Collins.

Even the *thought* of the minxy little tramp made his body react in a complicated way he found difficult to control—and he was a man who prided himself on control. A powerful combination of lust and regret flooded over him, although his overriding emotion was one of rage, and that was the one he hung onto.

'I cannot believe that she has had the nerve to show her face,' he bit out. 'I can't believe she's even here.'

'Well, she is. I invited her.'

'I thought you hadn't seen her since I withdrew you from that appalling school.'

Michela hesitated. 'Actually, we've…well, we've stayed in touch over the years,' she said. 'We emailed and phoned—and I used to see her whenever I was in England. And last year she came to New York and we took a trip to the Keys and it was just like old times. She was my best friend at school, Niccolò. We go back a long way.'

'And yet you told me nothing of this before?' he demanded. 'You maintain a secret friendship and then spring it on me on the eve of your marriage? Didn't you stop to consider how it might look—to have someone as notorious as this tawdry exhibitionist playing a major role in your wedding?'

Michela lifted her hands up to the sides of her head

in a gesture of frustration. 'Are you surprised I didn't tell you, when this is the kind of reaction I get?'

'What does Lucas say about your connection with her?' he demanded.

'It happened a long time ago. It's history, Niccolò. Most people in the States haven't even heard of *Stacked* magazine—it folded ages ago. And yes, I know that a video of the original shoot seems to have found its way onto YouTube—'

'What?' he exploded.

'But it's really quite tame by modern standards,' said Michela quickly. 'If you compare it to some of the music videos you see these days—well, it's almost suitable for the kindergarten! And Alannah doesn't do that kind of stuff any more. You've got her all wrong, Niccolò, she's—'

'She is a tramp!' he gritted out, his Sicilian accent becoming more pronounced as his temper rose once again. 'A precocious little tramp, who shouldn't be allowed within ten feet of decent society. When will you get it into your head, Michela, that Alannah Collins is—'

'Whoops!' A cool voice cut into his angry tirade and Niccolò turned to see a woman strolling into the room without bothering to knock and suddenly his words were forgotten. If somebody had asked him his name right then, he thought he might have trouble remembering it. And yet for a moment he almost didn't recognise her—because in his memory she was wearing very little and the woman in front of him had barely an inch of flesh on show. It was the sound of her naturally sultry voice which kick-started his memory and his libido. But it didn't take long for his eyes to reacquaint themselves with her magnificent body—nor to acknowledge the natural sensuality which seemed to shimmer from it in almost tangible waves.

She was wearing jeans and a white shirt with a high collar, but the concealing nature of her outfit did nothing to disguise the luscious curves beneath. Thick black hair like lustrous jet hung over her shoulders, and eyes the colour of denim were studying him with a hint of mockery in their depths. Niccolò swallowed. He had forgotten the pale creaminess of her complexion and the rosiness of her lips. He had forgotten that this half-Irish temptress with an unknown father could burrow underneath his skin, without even trying.

As she moved he could see the glitter of a little blue dragonfly brooch gleaming on her shirt-collar, which matched the amazing colour of her eyes. And even though he despised her, he could do nothing about the leap of desire which made his body grow tense. She made him think of things he'd rather not think about—but mostly she made him think about sex.

'Did I just hear my name being taken in vain?' she questioned lightly. 'Would you like me to walk back out and come in again?'

'Feel free to walk out any time you like,' he answered coldly. 'But why don't you do us all a favour, and skip the second part of the suggestion?'

She tilted her chin in a way which made her black hair ripple down her back, like an ebony waterfall. But the smile she slanted at him didn't quite reach her eyes.

'I see you've lost none of your natural charm,

Niccolò,' she observed acidly. 'I'd forgotten how you could take the word "insult" and give it a whole new meaning.'

Niccolò felt a pulse begin to pound in his temple as his blood grew heated. But much worse was the jerk of lust which made his groin feel unbearably hard. Which made him want to crush his mouth down over her lips and kiss all those insolent words away and then to drive deep inside her until she screamed out his name, over and over again.

Damn her, he thought viciously. Damn her, with all her easy confidence and her louche morals. And damn those sinful curves, which would compel a grown man to crawl over broken glass just to have the chance of touching them.

'Forgive me,' he drawled, 'but for a moment I didn't recognise you with your clothes on.'

He saw the brief discomfiture which crossed her face and something primitive gave him a heady rush of pleasure to think that he might have touched a nerve and hurt her. Hurt her as she had once hurt his family and threatened to ruin their name.

But she turned the look into a bright and meaningless smile. 'I'm not going to rise to that,' she said as she turned instead to his sister. 'Are you ready for your fitting, Michela?'

Michela nodded, but her eyes were still fixed nervously on Niccolò. 'I wish you two could be civil to each other—at least until the wedding is over. Couldn't you do that for me—just this once? Then you never need see one another again!'

Niccolò met Alannah's speculative gaze and the thought of her smiling serenely in a bridesmaid gown made his blood boil. Didn't she recognise that it was hypocritical for her to play the wide-eyed innocent on an important occasion such as this? Couldn't she see that it would suit everyone's agenda if she simply faded into the background, instead of taking on a major role? He thought of the powerful bridegroom's elderly grandparents and how they might react if they realised that this was the same woman who had massaged her own peaking nipples, while wearing a dishevelled schoolgirl hockey kit. His mouth hardened. How much would it take to persuade her that she was persona non grata?

He flickered his sister a brief smile. 'Why don't you let Alannah and I have a word or two in private, *mia sorella*? And let's see if we can sort out this matter to everyone's satisfaction.'

Michela gave her friend a questioning look, but Alannah nodded.

'It's okay,' she said. 'You're quite safe to leave me alone with your brother, Michela—I'm sure he doesn't bite.'

Niccolò stiffened as Michela left the suite and his unwanted feeling of desire escalated into a dark and unremitting tide. He wondered if Alannah had made that remark to be deliberately provocative. He would certainly like to bite *her*. He'd like to sink his teeth into that slender neck and suck hungrily on that soft and creamy skin.

Her eyes were fixed on him—with that infuriating look of mild amusement still lingering in their smoky depths.

'So come on, then, Niccolò,' she said insouciantly. 'Do your worst. Why don't you get whatever is bugging you off your chest so that we can clear the air and give your sister the kind of wedding she deserves?'

'At least we are agreed on something,' he snapped. 'My sister does deserve a perfect wedding—one which will not involve a woman who will attract all the wrong kind of publicity. You have always been wild—even before you decided to strip for the cameras. And I don't think it's acceptable for every man at the ceremony to be mentally undressing the bridesmaid, instead of concentrating on the solemn vows being made between the bride and groom.'

'For someone who seems to have spent all his life avoiding commitment, I applaud your sudden dedication to the marriage service.' Her cool smile didn't slip. 'But I don't think most men are as obsessed with my past as you are.'

'You think I'm obsessed by your past?' His voice hardened. 'Oh, but you flatter yourself if you imagine that I've given you anything more than a fleeting thought in the years since you led my sister astray.' His gaze moved over her and he wondered if the lie showed in his face because he had never forgotten her, nor the effect she'd had on him. For a long time he had dreamt of her soft body and her sweet kiss—before waking up in a cold sweat as he remembered what he had nearly done to her. 'I thought you were out of her life,' he said. 'Which is where I would prefer you to stay.'

Calmly, Alannah returned his stare and told herself not to react, no matter what the provocation. Didn't matter how angry he got, she would just blank it. She'd seen enough of the world to know that remaining calm—or, at least, *appearing* to—was the most effective weapon in dealing with an adversary. And Niccolò da Conti was being *very* adversarial.

She knew he blamed her for being a bad influence on his beloved sister, so maybe she shouldn't be surprised that he still seemed to bear a grudge. She remembered reading something about him in the press—about him not being the kind of man who forgot easily. Just as he wasn't the kind of man who was easily forgotten, that was for sure. He wore his wealth lightly; his power less so. He could silence a room by entering it. He could make a woman look at him and want him, even if he was currently staring at her as if she were something which had just crawled out from underneath a rock. What right did he have to look at her like that, after all these years? Because she'd once done something which had appalled his straight-laced sensibilities—something she'd lived to regret ever since? She was a different person now and he had no right to judge her.

Yet it was working, wasn't it? The contempt in his eyes was curiously affecting. That cold black light was threatening to destabilise a poise she'd spent years trying to perfect. And if she wasn't careful, he would try to crush her. *So tell him to keep his outdated opinions to himself. Tell him you're not interested in what he has to say.*

But her indignation was beginning to evaporate, because he was loosening the top button of his shirt and drawing attention to his body. Was he doing that on purpose? she wondered weakly, hating the way her stomach had suddenly turned to liquid. Was he deliberately reminding her of a potent sexuality which had once blown her away?

She became aware that her heart was pounding like mad and that her cheeks had grown hot. She might not like him. She might consider him the most controlling person she'd ever met—but that didn't stop her from wanting him in a way she'd never wanted anyone else. Didn't seem to matter how many times she tried to block out what had happened, or tried to play it down—it made no difference. All they'd shared had been one dance and one kiss—but it had been the most erotic experience of her life and she'd never forgotten it. It had made every other man she'd met seem as insubstantial as a shadow when the fierce midday sun moved over it. It had made every other kiss seem about as exciting as kissing your teddy bear.

She ran her gaze over him, wishing he were one of those men who had developed a soft paunch in the intervening years, or that his jaw had grown slack and jowly. But not Niccolò. No way. He still had the kind of powerful physique which looked as if he could fell a tree with the single stroke of an axe. He still had the kind of looks which made people turn their heads and stare. His rugged features stopped short of being classically beautiful, but his lips looked as if they had been made with kissing in mind—even if their soft sensuality was at odds with the hostile glitter in his eyes.

She hadn't seen him for ten years and ten years could be a lifetime. In that time she'd achieved a notoriety she couldn't seem to shake off, no matter how much she tried. She'd grown used to men treating her as an object—their eyes fixed firmly on her generous breasts whenever they were talking to her.

In those ten years she'd seen her mother get sick

and die and had woken up the day after the funeral to realise she was completely alone in the world. And that had been when she'd sat down and taken stock of her life. She'd realised that she had to walk away and leave the tawdry world of glamour modelling behind. She had reached out to try something new and it hadn't been easy, but she had tried. She was still trying—still dreaming of the big break, just like everyone else. Still trying to bolster up her fragile ego and hold her head up high and make out she was strong and proud, even if inside she sometimes felt as lost and frightened as a little girl. She'd made a lot of mistakes, but she'd paid for every one of them—and she wasn't going to let Niccolò da Conti dismiss her as if she were of no consequence.

And suddenly, she was finding it difficult to do 'calm', when he was staring at her in that contemptuous way. A flicker of rebellion sparked inside her as she met his disdainful gaze.

'While you, of course, are whiter than the driven snow?' she questioned sarcastically. 'The last thing I read was that you were dating some Norwegian banker, who you then dumped in the most horrible way possible. Apparently, you have a reputation for doing that, Niccolò. The article quoted her as saying how cruel you'd been—though I guess that shouldn't have really surprised me.'

'I prefer to think of it as honesty rather than cruelty, Alannah,' he answered carelessly. 'Some women just can't accept that a relationship has run its natural course and I'm afraid Lise was one of them. But it's interesting to know you've been keeping tabs on me all this time.' He gave her a coolly mocking smile. 'I guess single billionaires must have a certain appeal to women like you, who would do pretty much anything for money. Tell me, do you track their progress as a gambler would study the form of the most promising horses in the field? Is that how it works?'

Alannah tensed. Now he'd made it sound as if she'd been *stalking* him. He was trying to make her feel bad about herself *and she wasn't going to let him.* 'Now who's flattering themselves?' she said. 'You're best friends with the Sultan of Qurhah, aren't you? And if you go out for dinner with royalty, then the photos tend to make it into the tabloids—along with speculation about why your date was seen sobbing outside your apartment the following morning. So please don't lecture me on morality, Niccolò—when you know nothing of my life.'

'And I would prefer to keep it that way,' he said. 'In fact, I'd like to keep you as far away from any member of the da Conti family as possible. So why don't we get down to business?'

She blinked at him, momentarily disconcerted. 'Business?'

'Sure. Don't look so startled—you're a big girl now, Alannah. You know how these things work. You and I need to have a little talk and we might as well do it in some degree of comfort.' He waved his hand in the direction of the cocktail cabinet which stood at the far end of the glittering hotel suite. 'Would you like a drink? Don't good-time girls always go for champagne? I can't guarantee a high-heeled shoe for you to sip it from, but I can vouch for an extremely good vintage.'

Don't rise to it, she told herself, before fixing a

weary smile to her lips. 'I hate to challenge your stereotype, but I'm not crazy about champagne and even if I was I certainly wouldn't want to drink it with you. That might imply a cordiality we both know doesn't exist. So why don't you say whatever it is you're determined to say? And then we can end this conversation as quickly as possible so that I can concentrate on fitting Michela's wedding gown.'

He didn't answer for a moment, but instead leaned back against one of the giant sofas and looked at her, his arms folded across his broad chest. Yet for all his supposedly casual stance, Alannah felt a chill of foreboding as his eyes met hers. There was a patina of power surrounding him which she hadn't noticed in that long-ago nightclub. There was a hardness about him which you didn't find in your average man. Suddenly he looked formidable—as if he was determined to remind her just who she was dealing with.

'I think we both know a simple way to resolve this,' he said softly. 'All you have to do is step out of the spotlight right now. Do that and there will be no problem. Michela is about to marry a very powerful man. She is about to take on an important role as a new wife. In time, she hopes to have children and her friends will be role models to them. And…'

'And?' she questioned, but she knew what was coming. It was crystal clear from the look on his face.

'You are not an appropriate role model,' he said. 'You're not the kind of woman I want fraternising with my nephews and nieces.'

Her heart was beating very fast. 'Don't you dare judge me,' she said, but her voice wasn't quite steady.

'Then why not make it easy for yourself? Tell Michela you've changed your mind about acting as her bridesmaid.'

'Too late!' Forcing herself to stay strong, she held up her palms in front of her, like a policeman stepping into the road to stop the traffic. 'I've made my own dress, which is currently swathed in plastic in my room, waiting for me to put it on just before noon tomorrow. I'm wearing scarlet silk to emphasise the wedding's winter theme,' she added chattily.

'But it's not going to happen,' he said repressively. 'Do you really think I would let it?'

For a moment Alannah felt another shimmer of doubt flicker into the equation. The quiet resolution of his voice scared her and so did the forthright expression in his eyes. Somehow he was making her feel…vulnerable. *And she wasn't going to let that happen.* Because she didn't do vulnerable. Not any more. Vulnerable got you nowhere. It made you fall down when life landed one of its killer punches and think you'd never be able to get back up again. It made you easy prey to powerful predators like Niccolò da Conti. 'How wicked you make me sound,' she said.

'Not wicked,' he corrected silkily. 'Just misguided, out-of-control and sexually precocious. And I don't want any publicity generated by the presence of *Stacked* magazine's most popular pin-up.'

'But nobody—'

'Michela has already mistakenly tried to tell me that nobody will know,' he interrupted impatiently. 'But they will. The magazines you stripped for have become collectors' items and back issues now change hands for thousands of dollars. And I've just been informed that a film of you has made its way onto YouTube, raising your public profile even further. It doesn't matter what you wear or what you don't wear—you still have the kind of body which occupies a fertile part of the male imagination. Men still look at you and find themselves thinking of one thing—and only one thing.'

Alannah tried not to cringe, but unfortunately his words struck home. Clever, cruel Niccolò had—unwittingly or not—tapped into her biggest insecurity. He made her feel like an object. Like a *thing*. Not a woman at all, but some two-dimensional image in a magazine—put there simply for men to lust over.

The person she was now wouldn't dream of letting her nipples peek out from behind her splayed fingers, while she pouted at the camera. These days she would rather die than hook her thumbs in her panties and thrust her pelvis in the direction of the lens. *But she'd needed to do it, for all kinds of reasons. Reasons the uptight Niccolò da Conti wouldn't understand in a million years.*

'You were *notorious*, Alannah,' he continued. 'And that kind of notoriety doesn't just go away. It sticks like mud.'

She looked at him in despair. He was telling *her* that? Didn't he realise that she'd been living with the consequences of that job ever since? No, of course he didn't. He saw what he wanted to see and no more—he didn't have the imagination to put himself in someone else's shoes and think what their life might be like. He was protected by his wealth and position and his arrogance.

She wanted to go up and shake *him* and tell him

to think outside the box. To wipe that judgemental look from his face and to start seeing her as a person, instead of someone who'd once behaved rashly. She could see exactly why Michela had been so scared of him when they'd been at school together. Was it any wonder that the Italian girl had rebelled from the moment he'd dropped her off at the exclusive Swiss finishing school where Alannah's mother had worked as school matron?

'The most important thing for me,' she said slowly, 'is that Michela wants me there. It's her day and she's the bride. So, short of tying me up and kidnapping me—I intend to be there tomorrow.'

'Unless we come to some kind of mutually beneficial arrangement,' he said.

'Oh?' She tilted her head. 'Tell me more.'

'Oh, come on, Alannah.' He smiled. 'You're a streetwise woman. You've been around. There must be something in your life that you'd…*like*.'

'Something in my life that I'd like?' she repeated. 'You mean like a cure for the common cold, or an alarm that doesn't make you want to smash the phone every time you hear it?'

'Very amusing. No, nothing like that.' He paused, and his black eyes glittered. 'I am a very wealthy man—and I'm willing to make it worth your while to tell Michela that you've changed your mind.'

She stared at him in disbelief.

'Let me get this straight,' she said. 'You're offering me *money* to stay away from your sister and not be her bridesmaid?'

'Why not?' He gave a cold smile. 'In my experience, if you want something badly enough you can usually get it. The tricky thing is negotiating the right price—but that is something I should imagine you're very good at.'

'But that's…bribery.'

'Try thinking of it as common sense,' he suggested softly.

She was shaking her head. 'You know, Michela used to tell me how unbelievably controlling you were,' she said. 'And part of me thought she might have been exaggerating. But now I can see that every word was true.'

'I am not seeking your approval of my character,' he clipped out. 'Just think why I'm making you this offer.'

'Because you're a control freak?'

'Because Michela means everything to me,' he said, and suddenly his voice grew harsh as he remembered how he'd fought to protect his sister from the sins of their father. *And their mother.* He thought of their flight from Sicily—his mother pregnant with Michela and not knowing what lay ahead. Niccolò had been only ten, but he had been the one everyone had relied on. He had been the man around the house. And it was hard to relinquish that kind of role or those kinds of expectations…

'Michela is the only family I have left in the world and I would do anything for her,' he ground out.

'Except give her the freedom which a woman of her age has the right to expect?' she retorted. 'Well, I'm *glad* she's had the courage to stand up to you. To maybe make you realise that you can't keep snapping your fingers and expecting everyone else to just leap to attention. I'm not going anywhere until after the wedding. Better deal with it, Niccolò.'

Their gazes clashed and Niccolò felt the flicker of something unknown as he returned her stare. Oh, but she was a one-off. She took defiance to a whole new level and made it seem erotic. She made him want to take her in his arms and dominate her—to show her that he could not and would not be thwarted. He took a step towards her and a primitive surge of pleasure rippled over him as he watched her eyes darken. Because she still wanted him, he realised. Maybe not quite as much as he wanted her—but the desire he could read in her eyes was unmistakable.

And couldn't desire be the most powerful weapon of all? Didn't sex give a man power over a woman who wanted it?

'Why don't you think about what I've said?' he suggested. 'So that by the time I see you at the pre-wedding dinner later, you'll have had the sense to change your mind about my offer.'

Her eyes narrowed. 'But…'

He raised his eyebrows. Suddenly, she didn't look quite so defiant. Suddenly she looked almost unsure of herself. 'But?'

'I…' She shrugged her shoulders. 'It's just that… well, Michela said you were probably going to skip the dinner and that we wouldn't see you until tomorrow. Something to do with a business deal. Some new apartment block you've recently built in London.'

'Is that what she said?' He smiled. 'Well, not any more. I've decided business can wait, because something much more important has come up.' There was a pause as he looked at her and suddenly it was easy to forget the pressing needs of his billionaire clients and friends. 'What is it they say? Keep your friends close but your enemies closer. And I want you *very* close for all kinds of reasons, Alannah. You'd better believe that.'

CHAPTER TWO

ALANNAH PULLED UP the zip of her cocktail dress and stared at her pale-faced reflection in the mirror. She'd tried deep breathing and she'd done a quick bout of yoga, but her hands were still trembling and she knew why. Slipping on a pair of high-heeled shoes, she felt a wave of self-recrimination washing over her.

She thought about the things Niccolò had said to her earlier. The way he'd insulted her and looked down his proud, patrician nose. He'd been judging her in the most negative way possible, but that hadn't stopped her wanting him. She shuddered. Where was the self-respect she'd worked so hard to get back? She wondered what had happened to the cool, calm Alannah who wasn't going to let him get under her skin. How had he managed to puncture her self-possession with nothing more than a heated ebony gaze, which reminded her of things she'd rather forget?

Because memory was a funny thing, that was why—and sometimes you had no control over it. It flipped and jerked and jumped around like a flapping fish on the end of a hook. It took you to places you didn't want to visit. It could make ten years seem like a minute, or a minute seem like an hour.

It could put you back inside the skin of the person you'd once been.

And suddenly she was a teenager again. Seventeen years old and about to break the rules. Off to a party wearing the make-up which her Swiss finishing school strictly forbade, when really she should have been tucked up in bed in the dormitory. Wearing a tiny little micro-mini because she had been young and carefree—because back then she hadn't realised that a woman's body could become her enemy, instead of her friend…

By rights, someone like her shouldn't have been a pupil at the exclusive all-girls academy, tucked high in the beautiful mountains of Switzerland. She wasn't rich. She wasn't well-connected. She was just the illegitimate daughter of a single-parent mother who happened to be Matron at the fancy boarding school. And while this meant that Alannah got herself a great education, her 'charity' status meant that most of the girls simply tolerated her.

Michela da Conti was different. She was the only one who had held out the hand of genuine friendship—maybe because they had something in common, despite their rich-girl/poor-girl pairing. Alannah had spent her life rebelling against her super-strict mother while Michela had known real tragedy in her short life, plus she wanted to escape the strictures of her controlling brother, Niccolò.

Their youthful rebellion usually stretched no further than going out for illicit under-age drinks in one of the nearby bars after lights-out, or hanging out of the dormitory window, trying to inhale cigarettes without being sick.

But one night they heard about a party. A glitzy twenty-first birthday celebration for one of Niccolò's godsons—which was being held in one of the neighbouring mountain valleys.

'And we're going!' declared Michela excitedly.

Alannah remembered frowning. 'But what about your brother? Won't he be there?'

'You're kidding.' Michela had given a smile of satisfaction. 'Apparently, he's miles away in some obscenely expensive resort in Barbados, with his latest ghastly supermodel girlfriend. So we're safe.'

Alannah remembered walking into the crowded room, where coloured lights were flashing and music was blaring out loudly. Her borrowed silver minidress was clinging to her body like honey and she was getting lots of requests to dance, but she turned down every one because all the boys seemed too loud and too brash to be interesting.

She did her best to enjoy herself. She sipped a soft drink and admired the snowy view. Found a sleeping kitten on her way back from the loo and spent an enjoyable ten minutes stroking its furry tummy and wishing she could go home. When eventually she went back into the main room to find Michela to suggest they got a cab back to school, she couldn't find her anywhere. So she went and stood in a quiet corner of the room, losing herself in the shadows while everyone else partied—and that was when she saw him.

Him.

She had never forgotten that moment. It was like being struck by something with no sense of warning that it was coming. As if a velvet sledgehammer had hit her very hard. She was aware that he was tall and his hair was as black as the night sky. His eyes were black too—even from this distance she could see that. He was dressed in a dark suit, which made him look outwardly sophisticated, but she could sense something *primitive* about him. There was something predatory in the gleam of his eyes, which should have scared her as he began to walk towards her, with a sense of purpose in his step.

But she wasn't scared.

It was the most illogical thought she'd ever had, but at that moment she felt as if she'd been waiting all her life for him to arrive, and here he was.

Here he was.

He looked her up and down—as if it was his right to study a strange woman as he might study a car he was thinking of buying. But surely no car would make him smile like that—a smile which seemed to come from somewhere deep inside him, one that pierced her heart and made her knees feel as if they might have difficulty supporting her.

'I think you need to dance,' he said.

'I'm not a very good dancer.'

'That's because you've never danced with me. So come here and let me teach you how.'

Later, she would remonstrate with herself at the eagerness with which she fell into his arms. At the way she let him slide his hands around her back as if she'd known him for years. His hand moved to her hair and he started stroking it and suddenly she wanted to purr as loudly as that kitten had done earlier.

They said very little. The party was too loud for conversation and, anyway, it didn't seem to be conversation which was dominating Alannah's thoughts right then. Or his. Words seemed superfluous as he pulled her closer and, although the music was fast, they danced so slowly that they barely moved. Their bodies felt as if they were glued together and Alannah almost wept with the sheer pleasure of it all. Did he sense her enjoyment? Was that why he dipped his mouth to her ear, so that she could feel the warmth of his breath fanning her skin?

'You,' he said, his velvety voice underpinned with an accent which she recognised as Sicilian, 'are very beautiful.'

Wasn't it funny how some people you just seemed to spark off? So that she—inexperienced and raw as she was—didn't respond in a conventional way. She didn't blush and tell him she wasn't beautiful at all—but instead came out with something which sounded almost slick.

'And you,' she cooed back, looking straight into his black eyes, 'are very handsome.'

He smiled. 'A perfect match, then?'

She tipped her head back. 'Aren't you getting a little ahead of yourself?'

'Probably.' He leaned forward, so that her face was bathed in the dark spotlight of his gaze. 'Especially as we haven't even kissed. Don't you think that's a shocking omission, my beauty? So shocking that I think we ought to remedy it right now.'

She remembered the way her heart had crashed loudly against her ribcage. The way her mouth had dried with anticipation and the words had just come tumbling out of her mouth. 'Who says I'm going to kiss you?'

'I do.'

And he did.

In that shadowy corner of some anonymous house in the Swiss mountains, while outside flakes of snow floated past the window like big, white feathers, he kissed her.

He kissed her so intensely that Alannah thought she might faint. He kissed her for so long that she wanted him never to stop. It was like that pile of bone-dry sticks she'd once built on a long-ago holiday to Ireland—she remembered the way they'd combusted into flames the moment her aunt had put a match to them. Well, it was a bit like that now.

She was on fire.

His thumb brushed over her breast and Alannah wriggled with excitement. Because surely this was what she had been made for—to stand in this man's arms and be touched by him. To have him look at her as if she were the most beautiful woman in the world. He deepened the kiss to one of added intimacy and as he pushed his thigh between hers the atmosphere suddenly changed. It became charged. She could feel the flood of liquid heat to her groin and the sudden, almost painful hardening of her nipples as they pushed insistently against his chest. His breath was unsteady as he pulled away from her and there was a primitive emotion on his face which she didn't recognise.

'We'd better think about moving somewhere more comfortable,' he said roughly. 'Somewhere with a bed.'

Alannah never had a chance to reply because suddenly the mood was broken by some kind of commotion at the door. She felt him tense as Michela burst into the room with snow melting on her raven hair, and the guilty look on her friend's face when she saw Niccolò told its own story.

It was unfortunate that Michela was surrounded by the miasma of sickly-sweet marijuana smoke—and even more unfortunate when Niccolò's discreet enquiries the next day yielded up the information that both girls were already on a formal warning from the school. A small matter of the building's elaborate fire-alarm system having been set off by the two of them hanging out of a dormitory window, smoking.

Alannah would never forget the look of passion dying on Niccolò's face, only to see it being replaced with one of disgust as he looked at her. She remembered wanting to wither beneath it.

'You are my sister's friend?' he questioned incredulously. 'Her *school friend*?'

'Y-yes.'

'How old are you?'

'Seventeen.'

All the colour drained from his face and he looked as if she'd hit him. 'So Michela associates with a *puttana*, does she?' he hissed. 'A cheap little tart who puts out for strangers at parties.'

'I d-don't remember you objecting,' she stammered, stung into defending herself, even if deep down she felt she had no real defence to offer.

'No man objects when a woman offers herself to him on a plate like that,' he snapped.

The following day he had withdrawn Michela from the school and shortly afterwards the head teacher had summoned Alannah and her mother to her office. The head had clearly been furious at the prospect of having to say goodbye to Niccolò da Conti's generous donations to the school. She had told Alannah that her behaviour was unacceptable and her mother had pre-empted the inevitable expulsion by offering up her resignation.

'I'm not having my girl scapegoated by some rich financier,' she'd said fiercely. 'If you're going to heap all the blame on her, then this is not the kind of school for her.'

Of course, that was not an end to it—merely the beginning of a nightmare which put the whole Niccolò incident to the back of her mind.

But she'd never grassed up Michela and Michela had remained loyal to her ever since.

Her thoughts cleared and she saw her friend looking at her in the dressing-table mirror, her face still glowing from her pre-wedding facial, and Alannah sighed as she met Michela's questioning gaze. 'Maybe it would be better if I just bowed out, if it's going to cause a massive row between you and your brother. I'll just stand at the back like everyone else and throw rose petals. I can live with that.'

Michela glared as she put her hairbrush down.

'And let Niccolò have his own way? I don't think so. You've been the best of friends to me, Alannah—and I want you there. In fact, it'll probably do Niccolò good on all kinds of levels. I've never heard *anyone* speak to him the way you do.' She smirked. 'Nobody else would dare.'

Alannah wondered what Michela would say if she realised how much of her reaction to her powerful brother was bravado. That her feelings for him were… *complicated.* Would she be shocked if she knew the truth? That she only had to look at him to want to rip the shirt from his body and feast her eyes on all that silken olive flesh? That somehow he brought out a wildness in her which frightened her. Which she knew was wrong. And not only wrong…she knew only too well that those supposedly seamless sexual fantasies were nothing but an illusion.

She forced a smile. 'Okay, if you insist…it'll be business as usual. In which case, we'd better get going. I know it's traditional for the bride to keep her groom waiting on the big day, but not on the eve-of-wedding dinner!'

They took the elevator down to the iconic Midnight Room, where a large clock was set permanently at the witching hour. It was a spectacular party room designed by Emma Constantinides, the hotel owner's wife—and had won countless industry prizes since its opening. Circular tables had been set for dinner and the dark velvet ceiling was punctured with tiny lights, so that it resembled a star-filled sky. In the silvery light from hundreds of candles, people in evening dress stood drinking champagne as the scent of dark blue hyacinths wafted through the air.

A roar of delight greeted the bride-to-be's appearance and Alannah leaned forward to whisper in Michela's ear as people began to surge towards them. 'You go and sparkle,' she said. 'Anything you need me to check?'

Michela shook her head. She had already spotted Lucas on the opposite side of the room, talking to his mother. 'No. You go and sparkle too,' she said. 'And for goodness' sake, have a very large cocktail before we sit down to dinner. You look completely washed out, Alannah.'

But Alannah refused a drink. A drink on an empty stomach was a recipe for disaster and hers was already in knots. All she had to do was to get through the next thirty-six hours without crumbling, and surely she could do that.

And then she looked around the room and saw Niccolò—and every empowering thought flew straight from her mind as her gaze focused on him.

He was standing talking to a blonde whose sequined dress left little to the imagination and Alannah found herself thinking that he didn't seem to have a problem with *that.* The woman was gazing up at him and nodding intently, as if nothing but pearls of wisdom were falling from those cruel and kissable lips. There were other women clustering nearby, too—as if he were a dark shark and they were all hungry little pilot fish, just waiting for whatever scraps he cared to leave for them.

He lifted his head as if he had sensed her watching him—glancing across the room to where she stood. And suddenly it was too late to look away. His gaze captured hers and held it and it felt as if some fierce dark light were piercing through her skin. She felt sensitive. Exposed and raw. Terrified he would see through to the dark mass of insecurities hidden beneath her cool exterior, she tried to look away, but she couldn't. *She couldn't.* He seemed to be drawing her in by the force of his formidable will.

Desperately, she tried to compose herself. To concentrate on something other than how beautifully the dark suit caressed his hard body, but she failed at that, too. Instead she found herself staring at the snowy edge of his dinner-shirt and the way his olive skin gleamed like burnished gold above it.

He bent his head to say something to the blonde, who turned to look at her, and Alannah thought she saw faint surprise clouding the other woman's eyes. Had her uncomfortable stance given her away—making the woman guess that she was the outsider here?

She forced herself to turn away to talk to some of the other guests, who seemed genuinely charmed by her English accent, and for a while she allowed herself to relax before the bell rang for dinner. But a glance at the seating plan showed her that she was next to Niccolò—*of course she was,* for hadn't Michela made it clear that she wanted the two of them to get along better? She wondered when her friend was going to realise that it simply wasn't going to happen. Or at least, not in this lifetime. Her heart began thumping painfully as she made her way towards the top table.

She felt his presence behind her even before his shadow fell over the table. The palms of her hands were clammy and the race of her heart was thready, but somehow she managed to fix a wide smile to her lips as she turned to look at him.

'Niccolò!' she said brightly.

'Just the person you wanted to sit beside, right?'

'How did you guess?' Solely for the benefit of the other guests, she maintained that brittle rictus of a smile. 'You were right at the top of my list.'

But Alannah tensed as he leaned forward to kiss her on both cheeks, just as he would have done to any other female guest. She wondered if any other female guest would have reacted the way she did, with a pulse which was threatening to rocket out of control and a desire to tip her head up so that his mouth would meet hers, instead of grazing the innocent surface of her cheek. She found herself longing to reach up to touch that hard, chiselled jaw and to feel it scrape against her fingertips. She wanted to press her lips against his ear and kiss it. And how crazy was that? How could you want a man so much when you didn't even *like* him?

Stop it, she told herself as he pulled out her chair with an exaggerated courtesy, which seemed to be at odds with the mockery gleaming from his eyes. Did he know what kind of effect he had on her? Did he realise that her legs were weak and her breasts growing heavy? He sat down next to her and she could smell his warm, male flesh—as subtle and spicy as sandalwood—and all she wanted to do was to breathe it in. Reaching out, she picked up her champagne flute and took a gulp.

She could feel him watching as she drank the cold, fizzy wine but the champagne tasted as sour as a remedy you might take for an upset stomach. She put down her glass and looked at him, because they couldn't go on like this. Not with a whole day and a half to get through.

'I think Michela has sat us together deliberately,' she said.

He raised his eyebrows. 'Because?'

'I think she's hoping that we're going to declare some sort of truce.'

'Why—are we engaged in some sort of battle?'

'Please don't be disingenuous, Niccolò. You know we are. We've done nothing but argue since we reconnected.' She shrugged. 'And while that seems to be what you seem to want—I'd prefer it, and your sister would prefer it, if we could manage to be non-confrontational. At least, in public.'

Niccolò met her denim-blue eyes and gave a small dissenting shake of his head—thinking how wrong she'd got it. Because battle was the last thing he wanted. His needs around Alannah Collins were much more fundamental. He might even have contemplated a more conventional route by asking her out on a date, if she hadn't been the kind of woman he despised.

Yet there was nothing of the precocious teenager or sexy glamour model about her tonight. The image she presented was almost *demure*. Her navy silk dress was high-necked and the hemline showed nothing more than an couple of inches of slender knee. A small, glittering brooch in the shape of a fluttering moth was her only jewellery. Her most magnificent assets—the breasts which had once so captured the imagination of the British public—were only hinted at and certainly not on show. All he could see was the occasional glimpse of a soft curve as the material brushed against them. He swallowed. Was she aware that it was just as provocative to conceal something, as to reveal it?

Of course she was.

Trading on her own sexuality had been her stock-in-trade, hadn't it? She knew everything there was to know about how to pull in the punters and leave them slavering for more.

Shaking out his napkin, he placed it in his lap and scowled, recalling the first time he'd seen her at his godson's birthday party.

He remembered looking in amazement at the silver dress, which had clung to her curvy body like melted butter, and thinking that he'd never seen anyone looking quite so alluring. Had he been frustrated? Too long without a woman? Unlikely. All he knew was that he hadn't been able to tear his eyes away from her.

The look which had passed between them had been timeless. The lust which had overwhelmed him had been almost tangible. He had never experienced anything like it in his life—not before, nor since. The hardness at his groin had been almost unbearable as he had danced with her. Something elemental had caught him in its grip and he'd felt almost…*lost.* The dance had been simply a formality—paving the way for their first kiss. He had kissed her for a long time, tempted by a need to pull her into a dark and anonymous corner and just *take* her. And even though he detested being out of control…even though his own history had warned him this was not the way to go—it hadn't been enough to deter him from acting on it.

He had been just about to drive her back to his hotel, when there had been some sort of commotion by the door. He remembered turning to see Michela giggling as she'd entered the room, accompanied by a group of boys. His *sister.* Large flakes of snow had been melting on her raven hair and her look of guilt when she had seen him had told its own story.

And that was when Niccolò had discovered that Alannah Collins wasn't some twenty-something party guest, but the teenage best friend of his only sister. A wild-child who had been threatening to ruin Michela's reputation and bring shame on the da Conti name, after he'd spent years meticulously dragging it from the mud.

Was it any wonder that he despised her?

Was it any wonder that he despised himself, knowing what he had nearly done to her?

What he still wanted to do to her.

He leaned back in his chair, paying little attention to the plates of smoked salmon which were being placed in front of them. 'Did you ever tell Michela what happened between us?' he questioned suddenly.

She stiffened a little before turning to look at him, her eyes narrowing warily. 'But nothing did happen.'

'Oh, come on.' He gave a harsh laugh. 'It might as well have done. It would have done, if my sister hadn't arrived. I've never had a dance quite so erotic as the one I had with you. It was a dance which was headed straight for the bedroom.'

'Oh, for heaven's sake—'

'Does Michela realise that you would have spent the night with me if she hadn't turned up when she did?'

'You can't know that.'

'Yes, I can. And so can you. Why don't you try being honest with yourself for once, Alannah?' He leaned forward and his voice roughened. 'I know enough about women to realise when they want a man to make love to them—and you were screaming out to have me do it to you that night.'

'Really?' She took a nervous sip of her drink.

'And you've avoided answering my question,' he persisted. 'What exactly did you tell Michela?'

There was a pause. 'I didn't tell her anything.'

'Why not?'

Alannah shrugged, reluctant to admit the truth—that she'd been too ashamed of her own reaction to want to acknowledge it to anyone and certainly not to her best friend. That she'd felt dirty and cheap. Michela had warned her that her big brother was a 'player'. That he changed his women nearly as often as he changed his shirts. She remembered the two of them agreeing that any woman who went out with a man like him was *sad*. But she'd nearly been one of those women, hadn't she? Because he was right. If Michela hadn't walked in right then, she would have…

Briefly, she let her eyes close. She'd been so in thrall to him that he probably could have taken her outside and taken her virginity pressed up against a cold and snowy tree. She had certainly been up for going back to his hotel with him.

She opened her eyes and looked at him. 'Why not? Because even though Michela has always thought you a total control freak, she absolutely idolised you—and I knew you were the only family she had. It wasn't for me to disillusion her by telling her that you'd been hitting on her best friend.'

'Hitting on her best friend?' He gave a cynical smile. 'Oh, please. Unfortunately, I didn't realise I was dealing with *jailbait* at the time. You kept that one crucial fact to yourself.'

'Is that why you got me expelled?' she said, without missing a beat.

He shook his head. 'I didn't mention your name when I withdrew Michela from the school.'

Her eyes narrowed. 'Are you serious?'

He shrugged. 'There was no need. I thought I was removing Michela from your bad example—what I didn't realise was that you were going to continue the friendship behind my back.'

Alannah ran her fingertip down over her champagne glass, leaving behind a transparent stripe in the condensation. 'But all that happened a long time ago,' she said slowly.

'I guess it did.' He leaned back in his chair. 'And since your role seems to be non-negotiable, I guess I'm just going to have to be nice to you.'

'Is that possible?'

'Me being nice?' He watched the golden flicker of candlelight playing on her pale skin. 'You don't think so?'

'Not really. I think it would be like someone hand-rearing a baby tiger and then expecting it to lap contentedly from a saucer of milk when it reaches adulthood. Naïve and unrealistic.'

'And nobody could ever accuse you of that.'

'Certainly not someone with as cutting a tongue as you, Niccolò.'

He laughed, his gaze drifting over fingers which he noticed were bare of rings. 'So what has been happening to you in the last ten years? Bring me up to speed.'

Alannah didn't answer for a moment. He didn't want to know that her life had imploded like a dark star when her mother had died and that for a long time she had felt completely empty. Men like Niccolò weren't interested in other people's sadness or ambition. They asked polite questions at dinner parties because that was what they had been taught to do—and all they required was something fairly meaningless in response.

She shook her head at the waitress who was offering her a basket heaped with different breads. 'I'm an interior designer these days.'

'Oh?' He waited while the pretty waitress stood close to him for slightly longer than was necessary, before reluctantly moving away. 'How did that happen? Did you wake up one morning and decide you were an expert on soft furnishings?'

'That's a very patronising comment.'

'I have experience of interior designers,' he said wryly. 'And of rich, bored women who decide to set themselves up as experts.'

'Well, I'm neither rich, nor bored. And I think you'll find there's more to the job than that. I studied fashion at art school and was planning to make dresses, but the fashion world is notoriously tough—and it's difficult to get funding.' Especially when you had the kind of past which meant that people formed negative judgements about you.

'So what did you do?'

'I worked for a big fashion chain for a while,' she continued, pushing her fork aimlessly around her plate. 'Before I realised that what I was best at was putting together a "look". I liked putting colours and fabrics together and creating interesting interiors. I spent a few years working for a large interiors company to gain experience and recently I took the plunge and set up on my own.'

'And are you any good?' he questioned. 'How come I've never heard of you?'

'I think I'm good—have a look at my website and decide for yourself,' she said. 'And the reason you haven't heard of me is because there are a million other designers out there. I'm still waiting for my big break.'

'And your topless modelling career?' he questioned idly. 'Did that fall by the wayside?'

Alannah tried not to flinch, terrified he would see how much his question had hurt. For a minute back then she'd actually thought they were sticking to their truce and talking to each other like two normal human beings. 'This is you being "nice", is it, Niccolò? Behaving as if I was something you'd found on the sole of your shoe?'

His eyes didn't leave her face. 'All I'm doing is asking a perfectly legitimate question about your former career.'

'Which you can't seem to do without that expression of disgust on your face.'

'Wouldn't anyone be disgusted?' he demanded hotly. 'Isn't the idea of a woman peddling her flesh to the highest bidder abhorrent to any man with a shred of decency in his bones? Although I suspect the end-product must have been spectacular.' There was a pause before he spoke. 'Alannah Collins *shaking her booty.*'

His last few words were murmured—and Alannah thought how unexpected the colloquialism sounded when spoken in that sexy Sicilian accent of his. But his words reminded her that what you saw wasn't necessarily what you got. Despite his cosmopolitan appearance and lifestyle, Niccolò da Conti was as traditional as they came. His views and his morals came straight from another age. No wonder his sister had been so terrified of him. No wonder she'd gone off the rails when she had been freed from his claustrophobic presence and judgemental assessment.

'Those photographs were stills,' she said tonelessly. 'I never *shook* anything.'

'Ah, but surely you're just splitting hairs.' He gave a dangerous smile, his finger idly circling the rim of his untouched champagne glass. 'Unless you're trying to tell me that cupping your breasts and simulating sexual provocation for the camera while wearing a school uniform is a respectable job for a woman?'

Alannah managed to twist a sliver of smoked salmon onto the end of her fork, but the food never made it to her mouth. 'Shall I tell you why I did that job?'

'Easy money, I'm guessing.'

She put the fork back down. Oh, what was the point? she thought tiredly. He didn't *care* what had motivated her. He had judged her—he was still judging her—on the person she appeared to be. Someone who had danced too intimately with a stranger at a party. Someone who had gone off the rails with his beloved sister. Someone who had discovered that the only way to keep hope alive had been by taking off her clothes…

Who could blame him for despising her—for not realising that she was so much more than that?

She dabbed at her lips with her napkin. 'On second thoughts, I don't think polite interaction is going to be possible after all. There's actually too much history between us.'

'Or not enough?' he challenged and suddenly his voice grew silky. 'Don't you think it might be a good idea to forge some new memories, Alannah? Something which might cancel out all the frustrations of the past?'

Alannah stiffened. Was he suggesting what she *thought* he was suggesting? Was he *flirting* with her? She swallowed. And if he were? If he were, she needed to nip it in the bud. To show him she respected herself and her body.

She slanted him a smile. 'I don't think that's going to happen. I think we need to avoid each other as much as possible. We'll support Michela all the way and try not to let our mutual animosity show, but nothing more than that. So why don't you do me a favour and talk to the woman on your other side? She's been trying to get your attention since you first sat down and she's very beautiful.' She picked up her wine glass and took a sip, her eyes surveying him coolly over the rim. 'I'm surprised you hadn't noticed that, Niccolò.'

CHAPTER THREE

It was the worst night he'd had in a long time, or maybe it was just that Niccolò couldn't remember ever losing sleep over a woman before. He lay tossing and turning in the king-size bed of his hotel room, trying to convince himself that Alannah had been right and the less time they spent together, the better. But every time he thought about distancing himself from those denim-blue eyes and that pouting, provocative mouth he felt an uncomfortable ache deep inside him.

What was the matter with him?

Kicking away the rumpled sheet, he told himself she wasn't his kind of woman—that she represented everything he despised in a sometimes trashy and disposable society.

Abandoning all further attempts to sleep, he dealt with his emails and spoke to his assistant in London, who informed him that Alekto Sarantos was still unhappy with the interior of the penthouse suite. The Greek billionaire had let it be known that the apartment's design was too 'bland' for his tastes and, despite a close association going back years, he was now considering pulling out of the deal and buying in Paris instead. Niccolò silently cursed his temperamental friend as he terminated the phone-call and wondered how soon he could decently leave after the wedding to return to work.

Pulling on his gym gear, he went for a run in Central Park, where the bare trees were etched dramatically against the winter sky. Despite his restless night and the fact that little was in bloom, his senses seemed unusually receptive to the beauty which surrounded him on this cold winter morning. There were ducks and gulls on the lakes and woodpeckers were tapping in the trees. Other runners were already out pounding the paths and an exquisite-looking blonde smiled hopefully at him, slowing down as he approached. But he didn't even bother giving her a second look. Her eyes were glacial green, not denim blue—and it was that particular hue which had been haunting his sleep last night.

The run took the edge off his restlessness, even if it didn't quell it completely, and after he'd showered and dressed he found a series of increasingly frantic texts from his sister queuing up on his smartphone. The final one was followed by a wobbly voicemail message, demanding to know where he was.

He went along the corridor and knocked at her door—stupidly unprepared for the sight of Alannah opening the door, even though he'd known she was sharing a suite with his sister. He felt almost *high* as he looked at her and could feel the aching throb of longing which stabbed at his groin. She was wearing a denim shirt-dress which matched her eyes and a tiny ladybird brooch which twinkled red and black on the high collar. For a moment it occurred to him that she was dressed as sedately as a schoolteacher and he watched as a complicated series of expressions flitted across her face as she looked at him, before producing a smile which was clearly forced.

'Hi,' she said.

'Hi.' He tried his own version of that fake smile. 'Sleep well?'

She raised her eyebrows. 'You're here to enquire how I slept?'

No, I'm here because I'd like to take your panties down and put my tongue between your thighs. He shrugged. 'Michela has been bombarding my phone with texts. Is she here?'

'She's…' cocking her head in the direction of one of the closed doors behind her, she pulled a face '…in the bathroom.'

'Is something wrong?'

'She's broken a nail.'

He frowned. 'Is that supposed to be some kind of a joke?'

'No, Niccolò, it's not a joke. It's the finger her wedding ring will go on and everyone will notice. To a bride who's just hours away from the ceremony, something like this is nothing short of a catastrophe. I've called the manicurist, who's on her way up.'

'First World problems,' he said caustically. 'So everything is under control?'

'Well, that depends how you look at it.' She met his gaze and seemed to be steeling herself to say something. 'Her nerves aren't helped by the worry that you're going to lose your temper at some point today.'

'What makes her think that?'

'Heaven only knows,' she said sarcastically, 'when you have a reputation for being so mild-mannered and accommodating. Could it have something to do with the fact that you and I were at loggerheads throughout dinner last night, and she noticed?'

He raised his eyebrows. 'So what does she want us to do—kiss and make up?'

'Hardly,' she snapped. 'That might be stretching credibility a little too far.'

'Oh, I think I could manage to put on a convincing enough performance,' he drawled. 'How about you?'

So she *hadn't* been imagining it last night. Alannah stiffened. He really *was* flirting. And she was going to have to put on the performance of a lifetime if she wanted to convince him that it wasn't working.

She raised her eyebrows. 'So can I tell Michela that you're planning to be a good boy today? Do you think you're a competent enough actor to simulate enjoyment and behave yourself for the duration of the wedding?'

'I don't usually have to simulate anything—and I've never been called a *good boy* in my life,' he answered softly. 'But if Michela wants reassurance that I'm going to behave myself, then tell her yes. I will be extremely virtuous. And I will be back here at three, to take you both down to the wedding.'

Alannah gave a brief nod and her cool, careful smile didn't slip until she had shut the door on him, though her pulse was pounding loudly.

At least an air of calm had descended by the time the manicurist arrived to repair the tattered nail and the mood was elevated still further as Alannah helped Michela slide into her delicate white gown. Because this was *her* territory, she reminded herself fiercely.

She was proud of the dress she'd made for the bride and she wasn't going to let Niccolò da Conti whittle away at her confidence.

Her movements became sure and confident as she smoothed down the fine layers of tulle and soon she felt like herself again—Alannah Collins, who was living life according to her own rules, and ignoring the false perceptions of other people.

But the moment Niccolò arrived all that composure deserted her. She was aware of his piercing gaze as he watched her adjusting the floral circlet which held Michela's veil in place and it was difficult to keep her fingers steady. She could feel his dark eyes moving over her and the only comfort she got was by reminding herself that after this day was over, she need never see him again.

So why did that make her heart plummet, as if someone had dropped it to the bottom of a lift-shaft?

'You look beautiful, *mia sorella*,' he said, and Michela gave a smile of delight as she did a twirl.

'*Do* I?'

'Indeed you do.' His voice was indulgent. 'Lucas is a very lucky man.'

'Well, I have Alannah to thank for my appearance,' said Michela brightly. 'She's the one who made the dress. It's gorgeous, isn't it, Niccolò?'

Alannah wanted to tell her friend to stop trying so hard. To tell her that she and her brother were never going to achieve anything more than a forced civility. But she maintained the fiction necessary to soothe the bride's frazzled nerves by smiling at him in what she hoped looked like a friendly way.

'It is indeed a very beautiful dress,' he agreed

softly, his eyes gleaming out a silent message which she didn't dare analyse.

Alannah tried to relax as she handed Michela her bouquet and the three of them made their way to the Pembroke's celebrated wedding room, where the assembled guests were waiting. A harpist began to play and Alannah saw the sudden look of tension which hardened Niccolò's features into a grim mask as he gave his sister away to be married.

Maybe he just didn't like weddings, she thought.

She tried not to stare at him as the vows were made and to ignore the women who were clearly trying to catch his eye. And after the rings had been exchanged, Alannah tried to be the best guest she possibly could. She chatted to the groom's sister and offered to suggest some new colour schemes for her house in Gramercy Park. After the wedding breakfast, she took time to play with several of the frilly-dressed little girls from Lucas's huge extended family. And when they were all worn out, she lined them all up to twist their long hair into intricate styles, which made them squeal with delight.

By the time the tables had been cleared and the band had struck up for the first dance, Alannah felt able to relax at last. Her duties had been performed to everyone's satisfaction and the wedding had gone off without a hitch. Drink in hand, she stood on the edge of the dance-floor and watched Michela dancing in the arms of Lucas—soft white tulle floating around her slender body and a dreamy smile on her face as she looked up at her new husband.

Alannah felt her heart contract and wished it wouldn't. She didn't want to feel *wistful,* not today—

of all days. To wonder why some people found love easy while others seemed to have a perpetual struggle with it. Or to question why all that stuff had never happened to her.

'How come I always find you standing alone on the dance-floor?'

Alannah's heart clenched at the sound of Niccolò's Sicilian accent, but she didn't turn round. She just carried on standing there until he walked up to stand beside her.

'I'm just watching the happy couple,' she said conversationally.

He followed the direction of her gaze and for a moment they stood in silence as Lucas whirled Michela round in his arms.

'Do you think they'll stay happy?' he asked suddenly.

The question surprised her. 'Don't you?'

'If they are contented to work with what they've got and to build on it, then, yes, they have a chance. But if they start to believe in all the hype…' His voice grew hard. 'If they want stardust and spangles, then they will be disappointed.'

'You obviously don't rate marriage very highly.'

'I don't. The odds against it are too high. It's a big gamble—and I am not a gambling man.'

'And love?' she questioned as she turned at last to look at him. 'What about love?'

His mouth hardened and for a moment she thought she saw something bleak flaring at the depths of his black eyes.

'Love is a weakness,' he said bitterly, 'which brings out the worst in people.'

'That's a little—'

'Dance with me,' he said suddenly, his words cutting over hers, and Alannah tensed as his fingers curled over her bare arm.

They were a variation on the words he'd spoken all those years ago. Words which had once turned her head. But she was older now and hopefully wiser—or maybe she was just disillusioned. She no longer interpreted his imperious command as masterful—but more as an arrogant demonstration of the control which was never far from the surface.

She lifted her face to his. 'Do I get a choice in the matter?'

'No.' Removing the glass from her hand, he placed it on the tray of a passing waitress, before sliding his hand proprietorially around her waist and propelling her towards the dance floor. 'I'm afraid you don't.'

She told herself that she didn't have to do this. She could excuse herself and walk away. Because he was unlikely to start behaving like a cave-man by dragging her onto the dance-floor—not with all his new in-laws around.

Except that she left it a split second too long and suddenly it was too late for objections. Suddenly, she was on the dance-floor and his arms were round her waist and the worst thing of all was that she *liked* it. She liked it way too much.

'You can't do this, Niccolò,' she said breathlessly. 'It's over-the-top alpha behaviour.'

'But I just can't help myself,' he said mockingly. 'I'm an over-the-top alpha man. Surely you knew that, Alannah.'

Oh, yes. She knew that. A block of stone would

have known that. Alannah swallowed because his hands were tightening around her waist and making her feel there was no place else she would rather be. She told herself it would cause a scene and reflect badly on both of them if she pulled away from him. *So endure it. One dance and it will all be over.*

She tried to relax as they began to move in time with the music and for a while they said nothing. But it wasn't easy to pretend that it meant nothing to be wrapped in his arms again. Actually, it was close to impossible. His body was so hard and his arms were so strong. His unique scent of sandalwood and raw masculinity seemed to call out to something deep inside her—to touch her on a subliminal level which no one else had even come close to. She could hear the thunder of her heart as he lowered his head to her ear and even his voice seemed to flood over her like velvety-dark chocolate.

'Enjoying yourself?' he said.

She swallowed. 'I was before you forced me into this farce of pretending we have a civilised enough relationship to be dancing together.'

'But surely you can't have any complaints about what we're doing, *mia tentatrice*. Aren't I behaving like a perfect gentleman?'

'Not with…' Her words tailed away, because now he had moved his hands upwards and his fingers were spanning her back. She could feel their imprint burning through the delicate material of her bridesmaid dress and her throat constricted.

'With what?'

'You're holding me too tightly,' she croaked.

'I'm barely holding you at all.'

'You are a master of misinterpretation.'

'I am a master of many things,' came the silken boast, 'but misinterpretation wouldn't have been top of my list.'

She looked up from where she had been staring resolutely at his black tie and forced herself to meet the mocking light in his eyes. 'Why are you doing this?' she whispered.

'Dancing with you? Isn't it customary for the brother of the bride to dance with the bridesmaid at some point—particularly if both of them are single? Or were you holding out for the best man?'

'I'm not holding out for anyone. And I don't remember telling you I was single.'

'But you are, aren't you? And if you're not, then you might as well be.' He met her eyes. 'Because you are responding like a woman who hasn't been touched by a man for a very long time.'

She was tempted to snap back at him with indignation, but how could she? Because he was right. It *was* a long time since she had been touched by a man. It was a long time since she had danced with a man too, and it had never felt like this. Not with anyone. *It had only ever felt like this with him.*

'I don't understand what it is you want,' she said. 'Why you're dancing with me. Taunting me. Trying to get underneath my skin. Especially when you don't even *like* me—and the feeling is mutual.'

He pulled her closer. 'But not liking doesn't stop us *wanting*, does it, Alannah? Desire doesn't require affection in order to flourish. On the contrary, sometimes it works better without it. Don't you find that, *mia tentatrice*?' He stroked a reflective finger along her waist. 'That sex can be *so* much more exciting when there is a frisson of animosity between a man and a woman?'

Her skin still tingling from the lazy caress of his finger, she pulled away from him, trying to focus on the presumptuous things he was saying, rather than the way her body was reacting. 'Stop it,' she said weakly.

'But you haven't answered my question.'

'And I don't have to. Just as I don't have to stand here and take any more provocative comments. My duty dance is over.' With a monumental effort, she pulled away from him. 'Thanks for reminding me what a consummate player you are, Niccolò. And thanks for reminding me that ten years might have passed but you don't seem to have changed. You still treat the opposite sex as if—'

'I wouldn't generalise if I were you,' he interjected and now his voice was edged with steel. 'Because you have no idea how I treat women. And believe me when I tell you that I've never had any complaints.'

The sexual boast was blatant and Alannah suddenly felt as if her skin were too tight for her body. As if her flesh wanted to burst out of her bridesmaid dress. Her breasts were tingling and she knew she had to get away from him before she did something she regretted—or said something she would never live down. 'Goodnight, Niccolò,' she said, turning away and beginning to walk across the dance-floor. 'I think we can officially declare our truce to be over.'

Niccolò watched her go and felt frustration mount inside him, along with an even greater feeling of disbelief. She had gone. She had walked away with her head held high and her shoulders stiff and proud, and all his hunter instincts were aroused as he watched the retreating sway of her silk-covered bottom.

He swallowed.

He had played it wrong.

Or maybe he had just read her wrong.

She had been right. He didn't particularly like her and he certainly didn't *respect* her. But what did that have to do with anything? He still wanted her in a way he'd never wanted anyone else.

And tomorrow she would be gone. Leaving New York and going back to her life in London. And even though they lived in the same city, their paths would never cross, because their two lives were worlds apart. He would never know what it was like to possess her. To feel those creamy curves beneath his fingers and her soft flesh parting as he thrust deep inside. He would never know what sound she made when she gasped out her orgasm, nor the powerful pleasure of spurting his seed deep inside her. She might be the wrong type of woman for him on so many levels—but not, he suspected, in bed.

Still mesmerised by the sway of her bottom, he began to follow her across the dance-floor, catching up with her by one of the bars, where she was refusing a cocktail.

She barely gave him a glance as he walked up beside her.

'You're not leaving?' he said.

'I can't leave. At least, not until Michela has thrown her bouquet and driven off into the night with Lucas. But after that, you won't see me for dust, I promise.'

'Before you make any promises—I have a proposition you might like to hear.'

'I don't need to hear it,' she said flatly. 'I wouldn't need to be a genius to work out what you might have in mind, after the things you said on the dance-floor and the way you were holding me. And it doesn't make any difference.' She sucked in a deep breath and met his gaze. 'I'm not interested in having sex with you, Niccolò—got that?'

Niccolò wondered if she knew how blatantly her nipples were contradicting her words—but maybe now wasn't the time to tell her.

'But what if it was a business proposition?' he questioned.

Her eyes narrowed. 'What kind of business proposition?'

He looked at the waxy white flowers which were woven into her hair and he wanted to reach out and crush them between his fingers. He wanted to press his lips on hers. He wanted to undress her and feast his eyes on that soft, creamy body. In a world where he had managed to achieve every single one of his objectives, he suddenly recognised that Alannah Collins had been a residual thorn in his flesh. A faint but lingering memory of a pleasure which had eluded him.

But not for much longer.

He smiled. 'You said you were an interior designer and suggested I have a look at your website, which I did. And you *are* good. In fact, you are very good. Which means that you have a skill and I have a need,' he said.

Her mouth thinned into a prudish line. 'I don't think that your needs are the kind I necessarily cater for.'

'I think we're talking at cross purposes, Alannah. This has nothing to do with sex.' He slanted her a thoughtful look. 'Does the name Park View ring any bells?'

'You mean that enormous new apartment block overlooking Hyde Park which has been disrupting the Knightsbridge traffic for months?'

'That's the one.'

'What about it?'

'It's mine. I own it. I built it.'

Alannah blinked. 'But it's the most…'

'Don't be shy, Alannah,' he said softly as her voice tailed off. 'One should never be shy when talking about money. It's the most expensive building of its kind in the world—isn't that what you were going to say?'

She shrugged. 'I fail to see how your property portfolio could possibly interest me.'

'Then hear me out. A friend of mine—a brilliant Greek named Alekto Sarantos—is about to complete one of the penthouse apartments.'

She lifted her hand to adjust a stray petal on her headdress. 'And is there a problem?'

'*Sì*. Or at least—he certainly seems to think there is.' A note of irritation entered his voice. 'The problem is that Alekto doesn't like the décor, even though it has been overseen by one of the most popular designers in the city.'

'Let me guess.' She raised her eyebrows. 'Cream walls? Bowls of big pebbles lying around the place? Lots of glass and neutral-coloured blinds?'

He frowned. 'You must have seen photos.'

'I don't need to, but I'd recognise a bandwagon

anywhere—and every interior designer in the business seems to be jumping on it. Presumably this friend of yours doesn't do bland and that's why he doesn't like it.'

'No, Alekto doesn't do bland—in fact, he is the antithesis of bland. He described the décor to my assistant as a "tsunami of beige" and unless I can transform the place to his satisfaction before the Greek new year, then he says he'll pull out of the deal and go to Paris instead. It has become a matter of pride for me that he chooses London.' He gave a hard smile. 'And maybe that's where you could come in.'

'Me?'

'You want a break, don't you? I don't imagine they get much bigger than this.'

'But...' Somehow she managed to keep the tremble of excitement from her voice. 'Why me? There must be a million other designers itching to accept a job like this.'

His gaze swept over her like an icy black searchlight—objective, speculative and entirely without emotion.

'Because I like your style,' he said unexpectedly. 'I like the way you dress and the way you look. I always have. And if you can satisfy my exacting friend with your designs—then the job is yours.'

Alannah felt ridiculously thrilled by his praise, yet she didn't want to be thrilled. She wanted to feel nothing. To give nothing and take nothing. She met his dark gaze. 'And the fact that you want to go to bed with me has nothing to do with your offer, I suppose?'

He gave a soft laugh. 'Oh, but it has everything to do with it, *mia sirena*,' he said. 'As you said yourself, there are a million interior designers out there, but your desirability gives you a distinctive edge over your competitors. I cannot deny that I want you or that I intend to have you.' His black eyes gleamed. 'But I wouldn't dream of offering you the job unless I thought you were capable of delivering.'

CHAPTER FOUR

'NICCOLÒ WILL SEE you in just a moment, Alannah.' The redhead sitting outside Niccolò's office wore a silk blouse the colour of the lilies on her desk and when she smiled her lips were a neat coral curve. 'My name's Kirsty, by the way—and I'm one of Niccolò's assistants. Take a seat over there. Can I get you a coffee? Some tea perhaps?'

'No. I'm fine, thanks.' Carefully putting down her mood-boards, Alannah sank onto a seat, wondering if any of her reservations showed in her face. Whether her nerves or sick dread were visible to the impartial observer.

Ever since she'd left New York, she had listed all the reasons why she should say no to Niccolò's offer of work and during the cramped flight she had checked them off on her fingers. He was arrogant. Tick. He was dangerous. Double tick. He was also completely unapologetic about wanting to take her to bed. Only he hadn't even said *that* in a flattering way. He'd made it sound as if she was just something he needed to get out of his system. Like an itch. Or a fever. She bit her lip because his attitude brought too many memories flooding back. She hated men who regarded a woman as some kind of *object*, so surely self-respect and pride should have made her turn his offer down, no matter how lucrative?

But he was offering her work—legitimate work. His proposition had been like a cool drink when your throat was parched. Like finding a crumpled ten-pound note in your jeans before you washed them. She thought about the scarcity of jobs in her highly competitive field, and the ridiculously high mortgage on her tiny bedsit. She couldn't *afford* to turn him down—which was why she'd spent all weekend coming up with ideas she thought might appeal to a Greek billionaire who didn't like beige. And through it all she had realised that this was the vital springboard her career needed and she was going to grab at it with both hands.

She stared at the cream lilies on Kirsty's desk, trying to concentrate on their stark beauty, but all she could think about was the way Niccolò had stroked his finger over her when they'd been dancing at the wedding. Her heart began to pound. It had been an almost *innocent* touch and yet her response had been anything but innocent. The intensity of her feelings had shocked her. She had wanted him to peel the bridesmaid dress from her body and touch her properly. She had wanted him to kiss her the way he'd done all those years before—only this time not to stop.

And that was the problem.

She still wanted him.

She had done her best to quash that thought when she'd emailed him some suggestions. And had attempted to ignore her spiralling feeling of excitement when his reply came winging into her inbox late last night.

These are good. Be at my offices tomorrow at 7p.m.

It hadn't been the most fulsome praise she'd ever received, but it was clear he considered her good enough for the job and that pleased her more than it should have done. And hot on the heels of professional pride came a rather more unexpected feeling of gratitude. She had stared at his email and realised that, no matter what his motives might be, Niccolò was giving her the chance to make something of herself.

So she'd better show him that his faith had not been misplaced.

A buzzer sounded on Kirsty's desk and she rose to her feet, opening a set of double doors directly behind her.

'Niccolò is ready for you now, Alannah.' She smiled. 'If you'd like to come this way.'

Alannah picked up her mood-boards and followed Kirsty into a huge and airy office, blinking a little as she looked around her, because she'd never been anywhere like this before. She gulped. It was...*spectacular.* One wall consisted entirely of glass and overlooked some of London's more familiar landmarks and Alannah was so dazzled by the view that it took a moment for her to notice Niccolò sitting there and to realise that he wasn't alone.

Her first thought was how at home he looked in the luxury of his palatial surroundings. Long legs stretched out in front of him, he was reclining on a large leather sofa in one corner of the vast office—and opposite him was a man with black hair and the bluest eyes she'd ever seen. This must be Alekto Sarantos, Alannah thought, but she barely noticed him. Despite his unmistakable gorgeousness, it was Niccolò who captured her attention. Niccolò whose outwardly relaxed stance couldn't quite disguise the tension in his powerful body as their gazes clashed and held. She could read the mockery in his eyes. *I know how much you want me,* they seemed to say. And suddenly she wished that the floor could swallow her up or that the nerves which were building up inside her would show her some mercy and leave her alone.

'Ah, Alannah. Here you are.' Black eyes glittered with faint amusement as he looked her up and down. 'Not jet-lagged, I hope?'

'Not at all,' she lied politely.

'Let me introduce you to Alekto Sarantos. Alekto—this is Alannah Collins, the very talented designer I was telling you about.'

Alannah gave an uncertain smile, wondering exactly *what* he'd said about her. They were friends, weren't they? And didn't men boast to their mates about what they'd done with a woman? She could feel her cheeks growing slightly warm as she looked at Alekto. 'I'm very pleased to meet you.'

'Do sit down,' he said, in a gravelly Greek accent.

Alannah saw Niccolò pat the space beside him on the sofa—and she thought it looked a bit like someone encouraging a dog to leap up. But she forced herself to smile as she sat down next to him, unwinding the vivid green pashmina which was looped around her neck.

Alekto turned his startling blue gaze on her. 'So…

Niccolò assures me that you are the person who can replace the existing décor with something a little more imaginative.' He grimaced. 'Although frankly, a piece of wood could have produced something more eye-catching than the existing scheme.'

'I'm confident I can, Mr Sarantos.'

'No. *Parakalo*—you must call me Alekto,' he said, a hint of impatience hardening his voice, before giving a swift smile. 'I always like to hear a beautiful woman saying my name.'

Beautiful? No woman ever thought she was beautiful and that certainly hadn't been the effect Alannah had been striving for today. She'd aimed for a functional, rather than a decorative appearance—tying her hair back in a thick plait to stop it being whipped up by the fierce December wind. She had wanted to project style and taste as well as hoping her clothes would be like armour—protecting her from Niccolò's heated gaze.

Her Japanese-inspired grey dress bore the high neckline which had become her trademark and the fitted waist provided structure. A glittering scarab beetle brooch and funky ankle-boots added the unconventional twists which she knew were necessary to transform the ordinary into something different. It was the detail which counted. Everyone knew that.

'If you insist,' she said, with another polite smile. 'Alekto.'

Niccolò raised his eyebrows. 'Perhaps you'd like to show *Alekto* what ideas you have in mind for his apartment, while he concentrates on your undoubted beauty,' he suggested drily.

Trying to ignore the sarcasm in his voice, Alannah

spread out the mood-boards she'd been working on and watched as Alekto began to study them. Squares of contemporary brocade were pasted next to splashes of paint colour, and different swatches of velvet and silk added to the textural diversity she had in mind.

'We could go either traditional or contemporary,' she said. 'But I definitely think you need something a little bolder in terms of colour. The walls would work well in greeny-greys and muted blues—which would provide a perfect backdrop for these fabrics and textiles and reflect your love of the sea.'

'Did Niccolò tell you that I love the sea?' questioned Alekto idly.

'No. I searched your name on the Internet and had a look at your various homes around the world. You do seem rather fond of sea views and that gave me a few ideas.'

'Enterprising,' Alekto commented, flicking through each page, before lifting his head. '*Neh.* This is perfect. All of it. You have chosen well, Niccolò. This is a huge improvement. You have pleased me, Alannah—and a woman who pleases a man should always be rewarded. I think I shall take you out for dinner tonight, to thank you.'

'I'm sure Alannah would love nothing more,' interjected Niccolò smoothly, 'but, unfortunately, she is already committed this evening.'

'Really?' Alekto raised dark and imperious brows. 'I'm sure she could cancel whatever it is she is *committed* to.'

'Possibly.' Niccolò shrugged. 'But only if you are prepared to wait for your apartment to be completed, my friend. Time is of the essence if you expect it to be ready for your new year party. Isn't that what you wanted?'

The gazes of the two men clashed and Alekto's eyes suddenly hardened with comprehension.

'Ah,' he said softly as he rose to his feet. 'Suddenly, I begin to understand. You have always been a great connoisseur of beauty, Niccolò. And since good friends do not poach, I shall leave you in peace.' His blue eyes glittered. 'Enjoy.'

Alekto's chauvinistic innuendo took Alannah by surprise but she reminded herself that she was simply working for him—she wasn't planning on having him as her friend. Keeping her lips clamped into a tight smile, she stood up to let him shake her hand, before Niccolò led him into the outer office.

She waited until the Sicilian had returned and closed the door behind him before she turned on him.

'What was that all about?' she questioned quietly.

'What?' He walked over to his desk, stabbing at a button on his telephone pad, so that a red light appeared. 'The fact that your designs pleased him? Alekto is one of the wealthiest men I know. You should be delighted. The patronage of a man like that is more priceless than rubies.' He looked at her, his eyes curiously flat and assessing. 'Who knows what kind of opportunities could now come your way, Alannah. Especially since he clearly finds you so attractive.'

'No, none of that!' She shook her head—hating the way he was looking at her. Hating the way he was talking about her. 'I don't care that he's rich—other than it means I will have a very generous budget to work with. And I don't care whether or not he finds me attractive. I'd like it if for once we could keep my looks out of it, since I'm supposed to be here on merit.' She stared at him. 'What I'm talking about is you telling him I was busy and couldn't have dinner with him tonight.'

'Did you want to have dinner with him?'

'That's beside the point.'

He slanted her a look. 'I'm not sure what your point is.'

'That I don't want you or anyone else answering for me because I like to make my own decisions. And…' she hesitated '…you have no right to be territorial about me.'

'No,' he said slowly. 'I realise that.'

She narrowed her eyes warily. 'You mean you're agreeing with me?'

He shrugged. 'For a man to behave in a territorial way towards a woman implies that she is his. That she has given herself to him in some way. And you haven't, have you, Alannah?' The eyes which a moment ago had looked so flat now gleamed like polished jet. 'Of course, that is something which could be changed in a heartbeat. We both know that.'

Alannah stiffened as his gaze travelled over her and she could feel her throat growing dry. And wasn't it crazy that, no matter how much her mind protested, she couldn't seem to stop her body from responding to his lazy scrutiny. She found herself thinking how easy it would be to go along with his suggestion. To surrender to the ache deep inside her and have him take all her frustration away. All she had to do was smile—a quick, complicit smile—and that would be the only green light he needed.

And then what?

She swallowed. A mindless coupling with someone who'd made no secret of his contempt for her? An act which would inevitably leave him triumphant and her, what? *Empty*, that was what.

A lifetime of turning down sexual invitations meant that she knew exactly how to produce the kind of brisk smile which would destabilise the situation without causing a scene. But for once, it took a real effort.

'I think not,' she said, scooping up her pashmina from the sofa. 'I have a self-protective instinct which warns me off intimacy with a certain kind of man, and I'm afraid you're one of them. The things I require from you are purely practical, Niccolò. I need a list of craftsmen—painters and decorators—who you use on your properties and who I assume will be available to work for me—and to work very quickly if we're to get this job in on time.'

The impatient wave of his hand told her that painters and decorators were of no interest to him. 'Speak to Kirsty about it.'

'I will.' She hitched the strap of her bag further over her shoulder. 'And if that's everything—I'll get going.'

He nodded. 'I'll drive you home.'

'That won't be necessary.'

'You have your own car?'

Was he kidding? Didn't he realise that car parking costs in London put motoring way beyond the reach of mere mortals? Alannah shook her head. 'I always use public transport.'

'Then I will take you. I insist.' His eyes met hers

with cool challenge. 'Unless you'd prefer to travel by train on a freezing December night, rather than in the warm comfort of my car?'

'You're boxing me into a corner, Niccolò.'

'I know I am. But you'll find it's a very comfortable box.' He took his car keys from his jacket pocket. 'Come.'

In the elevator, she kept her distance. Just as she kept her gaze trained on the flashing arrow as it took them down to the underground car park, where his car was waiting.

He punched her postcode into his satnav and didn't say another word as they drove along the busy streets of Knightsbridge, where Christmas shoppers were crowding the frosty pavements. Alannah peered out of the window. Everywhere was bright with coloured lights and gifts and people looking at the seasonal displays in Harrods's windows.

The car turned into Trafalgar Square and the famous Christmas tree loomed into view and suddenly Alannah felt the painful twist of her heart. It was funny how grief hit you when you least expected it—in a fierce wave which made your eyes grow all wet and salty. She remembered coming here with her mother, when they were waiting for the result of her biopsy. When standing looking up at a giant tree on an icy winter night had seemed like the perfect city outing. There'd been hardly any money in their purses, but they'd still had hope. Until a half-hour session with a man in a white coat had quashed that hope and they'd never been able to get it back again.

She blinked away the tears as the car began to speed towards West London, hoping that Niccolò's concentration on the traffic meant he hadn't noticed. He reached out to put some music on—something Italian and passionate, which filled the air and made her heart clench again, but this time with a mixture of pleasure and pain.

Closing her eyes, she let the powerful notes wash over her and when she opened them again the landscape had altered dramatically. The houses in this part of the city were much closer together and as Niccolò turned off the main road a few stray traces of garbage fluttered like ghosts along the pavement.

'Is this where you live?' he questioned.

She heard the faint incredulity in his voice and realised that this was exactly why she hadn't wanted this lift. *Because he will judge you. He will judge you and find you wanting, just as he's always done.* 'That's right,' she said.

He killed the engine and turned to look at her, his dark features brooding in the shadowed light.

'It's not what I expected.'

Her question was light, almost coquettish. She wondered if he could tell she'd been practising saying it in her head. 'And what *did* you expect?'

For a moment Niccolò didn't answer, because once again she had confounded his expectations. He had imagined a pricey location—a fortified mansion flat bought on the proceeds of the money she'd earned from *Stacked* magazine. Or a cute little mews cottage in Holland Park. Somewhere brimming with the kind of wealthy men who might enjoy dabbling with a woman as beautiful as her.

But *this*...

The unmistakable signs of poverty were all around

them. The rubbish on the pavement. A battered car with its wing-mirror missing. The shadowy group of youths in their hoodies, who stood watching their car with silent menace.

'What happened to all your money?' he questioned suddenly. 'You must have earned—'

'Stacks?' she questioned pointedly.

His smile was brief as he acknowledged the pun. 'A lot.'

She stared down at her handbag. 'It was a short-lived career—it didn't exactly provide me with a gold-plated pension.'

'So what did you do with it?'

I paid for my mother's medical bills. I chased a miracle which was never going to happen. I chased it until the pot was almost empty though the outcome hadn't changed one bit. She shrugged, tempted to tell him that it was none of his business—but she sensed that here was a man who wouldn't give up. Who would dig away until he had extracted everything he needed to know. She tried to keep her words light and flippant, but suddenly it wasn't easy. 'Oh, I frittered it all away. As you do.'

Niccolò looked at the unexpected tremble of her lips and frowned, because that sudden streak of vulnerability she was trying so hard to disguise was completely unexpected. Was she regretting the money she had squandered? Did she lay awake at night and wonder how the hell she had ended up in a place like this? He tried and failed to imagine how she fitted in here. Despite all her attempts to subdue her innate sensuality and tame her voluptuous appearance, she must still stand out like a lily tossed carelessly into a muddy gutter.

And suddenly he wanted to kiss her. The street-light was casting an unworldly orange light over her creamy skin, so that she looked like a ripe peach just begging to be eaten. He felt temptation swelling up inside him, like a slow and insistent storm. Almost without thinking, he found himself reaching out to touch her cheek, wondering if it felt as velvety-soft as it appeared. And it did. Oh, God, it did. A whisper of longing licked over his skin.

'What...what do you think you're doing?' she whispered.

'You know damned well what I'm doing,' he said unsteadily. 'I'm giving into something which has always been there and which is refusing to die. Something which gets stronger each time we see each another. So why don't we just give into it, Alannah—and see where it takes us?'

She knew it was coming. Of course she did. She'd been kissed by enough men to recognise the sudden roughening of his voice and opaque smoulder of his black eyes. But no man had ever kissed her the way Niccolò did.

Time slowed as he bent his face towards hers and she realised he was giving her enough time to stop him. But she didn't. How could she when she wanted this so much? She just let him anchor her with the masterful slide of his hands as they captured the back of her head, before he crushed his lips down on hers.

Instantly, she moaned. It was ten long years since he'd kissed her and already she was on fire. She felt *consumed* by it. Powered by it. Need washed over her as she splayed her palms against his chest as his tongue licked its way into her mouth—her lips opened greedily, as if urging him to go deeper. She heard his responding murmur, as if her eagerness pleased him, and something made her bunch her hands into fists and drum them against his torso—resenting and wanting him all at the same time.

He raised his head, dark eyes burning into her like fire. But there were no subtle nuances to his voice now—just a mocking question in an accent which suddenly sounded harsh and *very* Sicilian. 'Are you trying to hurt me, *bella*?'

'I—yes! *Yes!*' She wanted to hurt him first—before he had the chance to do it to her.

He gave a soft laugh—as if recognising his own power and exulting in it. 'But I am not going to let you,' he said softly. 'We are going to give each other pleasure, not pain.'

Alannah's head tipped back as he reached down to cup her breast through the heavy silk of her dress. And she let him. Actually, she did more than let him. Her breathless sighs encouraged him to go even further, and he did.

He kissed her neck as his hand crept down to alight on one stockinged knee. And wasn't it shameful that she had parted her knees—praying he would move his hand higher to where the ache was growing unbearable? But he didn't—at least, not at first. For a while he seemed content to tease her. To bring her to such a pitch of excitement that she squirmed with impatience—wriggling restlessly until at last he moved his hand to skate it lightly over her thigh. She heard him suck in a breath of approval as he encountered the bare skin above her stocking top and she shivered as she felt his fingers curl possessively over the goose-pimpled flesh.

'I am pleased to see that despite the rather staid outfits you seem to favour, you still dress to tantalise underneath,' he said. 'And I need to undress you very quickly, before I go out of my mind with longing. I need to see that beautiful body for myself.'

His words killed it. Just like that. They shattered the spell he'd woven and wiped out all the desire—replacing it with a dawning horror of what she'd almost allowed to happen.

Allowed?

Who was she kidding? She might as well have presented herself to him in glittery paper all tied up with a gift ribbon. He'd given her a lift home and just assumed…*assumed…*

He'd assumed he could start treating her like a pin-up instead of a person. Somewhere along the way she had stopped being Alannah and had become a body he simply wanted to ogle. Why had she thought he was different from every other man?

'What am I doing?' she demanded, jerking away from him and lifting her fingertips to her lips in horror. 'What am I *thinking* of?'

'Oh, come on, Alannah.' He began to tap his finger impatiently against the steering wheel. 'We're both a little too *seasoned* to play this kind of game, surely? You might *just* have got away with the outraged virgin scenario a decade ago, but not any more. I'm pretty sure your track record must be almost as extensive as mine. So why the sudden shutdown at exactly the wrong moment, when we both know we want it?'

It took everything she had for Alannah not to fly at him until she remembered that, in spite of everything, he was still her boss. She realised she couldn't keep blaming him for leaping to such unflattering conclusions, because why *wouldn't* he think she'd been around the block several times? Nice girls didn't take off their clothes for the camera, did they? And nice girls didn't part their legs for a man who didn't respect them.

'You might have a reputation as one of the world's greatest lovers, Niccolò,' she said, 'but right now, it's difficult to see why.'

She saw his brows knit together as he glowered at her. 'What are you talking about?'

Grabbing the handle, she pushed open the car door and a blast of cold air came rushing inside, mercifully cooling her heated face. 'Making out in the front of cars is what teenagers do,' she bit out. 'I thought you had a little bit more finesse than that. Most men at least offer dinner.'

CHAPTER FIVE

EVERY TIME NICCOLÒ closed his eyes he could imagine those lips lingering on a certain part of his anatomy. He could picture it with a clarity which was like a prolonged and exquisite torture. He gave a groan of frustration and slammed his fist into the pillow. Was Alannah Collins aware that she was driving him crazy with need?

Turning onto his back, he stared up at the ceiling. Of course she was. Her *profession*—if you could call it that—had been pandering to male fantasy. She must have learnt that men were turned on by stockings—and socks. By tousled hair and little-girl pouts. By big blue eyes and beautiful breasts.

Had she subsequently learnt as she'd grown older that teasing and concealment could be almost as much of a turn-on? That to a man used to having everything he wanted, even the *idea* of a woman refusing sex was enough to make his body burn with a hunger which was pretty close to unbearable. Did she often let men caress the bare and silky skin of her thigh and then push them away just when they were in tantalising reach of far more intimate contact?

Frustratedly running his fingers through his hair, he got out of bed and headed for the bathroom.

If she hadn't been such a damned hypocrite when she'd slammed her way out of his car last night, then he wouldn't be feeling this way. If she'd been honest enough to admit what she really wanted, he wouldn't have woken up feeling aching and empty. She could have invited him in and turned those denim-blue eyes on him and let nature take its course. They could have spent the night together and he would have got her out of his system, once and for all.

He turned on the shower, welcoming the icy water which lashed over his heated skin.

True, her home hadn't looked particularly *inviting*. It didn't look big enough to accommodate much more than a single bed, let alone any degree of comfort. But that was okay. His mouth hardened. Mightn't the sheer *ordinariness* of the environment have added a piquant layer of excitement to a situation he resented himself for wanting?

Agitatedly, he rubbed shampoo into his hair, thinking that she made him want to break every rule in the book and he didn't like it. The women he dated were chosen as carefully as his suits and he didn't do *bad girls*. His taste tended towards corporate bankers. Or lawyers. He liked them blonde and he liked them cool. He liked the kind of woman who never sweated…

Not like Alannah Collins. He swallowed as the water sluiced down over his heated skin. He could imagine *her* sweating. He closed his eyes and imagined her riding him—her long black hair damp with exertion as it swung around her luscious breasts. He turned off the shower, trying to convince himself that the experience would be fleeting and shallow. It would be like eating fast food after you'd been on a health kick. The first greasy mouthful would taste like heaven but by the time you'd eaten the last crumb, you'd be longing for something pure and simple.

So why not forget her?

He got ready for the office and spent the rest of the week trying to do just that. He didn't go near Alekto's apartment, just listened to daily progress reports from Kirsty. He kept himself busy, successfully bidding for a new-build a few blocks from the Pembroke in New York. He held a series of back-to-back meetings about his beach development in Uruguay; he lunched with a group of developers who were over from the Middle East—then took them to a nightclub until the early hours. Then he flew to Paris and had dinner with a beautiful Australian model he'd met at last year's Melbourne Cup.

But Paris didn't work and neither did the model. For once the magic of the city failed to cast its spell on him. Overnight it had surrendered to the monster which was Christmas and spread its glittering tentacles everywhere. The golden lights which were strung in the trees along the Champs Élysées seemed garish. The decorated tree in his hotel seemed like a giant monument to bad taste and the pile of faux-presents which rested at its base made his mouth harden with disdain. Even the famous shops were stuffed with seasonal reminders of reindeer and Santa, which marred their usual elegance.

And all this was underpinned by the disturbing fact that nothing was working; he couldn't seem to get Alannah out of his mind. *Even now.* He realised that something about her was making him act out of character. There were plenty of other people whose style he liked, yet he had hired her without reference and only the most cursory of glances at her work. Governed by a need to possess her, he had ignored all reason and common sense and done something he'd sworn never to do.

He had taken a gamble on her.

He felt the icy finger of fear whispering over his spine.

He had taken a gamble on her and he never gambled.

He ordered his driver to take him to the towering block which rose up over Hyde Park. But for once he didn't take pride in the futuristic building which had been his brainchild, and which had won all kinds of awards since its inception. All he could think about was the slow build of hunger which was burning away inside him and which was now refusing to be silenced.

His heart was thudding as he took the elevator up to the penthouse, his key-card quietly clicking the door open. Silently, he walked through the bare apartment, which smelt strongly of paint, and into the main reception room where he found Alannah perched on a stepladder, a tape measure in her hand.

His heart skipped a beat. She wore a loose, checked shirt and her hair was caught back in a ponytail. He didn't know what he'd been planning to say but before he had a chance to say anything she turned round and saw him. The stepladder swayed and he walked across the room to steady it and some insane part of him wished it would topple properly, so that he could catch her in his arms and feel the soft crush of her breasts against him.

'N-Niccolò,' she said, her fingers curling around one of the ladder's rungs.

'Me,' he agreed.

She licked her lips. 'I wasn't expecting you.'

'Should I have rung to make an appointment?'

'Of…of course not,' she said stiffly. 'What can I do for you?'

His eyes narrowed. She was acting as if they were strangers—like two people who'd met briefly at a party. Had she forgotten the last time he'd seen her, when their mouths had been hot and hungry and they'd been itching to get inside each other's clothes? Judging from the look on her face, it might as well have been a figment of his imagination. He forced himself to look around the room—as if he were remotely interested in what she was doing with it. 'I thought I'd better see how work is progressing.'

'Yes, of course.' She began to clamber down the ladder, stuffing the tape measure into the pocket of her jeans. 'I know it doesn't look like very much at the moment, but it will all come together when everything's in place. That…' Her finger was shaking a little as she pointed. 'That charcoal shade is a perfect backdrop for some of the paintings which Alekto is having shipped over from Greece.'

'Good. What else?' He began to walk through the apartment and she followed him, her canvas shoes squeaking a little on the polished wooden floors.

'Here, in the study, I've used Aegean Almond as a colour base,' she said. 'I thought it was kind of appropriate.'

'Aegean Almond?' he echoed. 'What kind of lunatic comes up with a name like that?'

'You'd better not go into the bathroom, then,' she warned, her lips twitching. 'Because you'll find Cigarette Smoke everywhere.'

'There's really a paint called Cigarette Smoke?'

'I'm afraid there is.'

He started to laugh and Alannah found herself joining in, before hurriedly clamping her mouth shut. Because humour was dangerous and just because he'd been amused by something she'd said it didn't mean he'd suddenly undergone a personality transplant. He had an *agenda.* A selfish agenda, which didn't take any of *her* wishes into account and that was because he was a selfish man. Niccolò got what Niccolò wanted and it was vital she didn't allow herself to be added to his long list of acquisitions.

She realised he was still looking at her.

'So everything's running according to schedule?' he said.

She nodded. 'I've ordered velvet sofas and sourced lamps and smaller pieces of furniture.'

'Good.'

Was that enough? she wondered. How much detail did he need to know to be convinced she was doing a good job? Because no matter what he thought about her past, he needed to know she wasn't going to let him down. She cleared her throat. 'And I've picked up some gorgeous stuff on the King's Road.'

'You've obviously got everything under control.'

'I hope so. That is what you're paying me for.'

Niccolò walked over to the window and stared out at the uninterrupted view of Hyde Park. The wintry trees were bare and the pewter sky seemed heavy with the threat of snow. It seemed as if his hunch about her ability had been right. It seemed she was talented, as well as beautiful.

And suddenly he realised he couldn't keep taking his anger out on her. Who *cared* what kind of life she'd led? Who cared about anything except possessing her? Composing his face into the kind of expression which was usually guaranteed to get him exactly what he wanted, Niccolò smiled.

'It looks perfect,' he said. 'You must let me buy you dinner.'

She shook her head. 'Honestly, you don't have to do that.'

'No?' He raised his eyebrows in mocking question. 'The other night you seemed to imply you felt short-changed because I'd made a pass at you without jumping through the necessary social hoops first.'

'That was different.'

'How?'

She lifted her hand to fiddle unnecessarily with her ponytail. 'I made the comment in response to a situation.'

'A situation which won't seem to go away.' His black eyes lanced into her. 'Unless something has changed and you're going to deny that you want me?'

She sighed. 'I don't think I'm a good enough actress to do that, Niccolò. But wanting you doesn't automatically mean that I'm going to do anything about it. You must have women wanting you every day of the week.'

'But we're not talking about other women. What if I just wanted the opportunity to redeem myself?

To show you that I am really just a…what is it you say?' He lifted his shoulders and his hands in an exaggerated gesture of incomprehension. 'Ah, yes. A regular guy.'

'Of course you are.' She laughed, in spite of herself. 'Describing you as a regular guy would be like calling a thirty-carat diamond a trinket.'

'Oh, come on, Alannah,' he urged softly. 'One dinner between a boss and his employee. What's the harm in that?'

Alannah could think of at least ten answers, but the trouble was that when he asked her like that, with those black eyes blazing into her, all her reservations slipped right out of her mind. Which was how she found herself in the back of a big black limousine later that evening, heading for central London. She was sitting as far away from Niccolò as possible but even so—her palms were still clammy with nerves and her heart racing with excitement.

'So where are we going?' she questioned, looking at the burly set of the driver's shoulders through the tinted glass screen which divided them.

'The Vinoly,' Niccolò said. 'Do you know it?'

She shook her head. She'd heard about it, of course. Currently London's most fashionable venue, it was famous for being impossible to get a table though Niccolò was greeted with the kind of delight which suggested that he might be a regular.

The affluence of the place was undeniable. The women wore designer and diamonds while the men seemed to have at least three mobile phones lined up neatly beside their bread plates and their gazes kept straying to them.

Alannah told herself she wasn't going to be intimidated even though she still couldn't quite believe she'd agreed to come. As she'd got ready she had tried to convince herself that exposure to Niccolò's arrogance might be enough to kill her desire for him, once and for all.

But the reality was turning out to be nothing like she'd imagined. Why hadn't she taken into account his charisma—or at least prepared herself for a great onslaught of it? Because suddenly there seemed nothing in her armoury to help her withstand it.

She had never been with a man who commanded quite so much attention. She saw the pianist nodding to him, with a smile. She saw other diners casting surreptitious glances at him, even though they were pretending not to. But it was more than his obvious wealth which drew people's gaze, like a magnet. Beneath the sophisticated exterior, he radiated a raw masculinity which radiated from his powerful body like a dark aura.

They sat down at a discreet table but suddenly the complex menu seemed too rich for a stomach which was sick with nerves. Alannah found herself wishing she were eating an omelette at her own kitchen table rather than subjecting herself to a maelstrom of emotions which were making her feel most peculiar.

'What are you going to have?' asked Niccolò as the waiter appeared.

The words on the menu had blurred into incomprehensible lines and she lifted her gaze to him. 'I don't know. You order for me,' she said recklessly.

He raised his eyebrows before giving their order but once the waiter had gone he turned to study her, his black eyes thoughtful. 'Are you usually quite so accommodating?'

'Not usually, no.' She smoothed her napkin. 'But then, this isn't what you'd call *usual*, is it?'

'In what way?'

'Well.' She shrugged. 'You made it sound like a working dinner, but it feels a bit like a date.'

'And what if we pretended it was a date—would that help you relax a little more?'

'To be honest, it's been so long since I've been on a date that I've almost forgotten what it's like,' she said slowly.

He took a sip of water which didn't quite disguise the sudden cynicism of his smile. 'I find that very difficult to believe.'

She laughed. 'I'm sure you do—given your apparent love of stereotypes. What's the matter, Niccolò—doesn't that fit in with your image of me? You think that because I once took off my clothes for the camera, that I have men queuing up outside the bedroom door?'

'Do you?'

'Not half as many as you, I bet,' she said drily.

They were staring at one another across the table, their eyes locked in silent battle, when suddenly he leaned towards her, his words so low that only she could hear them.

'Why did you do it, Alannah?' he questioned roughly. 'Wasn't it bad enough that you were kicked out of school for smoking dope and playing truant? Why the hell did you cheapen yourself by stripping off?'

The waiter chose precisely that moment to light the

small candle at the centre of the table. And that short gap provided Alannah with enough time for rebellion to flare into life inside her.

'Why do you think I did it?' she demanded. 'Why do people usually do jobs like that? Because I needed the money.'

'For what?' His lips curled. 'To end up in a poky apartment in one of the tougher ends of town?'

'Oh, you're so quick to judge, aren't you, Niccolò? So eager to take the moral high ground, when you don't have a clue what was going on in my life and you never did! Did you know that when my mother handed in her notice, she never found another job to match that one—probably because the reference the school gave her was so grudging. Did you know that they got all their clever lawyers to pick over her contract and that she lost all her rights?'

His eyes narrowed. 'What kind of rights?'

'There was no pension provision made for her and the salary she got in lieu of notice was soon swallowed up by the cost of settling back in England. She couldn't find another live-in job, so she became an agency nurse—with no fixed contract. I had to go to a local sixth-form college to take my exams and at first, I hated it. But we were just beginning to pick ourselves up again when…'

Her voice tailed off and his words broke into the silence.

'What happened?' he demanded.

She shook her head. 'It doesn't matter.'

'It *does*.'

Alannah hesitated, not wanting to appear vulnerable—because vulnerability made you weak. But wasn't anything better than having him look at her with that look of utter *condemnation* on his face? Shouldn't Niccolò da Conti learn that it was wise to discover all the facts before you condemned someone outright?

'She got cancer,' she said baldly. 'She'd actually had it for quite a long time but she'd been ignoring the symptoms so she didn't have to take any unnecessary time off work. By the time she went to see the doctor, the disease was advanced and she was scared,' she said, swallowing down the sudden lump in her throat. They'd both been scared. 'There was nobody but me and her. She was only a relatively young woman and she didn't want…' The lump seemed to have grown bigger. 'She didn't want to die.'

'Alannah—'

But she shook her head, because she didn't want his sympathy. She didn't *need* his sympathy.

'Our doctor told us about an experimental drug trial which was being done in the States,' she said. 'And early indications were that the treatment was looking hopeful, but it was prohibitively expensive and impossible to get funding for it.'

And suddenly Niccolò understood. Against the snowy tablecloth, he clenched his hands into tight fists. *'Bedda matri!'* he said raggedly. 'You did those photos to pay for your mother to go to America?'

'Bravo,' she said shakily. 'Now do you see? It gave me power—the power to help her. The thought of all that money was beyond my wildest dreams and there was no way I could have turned it down.' *No matter how many men had leered in her face afterwards. No matter that people like Niccolò judged her and looked down their noses at her or thought that she'd be up for easy sex because of it.* 'My unique selling point was that I'd left one of the most exclusive Swiss finishing schools under rather ignominious circumstances and I guess I can't blame them for wanting to capitalise on that. They told me that plenty of men were turned on by girls in school uniform, and they were right. That's why that issue became their best-seller.'

Alarmed by the sudden whiteness of her face, he pushed the wine glass towards her, but she shook her head.

'It wasn't narcissism which motivated me, Niccolò—or a desire to flash my breasts like the exhibitionist you accused me of being. I did it because it's the only way I could raise the money. I did it even though I sometimes felt sick to the stomach with all those men perving over me. But I hid my feelings because I wanted to bring a miracle to my mother, only the miracle never happened.' Her voice wavered and it took a moment or two before she could steady it enough to speak. 'She died the following spring.'

She did pick up her glass then, swilling down a generous mouthful of red wine and choking a little. But when she put the glass back down, she had to lace her fingers together on the table-top, because she couldn't seem to stop them from trembling.

'Alannah—'

'It's history,' she said, with a brisk shake of her head. 'None of it matters now. I'm just telling you what happened. I used the rest of the money to put myself through art school and to put down a deposit on a home. But property is expensive in London.

That's why I live where I do. That's why I chose to live in one of the "tougher" parts of London.'

Niccolò put his glass down with a hand which was uncharacteristically unsteady as a powerful wave of remorse washed over him. It was as if he was seeing her clearly for the first time—without the distortion of his own bigotry. He had judged her unfairly. He saw how she must have fought against the odds to free herself from a trap from which there had been no escaping. He'd fought against the odds himself, hadn't he? Though he realised now that his own choices had been far less stark than hers. And although he hated the solution she had chosen, he couldn't seem to stop himself from wanting to comfort her.

'I'm sorry,' he said huskily. 'For what happened and for the choices you had to make.'

She shrugged. 'Like I said, it's history.'

'Your mother was lucky to have a daughter like you, fighting for her like that,' he said suddenly. He found himself thinking that anyone would be glad to have her in their corner.

Her head was bent. 'Don't say any more,' she whispered. 'Please.'

He stared down at the plateful of cooling risotto which lay before him. 'Alannah?'

'What?'

Reluctantly, she lifted her head and he could see that her eyes were unnaturally bright. He thought how pale and wan she looked as he picked up his fork and scooped up some rice before guiding it towards her mouth. 'Open,' he instructed softly.

She shook her head. 'I'm not hungry.'

'Open,' he said again.

'Niccolò—'

'You need to eat something,' he said fiercely. 'Trust me. The food will make you feel better. Now eat the risotto.'

And although Alannah was reluctant, she was no match for his determination. She let him feed her that first forkful—all warm and buttery and fragrant with herbs—and then another. She felt some of the tension seep away from her, and then a little more. She ate in silence with his black eyes fixed on her and it felt like a curiously intimate thing for him to do, to feed her like that. Almost *tender*. Almost *protective*. And she needed to remember it was neither. It was just Niccolò appeasing his conscience. Maybe he'd finally realised that he'd been unnecessarily harsh towards her. This was probably just as much about repairing his image, as much as trying to brush over his own misjudgement.

And he was right about the food. Of course he was. It *did* make her feel much better. She could feel warmth creeping through her veins and the comforting flush of colour in her cheeks. She even smiled as he swopped plates and ate some himself while she sat back and watched him.

He dabbed at his lips with a napkin. 'Feel better now?'

'Yes.'

'But probably not in the mood to sit here and make small talk or to decide whether or not your waistline can cope with dessert?'

'You've got it in one,' she said.

'Then why don't I get the check, and we'll go?'

She'd assumed he would take her straight back to

Acton but once they were back in the car he made the driver wait. Outside, fairy lights twinkled in the two bay trees on either side of the restaurant door, but inside the car it was dark and shadowy. He turned to study her and all she could see was the gleam of his eyes as his gaze flickered over her face.

'I could take you home now,' he said. 'But I don't want the evening to end this way. It still feels…unfinished.'

'I'm not in the mood for a nightcap.'

'Neither am I.' He lifted his hand to her face and pushed back a thick strand of hair. 'I'm in the mood to touch you, but that seems unavoidable whenever you're near me.'

'Niccolò—'

'Don't,' he said unsteadily. 'Don't say a word.'

And stupidly, she didn't. She just sat there as he began to stroke her cheek and for some crazy reason she found that almost as reassuring as the way he'd fed her dinner. Was she so hungry for human comfort that she would take anything from a man she suspected could offer nothing but heartbreak?

'Niccolò—'

This time he silenced her protest with the touch of his lips against hers. A barely-there kiss which started her senses quivering. She realised that he was teasing her. Playing with her and tantalising her. And it was working. Oh, yes, it was working. She had to fight to keep her hands in her lap and not cling onto him like someone who'd found themselves a handy rock in a rough sea.

He drew away and looked into her face and Alannah realised that this was a Niccolò she'd never seen before. His face was grave, almost…assessing. She imagined this was how he might look in the boardroom, before making a big decision.

'Now we could pretend that nothing's happening,' he said, as calmly as if he were discussing the markets. 'Or we could decide to be very grown-up about this thing between us—'

'Thing?' she put in indignantly, but his fingers were still on her face and she was shivering. And now the pad of his thumb had begun to trace a line across her lower lip and that was shivering, too.

'Desire. Lust. Whatever you want to call it. Maybe I just want to lay to rest a ghost which has haunted me for ten long years, and maybe you do, too.'

It was his candour which clinched it—the bald truth which was her undoing. He wasn't dressing up his suggestion with sentimental words which didn't mean anything. He wasn't insulting her intelligence by pretending she was the love of his life or that there was some kind of future in what he was proposing. He was saying something which had been on her mind since Michela's wedding. Because he was right. This *thing* between them wouldn't seem to go away. No matter how much she tried, she couldn't stop wanting him.

She wondered if he could read the answer in her eyes. Was that why he leaned forward to tap briefly on the glass which separated them from the driver, before taking her in his arms and starting to kiss her?

And once he had done that, she was left with no choice at all.

CHAPTER SIX

He didn't offer her a coffee, nor a drink. He didn't even put the lamps on. Alannah didn't know whether Niccolò had intended a slow seduction—but it didn't look as if she was going to get one. Because from the moment the front door of his Mayfair apartment slammed shut on them, he started acting like a man who had lost control.

His hands were in her hair, he was tugging her coat from her shoulders so that it slid unnoticed to the ground and his mouth was pressing down on hers. It was breathless. It was hot. It was…*hungry*. Alannah gasped as he caught her in his arms. He was burying his mouth in her hair and muttering urgent little words in Sicilian and, although her Italian was good, she didn't understand any of them. But she didn't need to. You wouldn't have to be a linguist to understand what Niccolò was saying to her. The raw, primitive sounds of need were international, weren't they?

He placed his hands on either side of her hips and drew her closer, so that she could feel the hard cradle of him pressing against her. He kissed her again and as the kiss became deeper and more urgent she felt him moving her, until suddenly she felt the hard surface of the wall pressed against her back and her eyelids flew open.

He drew back, his eyes blazing. 'I want you,' he said. 'I want to eat you. To suck you. To bite you. To lick you.'

She found his blatantly erotic words more than a little intimidating and momentarily she stiffened—wondering if she should confess that she wasn't very good at this. But now his palms were skating over her dress to mould the outline of her hips and the words simply wouldn't come. She felt his hand moving over her belly. She heard him suck in a ragged breath of pleasure as he began to ruck up her dress.

'Niccolò,' she said uncertainly.

'I want you,' he ground out. 'For ten years I have longed for this moment and now that it is here, I don't think I can wait a second longer.'

Niccolò closed his eyes as he reached her panties and impatiently pushed the flimsy little panel aside, because she was wet. She was very wet. He could detect the musky aroma of her sex as he slid his fingers against her heated flesh and began to move them against her with practised ease.

'Niccolò,' she whispered again.

'I want to see your breasts,' he said, moving his shaking fingers to the lapels of her silky dress and beginning to unbutton it. Within seconds two luscious mounds were revealed—their creamy flesh spilling over the edge of her bra. He narrowed his eyes to look at them. *'Madre di Dio,'* he breathed, his fingertips brushing over the soft skin. 'In the flesh it is even better. You have the most beautiful body I have ever seen.'

And suddenly he knew he really couldn't wait a second longer. Besides, she seemed more than ready for him. He felt as if something had taken hold of him and made him into someone he didn't recognise. As if this wasn't him at all but an imposter who'd entered his body. Unsteadily, he unzipped himself and he wanted to explode even before he positioned himself against her honeyed warmth.

She went very still as he entered her and for a moment he paused, afraid that he might come straight away—and when had *that* ever happened? But somehow he managed to keep it together, drawing in a deep breath and expelling it on another shuddering sigh as he began to move.

One hand was spread over her bare bottom as he hooked her legs around his hips and drove into her as if there were no tomorrow. As if there had been no yesterday. Her nails were digging into his neck as he kissed her, but he barely noticed the discomfort. He tried to hold back—to wait for her orgasm before letting go himself—but suddenly it was impossible and he knew he was going to come.

'Alannah!' he said, on a note of disbelief—and suddenly it was too late.

Wave after wave took him under. His frame was racked with spasms as he gasped out her name, caught up in a feeling so intense that he thought he might die from it. It felt like the first orgasm he'd ever had. He closed his eyes. The only orgasm he'd ever had. And it wasn't until his body had grown completely still that he noticed how silent and how still she was.

He froze.

Of course she was.

Remorse filled him as she put her hand against his chest and pushed him away. And although withdrawing from her succulent heat was the last thing he felt like doing he could see from the tight expression on her face that she wanted him to. And who could blame her?

There had been no answering cry of fulfilment from her, had there? He had given her no real *pleasure.*

With a grimace, he eased himself from her sticky warmth, bending to pull up his trousers before carefully zipping them up. 'Alannah?'

She didn't answer straight away—she was too busy fastening her dress, her fingers fumbling to slide the buttons back in place. He went to help her, but her voice was sharp.

'Don't.'

He waited until she'd finished buttoning and whatever little insect brooch she was wearing was surveying him with baleful eyes, before he lifted her chin with his finger, so that their eyes were locked on a collision course. 'I'm sorry,' he said.

She shook her head. 'It doesn't matter.'

'It does.' He heard the flatness in her voice. 'I'm not usually so…out of control.'

She gave a wry smile. 'Don't worry, Niccolò. I won't tell anyone. Your reputation is safe with me.'

His mouth hardened and his body tensed. It was her cool response which made something inside him flare into life—a feeling of anger as much as desire. A feeling set off by wounded male pride and an urgent need to put things right. This had never happened to him before. He was usually the master of control. He had always prided himself on his lovemaking skills; his ability to give women physical pleasure—even if he could never satisfy them emotionally.

A shudder of comprehension made his blood run cold.

Did he really want her to walk away thinking of him as a selfish lover? As a man who took, but gave nothing back? Was that how he wanted her to remember him?

'Let's hope you don't have to,' he said, his voice full of sudden resolution as he bent down to slide his arm behind her knees and then lifted her up.

'What…what the hell do you think you're doing?' she spluttered as he began to carry her along the wide corridor.

'I'm taking you to bed.'

'Put me down! I don't want to go to bed. I want to go home.'

'I don't think so,' he said, kicking open his bedroom door and walking over to the vast bed, before setting her down in the centre of the mattress. His knees straddling her hips, he began to unbutton her dress, but she slapped his hand away and he realised that his normal methods of seduction weren't going to work with her. Come to think of it, nothing felt remotely normal with her—and right now, this felt a million miles away from seduction.

He smoothed the tousled hair away from her face, staring down into the reproachful belligerence of her blue eyes, before slowly lowering his head to kiss her.

It wasn't a kiss, so much as a duel.

For a few seconds she held back, as if he were kissing some cold, marble statue. She lay there like a human sacrifice. He could sense her anger and frustration, so he forced himself to take it slowly—so slowly that it nearly killed him. He explored her lips with a thoroughness which was new to him—until he felt he knew them almost better than his own. And as she gradually opened them up to him—when she had relaxed enough to let his tongue slide inside her mouth—it felt like one of the most intimate acts he'd ever taken part in.

Her hands reached for his shoulders and he took the opportunity to press his body close to hers, but the shudder of delight as their bodies crushed against each other was entirely new to him. And still he took it slowly—still feasting on her lips until he was certain that her own desire was strong enough to make her wriggle against him with a wordless message of frustration.

He didn't speak. He didn't dare. Something told him that she didn't want him to undress her and he suspected that doing so would shatter a mood which was already dangerously fragile. His hands were trembling as they slid beneath her dress to reacquaint themselves with the hot, moist flesh beneath her panties. He heard her give a little moan—a sound of pleasure and submission—and his heart hammered as he unzipped himself and tugged her panties down over her knees.

He was only vaguely aware of the awkward rumpling of their unfastened clothing, because by then he was caught up with a hunger so powerful that he groaned helplessly as he slid inside her for a second time. It felt… For a moment he didn't move. It felt out of this world. He looked down to see an unmistakable flare of wonder in her eyes as he filled her, but just as quickly her dark lashes fluttered down to veil them. As if she was reluctantly granting him access to her body—but not to her thoughts.

He moved slowly. He kept her on the edge for a long time—until she was relaxed enough to let go. She wrapped her legs and her arms around him and held him close and Niccolò thought he'd never been quite so careful before. He'd learnt a lot about women's bodies during a long and comprehensive sexual education, but with Alannah it became about much more than technique.

Her body began to change. He could feel the tension building until it was stretched so tightly that it could only shatter—and when it did, she made a series of gasping little sighs, before she started to convulse helplessly around him. He was dimly aware of the groan he gave before he too let go, his every spasm matching hers, and he could feel her heart beating very fast against his as his arms tightened around her.

He must have fallen asleep, because when he next became aware of his surroundings it was to feel her shifting out from under him. His fingers curled automatically around her waist. 'What are you doing?' he questioned sleepily, moving his head so that her lips were automatically redirected to his and his voice was indistinct as his tongue slid into her mouth. 'Mmm?'

She let him kiss her for a moment before putting distance between them. He felt her lips ungluing themselves from his as she moved away.

'It's late, Niccolò—and this is a school night.'

He knew what she was doing. She was giving him

the opportunity to end the evening now, without either of them losing face. He wondered if this was what she normally did—give into a hot and mindless lust without much forethought, before following it up with a cool smile as if nothing had happened?

Without much forethought.

The words struck him and imprinted themselves on his consciousness. Suddenly he went hot and then cold as he realised their implication and he stared at her with growing horror.

'You know what we've just done?' he questioned and there was a note in his voice he'd never heard before.

She tilted her chin, but he could see the way she had instinctively started to bite her lip. 'Of course. We've just had sex. Twice.'

His fingers dug into her forearms, his voice suddenly urgent. 'Are you on the pill?'

He saw the exact moment that it registered. That would be the moment when her blue eyes widened and her lips began to tremble.

'We…' she whispered. 'We've…'

'Yes,' he completed grimly. 'We've just had unprotected sex.'

She swallowed. 'Oh, God,' she breathed. 'What are we going to do?'

He didn't answer at once. It was pointless to concentrate on the anger and frustration which were building up inside him, because he could see that harsh words of recrimination would serve no useful purposc. His mouth hardened. He should have known better. How could he have failed to take contraception into account?

'I think that there is only one thing we can do,' he said. 'We wait.'

'I…guess so.'

He frowned as he noticed that her teeth had started to chatter. 'You're shivering. You need to get into bed.'

'I don't—'

'I'm not listening to any objections,' he said emphatically. 'I'm going to undress you and put you to bed and then I'm going to make you tea.'

She wriggled. 'Why don't you go and make the tea and I'll undress myself?'

He frowned, and there was a heartbeat of a pause. 'Alannah, are you *shy*?'

She attempted a light little laugh, which didn't quite come off. 'Me? Shy? Don't be ridiculous. How could I possibly be shy when I've exposed my body to the harsh glare of the camera?'

Placing his palms on either side of her face, he stared down into her wide blue eyes. 'But stripping for a camera is a very anonymous thing to do,' he said slowly. 'While stripping for a man is intensely personal.'

She pulled a face. 'Stick with the day job, Niccolò—I don't think analysis is really your thing.'

Niccolò frowned. No, it wasn't his thing at all. Normally he ran a million miles from trying to work out what was going on in a woman's head. But most women weren't perplexing enigmas, were they? They didn't answer one question and immediately make you want to ask them a hundred more.

'You're shy,' he repeated. 'Are you going to tell me why?'

Alannah stifled a sigh as she looked at him, because telling Niccolò anything was the last thing she wanted. His lovemaking had left her feeling soft and vulnerable enough to have her defences weakened. And she wasn't stupid. She might despise the men who persisted in thinking of her as nothing but a body—yet surely that was the main attraction for Niccolò, no matter how much he might try to deny it. Wouldn't he be disappointed to discover the mundane truth about her?

Because iconic glamour models were supposed to typify sexuality, not belong to a band of women who had always found sex rather overrated until now.

'Yes, I'm shy,' she admitted grudgingly. 'I don't really like men looking at my body. I'm hung up about it. I hate being thought of as nothing but a pair of gravity-defying breasts. That's probably why I'm not usually able to relax very much. Why my sex life has been…'

Her words tailed off as she became aware that she'd said too much and she braced herself as she waited for him to distance himself, like a man who thought he'd bought a racy sports-car—only to find that he'd landed himself with a second-hand model which kept breaking down.

'Why your sex life has been, what?' he prompted softly.

She pulled a face. 'You really want me to spell it out for you? Isn't your ego healthy enough already without the added boost of me telling you how good you are in bed?'

He took her hand and lifted it to his lips, unable to hide his slow, curving smile of satisfaction. 'Am I?'

'You know you are.' She pulled her hand away. 'I'm sure I'm not the first woman to tell you that.'

'No, but you're the first woman who is such a mass of contradictions that you have my head spinning. You have a wildness…'

'Niccolò—'

He silenced her with a long kiss and when he finally raised his head, it was to subject her to a look of narrow-eyed thoughtfulness. 'I think we've done the subject to death for tonight,' he said. 'You're tired and so am I, and you're right—it *is* a school night. Bedtime,' he added firmly.

'I'm not sure,' she said.

'Well, I am. Relax, *mia tentatrice*.'

He was unbuttoning her dress again and suddenly Alannah had no desire to stop him. She lay there as he slid the silky garment from her body until she was left in just her hold-ups and her bra and, automatically, her palms moved towards her breasts—to protect them from his seeking gaze. But to her surprise he wasn't even looking at her breasts. He was sliding down her hold-ups as impersonally as if he'd been undressing a child who had been caught in a storm. Even her bra was removed with nothing but deft efficiency, so that she was naked and snuggled beneath the warm duvet almost before she'd realised it.

She blinked as he captured her in that searing ebony gaze.

'Now…was that so traumatic?' he questioned silkily.

She shook her head. 'I wasn't expecting…' Her words tailed off.

'You thought I would be unable to resist drooling

as I ogled your breasts? That you find yourself surprised by my sensitivity?'

'Something like that,' she mumbled.

He smiled, the pad of his thumb trailing a path over her bottom lip and causing it to tremble. 'You and me both,' he said drily, before getting up to let himself quietly out of the room.

While he was gone, Alannah took the opportunity to look around what was one of the most impersonal bedrooms she'd ever seen. There were no photos on display. No real hints as to what kind of man Niccolò really was. She knew his parents were dead—but there was no misty-eyed memorial of their wedding day. She remembered Michela clamming up whenever anyone had asked her about her folks—and hadn't she been a bit like that herself if people wanted to know about *her* father? It had seemed too crass to tell them the truth. *Oh, my mother was fresh out of Ireland and she had her drink spiked...*

She hadn't found out the whole story until three days before her mother had died. That Bridget Collins had woken up in her dingy hostel room with a splitting headache and vague, shifting memories of what had happened the night before—as well as a terrible soreness between her legs. She'd never seen the man again and the shame of it was that she didn't even know his surname. Nine months later Alannah had been born and her mother's over-protectiveness had kicked in.

Alannah stared at the photograph opposite the bed—a smoky, atmospheric monochrome study of a brooding Mount Vesuvius. If she'd known all that stuff before…if she'd been able to make sense of why her mother had been so unbelievably strict with her—would it have changed anything?

Probably not. And even if it had—it was all irrelevant now. Because you could never go back. You could never wipe out the things you'd done. Everyone knew that.

She was almost asleep by the time Niccolò returned, carrying a tray of camomile tea. Her eyelashes fluttered open as he sat down and the bed sank beneath his weight.

'This will help you sleep,' he said.

She didn't think she needed any help, but she drank the flower-filled brew anyway and then settled back down against the bank of pillows while Niccolò gently stroked her hair.

She wriggled her bare toes and stretched out her body and at that precise moment she didn't think she'd ever felt quite so blissfully content. Until a dark memory flickered into her mind like an evil imp—reinforcing the disturbing thought that they hadn't remembered to use protection….

CHAPTER SEVEN

'ANYONE WOULD THINK,' said Niccolò slowly, 'that you were trying to avoid me.'

Alannah looked up to find herself caught in the spotlight of a pair of ebony eyes, which cut into her like dark twin lasers. Winter light was flooding into the main reception room of the still bare Sarantos apartment, emphasising its vast and elegant dimensions. She had been there all morning, sitting on the newly upholstered window seat and sewing tassels onto a cushion, but the sight of the Sicilian standing in the doorway made her suspend her needle in mid-air.

She tried to compose herself and to say the right thing. Just as she'd been trying to do the right thing, ever since she'd crazily decided to have sex with him. She needed to treat what had happened as a one-off, and keeping their relationship on a purely professional footing was the only sane solution.

For both of them.

She put the needle down and pushed her empty coffee mug along the floor with the tip of her sneaker. 'Of course I'm not trying to avoid you,' she said lightly. 'You're my boss—I wouldn't dare.'

'Is that so?' He walked towards her. 'So why wouldn't you have dinner with me last night?'

'I explained that,' she protested. 'I had to travel to Somerset to buy some paintings and the man who owned the shop was just about to close up for the holidays, so it was the only day I could go. And then on the way back, there were loads of leaves on the line so the train was delayed. Didn't you get my voicemail message?'

'Oh, yes, I got your voicemail message,' he said impatiently. He stood looking down at her, feeling perplexed and more than a little frustrated. This had never happened to him before. Usually he had to barricade his bedroom once a woman had been granted access to it—he couldn't remember a lover ever being so reluctant to return. His mouth tightened. 'But the fact remains that on Tuesday we had sex and I've barely seen you since.'

She shrugged. 'That's just the way it's worked out. You're employing me to get this apartment done in a hurry and that's what I'm trying to do. That's my primary role, isn't it? You're not paying me to keep appearing at your office door and haunting you.'

Niccolò felt his mouth dry. He wouldn't mind her appearing at his office door. She was making him think of a few very creative uses for his desk… He swallowed. 'Am I going to see you later?'

Alannah sucked in a breath, trying not to be flattered at his persistence, but it wasn't easy. Because she had been dreading this meeting. Dreading and yet longing for it, all at the same time. Ever since she'd slipped out of his Mayfair apartment on Tuesday she'd told herself that it would be safer to stay away from Niccolò and not pursue the affair any further. She liked him. She liked him way more than was sensible for what she was sure he'd only ever intended to be a casual hook-up. And she didn't do casual. Just as she didn't do the kind of affair which would end up with her getting her heart smashed into a hundred little pieces.

'You're my boss, Niccolò,' she said.

'I haven't lost sight of that fact, *mia tentatrice*. But what does that have to do with anything?'

'You know very well. It's…unprofessional.'

He gave a soft laugh. 'You don't think we might already have crossed that boundary when you lay gasping underneath me for most of the night?' He narrowed his eyes. 'And on top of me at one point, if my memory serves me well.'

'Stop it,' she whispered, feeling colour flooding into her cheeks. 'That's exactly what I'm talking about. It blurs the lines and confuses things. I'm trying to concentrate on my work and I can't when you—'

'Can't stop wanting a rerun?'

'A rerun is what you do with movies. And it's a bad idea.'

'Why?'

She sighed. 'What happened last week was…' Her words tailed off. How best to describe it? The most amazing sex she'd ever had? Well, yes. She had certainly never realised it could be so intense, or so powerful. But there had been another blissful side to that night which was far more worrying. She'd realised that she could get used to waking up with Niccolò lying asleep beside her, his arms wrapped tightly around her. Just as she could get used to thinking about him at odd moments of the day and wishing he were there to kiss her. And those kind of daydreams would get her nowhere.

Because where would that leave her when the whole thing imploded? She'd just be another heart-broken woman crying into her gin and tonic, trying to resist the urge to send him a 'casual' late-night text. She would run the risk of making herself vulnerable and she wasn't going to let that happen. She felt a new resolve steal over her. 'A mistake,' she said.

'A mistake,' he repeated.

'Maybe that's a bad way to put it. It was obviously very enjoyable.' She pushed the cushion away and forced herself to face the truth, no matter how unpalatable it was. 'But the fact remains that you don't really like me. You told me that.'

He smiled. 'I like you a lot more now.'

'You described what you felt for me as, and I quote—"a wildness". You made me sound like a mild version of the bubonic plague.'

'I don't think any plague feels quite like this—except maybe for the fever in my blood when I close my eyes at night and find it impossible to sleep because I can't get you out of my mind.' His eyes gleamed. 'And you look incredibly beautiful when you're being defiant. Do you do it because you know how much it turns me on?'

'It's not defiance for the sake of it,' she said. 'It's defiance for a reason. I'm not doing it to try to entice you.' She forced herself to say it. To put the words out there instead of having them nagging away inside her. 'This relationship isn't going anywhere. We both know that.'

'So you're not pregnant?'

His words completely shattered her fragile façade and she stared at him, her heart pounding. During the day, when she was busy working, it was easy to push that thought to the back of her mind. It was at night-time when it became impossible. That was when the fear flooded through her body as she tried to imagine just how she would cope with having Niccolò da Conti's baby. That was when she had to fight to stop herself imagining a downy little black head, glugging away contentedly at her breast.

'I don't know,' she said. 'It's too early to do a test.'

'Which means we may be about to be parents together, *sì*? I think that constitutes some sort of relationship, don't you?'

'Not the best kind,' she said.

'Maybe not. But I need to know that if you are pregnant—*if you are*—whether I am the only man in the frame who could be the father.' His black eyes burned into her, but he must have seen her flinch because his voice softened by a fraction. 'Is that such an unreasonable request?'

She met his gaze, telling herself that in the circumstances he had every right to ask. But that didn't make it hurt any less and some of that hurt came spilling out.

'Yes. You are the only man in the frame. Did you think that because of my previous line of work that there would be a whole load of contenders?' She shook her head in despair. 'You really are fond of stereotypes, aren't you, Niccolò? Well, for your information, there isn't. If you really must know, I could count my previous lovers on one hand and still have some fingers free—and there's been no one in my life for the last three years.'

Niccolò let out the breath he'd been holding, unprepared for the powerful hit of pleasure which flooded through his body in response to her words. *He was the only man in the frame. There had been no one else in her life for the past three years.*

He stared at her, his eyes taking in the way she was illuminated in the harsh winter light. Her thick hair looked blue-black, like the feathers of a raven. He swallowed. *Dai capelli corvini.*

In her jeans and loose shirt she shouldn't have looked anything special, but somehow she looked unbelievably beautiful. Against her hair, her skin was creamy and her pallor emphasised the dramatic blue of her eyes. A little brooch in the shape of a dragonfly glittered on her lapel and suddenly he found himself envying the proximity of that worthless piece of jewellery to her body.

What if there were a baby?

His mouth hardened.

He would cross that bridge when he came to it.

The shrill sound of the doorbell shattered the silence.

'That'll be one of the painters,' she said. 'He rang up to say he'd left his keys behind.' Rising to her feet, she walked over and picked up a shoal of silver keys from where they lay on another window seat. 'I won't be long.'

Alannah was aware of his eyes burning into her as she left the room. Her shoes were squeaking as she went to open the front door where one of the painters stood. There were four of them in total and they'd been working around the clock—and although she'd stopped short of making cups of tea for them, she'd been friendly enough. This one had plaster dust in his hair and he was grinning.

She forced a smile as she held out the clump of keys. 'Here you go, Gary.'

But after he'd taken them and shoved them into his dust-covered jeans, he caught hold of her wrist. His big, calloused fingers curled around her skin and his face had suddenly gone very pink. 'I didn't realise you were *the* Alannah Collins,' he said suddenly.

Her heart sank as she snatched her hand away because she knew what was coming next. She wondered if it would be better to call his bluff or to slam the door in his face. But there were only a few days of the project left and it *was* nearly Christmas…why alienate one of the workforce unless it was absolutely necessary?

'Will there be anything else?' she questioned pointedly. 'Because I have work to do.'

'The schoolgirl,' he said thickly. 'With the big—'

A figure seemed to propel itself out of nowhere and it took a moment for Alannah to realise it was Niccolò and he was launching himself at Gary with a look of undiluted rage on his face.

Grabbing hold of the workman's shirt collar, he half lifted him from the ground and shoved his face very close.

'Che talii bastardu?' he spat out. *'Ti scippo locchi e o core!'*

'Niccolò!' protested Alannah faintly, but he didn't seem to be listening.

'How dare you speak to a woman like that?' he demanded. 'What's your name?'

The man blanched. 'G-Gary.'

'Gary what?'

'G-Gary Harkness.'

'Well, take it from me that you won't ever work in this city again, Gary Harkness—I shall make sure of that.' Releasing the shirt collar, Niccolò pushed him away and the man staggered a little. 'Now get out of here—get out before I beat your worthless body to a piece of pulp.'

Alannah didn't think she'd ever seen anyone look so petrified as the workman turned and ran down the corridor towards the elevator.

She lifted her gaze to Niccolò and met the furious blaze firing from his eyes as he clicked the door shut.

'What was that you said to him in Sicilian?'

'I asked him what he was looking at.' He paused as he steadied his breath. 'And I told him I would wrench out his eyes and his heart.'

Alannah gulped. 'You don't think that was a little…over the top?'

'I think he's lucky he didn't end up in hospital,' he ground out and his jaw tightened as he stared at her. 'How often does that happen?'

'Not much. Not these days.' She shrugged as she began to walk back into the main reception room, aware that he was following her. Aware that her heart was pounding. This wasn't a conversation she usually had—not with anyone—but maybe Niccolò was someone who needed to hear it. She turned to look at him. 'It used to be a lot worse. People only ever seemed able to have a conversation with my breasts—

or think that I would instantly want to fall into bed with them.'

Guilt whispered over his skin and Niccolò swallowed down the sudden dryness in his throat. Because hadn't he done something very similar? Hadn't he judged her without really knowing the facts and assumed a promiscuity which simply wasn't true?

'And I did the same,' he said slowly.

Her gaze was fearless. 'Yes, you did.'

'That was why you suddenly froze in the hallway of my house when I was making love to you, wasn't it?' he questioned suddenly.

His perception was nearly as alarming as the realisation that the conversation had taken an even more intimate twist. Despite her determination to stay strong, Alannah couldn't prevent the rush of heat to her cheeks. 'Yes,' she said quietly.

She started to turn her head away, but suddenly he was right there in front of her and his fingers were on her arm. They felt good on her arm, she thought inconsequentially.

'Tell me,' he urged.

It was hard to get the words out. Baring her soul wasn't something she normally did—and she had never imagined herself confiding in Niccolò da Conti like this. But for once his gaze was understanding and his voice was soft and Alannah found herself wanting to analyse the way she'd reacted—not just because he'd asked, but because she needed to make sense of it herself. 'I just remember you saying something about my body being even better in the flesh and I started to feel like an object. Like I wasn't a real person—

just a two-dimensional image in a magazine, with a staple in her navel. Like I was *invisible*.'

'That was not my intention,' he said slowly. 'I think I found myself overwhelmed by the realisation that I was finally making love to you after so many years of thinking about it.' There was a pause as he looked at her. 'Do you think you can forgive me for that, *mia tentatrice*?'

She studied him, and the flicker of a smile nudged at her lips because it was strange seeing him in this conciliatory mood. 'I'll think about it.'

Niccolò pulled her into his arms and she didn't object. She didn't object when he bent his head to kiss her either. Her breath was warm and flavoured with coffee and he wanted to groan with pleasure. She tasted as good as he remembered—in fact, she tasted even better—and there seemed something awfully decadent about kissing her in the near-empty apartment. This wasn't the kind of thing he usually did between meetings, was it? His heart skipped a beat as his fingertips skated over her breast, feeling it swell as he cupped it, and he heard her breath quicken as he began to unbutton her shirt.

It pleased him that she let him. That she really did seem to have forgiven him for his out-of-control behaviour of the other night. That she was relaxed enough not to freeze again.

He deepened the kiss, rubbing at her taut nipple with his thumb, and she gave a little sigh of pleasure. He kissed her for a long time until she was squirming impatiently and kissing him back. Until he forced himself to pull away from her, his voice unsteady as he looked into the darkening of her denim eyes and he felt a rush of triumph fuse with the headiness of sexual hunger.

'I would like to lay you down on the bare floor and make love to you, but I am short of time and must go straight from here to a meeting. And I don't feel it would do my reputation much good if I walked in so dishevelled.' He grimaced as he remembered that time in the hallway of his apartment, when he had shown all the finesse of a teenage boy. 'And I am aware that perhaps you like your lovemaking to be a little more slow and considered.'

'I...thought I did.'

He heard the reluctance in her voice but noticed she was still gripping tightly onto his arms. Her lips were trembling, even though she was biting down on them in an effort to stop it—and he realised just how turned on she was.

'Of course...' He moved his hand down to the ridge of hard denim between her legs. 'I probably do have enough time for other things. Things which you might enjoy.'

'Niccolò,' she said breathlessly.

'What do you think?' he said as he edged his middle finger forward and began to stroke her. 'Yes, or no?'

'Y-yes,' she gasped.

'Keep still,' he urged—but to his delight she didn't obey him. Or maybe she just couldn't. Her head was tipping back and suddenly she didn't look remotely shy...she looked *wild*. Beautiful. He felt her thighs part and heard her moaning softly as he increased the relentless pressure of his finger.

She came very quickly, tightening her arms around

his neck and making that shuddering little crescendo of sighs with which he'd become so familiar on Tuesday night. As he kissed her again her fingers began to claw at his shirt, as if she wanted to tear it from his chest, and for a moment he thought about changing his mind and taking her in the most fundamental way possible.

Temptation rushed over him in a dark wave. Impatiently, his hand strayed to the belt of his trousers, until some remaining shred of reason forced him to play out the ensuring scene. What did he have in mind? Rushing into his meeting with his shirt creased and a telltale flush darkening his skin? Using Alekto's apartment to have sex with a woman—wouldn't that be kind of *cheap*? On every single level, it wouldn't work—but that didn't make it any easier to pull away from her.

She started buttoning her shirt back up with trembling fingers and he walked over to the window to compose himself, willing his frustration to subside.

Outside, a light flurry of snowflakes was whirling down and he felt a sudden sense of restlessness. He thought about the impending holiday and what he would be forced to endure, because one thing he'd learned was that unless you were prepared to live in a cave—it was impossible to ignore Christmas. Already there was a glittering tree which he'd been unable to ban from the main reception of his offices. He thought about the horrendous staff party he'd been forced to attend last night, with those stodgy mince pies they were so fond of eating and several drunken secretaries tottering over to him with glassy smiles and bunches of mistletoe.

He turned round. Alannah had finished buttoning up her shirt, though he noticed her hands were shaking and her cheeks still flushed.

'What are you doing for Christmas?' he questioned suddenly.

'Oh, I'm wavering between an invitation to eat nut roast with some committed vegans, or having an alternative celebration all of my own.' She glanced over his shoulder at the snowflakes. 'Like pretending that nothing's happening and eating beans on toast, followed by an overdose of chocolate and trash TV. What about you?'

He shrugged. 'I have an invitation to ski with some friends in Klosters, but unfortunately my schedule doesn't allow it. I hate Christmas. What I would really like is to fast-forward the calendar and wake up to find it was the new year.'

'Oh, dear,' she said softly.

His eyes met hers and another wave of desire washed over him. 'But since we are both at a loose end, it seems a pity not to capitalise on that. We could ignore the seasonal madness and just please ourselves.'

She opened her eyes very wide. 'Are you asking me to spend Christmas with you, Niccolò?'

There was a pause. 'It seems I am.' He gave a cool smile. 'So why don't you speak to Kirsty and have her give you one of my credit cards? You can book us into the best suite in the best hotel in the city—somewhere you've always wanted to stay. Forget the nut roast and the beans on toast—you can have as much caviar and champagne as you like.' He gave a slow smile as he touched his fingertips to her raven hair. 'Maybe I can make some of your Christmas wishes come true.'

* * *

Alannah felt like taking her sharpest pair of scissors and snipping the small square of plastic into tiny pieces. She thought about what Niccolò had said to her. Make her wishes come true. *Really?* Did he honestly think that staying in a fancy hotel suite was the sum total of her life's ambition, when right now her biggest wish would be to tell him that she didn't need his fancy platinum credit card and she'd rather spend Christmas day alone than spend it with him?

Except that it wouldn't be true, would it? She might *want* it to be true, but it wasn't. Why else would she be sitting hunched in front of her computer, about to book a two-night break in a London hotel? She wondered what had happened to her determination to forget the night she'd spent with him and maintain a professional relationship.

She bit her lip. It had been shattered by Niccolò's resolve—that was what had happened. She had been lost the moment he'd kissed her. A single touch had been enough to make all her good intentions crumble. All her silent vows had been a complete waste of time—because she'd gone up in flames the moment he'd taken her in his arms.

She remembered the way his fingertip had whispered over the crotch of her jeans and her face grew hot. She hadn't been so shy then, had she? He'd soon had her bucking beneath him, and he hadn't even had to remove a single item of clothing. And still in that dreamy, post-orgasmic state she had agreed to spend Christmas with him.

That was something it was hard to get her head round. There must be millions of things he could be doing for the holiday—but he wanted to spend it with her. *Her.* Didn't that mean something? Her mouth grew dry. Surely it *had* to.

She stared at the credit card, which Kirsty had crisply informed her had no upper limit. Imagine that. Imagine having enough money to buy whatever you wanted. *The best suite in the best hotel.* How fancy would a hotel have to be for Niccolò not to have seen it all before, and be jaded by it? She ran through a list of possibilities. The Savoy. The Ritz. The Granchester. London had heaps of gorgeous hotels and she'd bet that he'd stayed in all of them. Had constant exposure to high-end affluence helped contribute to his inbuilt cynicism?

She was just about to click onto the Granchester when something made her hesitate. Perhaps it was a desire to shift him out of his comfort zone—away from the usual protective barriers which surrounded him. He had knocked down some of her defences, so why shouldn't she do the same with him? Why *shouldn't* she try to find out more about the real Niccolò da Conti?

She thought of a fancy hotel dining room and all the other people who would be congregated there. People who had no real place to go, who just wanted the holiday to be over. Or even worse—the wink-wink attitude of Room Service if they started asking for turkey sandwiches and champagne to be brought to their room.

An idea popped into her mind and it started to grow more attractive by the minute. She stared at the long number on the credit card. She might not have much money of her own, but she did have her imagination. Surely she was capable of surprising him with something unexpected. Something simple yet meaningful, which would incorporate the true meaning of Christmas.

His power and privilege always gave him an edge of superiority and that couldn't be good for him. An expensive tab in a smart hotel would only reinforce the differences between them. Wouldn't it be great to feel more like his *equal* for a change?

Because what if she *was* pregnant? She was going to have to get to know him better, no matter what the outcome. Her heart gave a painful lurch as she waited for that intrusive yet strangely compelling image of Niccolò da Conti's baby to subside.

She waited a minute before typing *cute Christmas cottage* into her browser. Because cute was exactly what she needed right now, she told herself. Cute stood a chance of making a cynical man melt so you might be able to work out what made him tick. Scrolling down, she stared at the clutch of country cottages which appeared on the screen.

Perfect.

CHAPTER EIGHT

THE FLURRIES WERE getting stronger and Niccolò cursed as he headed along the narrow country lane.

Why could nothing ever be straightforward? Glancing in his rear-view mirror at the swirl of snowflakes which was obscuring his view, he scowled. He'd given Alannah a credit card and told her to book a hotel in town and she'd done the exact opposite—directing him to some godforsaken spot deep in the countryside, while she went on ahead earlier.

Well, in terms of distance he wasn't actually *that* far from London but he might as well be in middle of his friend Murat's Qurhahian desert for all the sense he could make of his bearings. The sudden onset of heavy snow had made the world look like an alien place and it was difficult to get his bearings. Familiar landmarks had disappeared. The main roads were little more than white wastelands and the narrow lanes had begun to resemble twisting snakes of snow.

Glancing at his satnav, he could see he was only four minutes away, but he was damned if he could see any hotel. He'd passed the last chocolate-boxy village some way back and now an arrow was indicating he take the left fork in the road, through an impenetrable-looking line of trees.

Still cursing, he turned off the road, his powerful headlights illuminating the swirling snowflakes and turning them golden. Some people might have considered the scene pretty, but he wasn't in the mood for pretty scenery. He wanted a drink, a shower and sex in exactly that order and he wanted them now.

Following the moving red arrow, he drove slowly until at last he could see a lighted building in the distance, but it looked too small to be a hotel. His mouth hardened. Something that small could only ever be described as a cottage.

He could see a thatched roof covered with a thick dusting of snow and an old-fashioned lamp lit outside a front door, on which hung a festive wreath of holly and ivy. Through latticed windows a woman was moving around—her fall of raven hair visible, even from this distance. His hands tightened around the steering wheel as he brought the car to a halt and got out—his shoes sinking noiselessly into the soft, virgin carpet.

He rang the bell—one of those old-fashioned bells you only ever saw on ships, or in movies. He could hear the sudden scurrying of movement and footsteps approaching and then the door opened and Alannah stood there, bathed in muted rainbow light.

His body tensing, he stepped inside and the door swung violently shut behind him. His senses were immediately bombarded by the scene in front of him but, even so, the first thing he noticed was her dress. Who could fail to notice a dress like that?

It wasn't so much the golden silk, which skimmed

her curves and made her look like a living treasure, it was the scooped neck showing unfamiliar inches of creamy skin and the soft swell of her breasts. She had even positioned the glittery grasshopper brooch so that it looked poised to hop straight onto her nipple. Had she started to relax enough to stop covering her body up in that old puritanical way? he wondered.

But even this wasn't enough to hold his attention for long. His gaze moved behind her, where a fire was blazing—with two wing chairs on either side. Sprigs of holly had been placed above the paintings and, yes, there was the inevitable sprig of mistletoe dangling from the ceiling. On a low table a bowl was filled with clementines and in the air he could scent something cooking, rich with the scent of cinnamon and spice. But it was the Christmas tree which jarred most. A fresh fir tree with coloured lights looped all over the fragrant branches from which hung matching baubles of gold.

He flinched, but she didn't seem to notice as she wound her arms around his neck and positioned her lips over his. 'Merry Christmas,' she whispered.

Like a drowning man he fought against her feminine softness and the faint drift of pomegranate which clung to her skin. Disentangling her arms, he took a step back as he felt the clutch of ice around his heart.

'What's going on?' he questioned.

She blinked, as if something in his voice had alerted her to the fact that all was not well. 'It's a surprise.'

'I don't like surprises.'

Her eyes now held a faint sense of panic. Was she realising just how wrong she'd got it? he wondered grimly. He could see her licking her lips and the anger inside him seemed to bubble and grow.

'I thought about booking a hotel in London,' she said quickly. 'But I thought you'd probably stayed in all those places before, or somewhere like them. And then I thought about creating a real Christmas, right here in the countryside.'

'A *real* Christmas,' he repeated slowly.

'That's right.' She gestured towards a box of truffles on the table, as if the sight of chocolate were going to make him have a sudden change of heart. 'I went online at Selfridges and ordered a mass of stuff from their food hall. It was still much cheaper than a hotel. That's a ham you can smell cooking and I've bought fish too, because I know in Europe you like to eat fish at Christmas. Oh, and mince pies, of course.'

'I hate mince pies.'

'You don't…' Her voice faltered, as if she could no longer ignore the harsh note of censure in his voice. 'You don't *have* to eat them.'

'I hate Christmas, full stop,' he said viciously. 'I already told you that, Alannah—so which part of the sentence did you fail to understand?'

Her fingers flew over her lips and, with the silky dress clinging to her curves, she looked so like a medieval damsel in distress that he was momentarily tempted to pull her into his arms and blot out everything with sex.

But only momentarily. Because then he looked up and saw the Christmas angel on top of the tree and something about those gossamer-fine wings made his heart clench with pain. He felt the walls of the tiny cottage closing in on him as a dark tide of unwanted emotion washed over him.

'Which part, Alannah?' he repeated.

She held out the palms of her hands in a gesture of appeal. 'I thought—'

'What did you think?' he interrupted savagely. 'That you could treat me like your tame puppet? Playing happy couples around the Christmas tree and indulging in some happy-ever-after fantasy, just because we've had sex and I asked to spend the holidays with you, since we were both at a loose end?'

'Actually,' she said, walking over to the blaze of the fire and turning back to stare at him, 'I thought about how soulless it might be—having a corporate Christmas in some horrible anonymous hotel. I thought that with the kind of life you lead, you might like some home cooking for a change.'

'But I don't *do* home. Don't you get that?' he questioned savagely. He saw a small, rectangular present lying on the table and realised he hadn't even bought her a gift. *It wasn't supposed to be that kind of Christmas.* He shook his head. 'I can't stay here, Alannah. I'm sorry if you've gone to a lot of trouble but it's going to be wasted. So pack everything up while I put out the fire. We're going back to town.'

'No,' she said quietly.

His eyes narrowed. 'What do you mean…*no*?'

'You go if you want to, but I'm staying here.'

There was a pause. 'On your own?'

Alannah felt a sudden kick of rebellion as she met the incredulity in his eyes. 'You find that so surprising?' she demanded. 'You think I'm scared? Well, think again, Niccolò. I live on my own. I've spent pretty much the last seven years on my own. I don't need a man to protect me and look after me—and I certainly don't want to drive back to London with someone who can misinterpret a simple gesture with your kind of cynicism. So go to your anonymous hotel and spend the next few days splashing your cash and telling yourself how much you hate Christmas. I'll be perfectly happy here with my chocolate and mulled wine.'

His black eyes glittered. 'I'm telling you now that if you're calling my bluff, it won't work. I'm not staying here, but I'm not leaving without you, either.'

'I'm afraid you don't have a choice,' she said, walking across to the cocktail cabinet and pouring herself a glass of wine with a trembling hand. 'Like I said, I'm not going anywhere—and I don't imagine that even you are macho enough to drag me out by my hair. So leave. Go on. Just *leave*!'

Silently, they faced each other off before he pulled open the door and a fierce gust of wind brought a great flurry of snowflakes whirling into the room, before it slammed shut behind him.

Alannah didn't move as she heard the sound of his car starting up and then slowly pulling away on the snowy path. Her fingers tightened around her wine glass as she wondered how she could have judged him so badly. Had she thought that, because he'd murmured soft words in Sicilian when he'd been deep inside her, he'd lost the elements of ruthlessness and control which defined him?

Or was he right? Had she been naïve enough to imagine that a homespun meal might make him crave an intimacy which extended beyond the bedroom?

Her heart pounded.

Yes, she had.

Walking over to the sink, she threw away the wine, washing out the glass and putting it on the side to dry. She drew the curtains on the snowy darkness of the night and switched on the radio, just in time to hear the traditional Christmas service being broadcast from King's College, Cambridge. And as soon as the sound of carols filled the room she felt tears spring to her eyes, because it was so heartbreakingly beautiful.

She thought about the nativity scene—the helpless little child in a manger, and briefly she closed her eyes. She'd got it so wrong, hadn't she? She had taken him as her lover and ignored all the warning bells which had sounded so loudly in her ears. She had conveniently forgotten that everything was supposed to be on *his* terms and she'd tried to turn it into something it wasn't. Something it could never be. What had she been thinking of? She'd even bought herself a new and more revealing dress to send out the silent message that he had liberated her from some of her inhibitions. And she was almost as grateful to him for that as she was about the job he'd given her.

But he had thrown the offer back in her face.

She was cold now and ran upstairs to find a sweater, her heart contracting painfully as she looked around the bedroom. She had thought he would be charmed by the antique iron bedstead and the broderie-anglais linen. She'd imagined him picking up that old-fashioned jug and studying it—or telling her that he liked the view out into the snow-covered woods at the back of the house. She had planned to run him a bath when he arrived, and to light some of the scented candles she'd had delivered from London. She had pictured washing his back. Maybe even joining him, if he could persuade her to do so. She'd never shared a bath with anyone before.

What a fool she was, she thought viciously, dragging a mismatched blue sweater over the golden dress, and shaking her hair free. It wasn't as if she'd had no experience of life and the cruel lessons it could teach you. Hadn't she learnt that you had to just accept what you were given—warts and all? She should have taken what was already on the table and been satisfied with that. But she had been greedy, hadn't she? Niccolò had offered her something, but it hadn't been enough. She had wanted more. And still more.

The sound of the front door clicking open and closing again made her heart race with a sudden fear which made a mockery of her defiant words to Niccolò. Why the hell hadn't she locked it after he'd left—or was she hoping to extend an open invitation to any passing burglar? Except that no self-respecting burglar would be out on a snowy Christmas Eve like this. Even burglars probably had someone to share the holiday with.

'Who is it?' she called.

'Who do you think it is? Father Christmas?'

The sardonic Sicilian voice echoed round the small cottage and Alannah went to the top of the stairs to see Niccolò standing in the sitting room, snow clinging like frozen sugar to his black hair and cashmere coat. He looked up.

'It's me,' he said.

'I can see that. What happened?' she questioned

sarcastically as she began to walk downstairs. 'Did you change your mind about the mince pies?'

He was pulling off his coat and snow was falling in little white showers to the ground. She reached the bottom stair just as the poignant strains of 'Silent Night' poured from the radio. Quickly, she turned it off, so that all she could hear was the crackling of the fire and the sound of her own heartbeat as she stared at him. 'Why did you come back?'

There was a pause. His black eyes became suddenly hooded. 'It's a filthy night. I couldn't face leaving you here on your own.'

'And I told you that I would be fine. I'm not scared of the dark.' *I'm much more scared of the way you make me feel when you kiss me.*

'I'm not about to change my mind,' he said. 'I'm staying, and I need a drink.'

'Help yourself.'

He walked over to the bottle she'd opened earlier. 'You?'

A drink would choke me. 'No, thanks.'

She went and sat by the fire, wondering how she was going to get through the next few hours. How the hell did you pass the time when you were stuck somewhere with someone who didn't want to be there? After a couple of moments Niccolò walked over and handed her a glass of wine, but she shook her head.

'I said I didn't want one.'

'Take it, Alannah. Your face is pale.'

'My face is always pale.' But she took it anyway and drank a mouthful as he sat down in the other chair. 'And you still haven't really told me why you came back.'

Niccolò drank some of his wine and for a moment he said nothing. His natural instinct would be to tell her that he didn't have to justify his actions to her. To anyone. But something strange had happened as he'd driven his car down the snowy lane. Instead of the freedom he'd been expecting, he had felt nothing but a heavy weight settling somewhere deep in his chest. It had occurred to him that he could go and stay in a hotel. That if the truth were known, he could easily get a flight and join his friends and their skiing party. He could pretty much get a plane to anywhere, because the hosts of the many parties he'd declined would have been delighted if he'd turned up unexpectedly.

But then he'd thought of Alannah. Curled up alone by the fire with her raven hair aglow, while beside her that corny Christmas tree glittered. All that trouble she'd taken to create some sort of occasion and he'd just callously thrown it back in her face. What kind of a man did that? He thought of how much he'd anticipated making love to her again. How he'd spent the day aching to possess her and wanting to feel her arms wrapped tightly around him. What was *wrong* with him?

He put down his glass and his face was sombre as he turned to look at her.

'I came back because I realised I was behaving like an idiot,' he said. 'I shouldn't have taken it out on you and I'm sorry.'

Alannah sensed that sorry wasn't a word which usually featured highly in his vocabulary, but she wasn't letting him off that lightly. Did he think that a single word could wash away all the hurt he'd inflicted? 'But you did.'

'Yes. I did.'

'Because you always have to be in charge don't you, Niccolò?' she demanded, her anger starting to bubble up. 'You decided how you wanted Christmas to play out and that was it as far as you were concerned. What *you* want is paramount, and everyone else's wishes can just go hang. This is exactly what happened at Michela's wedding, isn't it? Niccolò wants it this way—so this is the way it must be.'

'That was different.'

'How?' she demanded. 'How was it different? How did you ever get to be so damned...*controlling*?'

The flames were flickering over his brooding features and illuminating his ebony hair, so that it glowed like fire-touched coal.

'How?' He gave a short laugh. 'You don't have any ideas?'

'Because you're Sicilian?'

'But I'm not,' he said unexpectedly. 'I'm only half Sicilian. My blood is not "pure". I am half Corsican.' He frowned. 'You didn't know that?'

She shook her head and suddenly his almost swashbuckling appearance made sense. 'No. I had no idea. Michela never really talked about that kind of thing. Boarding school is about reinvention—and escape. About painting yourself in the best possible light so that nobody feels sorry for you. All we knew was that you were unbelievably strict.' She put her glass down. 'Although you did used to take her to the Bahamas for Christmas every year, and we used to get pretty jealous about that.'

'She never told you why?'

'I knew that your parents were dead.' She hesitated. 'But nobody wants to talk about that kind of stuff, do they?'

Niccolò felt his mouth dry. No, they didn't. They definitely didn't. And when death was connected with shame, it made you want to turn your back on it even more. To keep it hidden. To create some kind of distance and move as far away from it as you could. He'd done that for Michela, but he'd done it for himself, too. Because some things were easier to forget than to remember.

Yet even though she was doing her best to disguise it, Alannah was looking at him with such hurt and confusion on her face that he felt it stab at his conscience. All she'd done was to try to make his Christmas good and he had thrown it back in her face in a way she didn't deserve. He'd given her a lot of stuff she didn't deserve, he realised—and didn't he owe her some kind of explanation?

'Mine was a very…unusual upbringing,' he said, at last. 'My mother came from a powerful Sicilian family who disowned her when she married my father.'

She raised her eyebrows. 'Wasn't that a little…dramatic?'

He shrugged. 'Depends which point of view you take. Her family was one of the wealthiest on the island—and my father was an itinerant Corsican with a dodgy background, who worked in the kitchens of one of her family hotels. It was never going to be thought of as an ideal match—not by any stretch of the imagination.' His gaze fixed on the flames which danced around one of the logs. 'My father was completely uneducated but he possessed a tremendous charisma.' He gave a bitter laugh. 'Along with a massive gambling addiction and a love of the finer things in life. My mother told me that her parents did everything in their power to prevent the marriage and when they couldn't—they told her she would only ever be welcome if she parted from him. Which for a strictly traditional Sicilian family was a pretty big deal.'

Alannah stared at him. 'So what did she do?'

'She defied them and married him anyway. She loved him. And she let that *love*—' His voice took the word and distorted it—so that when it left his lips it sounded like something dark and savage. 'She let it blind her to everything. His infidelity. His habitual absences. The fact that he was probably more in love with her inheritance, than with her. They took the boat to Italy when my mother was pregnant with me and we lived in some style in Rome—while my father flew to casinos all over the world and spent her money. My mother used to talk to me all the time about Sicily and I guess I became a typical immigrant child. I knew far more about the place of my birth than I did about my adopted homeland.'

Alannah leaned forward to throw another log on the fire as his words tailed off. 'Go on,' she said.

He watched the flames leap into life. 'When I was old enough, she used to leave me in charge of Michela so she could go travelling with him. She used to sit in casinos, just watching him—though I suspect it was mainly to keep the other women at bay. But he liked the attention—the idea that this rich and wealthy woman had given up everything to be with him. He used to tell her that she was his lucky charm. And I guess for a while that was okay—I mean, the situation certainly wasn't perfect, but it was bearable. Just that beneath the surface everything was crumbling and there was nothing I could do to stop it.'

She heard the sudden darkness in his voice. 'How?'

Leaning his head back against the chair, he half closed his eyes. 'My mother's inheritance was almost gone. The rent on our fancy apartment in Parioli was due and the creditors were circling like vultures. I remember her mounting sense of panic when she confided the bitter truth to me. I was eighteen and working towards going to college, though something told me that was never going to happen. My father found out about a big tournament in Monaco and they drove to France so that he could take part in it.' There was a pause. 'It was supposed to be the solution to all their problems.'

She heard the sudden break in his voice. 'What happened?'

'Oh, he won,' he said. 'In fact, he cleaned up big time. Enough to clear all his debts and guarantee them the kind of future my mother had prayed for.'

'But?' She sensed there was a *but* coming. It hung in the air like a heavy weight about to topple. He lowered his head to look at her and Alannah almost recoiled from the sudden bleakness in his eyes.

'That night they celebrated with too much champagne and decided to set off for Rome, instead of waiting until the morning. They were driving through the Italian alps when they took a bend too fast. They hit the side of the mountain and the car was destroyed.' He didn't speak for a moment and when he did, his words sounded as if they had been carved from stone.

'Neither of them would have known anything about it. At least, that's what the doctors told me.'

'Oh, Niccolò,' she breathed. 'I'm so sorry. Michela told me they'd died in a car crash, but I didn't know the background to the story.'

'Because I kept as much from her as I could. The post-mortem was inconclusive.' His voice hardened. 'Determining the level of alcohol in a…cadaver is always difficult. And no child should have the shame of knowing her father killed her mother because he was on a drunken high after winning at cards.'

She thought how *cold* he sounded—and how ruthless. But that was his default position, wasn't it—and wasn't it somehow understandable in the circumstances? Wasn't much of his behaviour explained by his dreadful legacy? 'You still must have been devastated?' she ventured.

He gave a bitter laugh. 'Do you want the truth? The real and shocking truth? My overriding emotion was one of relief that my father had won so big and that somehow the money got to me intact. It meant that I could pay the rent and clear the debts. It meant that I could send Michela away to school—at thirteen she was getting too much for me to handle. And it meant that I could live my own life. That I could capitalise on his win and make it even bigger. And that's what I did. I bought my first property with that money and by the end of that first year, I had acquired three.'

Alannah nodded. It was funny how when you joined up the dots the bigger picture emerged. Suddenly, she realised why he'd always been so strict with his sister. She saw now that his own controlling nature must have developed as an antidote to his father's recklessness. Financial insecurity had led him to go on and make himself a colossal fortune which nobody could ever bleed away. His wealth was protected, but in protecting it he had set himself in a world apart from other men.

'And did this all happen at Christmas?' she questioned suddenly. 'Is that why you hate the holidays so much?'

'No. That would have been neat, wouldn't it?' He gave a wry smile. 'It's just that Christmas came to symbolise the bleak epicentre of our family life. For me, it was always such an empty festival. My mother would spend vast amounts of money decking out the rooms of our apartment, but she was never there. Even on Christmas Eve she would be sitting like some passive fool on the sidelines while my father played cards. Supposedly bringing him luck, but in reality—checking out that some buxom hostess wasn't coming onto him.'

She winced at the phrase, but suddenly she could understand some of his prejudice towards her, too. For him, buxom women in skimpy clothes were the ones who threatened his parents' relationship. Yet in the end, his puritanical disapproval of her chosen career had done nothing to destroy his powerful lust for her, which must have confused him. And Niccolò didn't do confusion. She'd always known that. Black and white, with nothing in between.

'To me, Christmas always felt as if I'd walked onto a stage set,' he said. 'As if all the props were in place, but nobody knew which lines to say.'

And Alannah realised that she'd done exactly the same. She had tried to create the perfect Christmas.

She'd bought the tree and hung the holly and the mistletoe—but what she had created had been no more real than the empty Christmases of his past.

'Oh, Niccolò—I'm sorry,' she said. 'I had no idea.'

He looked at her and some of the harshness left his face. 'How would you have done? I've never talked about it. Not to anyone.'

'Maybe some time, it might be good to sit down and discuss it with Michela?' she ventured.

'And destroy her memories?'

'False memories are dangerous. And so are secrets. My mother waited until she was dying to tell me that her drink had been spiked and she didn't even know my father's name. I wish she'd shared it with me sooner. I would have liked to have let her know how much I admired her for keeping me.'

His eyes narrowed. 'She sounds an amazing woman.'

'She was.' His words pleased her but she felt vulnerable with his black eyes looking at her in that curiously assessing way. In an effort to distract herself, she got up and went to look out of the window. 'I'm afraid the snow shows no sign of melting?'

'No.'

She turned round. 'I suppose on a practical level we could take down all the decorations if that would make you feel better—and then we could watch that programme on TV which has been generating so much publicity. Have you heard about it? It's called "*Stuff Christmas*".'

Without warning, he rose from the chair and walked over to her, his shadow enveloping her and suddenly making her feel very small. His ebony gaze flickered over her and she saw that the bitterness in his eyes had been replaced by the much more familiar flicker of desire.

'Or we could do something else, *mia fata,*' he said softly. 'Something much more appealing. Something which I have been aching to do since I walked back in here. I could take you upstairs to bed and make love to you.'

His features were soft with lust and Alannah thought she'd never seen him looking quite so gorgeous. She wanted him just as she always wanted him, but this time her desire was underpinned with something else—something powerful and inexplicable. A need to hold him and comfort him, after everything he'd told her. A need to want to reach out and protect him.

But he'd only told her because of the situation in which they found themselves and she needed to face the truth. He wanted her for sex—*that was all*—and she needed to protect her own vulnerable heart. Maybe it was time to distance herself from him for a while. Give them both a little space.

But by then he was kissing her and it was too late to say anything. Because when he kissed her like that, she was lost.

CHAPTER NINE

SLOWLY, NICCOLÒ LICKED at the delicious rosy flesh of Alannah's nipple until eventually she began to stir. Raising her arms above her head, she stretched languorously as the silky tumble of her hair rippled over the pillow like a black banner.

'Niccolò,' she murmured, dark lashes fluttering open to reveal the sleepy denim eyes beneath.

He gave a smile of satisfaction as she somehow turned his name into a breathy little sigh—a variation of the different ways she'd said it throughout the night. She had gasped it. Moaned it. At one point she had even screamed it—her fingernails clawing frantically at his sweat-sheened body as she'd bucked beneath him. He remembered her flopping back onto the pillow afterwards and asking if was it always like this. But he hadn't answered her. He hadn't dared. For once there had been no words in his vocabulary to describe a night which had surpassed any other in his experience. He had come over and over again… in her and on her. And this time he'd remembered to use protection. Hell. Even doing *that* had felt as if it should be included in the pages of the Kama Sutra. He swallowed as he felt the renewed jerk of desire just from thinking about it. No orgasm had ever felt more powerful; no kisses that deep.

He was still trying to work out why. Because he had allowed her to glimpse the bleak landscape of his past—or because he had waited what seemed like a whole lifetime to possess her? He gave another lick. Maybe it was simply that he was discovering she was nothing like the woman he'd thought her to be.

'Niccolò?' she said again.

'Mmm?'

'Is it morning?'

'I think so.' His tongue traced a sinuous path over the creamy flesh and he felt her shiver. 'Though right now I don't really care. Do you?'

'I don't…' He could hear the note of dreamy submission in her voice. 'I don't think so.'

'Good.' He moved his tongue down over her body, feeling himself harden as it trailed a moist path to her belly. But the anatomical significance of that particular spot suddenly began to stab at his conscience and the thought he'd been trying to block now came rushing into his mind. *Was* she pregnant? He felt the painful contraction of his heart until he reminded himself that was a possibility, not a fact—and he only ever dealt with facts. There was nothing he could do about it right now—so why not continue tracking his tongue down over her salty skin and obliterating the nagging darkness of his thoughts with the brief amnesia of pleasure?

He wriggled down the bed and knelt over her, his legs straddling her as he parted her thighs and put his head between them. The dark triangle of hair at their apex was soft and for a moment he just teased at the curly strands with his teeth. She began to writhe as he flickered his tongue with featherlight accuracy against her clitoris, and the fingernails which had begun to claw restlessly at the sheet now moved to grip his shoulders.

She tasted warm and wet against his mouth and her urgent little cries only increased when he captured her circling hips and pinned them firmly against the mattress, so that he could increase the unremitting pressure of his tongue. He could hear her calling his name out. He could feel her spiralling out of control. And suddenly he felt her begin to spasm helplessly against his mouth.

'N-Niccolò!' she breathed. 'Oh, Niccolò.'

His mind and his body were at such a fever-pitch of hunger that he couldn't speak and, urgently, he reached for a condom and eased himself into her slick warmth.

He groaned. She felt so *tight.* Or maybe it was because he felt so big—as if he wanted to explode from the moment he thrust inside her. As if he wanted to come, over and over again. And yet surely she had drained every seed from his body, so that there was nothing left to give?

It seemed she had not. He drove into her until he didn't know where he ended and she began. Until her back began to arch and her eyes to close—each exquisite spasm racking through his body as time seemed to suspend itself, leaving him dazed and breathless.

The silence of the room was broken only by the sound of his own muffled heartbeat.

'I don't know how much more pleasure I can take,' she said eventually and he felt her face pressing against his shoulder.

He turned his head and blew a soft breath onto her cheek. 'Don't you know that you can never have too much pleasure, *mia tentatrice*?'

But Alannah wrinkled her nose as she stared up at the ceiling because she didn't agree. You could. You definitely could. There was always a snake in the garden of Eden—everyone knew that. She thought about all the things he'd confided in her last night. Her heart had softened when she'd heard his story. She'd felt so close to him—and flattered that he had trusted her enough to tell her all that stuff about his past. But that was dangerous, too. If she wasn't careful she could start weaving hopeless fantasies about something which was never intended to last.

She looked over at the window where bright light was shining against the closed curtains. And she realised that it was Christmas morning and last night he'd wanted to leave. She watched as he got out of bed and walked over to the window to pull back the curtains and she blinked as she gazed outside. Thick snow lay everywhere. Branches and bushes were blanketed with the stuff. Against a dove-grey sky the world looked blindingly white and not a sound could be heard and Alannah knew she mustn't let the fairy-tale perfection of the scene in front of her blind her to the reality of their situation.

She put her hands beneath the duvet, her warm belly instinctively recoiling from the icy touch of her fingers.

'We haven't really discussed what's going to happen if I'm pregnant.'

The words hung and shimmered in the air, like the baubles on the unwanted Christmas tree downstairs.

He seemed to choose his words carefully, as if he was walking through a minefield of possibilities.

'Obviously, if such a situation arises—then I will be forced to consider marrying you.'

Alannah did her best not to recoil because he made it sound like someone being forced to drink a bitter draught of poison. She didn't say anything for a moment and when she did, she chose her words as carefully as he had done.

'Before you do, I think there's something you should take into account,' she said quietly. 'Gone are the days when women could be forced to marry against their will—because there's a baby on the way. If I *am* pregnant, then I want my baby to have love—real love. I would want my baby to put contentment before wealth—and satisfaction before ambition. I would want my baby to grow up to be a warm and grounded individual—and, obviously, none of those things would be possible with you as a cynical role model. So don't worry, Niccolò—I won't be dragging you up the aisle any time soon.'

She had expected anger, or a righteous indignation—but she got neither. Instead, his expression remained cool and non-committal. She almost thought she saw a flicker of amusement in those ebony eyes.

'Have you finished?' he said.

She shrugged, wishing she didn't want him so much. 'I guess.'

'Then I'll make coffee.'

He didn't just make coffee. After a bath which

seemed to take for ever to fill, Alannah dressed and went downstairs to find him deftly cracking eggs into a bowl with one hand.

He glanced up. 'Breakfast?'

She grimaced. 'I don't know if I can face eggs.'

'You really should eat something.'

'I suppose so.' She sat down and took the cup of coffee he poured for her and, after a couple of minutes, a plate of scrambled eggs was pushed across the table. She must have been hungrier than she'd thought because she ate it all, before putting her fork down and watching while he finished his own. She thought how he could even make eating look sexy. *Keep your mind fixed on practicalities,* she told herself. 'We ought to investigate the roads,' she said. 'Maybe we can dig ourselves out.'

'Not yet.' His eyes were thoughtful as they surveyed her over the rim of his coffee cup. 'I think we should go for a walk. You look as if you could do with some colour in your cheeks.'

'That's what blusher is supposed to be for.'

He smiled. 'There's a cupboard below the stairs packed with boots and waterproof jackets—why don't we go and investigate?'

They found coats and wrapped up warm and as Niccolò buttoned up her coat Alannah kept reinforcing the same mantra which had been playing in her head all morning. That none of this meant anything. They were just two people who happened to be alone at Christmas, who happened to enjoy having sex with each other.

But the moment they stepped out into the snow, it

was impossible to keep things in perspective. It felt as if nature were conspiring against her. How could she not be affected when it felt as if she'd been transplanted into a magical world, with a man who made her feel so *alive*?

They walked along, their footsteps sinking into the virgin tracks, and she was surprised when he took her hand as they walked along. Funny how something so insignificant could feel so meaningful—especially when she thought about the many greater intimacies they'd shared. Because holding hands could easily masquerade as tenderness and tenderness was shot with its own special kind of danger…

As occasional stray flakes drifted down on their bare heads they talked about their lives. About the reasons he'd come to live in London and her summer holidays in Ireland. She asked how he'd met Alekto Sarantos, and he told her about their mutual friend Murat, the Sultan of Qurhah, and a long-ago skiing trip, when four very alpha men had challenged each other on the slopes.

'I didn't realise you knew Luis Martinez,' she said. 'That *is* Luis Martinez the world-champion racing driver?'

'Ex world champion,' he said, a little testily—and Alannah realised how competitive the four friends must have been.

He told her he hated litter and cars which hogged the middle lane of the motorway and she confided her dislike of drugs and people who ignored shop assistants by talking on their mobile phones. It was as if they had made an unspoken decision to keep the conversation strictly neutral and, unexpectedly, Alannah found herself relaxing. To anyone observing them, they probably looked like an ordinary couple who'd chosen to escape the mad rush of the city to create a dream holiday for themselves. And that was all it was, she reminded herself fiercely. A dream.

'Are you finding this…impossible?' she said. 'Being stuck here with this manufactured Christmas everywhere, when last night you were desperate to leave?'

He kicked at some snow, so that it created a powdery white explosion before falling to the ground. 'No,' he said eventually. 'It's easier than I imagined. You're actually very good company. In fact, I think I enjoy talking to you almost as much as I enjoy kissing you.' His eyes gleamed. 'Although, on second thoughts…'

She turned away, blinking her eyes furiously because kindness was nearly as dangerous as tenderness in helping you to distort reality. But he was getting to her—even though she didn't want him to. Wasn't it funny how a few kind words had the power to make everything seem different? The world suddenly looked bright and vivid, even though it had been bleached of colour. The snow made the berries on the holly bushes stand out like drops of blood and Alannah reached up to bend back a tree branch, watching as it sent a shower of snow arcing through the air, and something bubbled up inside her and made her giggle.

She turned around to find Niccolò watching her, his eyes narrowed against the bright light, and her mouth grew dry as she saw an instantly recognisable hunger in their black depths.

'What…what are we going to do if it doesn't melt?' she said, suddenly breathless.

He leaned forward to touch a gloved finger to her lips. 'Guess,' he said, and his voice was rough.

CHAPTER TEN

He made love to her as soon as they got back—while her cheeks were still cold from the snowy air and her eager fingers icy against his chest as she burrowed beneath his sweater. Alannah lay on the rug in front of the fire, with her arms stretched above her head, wearing nothing but a pair of knickers. And all her shyness and hang-ups seemed like a distant memory as he trailed his lips over every inch of her body.

His fingertips explored her skin with a curiously rapt attention and she found herself reaching for him with a sudden urgency, drawing in a shuddering breath as he eased into her and letting the breath out again like a slow surrender as he lowered his mouth to hers. She loved the contrast of their bodies—his so olive-skinned and dark against her own milky pallor. She liked watching the flicker of flames gilding his flesh and the way his limbs interlocked so perfectly with her own. She loved the way he tipped his head back when he came—and made that low and shuddered moan of delight.

Much later, he pulled his sweater over her head and set about cooking lunch, while she curled up on the sofa and watched him, and suddenly she felt relaxed.

Really and properly relaxed. The cushion behind her back was soft and feathery and her bare toes were warm in the fire's glow.

'It seems *weird*,' she said as he tipped a pile of clean vegetables from the chopping board into a saucepan, 'to see you in the kitchen, looking like you know exactly what you're doing.'

'That's because I do. It isn't exactly rocket science,' he answered drily. 'Unless you think cooking is too complicated for a mere man and that women are naturally superior in the kitchen?'

'Women are naturally superior at many things,' she said airily. 'Though not necessarily at cooking. And you know what I mean. You're a billionaire businessman who runs an international empire. It's strange to see you *scraping carrots*.'

Niccolò gave a soft laugh as he grabbed a handful of fresh herbs, though he recognised that she'd touched a nerve. Just because he *could* cook, didn't mean he did—and it was a long time since he'd done anything like this. Yet wasn't there something uniquely *comforting* about creating a meal from scratch? He'd cooked for his sister in those early days of loss but as she'd got older his responsibilities towards her had lessened. When he had sent her away to school, only the vacations had required his hands-on guardianship. But he had enjoyed his role as quasi-parent and he'd made sure that he carried it out to the best of his ability—the way he tackled everything in his life.

He remembered the trips to the famous Campagna Amica market, near the Circus Maximus. He had taken Michela with him and shown the sulky teenager how to select the freshest vegetables and the finest pieces of fruit. And all the stall-owners had made a fuss of her—slipping her a ripe pear or a small bunch of perfect grapes.

When Michela had finally left home, he had filled every available hour with work—building up his property portfolio with a determination to underpin his life with the kind of security he'd never had. And as his wealth had grown, so had his ability to delegate. These days he always ate out, unless a woman was trying to impress him with her culinary repertoire. His Mayfair fridge was bare, save for coffee and champagne. His apartment was nothing but a base with a bed. It wasn't a home because he didn't *do* home. But as he squeezed lemon juice over the grilled fish he realised how much he had missed the simple routine of the kitchen.

He glanced up to find Alannah still watching him, her bare legs tucked up beneath her. His sweater was much too big for her and it had the effect of making her look unbelievably fragile. Her black hair was spilling down over her shoulders and her blue eyes were shining and something about that almost innocent look of eagerness made his heart contract.

Deliberately, he turned away, reaching for a bottle of prosecco and two glasses. *She's just someone you're trying to get out of your system,* he reminded himself grimly.

His face was composed by the time he handed her a glass. 'Happy Christmas,' he said.

They drank prosecco, lit candles and ate lunch. Afterwards, he made love to her again and they fell asleep on the sofa—and when they awoke, the candles were almost burnt down and outside the starry sky was dark and clear.

Alannah walked over to the window and he wondered if she was aware that her bare bottom was revealed with every step she took.

'I think the snow might be melting,' she said.

He heard the unmistakable note of disappointment in her voice and something inside him hardened. Did she think they could exist in this little bubble for ever, and pretend the rest of the world wasn't out there?

He insisted on loading the dishwasher and making tea to eat with their chocolate. Because any kind of activity was better than sitting there letting his mind keep working overtime.

But action couldn't permanently silence the nagging thoughts which were building inside him and he thought about what she'd said earlier. About putting contentment before wealth and satisfaction before ambition. About not wanting to drag him up the aisle.

Because that was not a decision she alone could make. And if there *was* a baby, then surely there was only one sensible solution, and that solution was marriage.

His jaw tightened. Obviously it was something he'd thought about, in the same way that the young sometimes thought about getting old—as if it would never happen to them. He liked children—and was godfather to several. Deep down, he'd recognised that one day he wanted to be a father and would select a suitable woman to bear his child.

He'd imagined she would be blonde and slightly aloof. Maybe one of those American women who had been brought up on milk and honey and could trace their roots back over generations. The type who kept their emotions on an even keel. The type who didn't believe in fairy tales. The type he felt safe with. It wasn't their trust funds which excited him, but the satisfaction of knowing that they would unknowingly welcome the son of a Corsican bandit into their rarefied drawing rooms.

He stared across the room at Alannah. In no way was she aloof; he had never seen a woman looking quite so accessible. Even with her fingers wrapped chastely around a mug of herb tea, she looked…wild. He felt his throat dry. She touched something deep inside him, something which felt…*dangerous.* Something which took him to the very edges of his self-control. She always had. She spoke to him as nobody else did. She treated him in a way which no one else would dare try.

But the fact remained that she had a background even more unsettled than his own. He had already taken a gamble on her—but surely there was no need to take another. He might not have learnt many lessons at the knee of his father, but one thing he knew was that the more you gambled—the greater your chance of losing. The most sensible thing he could do would be to walk away from her. To keep on walking, without looking back.

He swallowed. Yet if she carried his child—he could walk nowhere. What choice would he have other than to stay with her? To tie himself to someone who no way fitted the image of the kind of woman he wanted to marry. Two mismatched people united by a single incident of careless passion. What future was there in that?

She looked up and her expression grew wary.

'Why are you frowning at me?'

'I didn't realise I was.'

'Actually, frowning isn't really accurate. You were glaring.'

'Was I?' He leaned back in his chair and studied her. 'I've been thinking.'

'Sounds ominous,' she said.

'You do realise that despite all your words of rebellion this morning—I'm going to marry you if you're having my baby?'

Her creamy skin went pink. He saw her fingertips flutter up to touch the base of her neck.

'What…what made you suddenly think of that?'

He saw the flare of hope in her eyes and knew he mustn't feed it, because that wasn't fair. He had a responsibility to tell her the truth and the last thing he wanted was her thinking he was capable of the same emotions as other men. He mustn't fool her into thinking that his icy heart might be about to melt. His mouth hardened. Because that was never going to happen.

'I suddenly realised,' he said slowly, 'that I could never tolerate my son or daughter growing up and calling another man Father.'

'Even though I am the last kind of person you would consider marrying under normal circumstances.'

He met her eyes—but hadn't he always been completely honest with her? Wouldn't she see through a placatory lie to try to make her feel better? 'I guess.'

She put her cup down quickly, as if she was afraid she was going to spill it. 'So this is all about possession?'

'Why wouldn't it be? This child is half mine.'

'*This child* might not even exist!' she choked out. 'Don't you think we ought to wait until we know, before we start having arguments about parental rights?'

'When *can* you find out?'

'I'll do the test when I get back to London,' she said, jumping up from the sofa and dabbing furiously at her eyes with shaking and fisted hands.

The warm and easy atmosphere of earlier had vanished. And how.

Alannah stormed upstairs to splash cold water onto her face and to try to stem the hot tears from springing to her eyes, and yet all she could feel was a growing sense of frustration. She didn't *want* to be like this. She couldn't blame him for what he'd said, just because it didn't fit in with her fantasies. He was only being straight with her. So maybe this was a wake-up call to start protecting herself. To start facing up to facts.

Their fairy-tale Christmas was over.

She went back downstairs and turned on the TV, giving an exaggerated sigh of relief when she heard the weatherman announce that a warm weather front was pushing up from Spain, and the snow was expected to have thawed by late morning.

'Great news,' she said. 'London here we come.'

Niccolò watched as she stomped out of her chair to throw away the untouched mince pies and chocolates and every attempt he made to start a conversation was met with a monosyllabic response. He realised that he'd never been given such cool treatment by a woman before.

But that didn't stop them having sex that night. Very good sex, as it happened. Their angry words momentarily forgotten, he reached for her in the darkness with a passion which she more than matched. In a room washed silver by the full moon, he watched as she arched beneath him and called out his name.

He awoke to the sound of dripping outside the window to find the weatherman's predictions had been accurate and that the snow was melting. Leaving Alannah sleeping, he packed everything up, made a pot of coffee, then went along the lane to find his car.

By the time he drove back to the cottage, she was up and dressed, standing in the middle of the sitting room, clutching a mug—her face pale and her mouth set. He noticed she'd turned the tree lights off and that the room now looked dull and lacklustre.

'Christmas is over,' she said brightly, as if he were a stranger. As if she hadn't been going down on him just a few sweet hours before.

'What about the tree?'

'The woman I hired the cottage from supplied it. She said she'll take it away.'

'Alannah—'

'No,' she said quietly. 'I don't want any protracted stuff, or silly goodbyes. I just want to get back to London and finish up the job you've employed me to do.'

Niccolò felt a flicker of irritation at her suddenly stubborn and uncompromising attitude, but there didn't seem to be a damned thing he could do about it. She was almost completely silent on the journey back as the car slushed its way through the unnaturally quiet streets and, for some reason, the passionate opera he usually favoured while driving now seemed completely inappropriate.

He drove her to Acton and parked up outside her

home, where most of the small nearby houses seemed to be decked with the most garish tinsel imaginable. Someone had even put an inflatable Santa in their cramped front yard.

'Thanks for the lift,' she said, as she reached for the door handle.

'Aren't you going to invite me in?'

She gave him a steady stare. 'Why would I do that?'

'Maybe because we've been sleeping together and I might like to see where you live?'

Alannah hesitated and hated herself for that hesitation. She wondered if secretly she was ashamed of her little home and fearful of how judgemental he might be. Or was it simply an instinctive reaction, because she was unwilling to expose any more of herself to him?

'Okay, come in, then,' she said grudgingly.

'Grazie,' came his sardonic reply.

It was shiveringly cold as she unlocked the door. She'd turned the heating down low before the taxi had arrived to take her to the cottage and now the place felt like an ice-box. Niccolò stood in the centre of her small sitting room as she adjusted the thermostat, looking around him like a man who had just found himself in a foreign country and wasn't quite sure what to do. She wondered how he managed to make her furniture look as if it would be better suited to a doll's house.

'Would you like a guided tour?' she said.

'Why not?'

The cramped dimensions meant she needed to be vigilant about tidiness and Alannah was glad there were no discarded pieces of clothing strewn around her bedroom and that the tiny bathroom was neat. But it still felt excruciating as she led him through an apartment in which she'd tried to maximise all available light in order to give an illusion of space. She'd made all the drapes herself from sari material she'd picked up at the local market, and the artwork which hung on the walls was her own. A friend from college had feng-shuied every room, there were pots of herbs lined up on the window sill in the kitchen, and she found the place both restful and creative.

But she wondered how it must seem through Niccolò's eyes, when you could practically fit the entire place into his downstairs cloakroom back in Mayfair.

They walked back into the sitting room and, rather awkwardly, she stood in front of him. He really did seem like a stranger now, she thought—and a terrible sense of sadness washed over her. How weird to think that just a few hours ago he was deep inside her body—making her feel as if she was closer to him than she'd ever been to anyone.

'I would offer you coffee,' she said. 'But I really do want to get on. If Alekto is going to have the apartment ready for his New Year's Eve party, then I need to get cracking.'

'You're planning to work *today*?'

'Of course. What did you think I'd be doing?' she questioned. 'Sobbing into my hankie because our cosy Christmas is over? I enjoyed it, Niccolò. It was an… interesting experience. And you're a great cook as well as a great lover. But you probably know that.'

She made a polite gesture in the direction of the door but he suddenly caught hold of her wrist, and all pretence of civility had gone.

'Haven't you forgotten something?' he iced out, his eyes glittering with unfeigned hostility.

She snatched her hand away, swallowing as she met his gaze. 'No, I haven't. It's not the kind of thing you can easily forget, is it? Don't worry, Niccolò. I'll let you know whether I'm pregnant or not.'

CHAPTER ELEVEN

'I'M NOT PREGNANT.'

Alannah's voice sounded distorted—as if it were coming from a long way away, instead of just the other side of his desk—and Niccolò didn't say anything—at least, not straight away. He wondered why his heart had contracted with something which felt like pain. Whether he'd imagined the cold taste of disappointment which was making his mouth bitter. He must have done. Because wasn't this the news he'd been longing for? The only sane solution to a problem which should never have arisen?

He focused his eyes to where Alannah sat perched on the edge of a chair opposite him and thought how pale she looked. Paler than the thick white lanes through which they'd walked on Christmas Day, when the snow had trapped them in that false little bubble. Her blue eyes were ringed with dark shadows, as if she hadn't been sleeping.

Had she?

Or had she—like he—been lying wide-eyed in the depths of the night, remembering what it had felt like when they'd made love and then fallen asleep with their limbs tangled warmly together?

He flattened the palms of his hands flat on the surface of his desk. 'You're sure?'

'One hundred per cent.'

He wondered why she had chosen to tell him here, and now. Why she had come to his office after successfully negotiating a ten-minute slot in his diary with Kirsty. And Kirsty hadn't even checked with him first!

'Couldn't you have chosen a more suitable time and place to tell me, rather than bursting into my office and getting my assistant to collude with you?' he questioned impatiently. 'Or is it just a continuation of your determination to keep me at arm's length?'

'I've been busy.'

That was usually *his* excuse. He leaned back in his chair and studied her. 'You won't even have dinner with me,' he observed coolly.

'I'm sure you'll get over it,' she said lightly.

His gaze didn't waver. 'I thought you said you'd enjoyed our "experiment" over Christmas—so why not run with it a little longer? Come on, Alannah.' A smile curved his lips. 'What harm could it do?'

Alannah stared at him. What *harm* could it do? Was he serious? But that was the trouble—he was. Unemotional, cynical and governed by nothing but sexual hunger—Niccolò obviously saw no reason why they shouldn't continue with the affair. Because it meant different things to each of them. For him, it was clearly just an enjoyable diversion, while for her it felt as if someone had chipped away a little bit of her heart every time she saw him. *It was being chipped away right now.*

She had chosen his office and a deliberately short

appointment in which to tell him her news in order to avoid just this kind of scene. She'd actually considered telling him by phone but had instinctively felt that such a move would have been counterproductive. That he might have insisted on coming round to confront her face to face and her defences would have been down.

It was bad enough trying to stay neutral now—even with the safety of his big oak desk between them. Sitting there in his crisp white shirt and tailored suit, Niccolò's face was glowing with health and vitality and she just wanted to go and put her arms around him. She wanted to lean on him and have him tell her that everything was going to be okay. But he didn't want a woman like her leaning on him and anyway—she was independent and strong. She didn't need a man who could never give her what she wanted, and what she wanted from him was love. *Join the queue,* she thought bitterly.

'You haven't *done* anything,' she said. 'You haven't made or broken any promises. Everything is how it's supposed to be, Niccolò. What happened between us was great but it was never intended to last. And it hasn't.'

'But what if…?' He picked up the golden pen which was lying on top of the letters he'd been signing and stared at it as if he had never really seen it before. He lifted his gaze to hers. 'What if I wanted it to last—at least for a little while longer? What then?'

Alannah tensed as fear and yearning washed over her—yet of the two emotions, the yearning was by far the deadlier.

'And how long did you have in mind?' she questioned sweetly. 'One week? Two? Would it be presumptuous to expect it might even continue for a *whole month*?'

He slammed the pen down. 'Does it matter?' he demanded. 'Not every relationship between a man and a woman lasts for ever.'

'But most relationships don't start out with a discussion about when it's going to end!' She sucked in a breath and prayed she could hold onto her equilibrium for a while longer. 'Look, nothing has changed. I'm still the same woman I always was—except that I have you to thank for helping me lose some of my inhibitions. But I still don't know who my father was and I still have the kind of CV which would make someone with your sensitive social antennae recoil in horror. Appearances matter to you, Niccolò. You know they do. So why don't you just celebrate the fact that you had a lucky escape and that we aren't going to be forced together by some random act of nature.' She rose to her feet. 'And leave me to finish off Alekto's apartment in time for his party. The caterers are arriving tomorrow, and there are still some last-minute touches which need fixing.'

'Sit down,' he said. 'I haven't finished yet.'

'Well, I have. We've said everything which needs to be said. It's over, Niccolò. I'm not so stupid that I want to hang around having sex with a man who despises everything I stand for!'

'I don't despise what you stand for. I made a lot of judgements about you and some of them were wrong.'

'Only *some* of them?' she demanded.

'Why can't you just accept what I'm offering? Why do you have to want more?'

'Because I'm worth it.' She hitched the strap of her handbag over her shoulder. 'And I'm going now.'

He rose to his feet. 'I don't want you to go!' he gritted out.

'Tough. I'm out of here. *Ciao.*'

And to Niccolò's amazement she picked up her handbag and walked out of his office without a backward glance.

For a moment he stood there, stunned—as the door slammed behind her. He thought about rushing after her, about pulling her into his arms and kissing her and *then* seeing whether she was so damned certain their relationship was over. But that would make it all about sex, wouldn't it? And sex had always been the least troublesome part of this equation. Besides, Kirsty was buzzing through to tell him that his eleven o'clock had arrived, so he was forced to concentrate on listening to what his architect was saying, rather than on a pair of stubborn pink lips he still wanted to crush beneath his own.

By seven o'clock that evening, he decided that Alannah had been right. Better to end it now, before she got in too deep—because it wouldn't be fair to break her heart as he had broken so many others. She would start falling in love with him. She would want more from him than he was capable of giving. Better they both recognised his limitations now.

He glanced up at the clock again. Maybe he should start as he meant to go on. Dinner with someone new would surely be the way to go. A civilised dinner with someone who didn't get under his skin the way she did.

He flicked through his address book, but none of the long list of names excited him enough to pick up the phone. He had his driver drop him home and worked in his study until way past midnight. But still he couldn't sleep. He kept remembering when Alannah had spent the night with him there and, even though the linen had been laundered, he thought he could still detect the unique scent of her skin on his sheets. He thought about the cottage. About the tree-lights and the snow. About that unreal sense of quiet satisfaction as he had cooked her Christmas lunch. The way they had fallen asleep on the sofa after they'd made love. Hadn't that been like the closest thing to peace he'd felt in a long, long time?

And that was all make-believe, he told himself fiercely. As insubstantial as Christmas itself.

He lay and watched the luminous numbers on his clock changing slowly and just before his alarm was due to go off a text arrived from Alekto Sarantos.

Don't be late for my party! Beautiful women and a beautiful apartment—what better way to see in the new year? A

Niccolò stared blankly at the screen of his mobile phone, telling himself that a party was exactly what he needed, and didn't Alekto throw some of the best parties he'd ever been to? But just the thought of it left him cold. Tugging on his running gear, he got ready for the gym and wondered why his eyes looked so shadowed and haunted.

But deep down, he knew exactly why.

'It is *spectacular*.' Alekto Sarantos smiled as he looked around the main reception room, his blue eyes gleaming. 'You have transformed my apartment, Alannah—and you have worked against the clock to get it done in time for my party. *Efkaristo poli.* I thank you.'

Alannah smiled back, even though just smiling seemed to take a massive effort these days. It was true that the place *did* look pretty amazing—especially when she thought back to the sea of beige it had been before. The woman who had made the curtains had got very excited about it and she had told someone, who had told someone else. Even during the short period between Christmas and new year, word had soon got round in an industry which survived by constantly seeking out new ideas and new faces. Already Alannah had received a phone call from one of the big interior magazines, asking if they could do a photo shoot there. She doubted whether Alekto would agree, since she got the idea he was very hot on privacy. Still, she could *always ask* him. And even if he didn't give his permission, she sensed that she had turned a corner—because this was the big break she had been waiting for. *And she had Niccolò to thank for it.*

Security and creative fulfilment were lying within her grasp. So why did it all feel so empty? Why was she having to force herself to look and sound enthusiastic about something she'd always dreamed of?

She sighed. She knew *exactly* why. *Because she'd made the fundamental mistake of falling in love with a man who had never offered her anything but sex.*

'I hope you're coming to my new year's party?' Alekto was saying. 'You really ought to be the guest of honour, after what you've achieved here. Unless, of course, you have already made plans?'

Alannah glanced out at the late afternoon sky, which was now almost dark. The only plans she had made were to buy the TV guide and turn up the central heating, while she waited for Big Ben to chime in a new year she couldn't seem to get worked up about. She thought about getting dressed up for a party attended by Alekto Sarantos and his glamorous friends, and how any sane person would leap at such an opportunity.

But what if Niccolò was there?

Her heart pounded. The possibility was high. It was more than high. They were best mates, weren't they? She shook her head. 'It's very sweet of you—but I think I'll just have a quiet evening in,' she said.

'Up to you.' Alekto shrugged. 'But if you change your mind…'

Alannah went home, bathed and washed her hair—before pulling on her dressing gown and a pair of slouchy socks and switching on the TV. She flicked channels. Crowds of people were already flocking into Trafalgar Square, even though it was still early. People were being interviewed, swigging from beer bottles and giggling—and Alannah suddenly saw herself as a fly on the wall might see her. A woman sitting on her own at nine o'clock on New Year's Eve, wearing a dressing gown and a pair of old socks.

What had she become?

She swallowed. She had become a cliché, that was what. She had fallen in love with someone who had always been out of reach. And yet, instead of accepting that and holding her head up high and just getting on with her life, the way she'd always done, she had caved in. She was like some sort of mole, living in darkness—cowering inside her own safe little habitat, because she was afraid to go out. It was the worst night of the year to be home alone—especially if your stupid heart was heavy and aching—and yet here she was. *Mole.*

What was she so worried about? That she might see Niccolò with another woman? Surely that would be the best of all possible outcomes—it would remind her of how easily he could move on. It would make her accept *reality*, instead of chasing after rainbows.

Tearing off her slouchy socks, she pulled out the gold dress she'd worn at Christmas and slithered into it. Then she slapped on a defiant amount of make-up, her highest heels—and a warm, ankle-length coat. People were milling outside pubs as she made her way to the station and more snow was falling as she caught the underground and got out at Knightsbridge.

It was much quieter in this part of town. There were few revellers out and about around here—this was the world of the private, rather than the street party. But by the time she reached Park View other partygoers were milling around in the foyer and the party atmosphere was contagious. She shared the elevator up to Alekto's apartment with several stunning women and a man who kept surreptitiously glancing at his phone.

The elevator pinged to a halt and the door to the penthouse was opened by a waitress dressed as a flamingo, a tray of exotic-looking cocktails in her hand. Alannah went off to hang up her coat and then wandered along the corridors she knew so well, back towards the sitting room. It was strange seeing the place like this—full of people—when she had only ever seen it empty. Most of the furniture she'd installed had been pushed back against the walls to maximise the space—but the room still looked spectacular. Even she could see that. The colours worked brilliantly—providing the perfect backdrop for Alekto's extensive art collection—and she was particularly proud of the lighting.

In spite of everything, she knew Niccolò would be pleased with her work. He might regret some things, but he would never regret giving her the job and she should take pride in that. A horrible dark pain washed over her, only this time it was underpinned with reproach. She wasn't supposed to be thinking about Niccolò. Wasn't that going to be her one and only new year resolution? That part of her life was over. She had to cut her losses and move on. And it was a waste of time to wonder what it would have been like if she *had* been pregnant. Or to dwell on that irrational and sinking sense of disappointment when she had stared at the test result and it had been negative.

A woman masquerading as a bird of paradise offered her a drink and Alannah took one, but the sweet concoction tasted deceptively powerful and she put the glass down as Alekto Sarantos came over to talk to her.

'You made it, then,' he said, with a smile. '*Thavmassios.* If I had a Euro for every person who has asked me who is responsible for the design of this apartment, then I would be a very rich man.'

'But I thought you *were* a very rich man,' she said, and he laughed, before giving her a thoughtful look. 'I might have some work for you in Greece, if you're interested?'

Alannah didn't even need to think about it. 'I'd be very interested,' she said immediately, because a different country might be just what she needed. What was it they said? A new year and a new start.

'Why don't you call my office on Monday?' he suggested, pulling out a business card and handing it to her.

'I will,' she said, putting it into her handbag as he walked away.

'Alannah?'

A familiar voice curled over her skin like dark velvet and she turned to see Niccolò standing there. His hair and shoulders were wet with melting snow and he was wearing a dark cashmere coat, which made him stand out from all the other guests. Alannah stiffened as his shadow fell over her and her heart began to hammer as she looked up into his shuttered features.

The knot of tension in her stomach grew tighter. But she had come here tonight to hold her head high, hadn't she? Not to hang it in shame. Nor to waste time wishing for something which could never be.

'Niccolò,' she said coolly. 'Fancy seeing you here.'

'What were you saying to Alekto?'

'That's really none of your business.'

'You do know he is world-famous for breaking women's hearts?'

'Why, has he lifted the crown from you?' she questioned acidly. 'And what are you doing still wearing your overcoat?'

'Because I have driven halfway across London looking for you,' he growled.

She frowned. 'Why?'

'Why do you think?' he exploded. 'I went round to your apartment, only you weren't there.' He had spent the afternoon psyching himself up, making careful plans about what he was going to say to her. He had decided to surprise her, because he…well, because he wanted to—and that in itself was uncharacteristic. He had naturally made the assumption that she would have been home alone, only when he'd got there Alannah's apartment had been shrouded in darkness and his heart had sunk. The sight of all those empty windows had suddenly seemed like a metaphor for his life and they had confirmed the certainty which had been growing inside him for days.

Instinct had made him pull out his telephone to speak to Alekto and his hunch was proved right. His friend had coolly informed him that, yes, Alannah *had* been invited to the party and although she'd told him she wasn't coming, she seemed to have changed her mind. In fact, she had just walked in, looking like a goddess in a spectacular golden dress.

Niccolò had turned his car around and driven from Acton, getting snarled up in the new-year traffic—his nerves becoming more and more frayed as an unfamiliar sense of agitation nagged away at him. And now he was here standing in front of her and nothing was as he thought it would be. He had not intended to launch into a jealous tirade because he'd seen her being chatted up by one of the world's biggest players.

Wasn't he supposed to be a 'player' himself?

His mouth hardened.

Not any more.

He was in a roomful of some of the most beautiful

women in the world and yet he could see only one. One who was staring at him with hostility and suspicion and, in his heart, he knew he couldn't blame her.

So why the hell was he demonstrating an arrogance which might cause her magnificent pride to assert itself, and tell him to take a running jump? He needed to keep her onside. To placate her. To make her realise why he had come here. *And to make her realise that it was the only possible solution.*

'I need to talk to you,' he said.

'Talk away.' She gave a careless shrug. 'I'm not stopping you.'

'In private.'

'I'd prefer to stay here, if you don't mind.'

'Unfortunately, *tentatrice*, I do mind.'

Without warning, he caught hold of her hand, his fingers enclosing her hammering pulse as he led her through the throng of partygoers until they had reached one of the bedrooms. He shut the door, just as she shook her hand free and glared at him.

'What do you think you're doing?' she demanded. 'You can't just waltz up to someone in the middle of a party and *manhandle* them like that! You can't just drag a woman from a room because you've decided you want a private word with her. Oh, sorry—I'd forgotten.' She slapped her palm against her brow. 'You can—and you do. Well, you might be Tarzan but I am not your Jane. I don't *do* Neanderthal and I don't *do* arrogant men who think they can just blaze into other people's lives doing exactly what they want. So will you please step aside and let me pass?'

'Not until you've heard me out,' he said, as a strange sense of calm washed over him. 'Please.'

She looked at him for a moment before pointedly glancing at her watch. 'You've got five minutes.'

Niccolò sucked in a breath but for a moment he couldn't speak. His calmness seemed to be deserting him as he realised that this wasn't going to be easy. He was going to have to do something unheard of—something he had instinctively always shied away from. He was going to have to pull out his feelings from the dark place where he'd buried them and he was going to have to admit them. To her. And even when he did, there was no guarantee that it might not be too late.

He looked into the wary blue of her eyes and his heart pounded. 'I need to ask your forgiveness,' he said. 'For all the unjust accusations I hurled at you. For my bull-headedness and my lack of compassion. For taking so long to realise the kind of woman you really are. Strong and proud and passionate and loyal. I've missed you, Alannah, and I want you back. Nobody talks to me the way you do, or makes me feel the way you do. Nobody else makes my heart skip a beat whenever I see her. I want to spend the rest of my life with you. To one day make the baby we didn't have this time. I want to make a real home—with you. Only with you.'

She took a step back, as if she'd just seen a ghost, and she started shaking her head. 'You don't want me,' she said in a hoarse voice. 'You only think you do, because I'm the one who walked away and that's probably never happened to you before. You want someone respectable, who is as pure as the driven snow—because that's the sort of thing you care about. Someone *suitable*. You didn't want me as bridesmaid because you were worried about what other people would think. Because you're hung up on appearances and how things look from the outside, no matter what you say.'

'I used to be,' he said savagely. 'But you have made me realise that appearances and social position don't matter. It's what's underneath which counts. And you have everything that counts. You are soft and smart and funny. You are kind and caring and talented. You didn't even smoke dope at school, did you—even though you were accused of it?'

Startled by this sudden conversational twist, Alannah narrowed her eyes suspiciously. 'Did Michela tell you that?'

He shook his head. 'She didn't have to. I worked it out for myself. I think you may just have covered up for my sister all this time.'

'Because that's what friends do,' she said fiercely. 'That's called loyalty.'

'I realise that now,' he said. 'It's just taken me a long and very circuitous route to get here. But I don't want to talk about the past any more… I want to concentrate on the future.'

He reached within the pocket of his snow-covered overcoat and pulled out a little box. 'This is for you,' he said, and his voice was slightly unsteady.

Alannah watched as he opened it and she was shamefully aware of a sinking sense of disappointment as she looked inside. Had she really thought it was an engagement ring? Was she really that fickle? Because glittering against the background of dark velvet was a brooch shaped like a little honey-bee. Its back was covered with yellow, black and white stones and she found herself thinking that she'd never seen anything so sparkly. She looked up at him, still disorientated.

'What's this?' she said.

'You collect insect brooches, don't you? They're diamonds. The black ones are quite rare. It's for you,' he said again. 'Because I didn't buy you a Christmas present.'

But Alannah felt a terrible lump in her throat as she began to blink her eyes rapidly. 'You just don't get it, do you?' she whispered. 'The brooches I have are all worth peanuts. I wear them because my mother gave them to me—because they *mean* something to me. I don't care if they're diamonds or paste, Niccolò. I don't care how much something is *worth*.'

'Then what if I tell you this is worth what I feel for you, and that is everything. *Everything*.' He moved closer. 'Unless you want me to go to a flea-market to find you something cheaper? Tell me, Alannah—are you going to set me a series of challenges before you will accept me?'

She almost laughed, except that now hot tears were springing to her eyes and she couldn't seem to stop them. 'I don't know what I'm going to do,' she whispered. 'Because I'm scared. Scared because I keep thinking this is all a dream and that I'm going to wake up in a minute.'

'No, not a dream,' he said, taking the brooch from the box and pinning it next to the little grasshopper which already adorned her golden dress. 'I bought you this because I love you. This is the reality.'

Her lips parted. 'Niccolò,' she said again, and now her voice was shaking. 'If this isn't true—'

He halted her protest by placing his finger over her lips. 'It *is* true. It has always been true. The first time I set eyes on you, I was hit by a thunderbolt so powerful that I felt as if you'd cast some kind of spell on me. And that spell never really faded. I love you, Alannah—even though I've been running away from the idea of love all my life. I saw what it did to my mother. I saw it as a weakness which sucked the life from everything in its path. Which blinded her even to the needs of her children.'

She bit her lip. 'I can understand that.'

He sensed her absolution, but he was not finished. 'But what I feel for you does not feel like weakness. I feel strong when I am with you, Alannah. As strong as a mountain lion. As if I could conquer the world.'

She let him put his arms around her and her head rested against his chest. 'That's funny, because right now I feel as weak as a kitten.'

His black eyes burned into her as he gently levered her face up so that she was looking directly at him. 'The only thing I need to know is whether you love me?'

'Of course I love you.' The words came tumbling out as if she'd been waiting all her life to say them. She thought about the first time she'd seen him, when they'd just clicked. It had been a thunderbolt for her, too, and she had never been able to forget him. She thought about how empty her life seemed when he wasn't there. He wasn't the man she'd thought him to be—he was so much more. 'I think I've always loved you.'

'Then kiss me, my beautiful Alannah,' he said softly. 'And let me show you my love.'

Slowly and tenderly, he traced his fingertip along the edges of her lips before lowering his head towards hers and Alannah's heart filled up with so much happiness that she felt as if she might burst with it.

EPILOGUE

'I USED TO think you hated weddings.'

Niccolò looked down into Alannah's face as he closed the door to their honeymoon suite, and smiled at her. 'I did. But that was before I found the woman I wanted to marry. Now it seems that I'm their biggest fan.'

'Mmm. Me, too.' She looped her arms around his neck. 'You did like the dress?'

'You looked beautiful. The most beautiful bride in the world. But then, you could wear a piece of sacking and I still wouldn't be able to tear my eyes away from you.'

'Oh, Niccolò.' She slanted him a look from between her lashes. 'Whoever would have guessed that beneath that cynical exterior beat the heart of a true poet?'

'It's true,' he said, mock-seriously. 'Though I must be careful not to lose my edge. If my competitors find out how much I'm softening, then I will soon be toast in the world of finance.'

'You?' She laughed easily. 'Yeah, sure. Like *that's* ever going to happen!'

He began to unzip her dress. 'Are you tired?'

'Not a bit. Even though it's been a very long day.'

She closed her eyes as the costly gown pooled to the ground around her feet. She had thought he would want a quiet wedding—something discreet, even a little hushed-up. Hadn't she thought he'd want to keep the risk of press interest to a minimum, despite his protestations that her past no longer bothered him? Probably. But once again he had surprised her. It was funny how love had the power to change people and to alter their views on what was important. He had told her that he was going to announce their engagement to the world's press and then he had gone out and bought her an enormous sapphire ring, which he said was the closest colour he could get to the denim-blue of her eyes.

Predictably, some of the old photos from *Stacked* magazine had made an appearance in the papers—but suddenly, they didn't seem to matter. It was slightly surreal to hear Niccolò echoing his sister's words—*and believing them*—by saying really they were very tame in comparison to a lot of the stuff you saw in contemporary music videos.

'I am proud of you, *tentatrice*,' he had murmured, crumpling the newspaper into a ball and hurling it into the bin. 'Proud of all you have achieved and how you have kept your dignity intact. Most of all, I am proud that you have consented to be my wife.'

And she had smiled. 'Oh, darling.'

The wedding was held in London's oldest Italian church, in Clerkenwell, and there was a stellar number of guests. A fully recovered Luis Martinez was there—as was the Sultan of Qurhah, Murat 'the Magnificent'. And naturally, Alekto Sarantos was at his dazzling best, even though he was barely visible through the sea of eager women who were clamouring round him. Michela was matron of honour—her silk gown cleverly hiding the beginning of a baby bump.

With Alannah's encouragement, Niccolò had told Michela the truth about their parents' death—and the admission had brought brother and sister much closer. Because secrets were always more dangerous than the truth, as he'd learned.

Alannah shivered with pleasure as Niccolò lifted her out of the discarded wedding dress and carried her over to the bed, wearing nothing but her underwear, sheer stockings and a pair of very high, white stilettos. As he undressed her she thought about the inhibitions which had once crippled her and which now seemed like a distant memory.

Tomorrow they were flying to the island of Niccolò's birth. He had only been back to Sicily once, after his mother's death—when he had been full of youthful rage and bitterness about the rejection she had suffered at the hands of her own family. But time had mellowed him and Alannah had helped him get some perspective. His maternal grandparents were dead—but he had cousins and uncles and aunts living there. A whole new family for them to get to know. And she was excited about that, too—looking forward to a big, extended family after so many years on her own.

He moved over her, his face suddenly very serious as he brushed her hair away from her cheek. 'Thank you,' he said softly.

She took his hand and kissed it. 'For?'

'For loving me. For being you.'

For being you. He didn't want anyone else, she had come to realise. He just wanted her exactly as she was, with no changes or modifications. He didn't want to rewrite her past, or pretend it hadn't happened, because her past had made her the woman she was today. And he loved that woman.

Alannah sighed.

Just like she loved her man.

* * * * *

THE SOLDIER'S HOLIDAY HOMECOMING

JUDY DUARTE

In memory of Lydia Bustos, who was called home sooner than any of us expected. I'm rejoicing for you, Tia – but missing you, especially during the holidays.

Chapter One

Brighton Valley, Texas, was the last place in the world Joe Wilcox had ever expected to step foot in again.

Well, not when it came to the good ol' U.S.A. He sure as hell wouldn't look forward to another deployment to Afghanistan. But he'd made a promise to deliver a letter for a friend, and if there was one thing that could be said about Joe—he always kept his word.

So he'd packed a few belongings, rented a car just outside of Camp Pendleton and left California. He'd stopped in El Paso long enough to spend the night with Red Conway, a retired marine he'd met on a bus ten years ago. Red had taken Joe in when he'd been a down-and-out teenage runaway, hell-bent on leaving everyone and everything he'd once known behind.

The two men had shared a couple of beers, a pizza and a few stories. The next day, Joe had continued on for another nine hundred miles, finally arriving in Brighton Valley exhausted and hungry.

The first thing Joe did after checking in to a cheap but clean room at the Night Owl, a motor lodge that catered to travelers who were low on funds and just passing through, was to shove his duffle bags under the bed. There was a closet he could have used, but that had never felt like a safe place when he'd been a kid determined to protect his valuables from an uncle who might not have enough cash to buy a pack of cigarettes and a pint of Jack Daniels.

He probably should have shaken the habit years ago, but being back in town brought back all kinds of weird memories, leaving him a bit unbalanced.

Next he took a long, hot shower, slipped into a comfortable pair of worn jeans and a black sweatshirt and hoofed it across the highway to the Stagecoach Inn.

In spite of the seasonal chill in the air, a cold beer would really hit the spot right about now, but he wasn't looking for a drink or any entertainment. He was on a mission. He had a letter to deliver to a blonde cocktail waitress named Chloe Dawson.

Once he found the coldhearted woman who'd broken Dave Cummings's heart, he'd give her the letter Dave had asked him to deliver.

Now, as he stood on the side of the busy highway, waiting for a lull in the traffic so he could cross, he pulled out Chloe's photograph, the one Dave had always carried. He studied the photo in the flickering streetlight overhead. The snapshot was a little grainy, so her facial features weren't especially clear, but it was easy to see that the platinum blonde had long, wavy hair and a dynamite shape.

To be honest, when he and Dave had been stationed in Afghanistan, all Dave could talk about was the woman he'd placed on a pedestal and the dreams he'd had for them. Joe had been a little envious. He'd never had a family—well, not one he'd wanted to claim—so he'd never dared to consider a white-picket-fence dream. But his buddy had grown up as an only child, adored by his parents. So why wouldn't he expect to have that same life for himself?

Joe had to admit that he'd wondered what such an attractive woman had seen in Dave. Not that his friend wasn't a good person. He was kind and generous to a fault, but he'd been so sheltered by his doting parents that he tended to be naive about life and other things.

Dave had been more sensitive than guys like Joe, who'd learned early on to get tough in order to survive, and as a result, he'd been hit hard by his father's unexpected death. Then, when his mom had been diagnosed with an aggressive form of cancer nine months later, he'd been devastated.

Obviously Chloe had seen how broken up and vulnerable Dave had been and used it against him when she'd set her gold-digging plan in motion.

From what Joe had gathered, she'd rented a room from Dave's widowed mother, and when Dave had gone home on leave last summer, he'd fallen hard for her. And, sadly, he'd been too caught up in grief and lust and starry-eyed wonder to see the writing on the wall.

After Mrs. Cummings's funeral, Chloe had promised to take care of the ranch and to wait for him until he returned from war. Dave, of course, had bought her line of bull and had promised her the moon.

The dream that they'd get married as soon as he got back from deployment and eventually raise "a passel of kids" on the family ranch had been the only thing that kept him going.

Dave might have joined the Marines, hoping to man up and become independent, but he hadn't been cut out for a life of combat, especially when his idea of happy ever after was in Texas.

Not that life in a war zone had been a cakewalk for Joe, either, but growing up with an abusive drunk uncle and then ending up in the foster care system had made him both street-smart and strong. He hadn't realized it at the time, but in a lot of ways his crappy childhood had been a blessing.

Either way, Dave's defense mechanism for dealing with his depression and fears had been to cling to his future with Chloe. It was all he'd talked about, all he'd looked forward to. But apparently Chloe had envisioned an entirely different future, one without Dave. And it looked like fate had granted her that wish.

As the last headlights of the oncoming traffic passed, Joe crossed the street, his boots crunching on the graveled parking lot as he made his way to the entrance of the Stagecoach Inn, where blinking Christmas lights adorned the front window.

He could have gone out to the ranch looking for Chloe, but from what Dave had told him, she worked at the honky-tonk to pick up extra money. And Dave had spent many nights in the war-ravaged deserts of Afghanistan, worrying that some rowdy cowboy might pick up his girl while she was there.

Was that what had happened? Had Chloe found someone better looking? Someone with more money and a bigger ranch?

Joe supposed it really didn't matter why she'd broken Dave's heart, just that she'd done it—callously and without any thought of how lonely and despondent the poor guy had been.

When her Dear John arrived, Dave's depression spiraled downward. And in his grief, he'd taken off after a group of combatants on his own, a reckless act that bordered on suicide and nearly got him killed.

Joe had run to his defense and gotten shot, too, which resulted in two career-ending injuries. All because of that damn cocktail waitress. Couldn't she have waited until Dave had gone home to break up with him? Her abandonment in his time of need had led to him having a death wish, which eventually came true.

As Joe neared the entrance of the rowdy honky-tonk, the country music as well as the hoots of laughter grew louder. He pulled open the door, then paused in the doorway, allowing his senses to adjust to the smell of booze and smoke, to the blaring jukebox and the chatter of people milling about.

He was looking for a woman—a sexy blonde who'd be taking orders and serving drinks. From Dave's description, Chloe was twenty-two years old, about five foot four and a knockout. The photograph wasn't going to be all that helpful, although Joe didn't have any reason to dispute Dave's claim. Either way, in a small place like this she shouldn't be too hard to find.

Joe made his way across the scarred wood floor to the bar, which stretched across the far wall. While the bartender filled a glass of beer for a cowboy sitting three seats to the left, Joe asked, "You know a woman by the name of Chloe Dawson?"

"Yeah. She used to work here for a while, but not anymore."

"What happened to her?"

"She quit."

"Know where I can find her?"

The barkeep surveyed him for a beat, as if he was

some kind of stalker or an abusive ex-boyfriend or something. "I got no idea where she is."

Joe didn't believe that for a minute, but there were plenty of others around here who might talk. Besides, he had a feeling she was still staying out at the Cummings ranch. Why wouldn't she be? Last he'd heard, Dave had left it to her in his will.

Did she know that already? Dave had already been discharged at the time of his death, so the military wouldn't have alerted her.

How long did it take for news from the outside world to reach a small town like this?

As the bartender delivered another round of drinks to a couple at the far end of the bar, Joe pulled out the stool and took a seat. It was pretty late to drive out to the ranch tonight. Besides, the sun had set several hours ago, and he was exhausted.

When the bartender finally returned, he wiped his hands on a dish towel. "What'll you have?"

Joe wasn't sure. Did he want something strong to help him unwind and go to sleep? Or something light and satisfying to wash down the road dust he'd swallowed since his trek from El Paso?

One thing he knew for sure, he was dead tired and running on fumes, although he doubted he'd be able to fall asleep right away.

"I'll have a Corona," he said.

The bartender continued to study him. "Can I see your ID?"

At twenty-six and after eight years in the military, Joe wasn't used to being carded. But then again, he'd only been out of the service and back in the States for a couple of months. He reached into the front pocket of his jeans, only to come up empty-handed.

Where the hell was…? Oh, crap. He'd showered back in the room and changed clothes. He must have left his wallet on the nightstand, next to his cell phone and… Damn. The key to the room had been right beside it. All he had on him was Dave's letter and the photograph, neither of which would do him much good tonight.

So much for hiding his valuables out of sight. Talk about being too tired to think straight. He blew out a ragged sigh. "I'm not trying to pull a fast one. I'm staying across the street at the Night Owl. Apparently, I left my wallet there."

"Sorry, buddy. The guy who worked here before me got fired for serving a minor, and I was told to card anyone who looked younger than thirty."

"I understand. I need to get my cash anyway. Keep that beer cold for me. I'll be back." Joe slid off the bar stool and headed for the door. He felt like a batter with two strikes against him already. What else could go wrong?

As he stepped outside and made his way to the parking lot, a drunk stumbled past him, walking toward a Silverado pickup, the keys in his hand.

"You got someone you can call?" Joe asked the guy.

"Get off my back," the drunk said. "You sound like my wife."

Joe was going to argue, but a woman came out a moment later and called out to the man. "Larry, I told you I'd drive. Wait for me. I can pick up my car tomorrow. Just let me get my purse and tell Shannon goodbye. I'll be right back."

Glad the guy had a ride, Joe headed for the Night

Owl. Did he want a beer badly enough to return to the bar once he got another key to his room? He wasn't so sure that he did. Just seeing the drunken man—Larry—was a reminder of his uncle and all the nights Tío Ramon had come stumbling home, slurring his words and raising his fists, ready to strike up a fight with his aunt or whoever crossed him.

For the most part, Joe didn't drink much at all. But tonight, he might be tempted to tie one on, just like Dave had been prone to do ever since they'd both been sent to the hospital in Germany.

Dave's injuries had been pretty severe. And just thinking that he'd have to go through life physically damaged had sent the already emotionally impaired man into a depression from which he hadn't been able to recover.

Hell, Joe had been bummed, too. His own gunshot wound had made him rethink his intention to reenlist, which was why he was here now—no longer officially in the corps, but always and forever a marine.

He'd shaken his own discouragement and disappointment, focusing instead on Dave's recovery and rehab. That is, until he'd been discharged and sent back to the States. Upon Dave's arrival two weeks ago, Joe had picked him up at the airport, determined to help him mend. But Dave's depression and attitude had sunk to an all-time low, and on one of his first nights back, he downed more than his prescribed dose of meds, followed by a glass of ninety proof, ending his pain forever.

The coroner had ruled Dave's death an accident, an unintentional overdose. But Joe believed otherwise.

There was a life insurance policy somewhere, which

wouldn't do anyone any good if the death was ruled a suicide. Joe had the power to throw a wrench into the machinery and blow things sky-high, which he was tempted to do. After all, Dave had told him that he'd made Chloe his beneficiary. And on top of that, he'd left her everything—his money, his family ranch in Brighton Valley.

How lucky could a heartless woman get?

As Joe started across the street, heading for the Night Owl, the Silverado started up, but something wasn't quite right about the sound. Instead of backing out in a normal fashion, the driver gunned the engine and the tires spun, kicking up gravel as it blasted forward and over the curb.

Joe's pause to look over his shoulder at drunk Larry cost him his opportunity to make it all the way across the street as oncoming cars zoomed by him, leaving him no safe retreat as the truck shot onto the highway, barreling right at him.

He'd thought his day couldn't get much worse and might have considered this strike three, but he was too busy trying to dodge the speeding truck as it nailed him in the side, sending him flying into the night.

When Chloe Dawson received the call from the Brighton Valley Medical Center asking her to come to the hospital and identify a hit-and-run victim, a patient they believed to be David Cummings, her heart dropped to the pit of her stomach, and her grip on the receiver tightened. "Is he...*dead?*"

"No, he's unconscious."

"I'll be right there."

The moment she hung up, she threw on a pair of

jeans, a white T-shirt and sweater. Then she climbed into one of the ranch pickups and drove to town, her hands clammy as they struggled to control both the steering wheel and the gearshift at the same time, her knee wobbly as she stepped on the clutch.

Thank God her dad had insisted she learn to drive a stick when she'd turned sixteen, although this beat-up old GMC wasn't anything like the little Honda Civic she'd once driven.

She kept her eyes on the darkened country road until she reached city limits twenty minutes later and turned down the highway that led to the medical center. She snagged the first parking space she could find and rushed to the E.R. entrance.

Once inside, she told the receptionist to alert Dr. Betsy Nielson of her arrival. It gave her some comfort to know that Dave was under the care of one of the best doctors at BVMC.

After making several visits to the emergency department with Teresa Cummings, Dave's mother, and also with some of the elderly residents at the Sheltering Arms Rest Home, where Chloe had once worked as a nurse's aide, Dr. Betsy Nielson and Chloe had become well acquainted.

Fortunately, within a matter of minutes, Betsy, an attractive redhead wearing a pair of light blue scrubs came out to the waiting room personally to find her. "Thanks for coming in, Chloe."

"No problem. I'm glad you called. How is he?"

"He's conscious now, but I'm afraid he's not going to be any help. He has amnesia—and no ID."

"And you think it's Dave?"

"I've never met Teresa's son, so I have no idea what

he looks like. But the patient is in his mid- to late-twenties. A tattoo of the marine insignia on his left biceps indicates he is or was in the military. So I made the assumption. Sheriff Hollister is checking into that."

Chloe hadn't heard from Dave in months—not since she'd had to take a direct approach and tell him that a couple of shared dinners in the hospital cafeteria didn't mean they were altar-bound. She'd felt badly about hurting him, especially with him being so far from home, but each letter he'd sent her from Afghanistan had included more and more marriage plans. And she'd needed to make it clear that she only wanted to be friends.

"How badly is he hurt?" Chloe asked. "Is he going to be okay?"

"He's bruised, with cuts and lacerations. But there aren't any broken bones. His most serious injury appears to be a concussion."

"Where did it happen?"

"On the highway outside the Stagecoach Inn."

Chloe had worked at the honky-tonk for a while, hoping to earn some spare cash so she could go back to nursing school once Dave got back home and was able to run the ranch himself. But she'd never liked getting involved in confrontations and tried to avoid them at all costs. Needless to say, she'd gotten tired of having to put some of the rowdier patrons in their places as the night wore on. So she'd quit last month.

"Did anyone inside the Stagecoach Inn know who he was? I mean, Dave wasn't much of a drinker—unless that changed while he was deployed." Had he stopped by the bar to look for her? He hadn't liked the idea of her working there, but since he'd quit writing to her and her last letter to him had been returned, he might not know that she'd quit.

"From what I understand," Betsy said, "he might have gone inside, but he never ordered a drink."

"So what happened? How'd he get hit by a car?"

"The sheriff's department is still investigating, so I'm not entirely sure. Apparently he was on foot. A bystander heard the squealing wheels and the thud, but only caught sight of the taillights of the vehicle. She called 9-1-1, and he was rushed to the hospital. But because he has no wallet, the only clue to his identity was the letter he was carrying."

"The letter?"

"Apparently it was written by Dave Cummings and addressed to you. That's why I called the ranch and wanted you to give us a positive ID."

"Where is he?" Chloe asked. "Can I see him?"

"Of course. Come with me."

The doctor led Chloe through the E.R. door and along a maze of exam rooms until she reached a small area just off the nurses' station and slowed to a stop. "He's right here." She pulled the curtain back.

But when Chloe spotted the man lying in bed and took in his dark hair—clipped short but not in the customary military high and tight—as well as his olive complexion and square cut jaw, she froze in her tracks. His eyes were closed, and he had a couple of scrapes on a notably handsome face.

While she'd like to be of help to the doctor, she realized that she wouldn't be. "I'm sorry, Betsy, but that's not Dave Cummings."

"Do you know who he is?"

"I've never seen him before." She certainly would

have remembered if she had. Even asleep and with bumps and bruises, the man definitely aroused a woman's soul and would leave a lasting impression.

Upon hearing their voices, he stirred. When his eyes opened, her breath caught at the sight of their stunning sky-blue color.

He zeroed in on her, and his brow furrowed. "Who are you?"

"My name's Chloe Dawson. You had a letter addressed to me."

He merely studied her, his gaze laced with confusion.

"Do you know Dave Cummings?" she asked.

"I suppose I should, since they tell me that's who wrote the letter I had in my pocket. But the name doesn't ring a bell." He reached up and stroked his head, massaging the temple.

"You could be one of Dave's friends," Chloe said. "I'd have to ask him, but I'm not sure how to get in touch with him. He was in Afghanistan the last I heard, although he could be back in the States now."

The handsome but wounded marine looked at the doctor, then back to Chloe. "Apparently, my brains were scrambled in that accident. And the pain medication the nurse gave me is really kicking in."

"Good," Betsy said. "Maybe you'll wake up fresh in the morning and remember who you are and what you're doing in Brighton Valley."

"About that letter that was addressed to me," Chloe said. "I'd like to see it. To be honest, I haven't heard from Dave in months, and I've been worried about him."

"I don't have it. The paramedics told me about it when they brought him in. From what I understand, the sheriff is using it as part of his investigation."

"You mean he thinks that letter may give him a clue as to who the driver was?" Chloe asked. "That doesn't make sense."

"It was probably just a random hit-and-run. But they want to rule out any criminal motivation."

Chloe stiffened. Had there been a crime committed? Had the handsome G.I. Doe done something illegal?

As if sensing Chloe's concern, Dr. Nielson placed a comforting hand on her shoulder. "I'm sure there's nothing to worry about. Sheriff Hollister used to be a detective with the Houston Police Department, so he's just being thorough. He's going to check with any witnesses or people working at any of the nearby businesses. He'll get to the bottom of this—probably by morning, if not sooner."

Chloe hoped so. She couldn't imagine how the poor guy must feel—injured, alone, confused.

"If the letter doesn't give us a clue to his identity," Chloe said, "it might let us know where we can find Dave. He ought to be able to shed some light on the problem."

"So I take it I'm the problem you're trying to solve," the handsome marine said. "That's a little unsettling."

"I didn't mean to imply that." Chloe eased closer to the bed. "Besides, I'd think that you'd want to get to the bottom of this."

"To say the least." G.I. Doe blew out a weary sigh. "So how do you know that guy—Dave Cummings?"

"I'm a family friend. I live on his ranch and have been house-sitting until he comes home. That's all."

Betsy glanced at the chart in her hand, then back to Chloe. "If you'll excuse me, I'm going to complete the paperwork to have him admitted for the night."

"All right. But under the circumstances—and assuming that he's a friend of Dave's—will you make a note of my name and number in his paperwork? I'd like to be kept informed about his condition."

The doctor addressed her injured patient. "Do you have a problem with that?"

"As long as you don't list her as next of kin, I'm okay with it."

"Why would it bother you to think that I was related to you?" Chloe asked.

A slow grin stretched across his face. "Because you're too damn pretty. If we were related by blood, I'd have to fight the guys off you—rather than fight to be at the top of your consideration list."

"Would you, now." So G.I. Doe was not only handsome, but a flirt. She glanced at his left hand, checking for a ring and not finding one.

Not that it mattered if he was already taken. She had enough on her plate these days without stressing over a romance.

Still, he was more than a little attractive, even in his injured state. But she wouldn't think about that now. The important thing was that he was her only link to Dave. And until Dave came home and could take over the ranch, Chloe was stuck in limbo and unable to get on with the future she had planned.

Chapter Two

The ranch foreman, Tomas Hernandez, had just left for the day when Chloe's cell phone vibrated in her pocket. She recognized the number to the Brighton Valley Medical Center and slid her finger across the screen. "Hello?"

"Chloe? This is Dr. Betsy Nielsen. Joe Wilcox is in stable condition and we're going to be discharging him soon."

She switched the phone to her other ear, thinking she hadn't heard correctly. *"Who?"*

"Joe Wilcox. The hit-and-run patient you came in to see last night."

"His memory returned?"

"No, I'm afraid it hasn't. Sheriff Hollister called shortly after you left the hospital last night. During the investigation, he learned who our patient is. Apparently, Mr. Joseph Wilcox arrived in town yesterday evening and checked into the Night Owl Motel. When the manager let the sheriff into his room, they found his wallet and the keys to a rental car, which also had been leased to Joseph Wilcox. The name on his California driver's license is a match, as well. I was told the photo bears his likeness. But they've yet to uncover any other information, so they still don't know much about him—or why he's in Texas."

Dave mentioned something about a buddy in the corps named Joe. The last name might have been Wilcox, but she wasn't sure.

"A deputy took his fingerprints," the doctor added, "Apparently he has a military record, although it will take more time to get any classified information. Unfortunately, we don't know how long that will be. And, like I said, physically, he's stable. So there's no legitimate reason for me to keep him another night."

Chloe knew Betsy wouldn't release a patient before it was wise to do so, but she didn't have the same confidence in the hospital administration who might be worried about him not being able to pay the bill. Her experience with the administrator of the Sheltering Arms Rest Home gave her cause to worry.

"Surely the hospital won't turn him out on the street," Chloe said. "He has no memory, nowhere to go and no one to take care of him."

"Of course not. That's why I called you. Since you left your name and number as his emergency contact, I was hoping that we could release him into your care."

Chloe didn't want to say no. After all, helping people was her natural calling, an intrinsic part of who she was. But she was living in the ranch house alone. And the man was a stranger.

"If you'd rather not take on the responsibility," Betsy said, "I understand."

Chloe might not know anything about the man, but he either was or had been a marine. And he had to be Dave's friend. Why else would he be delivering a letter to her?

"What time is he scheduled to be discharged?" She still needed to finish up her evening chores, and it was already pushing five o'clock.

"He should have been released a couple of hours ago, but I stalled the admin assistant until I had time to call you personally."

So much for finishing her chores before dark. She walked to the row of hooks just inside the back door and grabbed a red barn jacket to ward off the winter chill. "Then I'll leave now."

"That's great. He's on the third floor, in room 327. I'll have the paperwork ready for his discharge."

Five minutes later, Chloe climbed into the faded green GMC pickup and turned on the ignition. The old ranch truck roared to life, just as dependable as Chloe herself.

To be honest, she was apprehensive about taking in a stranger, but she chided herself as quickly as the thought crossed her mind. Teresa Cummings, Dave's mom, had let Chloe move to the Rocking C when she didn't have anywhere else to go. So taking in Joe Wilcox was her way of paying it forward. Besides that, Teresa would have taken the wounded marine under her wing in a heartbeat.

One night, before Teresa's death, she and Chloe had shared a pot of tea and talked about Teresa's terminal illness, her fears and her thoughts on life. The dying woman had also shared her regrets, one of which was about a kid she'd neglected to take in and offer a home.

Apparently, years ago, when Dave had been in high school, one of his friends had needed a home. The teenager had been living in foster care and had been miserable. So Teresa had asked her husband if the boy could move in with them. Her husband had been reluctant because the kid had gotten into trouble in the past and had even been suspended from school on several occasions. Still, he'd always been polite and helpful whenever he'd been on the Rocking C, and Teresa had suspected he'd only been acting out because of his sad childhood and difficult living situation.

Dave had begged them to let the boy stay with them, but his father had been firm in his decision. Teresa hadn't pushed her husband, although she always suspected she could have gotten him to see reason.

Shortly thereafter, the boy ran away from his foster home and was never heard from again. Dave had been inconsolable for nearly a year, and his relationship with his father had suffered terribly because of it.

Teresa had wished that she would have insisted that they take the boy in. And she'd always wondered what might have happened, how he might have fared if she had provided him a loving home. She also wondered if Dave and his father's relationship might have been a happier one, especially since her husband had died of a heart attack shortly after Dave joined the Marines in his one and only act of sheer rebellion.

To appease her guilt, Teresa had promised herself that, from then on, the Rocking C Ranch would always have its paddocks open for any stray, whether it had four legs or two.

And since Chloe had resolved to keep the ranch running exactly as Teresa would have done had she still been alive, that meant letting a hit-and-run victim who couldn't recall his own name recover there.

By the time she reached the medical center, it had grown dark outside and was threatening to rain. She turned into the hospital parking lot and pulled into a spot close to the entrance.

After entering the lobby, which had been decorated with twinkly lights and a big Christmas tree near the front window, she took the elevator to the third floor, where the nurses' station was a flurry of activity, reminding her of the shift changes at the Sheltering Arms. But thanks to the administrator at the nursing home who'd fired her rather than the incompetent nurse she'd reported, Chloe was no longer a part of the staff.

She checked out the room numbers until she spotted 327. The door was open, so she walked in. But she stopped short when she saw the wounded man standing near his bed, wearing a pair of tattered jeans, his broad chest bare.

Unable to help herself, she watched as he attempted to put on a torn black sweatshirt he must have been wearing at the time of the accident. His left hand was wrapped in an oversize bandage, and his muscled form struggled with the effort.

"Would you like… I mean, I could…"

He glanced over his shoulder, those amazing blue eyes locking in on hers and exposing something deep within, something vulnerable.

"Thanks, but I've got it." His handsome face bore a couple of scrapes, but other than that, he appeared strong and healthy. She could hardly tell that he'd been brought in on a gurney last night.

Maybe she should have taken a few extra minutes to freshen up and change out of her work clothes. Not that she was dirty or unkempt. It's just that he…well, she…

Oh, forget it. She didn't have time to let her thoughts drift into girlish, romantic notions.

"I don't mean to interfere if you'd rather do it yourself. It's just that, with the bandage and all, I thought..." She gave her head a little toss. "I'm sorry. I guess I shouldn't have just barged into your room like that. But...well, you're Joe Wilcox, right?"

"That's what they tell me." He pointed toward a stack of papers on the bed tray with his bandaged hand, yet her focus remained on his broad shoulders, on the scatter of dark chest hair that ran along taut abs and trailed into the waistband of his jeans.

"Do you remember me?" she asked.

"You're the woman who came in last night to identify me. Chloe Dawson, right?"

She tossed him a smile. "Yes, that's me. I'm glad you remembered."

"Don't be too optimistic," he said. "I can recall everything as far back as the ambulance ride. Anything before that is a giant black spot in my mind. Besides..." He patted the paperwork one more time. "Your name is on my discharge sheet."

"So Dr. Nielson told you that I was coming to pick you up?"

"Yep. Right before she signed off on my chart. I think she was eager to get home to her new baby. Not that I can blame her."

So he liked children? That ought to mean he was one of the white hats and that she had nothing to worry about by being alone with him.

"Do you have kids?" she asked.

He froze, and his blue eyes darted upward as if he had to look up the answer in his cranial database. "I have no idea. But that's not what I meant. I can't blame the doc for wanting to ditch this place as soon as she could. Hospitals give me the creeps."

Maybe, if she prodded him with enough questions, she'd latch on to the thread that would unravel all of his suppressed memories. "Have you been in the hospital before?"

"I don't know the answer to that, either. I'm going to guess that I have—and that I didn't like it."

"Why?"

"Because I can't wait to get out of here." He finally managed to slip on the sweatshirt. "You ready to go?"

"Sure. If you are."

He snatched a white plastic bag off the floor by his chair and headed out the door. As she tried to keep up with his determined pace, her dusty cowboy boots clicked along the polished corridor floor.

"Wait," she called out just before he reached the elevator. "I realize you're in a hurry to leave and would probably hitch a ride with the first ship setting sail, but Dr. Nielson is releasing you to my care. So let's slow down just a minute. Is there anything in that discharge paperwork that I need to know about before we hightail it out of here?"

"Sorry." He handed her the top sheet off his stack for her to read. "Listen, Miss Dawson."

When she looked up from the paper he'd given her and caught his gaze—or rather, when those amazing blue eyes caught hers—her tummy did a somersault.

He smiled. "It's *miss,* right?"

Was he asking if she was single? Or just trying to be polite?

While working at the Stagecoach Inn, she'd gotten used to men—old and young, drunk and sober—

hitting on her. And she was usually pretty quick on the draw when it came to letting them know she wasn't interested.

But she'd make an allowance for the sexy marine who was still probably disoriented from the accident and the shock of having his memory banks wiped clean—at least, temporarily.

"Yes, it is. But let's make that Chloe."

"All right," he said. "Thanks for picking me up, Chloe. And you might as well call me Joe, although, I may not answer to it."

Why? Had he realized that the sheriff might have mistaken him for someone else?

No, she'd been told that his photo and name lined up. "I suppose, if you don't remember who you are, your name wouldn't sound familiar."

"That's the problem. Something about that name doesn't feel right, although I have no idea why. Maybe because my brain is still so scrambled." He let out a weary sigh. "Anyway, you don't really have to be responsible for me. I waited for you to get here because Dr. Nielsen seems like a nice woman, and I don't want to get her in trouble with the hospital bigwigs. But you can just drop me off at a nearby homeless shelter or rescue mission. I'll be fine."

She couldn't possibly dump him just anywhere, especially in his condition. Yet he turned his back and continued on his way, his only goal the hospital exit.

"Joe," she called out.

At the sound of his name—or maybe just her voice—he turned in response.

With her boots still planted in the middle of the hall,

she asked, "Have you ever stayed in a homeless shelter or a rescue mission?"

"I don't know."

For a guy who didn't seem to know very much about himself, he had no problem putting one combat boot in front of the other and pretending that nothing was wrong.

"Have you ever been to Brighton Valley?" she asked.

"Don't know that, either."

She wondered if he was getting tired of sounding like a broken record. "We don't have any homeless shelters or rescue missions here. There's a community church that lets people sleep in the basement, but the pastor usually goes home before now, so I doubt that they're open."

"Then I appreciate your offer to give me a ride and a place to stay for a day or two—at least, until my memory returns."

"No problem. Dave and his family would have done the same."

The furrow in his brow deepened as if he was reaching deep into his memory banks, only to find them empty. Then he nodded and continued to the elevator.

She followed him. When the doors opened, they stepped inside.

His fingers lingered over the panel for longer than necessary, so she pressed the *L* for lobby. Again, she reminded herself that by taking him home she was doing the right thing. After all, she couldn't very well let him wander the streets if he couldn't even operate a simple elevator.

He glanced at her, and his blank stare tore at her heart. Had the gravity of his situation finally sunk in?

"You sure you don't mind me bunking with you?" he asked.

"Of course not. You're a friend of Dave's, and honestly, it's his ranch. I'm only doing what he and his mother would have done for any of their friends."

"I'll try to make it up to you—the inconvenience and what not—when I figure out who I am and what I'm good for."

"Judging by the dosage of painkillers Dr. Nielsen sent home with you, I don't think you'll be much good at anything for a few days. So let's get you well first." She nodded toward the main entrance to the lobby. "Come on, let's go."

He didn't need any convincing, soon taking the lead as they left the holiday-decorated lobby, leaving Bing Crosby crooning about dreams of a white Christmas behind.

Other than the soles of their boots tapping on the dusty concrete, they walked in silence until they reached the well-lit parking lot. Then Joe paused to look around.

Was he having a breakthrough?

"I'm not sure where we are," he said, "or what's nearby. But the doc told me to take the medicine when I eat. And for some weird reason, I have a real craving for Mexican food. Is there a taco shop nearby? Someplace where I can get some good *menudo* or *albondigas?*"

The way the Spanish words rolled off his tongue—as if he was a native speaker—surprised her. That was an interesting twist since Wilcox wasn't a typical Mexican surname.

Maybe he wasn't who they thought he was. That was a possible cause for alarm, but the USMC tattoo she'd seen before he'd put on that sweatshirt was enough to waylay at least some of her concern.

"Tía Juana's is a drive-through," she said. "And it's not too far from here. We can pick up something on the way back to the ranch."

"Thanks. That sounds great. And as a side note, I'd offer to pay, but you'll have to take my IOU. The sheriff was supposed to drop off my wallet at the hospital earlier today, but he hasn't done that yet."

"No problem," she said. "But as a side note of my own, I'm sorry."

"About what? Me not having any cash? That's the least of my problems."

"I know. And it must be horribly frustrating for you. I can't imagine what you're going through."

Fortunately, though, he'd just had a change in luck.

Joe Wilcox now had Chloe Dawson to watch out for him—and with no one else to nurse these days, she intended to focus all her TLC on him.

By the time they reached the ranch, Joe was beyond exhausted. It had taken all his energy to finish off the spicy Mexican soup he'd ordered at Tía Juana's and to eat a couple bites of a quesadilla. Then he'd washed down his pills with a glass of iced tea.

"I'll show you to the guest room," Chloe said.

He followed her out of the kitchen, through a cozy living room with a stone fireplace and a built-in bookshelf, past a staircase leading to the second floor. He wondered where she slept. He knew better than to ask, though. No need for her to think he had ulterior motives, although she was one hell of a pretty woman.

He'd always been attracted to blondes…

Hadn't he? While that bit of information seemed to be a memory, it certainly wasn't one that was going to be very useful.

Still, Chloe's hair was a platinum shade that hung down her back in soft, shimmering waves he was tempted to touch and to watch slip through his fingers.

He kept his hands to himself, though. The last thing he wanted to do was to step out of bounds before he'd spent ten minutes alone with her. Besides, he wasn't up to fighting weight yet.

And speaking of hands… He glanced at the oversize bandage that was more trouble than it was worth. The tape was already flapping up. He'd told the nurse who'd put it on that he hadn't needed it, but she'd insisted, and he'd been too tired and rheumy to argue.

As he followed Chloe to the hall, she pointed out a bathroom on the left, then led him to the first door on the right. "I'd give you Dave's room, but if he shows up, he'll need a place to sleep. So this will have to do."

"I'd be happy on the couch. All I need is a pillow and blanket."

"We can do better than that," she said.

"'We'?" He hadn't realized that she might not live alone.

"Sorry. I'm actually just a guest here myself, so I don't consider the house mine." She flipped on the light switch, illuminating a small room with a double bed, a single nightstand and a dresser that rested near the window. "Would you like me to find you something to sleep in? There should be some men's pajamas in Dave's room."

Something told him he'd prefer to sleep in the raw,

but he decided not to mention that. "No, thanks. My boxers will have to do."

"Okay." She bit down on her bottom lip, as though worried about something.

"I plan on crashing the minute my head hits the pillow," he added. "I doubt I'll wake up until morning."

"Good." She brightened a moment, and then her smile slipped away. "I mean, a good night's sleep ought to do wonders."

An awkwardness settled around them, but Joe was too far gone to ponder why—or to even care.

"I'll leave you alone so you can get some rest," she said. "I'll see you in the morning."

"Thanks again."

"You're more than welcome." She waited a beat, as if still struggling with something. Attraction maybe?

Well, that was too damn bad. As nice as he might have found that before his accident, his jumbled and sleepy brain was too intent upon hitting the sheets—alone.

Of course, that didn't mean he'd feel the same way tomorrow.

For a guy who didn't know who or where he was, Joe had gotten a fairly good night's sleep. But now, as the morning rays lit the guest bedroom, he winced and stretched out his bum knee, hoping the ache would ease. He must have exasperated an old injury, because he'd spotted some nasty scarring earlier.

He had no idea what had happened to him. A normal, healthy guy who hadn't jarred his brains on the highway would have remembered how he'd messed himself up like that, especially since it looked as though he'd had surgery to correct it.

Damn. He hated not knowing anything about himself—who he was, where he was from, where he'd planned to go next.

At the sound of footsteps padding down the hall, he turned to the doorway, where the pretty blonde stood holding a stack of folded clothes.

"Good morning," she said. "How are you feeling?"

"Okay, I guess. Last night, before dozing off, I convinced myself that I would wake up feeling completely back to normal and with my memory intact."

"And…?"

"My head doesn't feel nearly as bad as before. But my memory?" He clucked his tongue. "Still nothing."

"How about a cup of coffee? Maybe a jolt of caffeine will trigger something."

Just seeing his pretty caretaker wearing a snug black sweater, leaning sexily in the doorway was enough to jolt him wide awake. But he wasn't about to make a comment like that. "Sure, coffee sounds great."

"How do you like it?"

"Black." The fact that he'd had an answer for her was enough to make him think his memory might actually return before long. He just wished it would hurry up. The brain fog was enough to make him climb the walls.

"You got it," she said. "How about bacon and eggs? I could also whip up some oatmeal or maybe some hotcakes for you. Do you have a preference?"

Nothing jumped out at him. "I'll have whatever you're having."

"Nonfat Greek yogurt and bananas?"

No, he'd pass on the healthy crap. A slow grin tugged

at his lips. "Would hotcakes and bacon be too much trouble?"

She tossed him a sunny smile. "Not at all. Do you want me to serve you in here?"

While having a beautiful blonde sit on his bed, spoon-feeding him, triggered an intriguing vision and opened up some interesting possibilities, he didn't want her to think of him as an invalid. "No, I'll come out to the kitchen."

She lifted the folded clothing in her arms. "I brought you something you can wear—pants and shirts that belong to Dave. I also put fresh towels on the bathroom counter."

A shower sounded good. And so did having breakfast with her. "Thanks."

"Did you want to eat first?"

"If you don't mind. I want to take another dose of my pain medication, and I'm not supposed to do that on an empty stomach."

"You got it. I'll have it on the table in no time at all." She tossed him another smile, then placed the clothing on the top of the dresser.

When she turned and left the room, he threw off the covers, wincing when he bumped the scrape on his knuckles that was no longer protected by the bandage he'd removed, and got out of bed. He couldn't very well join her for breakfast without clothes. And since he was going to postpone the shower for later, he snatched the pair of folded jeans off the stack she'd set on top of the dresser, slipped them on and followed the aroma of sizzling bacon to the kitchen, where he found Chloe standing at the stove, her back to him. Her long blond hair had been pulled back into a ponytail.

Apparently, she hadn't heard him approach the kitchen, so he could just stand here and enjoy the view. But something told him not to get caught up in romantic dreams when he had no idea who he was or where he was going—or if there was a family waiting for him somewhere. So he decided to let his presence be known. "Something sure smells good."

At the sound of Joe's voice, Chloe turned to the kitchen doorway, where he stood wearing one of Dave's T-shirts and a pair of jeans. Yet that's where any similarities between the two men ended.

Dave had been fair-haired and on the thin side, while Joe was dark-haired with an olive complexion. His bulkier frame filled out that T-shirt in a way Dave never had.

"Is there anything I can do to help?" he asked.

"No, I have everything under control. Just come on in and have a seat."

As he complied, taking one of the kitchen chairs near the bay window that looked out into the nearest pasture, she poured him a mug of coffee and carried it to the table.

He thanked her, then took a sip. "You know, I really appreciate you providing me with a temporary place to stay, although I don't like the idea of causing you extra work."

"It's no problem."

"Maybe not, but I'd be happy to help out any way I can."

Since the ranch hand who usually helped Tomas with the chores had taken some time off to visit his family in Mexico, there was plenty to do. "That's nice of you to offer. And I might take you up on it—once you're feeling strong enough."

He smiled, revealing a pair of dimples and a glimmer in those amazing blue eyes. For a moment, she lost her train of thought.

"I'll start today," he said, "but don't worry. I'll take it slow and easy."

"Let's wait until tomorrow. I'd feel better if you had a little more time to rest."

"All right. Then I'll just have to hang out here at the house. But I promise not to get in your way or cause you any trouble."

Something told her that any trouble that came her way would be of her own making. "I'm sure you won't be. And to be honest with you, it'll be nice to have someone to talk to every now and then."

The big old ranch house could get lonely at times, especially in the evenings.

"So you're a guest here, too," he said.

She nodded, then turned back to the hotcakes that were browning on the griddle. She flipped each one over, then reached for a platter on which she could put them as soon as they were done.

"So what do you do when you're not nursing the injured?" he asked.

"I'm between jobs right now, which worked out okay in the long run. Tomas, the ranch foreman, is shorthanded, so I've been helping out when I can."

In truth, Tomas was a good worker—and he tried hard. But he'd never really had a supervisory role before. But when the previous foreman retired, Chloe had to find someone to step up to the plate. If she'd had more money to work with to offer a fair wage to someone better equipped, she would have. As it was, she promoted him based upon seniority.

"When you go back to job hunting," Joe said, "what kind of work do you do?"

"I used to be an aide at an assisted-living facility in town. I also plan to attend nursing school next semester."

"Pretty cool. I have my very own Florence Nightingale to help me get back on the mend."

She turned to face him again and smiled. "Nursing has always been a dream of mine."

Of course, after being terminated from the Sheltering Arms, she'd spent a little time wondering if she'd pinned her heart on the wrong dream.

Had Teresa Cummings, Dave's mother, still been alive, Chloe would have shared her disappointment and concern over her firing, which had seemed so unfair.

Then again, if Teresa had been alive, she would have advised Chloe to handle things differently at the time than she had, to confront her boss, to stir the pot. And if the administrator had seen fit to fire her anyway, Teresa might have encouraged her to file a wrongful termination suit.

But Chloe had never liked making waves. So she'd rolled over and walked away from the one job that had been the perfect fit for her.

She was tempted to share the details with Joe, but she bit her tongue. What did she really know about him?

Sure, she was drawn to him, although she blamed that on him being injured and her having a nurse's heart. She'd always been a nurturer, and she knew she'd make a good R.N. someday. But it wasn't just her heart Joe had touched. There was something about *him* she found attractive.

But she'd already had one bad relationship, if you could even call it that. Either way, she'd made a big mistake and didn't trust her judgment or instincts about men these days. And as long as she didn't act upon that attraction, they ought to get along just fine.

Chapter Three

By ten o'clock, Chloe had done two loads of laundry, cleaned the stove and washed the big bay window near the antique oak table. She enjoyed having her morning coffee where she could look out into the yard and pastures, so keeping the glass spotless had always been a priority.

While she worked, she kept the noise down. Joe might have offered to help her out on the ranch, but not long after eating breakfast and taking his pain medication, he'd mentioned being dizzy and had returned to the guest room and taken a nap. And she was glad that he'd done so.

Like it or not, he'd suffered a concussion. There was no way she would let him push himself too hard until he'd fully recovered.

She'd grown up as an army brat—the only girl with two older brothers, so she knew how stubborn men could be and how hard it was to admit their weakness. She'd keep that in mind the next time he offered to help. In the meantime, she continued to do her morning chores.

Next up was the kitchen floor. She'd just entered the mudroom to retrieve the plastic bucket and mop when the phone rang, so she hurried back to the kitchen and answered the old-style wall-mounted telephone before the noise disturbed Joe.

"Chloe," the caller said, "it's Betsy Nielson. How's our patient doing this morning?"

"He had a good breakfast. Now he's resting again."

"Good. Is he able to remember anything yet?"

"Not that I've seen so far."

"Give it some time. My husband, Jason, suffered from amnesia about four years ago. It was pretty tough on him, but his memories slowly began to return."

"How long did it take?"

"A couple of weeks. But each case is different, so it's impossible to predict. Just encourage Joe to be patient and let nature take its course."

"I will." Chloe wrapped the coiled phone cord around her index finger. "Has there been any news? I mean, how is the investigation going?"

"I haven't heard, but I'm sure Sheriff Hollister will be contacting Joe soon to give him an update."

"That's good. Joe will be eager to talk to him."

After the call ended, Chloe placed the receiver back in the cradle on the wall. She was eager to hear what the sheriff had to say, too. She hadn't heard from Dave in months and wondered where he was—and why he'd sent a letter to her through someone else.

A few weeks ago she'd written to him, but he hadn't responded. Then, just last Monday, she'd found her letter in the mailbox. The military had forwarded it to Dave, using the ranch address, which led her to believe his tour of duty had ended and that he'd been discharged.

If that was the case, then why hadn't he contacted her or come home yet? If he had actually been discharged, then he was no longer in Afghanistan. And that was a relief. Sure, his attachment to her had made her uncomfortable, but that didn't mean she didn't care about him.

She wasn't sure why he'd latched on to her like he had. She suspected that stress, battle fatigue and the recent death of his mother had all compounded and caused him to assume their friendship was something it had never been.

She'd done her best to explain that to him, but he couldn't seem to get the picture. Finally, when he began naming the children he'd imagined them having, she'd sent him a nice letter, trying to be kind, yet firm and direct.

Of course, she'd have to move off the ranch now that he was home. She couldn't risk having him think that there was any chance of her changing her mind about the two of them having a future together. Maybe, if he was out of the service and back in Brighton Valley, he could be more realistic about their relationship.

Either way, she would leave the Rocking C as soon as he arrived. She'd been looking after the ranch and trying to hold things together for him while he was gone, but her savings were just about gone, and the bills were still mounting up. She hoped he returned while he could still dig his way out of the hole he probably didn't know he was in.

"A penny for your thoughts."

Chloe turned to find Joe standing in the kitchen doorway. He was still wearing the same clothes. Even though he hadn't yet showered and appeared to be a bit battered, he looked as sexy as ever.

"My thoughts aren't worth much," she said, shaking off her worries and forcing a smile.

"Either way, I'm sorry, Chloe. I didn't mean to offer my services, then get dizzy and pass out on you."

Her smile deepened. "Don't give that a second thought. There'll be plenty to keep you busy when the time comes. It's best if you take it easy for now."

She couldn't help taking in his broad chest, the masculine bristle he'd yet to shave and those piercing blue eyes that seemed to see right through her. Again, she couldn't help comparing him to Dave, which wasn't fair to the other man. Not when Joe was drop-dead gorgeous.

He seemed to be checking her out just as closely as she'd been assessing him. Flushing, she tucked a strand of hair behind her car, wishing she'd put on something other than jeans this morning.

At the sound of an approaching vehicle's engine, Chloe peered out the window and into the yard, where a police car pulled up.

"The sheriff is here," she said.

Joe stiffened. A flicker of emotion tumbled across his face, while apprehension marred his brow.

The poor man. Chloe crossed the room, reached out and touched his forearm, felt the warmth of his body heat. "It'll be okay."

His gaze seemed to say, *I hope you're right,* yet the tension in his stance suggested he had his doubts. Then he pulled free and headed for the living room, with her following behind.

Joe opened the front door, where a uniformed law enforcement officer stood on the stoop.

"I'm Shane Hollister," the sheriff said. "I'm heading up the investigation into your hit-and-run accident."

The words wadded up in Joe's throat. What was he supposed to say, other than "Thank God. What news do you have?"

Yet for some reason, facing the lawman sent a wisp of apprehension through him.

Damn. Did he have some reason to feel guilty?

Rather than stew about all the memories that evaded him, he shook off the uneasiness and said, "Hello, Sheriff."

Hollister gave him a once-over. "It's good to see you up and around. How are you doing?"

"Not bad. But I still can't remember squat—if that's what you mean."

"Well, maybe I can help." The sheriff handed him a wallet. "I meant to give you this before you left the hospital, but I missed you."

"That's okay." Joe turned the dark leather over in his hands, then flipped it open. He pulled out the California driver's license.

Sure enough, that was his photo staring back at him, verifying his name was Joseph Wilcox, even if it still didn't sound familiar. According to his address, he lived on base at Camp Pendleton.

"Please," Chloe told the sheriff, "come in and have a seat."

Hollister chose one of the chairs near the fireplace, then pulled a small notepad from his breast pocket. He flipped through a couple of pages before launching into his reason for coming by.

"We got a hit on your military service record," he told Joe. "It looks like you were medically discharged from the Marine Corps a few months ago."

If that were the case, then his address was no longer valid.

"The military won't release much of your information," Hollister said, "but I have a buddy up at the Houston NCIS office looking into it for me."

"NCIS?" Chloe asked.

"It stands for Naval Criminal Investigative Service," Hollister explained. "They work with both the navy and the Marine Corps, so my friend should be able to access info for us. Hopefully we'll know more later this week."

"Was there any word about Joe serving with Dave?" Chloe asked. "Or do you have any idea where Dave might be?"

"Not yet. That's something my contact at NCIS might be able to provide." Hollister turned his focus back to Joe. "It looks like you joined the Marines about six months after your eighteenth birthday. You were a staff sergeant at the time of your discharge, which tells me that you probably had a stellar service record to move up the ranks so quickly."

Joe blew out a ragged sigh. "That's good to know, I suppose. It's too bad I can't recall some of that stellar service myself."

Chloe eased up to his chair and placed her hand on his shoulder. "Dr. Nielson said to give it some time. Her husband suffered from amnesia a few years back, and his memory returned slowly over the course of a few weeks."

"That sounds like ages to me," Joe said. "I've never had much patience."

"You haven't?" As if eager to grab on to anything positive, Chloe gave his shoulder a gentle squeeze. "I'd say that's good news."

Joe looked up at her and furrowed his brow. "What do you mean?"

"If you know that so readily about yourself, then it sounds like a memory has returned already."

Unfortunately, Joe didn't find that very helpful and returned his gaze to the sheriff. "Have you found out anything else about the person who hit me?"

"Judging from the tire tracks and a couple of eye-witness accounts, we think the perp was parked at the Stagecoach Inn and jumped the curb before hitting you. I have a couple of my deputies questioning all the patrons who were there that night—and looking over their cars to see if there's any corresponding bodywork damage. But that's assuming it was one of the locals. We're still gathering credit-card records in case it was someone who was just passing through on the highway and decided to stop off at the bar for a few drinks to wait out the evening traffic."

"I appreciate your efforts to find whoever it was who hit me," Joe said. "And for helping me piece my life back together."

"No problem." The sheriff put away his notepad and got to his feet. "That's my job. But you might want to consider that this wasn't a mere accident."

Chloe's hand slipped off Joe's shoulder. "Why do you say that?"

"There weren't any skid marks, so either the driver didn't see you or was aiming right at you."

The thought that someone might have been out to get him didn't sit well, but when Joe shot a glance at Chloe and saw the worry that marred her brow, his concern shifted.

He didn't like seeing her on edge, which was surely the case since she'd removed the warmth of her support when she'd taken her hand from his shoulder. Neither did he want to bring any trouble her way. But he wasn't about to reassure her with false promises, especially if he had no clue what kind of complications his presence could cause.

"I don't want to alarm you or be a conspiracy theorist," the sheriff added, "but there's a lot we still don't know about you. And with your temporary memory loss, you can't answer any of those questions for us. I can't ignore the fact that someone might have been out to hit you for some reason. Or that they might not want you in town."

Joe wished he could reassure both Chloe and the sheriff, but he couldn't. He might not feel like a wanted man, but how would he know for sure? The lawman was probably just trying to cover all the bases, which was wise. It made sense not to restrict his investigation to the easiest, most obvious case solution.

And while Joe had hoped that the sheriff's arrival would toss him a life raft of sorts, instead, it had only opened up more worries, more concerns, more what-ifs.

What little solid ground he'd once felt under his feet had been whisked away, leaving him alone, tossed about on a choppy sea with no compass, no oars and no sign of the shore.

"So what do we do?" Chloe asked.

We? He couldn't expect her to help. She'd done a lot already. But the thought of having someone in his corner of the rowboat helped a little.

"My suggestion would be for Mr. Wilcox to try to

keep a low profile," Hollister said. "It might be best if he stayed here at the ranch until we can investigate further."

"I'd hoped someone in town might recognize him and be able to tell us more about who he is—and why he's here," Chloe said.

Joe wasn't as concerned for his own safety as he was for hers. So far, she'd been a friend, an ally in his messed-up world, and he didn't want to do anything that might put her in jeopardy.

"Maybe it's best if I moved on," he said.

Chloe placed her hand back on his shoulder. And this time, her fingertips sent a whisper of heat through his veins. Her gaze met his, stirring something deep within. "Where would you go?"

He raked a hand through his hair. How the hell did he know? But he'd figure something out. He had to, before this beautiful stranger turned his mixed-up brain even more inside out.

"It has to be frustrating not to know who you are or why you're here," the sheriff said. "But from a safety standpoint, I think it's more important to get to the bottom of this accident first and then figure out the memory problem later."

Joe could see how Hollister would be more concerned with a crime being committed in his quaint small town. And while it was helpful of the sheriff to go above the call of duty and look for his personal records, it wasn't as if Joe was suffering from a simple little "memory problem." It was a full-blown loss of identity, a loss of control over his life. And his gut clenched at the thought, at the possibilities….

What if he had somewhere else to be at this exact second? Or what if someone needed him, but he was AWOL?

Crap. What if the person waiting for him was his wife?

"Uh, Sheriff," he said. "Do you know if my military file mentioned anything about me being married or having kids?"

"It didn't say specifically, but you don't have any military dependents listed. So my guess would be that you're single."

Joe released a pent-up sigh. At least he didn't have a family worrying about him. Not that he was completely off the hook. There could be someone else who needed him, someone who…

No, that wasn't true. He wasn't sure how he knew that there was no one else, that no one had ever worried about him. He just did.

"All right," Chloe said. "I'll keep Mr. Wilcox on the ranch while you finish looking into whoever did this."

"Sounds good." The sheriff made his way to the door, then turned and looked at Joe. "I'll keep you posted as to what else we uncover. And I'll call the minute I hear anything from the military."

"Thanks. I'd appreciate that." Joe supposed he should feel better, yet his jumbled mind couldn't wrap itself around so many possibilities. And that left him just as confused as he'd been the moment he'd woken up in the E.R.

Well, almost as confused.

"I'll walk you outside," Chloe told the sheriff.

As the two stepped onto the porch and continued toward the police car, Joe remained in the living room, feeling like a kid left behind so the grown-ups could have a discussion in private.

But he could see why Chloe might want to talk to the cop in private. No doubt she wanted to relay her fears and misgivings about living with a random stranger.

Hell, if she was afraid, he'd have to leave—no matter what Hollister had suggested. Too bad he had no idea where to go.

For the time being, he headed back to the kitchen, determined to mop the floor and to finish the chore Chloe had started before Hollister had arrived. He figured that he might as well make himself helpful around the house and the ranch so she wouldn't think of him as an obligation or a burden.

Okay. So he was also curious about what was going on outside, what was being said.

He placed the bucket into the sink, then turned on the faucet. While the water flowed out of the spigot, he looked out the big kitchen window, where Hollister and Chloe stood near the squad car.

The sheriff opened the driver's door and reached across the seat. Then he handed an envelope to Chloe.

Was that Dave's letter?

For just being a "family friend," she was certainly concerned about the guy. Not that Joe had any claim to his personal Florence Nightingale, but he couldn't stop the uneasy feeling rolling through his stomach.

Or the prickle of jealousy that sketched over him, urging him to try and make Chloe experience her own case of amnesia and forget whatever it was that she felt for Dave Cummings.

Chloe recognized Dave's loopy penmanship the moment Sheriff Hollister handed over the letter. She'd been tempted to tear into it right then and there, but she merely stared at the worn and smudged envelope that someone had folded in half, measuring the weight of it in her hand.

Apparently someone had been carrying it around for a while—either Dave or Joe. Maybe even both of them.

"I'm curious about the contents of that letter," the sheriff said.

She could understand why, but she was reluctant to read what Dave had to say in front of anyone. She wasn't sure what he'd written—or how it would make her feel. She'd never liked hurting anyone's feelings or angering them, and realizing that she'd either hurt or angered Dave didn't sit well with her.

"There might be something inside that would suggest why Wilcox is here," Sheriff Hollister added.

"I thought you would have opened it as part of your investigation," Chloe said.

"It's a sealed envelope. I can't read it without a warrant, and since Dave Cummings wrote it to you, there's no reason for me to request one." Sheriff Hollister reached into his pocket and pulled out a business card. "If you find any clues that might help with my investigation, I'd appreciate it if you'd let me know."

"Of course."

He nodded, then climbed into his squad car. "Everything I've learned about Wilcox suggests that he's law-abiding. But if you have reason to believe otherwise, give me a call."

"I will. Thank you." She refolded the envelope, then shoved it into the back pocket of her jeans.

Rather than return to the house, she waited until the sheriff left and watched the black-and-white vehicle head down the drive, biding her time and tamping down her compulsion to tear into the missive.

While tempted to dash upstairs and pore over the contents so she could get an idea where Dave was and why Joe had possession of the letter in the first place, she reined in her curiosity. She'd already left Joe alone in the house long enough and didn't want him to think she was rude—or worse, suspicious of him. So she walked up the porch steps and entered the living room.

She thought her houseguest might have gone back to bed—and if he had, she wouldn't have blamed him. Those head injuries could really take a lot out of a person. But when she heard noise coming from the kitchen, she went looking for him there. She wouldn't have been surprised to see him fixing himself a snack. But she hadn't expected to find a bucket on the wet floor and to see him wringing out the mop.

"What are you doing?" she asked.

His movements stilled, and he leaned against the wooden handle, the muscles in his forearms flexed and primed for heartier work. "Thought I'd better help out and pay for my keep."

"You don't need to do that."

"Yes, I do. I don't like taking handouts." His eye twitched, and his brow furrowed, his words drifting off. Had a memory crossed his mind?

She was afraid to ask since she'd already jumped to that conclusion a couple of times, and she'd been wrong.

"At least, I don't think I do," he added.

"Dr. Nielson said that you should take it easy."

"Yeah, and she also told me to be patient, but something tells me I'm not one to sit around and wait for things to happen."

She continued to stand in the doorway, the letter burning a hole in her back pocket.

"I'll tell you what," Joe said. "I'm almost finished here. As soon as I dump out the dirty water, I'll go to the barn and check out the stables. That way, you can read the letter the sheriff gave you in private."

Chloe smoothed her hand over the front of her jeans, fingering the hemmed edge of the pocket, making sure it was still hidden inside. Had she been that obvious?

"I saw Hollister give it to you outside, and if I were in your boots, I'd be dying to read it, too. Especially if it says Joe Wilcox is a nutcase and you shouldn't let him within a hundred feet of you." He smiled, but she knew he was itching for a clue as to why he was here.

Still, she wanted to be alone when she read whatever Dave hadn't wanted to tell her in person.

If truth be told, she felt badly about possibly hurting his feelings while he was in a war zone, no matter how gentle she'd tried to be. And she regretted the distance her honesty had created between them.

"Thanks for understanding," she said. "I'll let you know if it says anything about you."

Joe nodded. Then he began to mop the floor under the table, which was the only dry spot left. After he finished, he leaned the mop against the wall and carried the bucket through the mudroom and out into the yard.

When Chloe was finally alone, she went into the living room, took a seat in the chair in which Sheriff Hollister had once sat and took the envelope from her pocket. After opening it, she withdrew the letter and unfolded the single sheet of paper.

Chloe,

If you're reading this letter, then that means Joe found you for me and hand-delivered it.

I can never thank you enough for what you did for my mom during her last days, and I'm sorry that my love and gratitude made you uncomfortable. Even though my feelings weren't reciprocated, that doesn't mean that I felt them any less.

I can't think of anywhere else I'd rather be than with you. But if you're not interested in what we could have together, then I won't bother you again.

Goodbye.

Dave

Chloe read the short note several times, focusing on the last cryptic part. Dave had a penchant for the melodramatic, so it was hard to know what he meant. Still, he didn't have to stay away. The ranch belonged to him, and she would gladly turn the reins back over to him when he came home.

If he came home. Joe clearly knew where he could be found—that is, if his memory ever returned. When it did, she'd ask him to contact Dave and tell him she was leaving, that she couldn't stay on the Rocking C forever.

But why hadn't Dave contacted her in person? And why had he wanted the letter delivered when it would have been much easier to mail it? Or even to call?

Had Dave asked Joe to evict her? Maybe, once she'd cleared out of the house, Joe was to inform Dave so that he could return to the Rocking C without having to see her.

But if that was the case, all he'd had to do was say the word and she'd start packing.

However, she wouldn't leave the ranch unattended until he actually arrived. So he'd just have to man up and deal with her temporary presence.

In the meantime, what in the world was she going to do with Joe?

And what would he tell her once his memory returned? She had no idea.

For a moment, she pondered showing him Dave's letter, thinking it might jar his memory. But she didn't consider that option very long. She'd just tell Joe that Dave had asked him to deliver it in person.

Perhaps just her reassurance that Joe was actually Dave's friend was enough. It would have to be—until she figured out just what Dave meant when he said, "But if you're not interested in what we could have together, then I won't bother you again. Goodbye. Dave."

What if he'd actually been saying goodbye forever? What if Dave had…?

Oh, God. And what if, somehow, it had been her fault?

Chapter Four

As Joe made his way through the Rocking C barn, the smell of straw and dust stirred more than his senses. He stopped for a moment, scanning the walls where the tack hung and pondering the feeling of déjà vu that settled over him.

Had he actually been here before? It seemed as though he had.

Or was it something about the ranch or the scent of feed and leather that made him feel at home?

A horse whinnied, and he continued to walk to the back of the barn, where an Appaloosa was stabled.

"Hey there," he told the mare. "How's it going?"

She snorted, threw back her head, then stepped closer.

He reached in to stroke her neck. He didn't know how long he stood there, talking to the horse, striking up a friendship of sorts. Certainly long enough for Chloe to have read her letter from Dave.

He supposed he could go back into the house now, but he lingered in the barn, trying to wrap his mind around the cloak of familiarity. Too bad he wasn't having much luck.

Behind him, boot steps sounded. He glanced over

his shoulder and spotted the approach of a stocky, middle-aged cowboy.

When their eyes met, the man introduced himself. "I'm Tomas Hernandez, the ranch foreman. You must be Joe Wilcox."

For some reason, even though he'd been assured that his identity had been confirmed, the name still didn't seem to fit. That was probably to be expected with amnesia.

Shaking off the lingering uneasiness, Joe turned away from the horse and reached out a hand to greet the foreman.

"It's good to see you out and about," Hernandez said. "I heard about the accident. Sounds like you were lucky."

Joe didn't feel so lucky. He felt lost and out of control. But he wasn't about to whine about it. "I suppose it could have been a whole lot worse."

Hernandez nodded. "You're right. You still could be laid up in the hospital."

Or in the morgue.

Again, Joe let the reality of the thought pass. "The doctor said to take it easy, but I'm going stir-crazy. I never have been able to sit still."

He wasn't sure how he knew that. Maybe because he was chomping at the bit to get back to normal, whatever that might be.

"If you have any work that needs to be done," Joe added, "just say the word. I'd like to help out any way I can."

"Chloe said you're still recovering and won't be available for a while."

So they'd talked about him. Joe couldn't blame

them, he supposed. But he didn't like the idea of being a burden—or someone's problem. In fact, his gut twisted at the thought, and a shadow of uneasiness draped over him once more, this time weighing him down even worse than the amnesia did.

"I figure I'll take it easy today," he told Hernandez. "But I'll be ready to pitch in tomorrow."

"That's good to hear. I'm down a ranch hand, so there's plenty to keep us both busy for a while."

As the silence stretched between them, they assessed each other like two stray dogs wondering if they should be friends or foes.

Joe nodded toward the mare. "She's a pretty horse."

"Yes, she is. And she has good bloodlines, too. Her name's Lola. She's going to foal soon, so I brought her in and stabled her until her time comes."

Joe still couldn't shake the feeling that he'd been on the ranch before. And in the barn. Did Hernandez recognize him?

"Have you worked here long?" he asked the foreman.

"About four years." Hernandez lifted his hat, revealing a balding head. "It'll be five this coming February."

"I don't suppose you recognize me," Joe said.

"No, I'm afraid not."

"I thought maybe Dave had brought me around," he told the foreman.

"Not that I'm aware of."

That shot down his theory, he supposed. Maybe he'd grown up on a ranch. But where?

He scanned the barn again. So why did he have this feeling of déjà vu? Was his scattered brain playing tricks on him? Maybe. Still, Hernandez wasn't very forthcoming.

"When did Dave join the Marines?" he asked the foreman.

"About two and a half years ago. He and his father had a big falling out over something or other. And Dave enlisted to spite him."

"What'd they fight about?"

"Almost everything. But that last time was the worst. And I'm sure Dave was sorry about it afterward."

"You mean joining the corps?"

"Leaving home, mostly. His father died of a heart attack shortly after Dave finished recruit training. And I think Dave blamed himself for it. Last time he was here, to attend his mother's funeral, he told me he'd be home soon and wouldn't ever leave again. He asked me to look out for things until he did. But he hasn't contacted any of us in quite a while."

No wonder Chloe was eager to read that letter.

And now Joe was even more curious than ever to know what it said. He and Dave might be buddies, but they hadn't enlisted at the same time. According to what the sheriff had said, Joe had joined five years earlier.

He stroked his chin, felt the stubble of the beard he hadn't shaved this morning. That shower he'd been meaning to take after he'd taken his morning pain meds was long overdue.

"Well," he said to Hernandez, "I'm going to head back to the house. If you start making a list of chores you'd like me to do, I'll get started on them tomorrow."

"All right. I'll do that."

Joe gave Lola's neck one last stroke, then strode toward the barn door. He hated not knowing anything about himself. And while he continued to get some fleeting thoughts about his character and things he liked or disliked, he had no idea how to cobble them together.

After entering the living room, he took a moment to survey the leather furnishings, the built-in bookshelf in the far wall, the stone fireplace with photos lining the mantel. When he noticed one of a smiling marine in uniform, he made his way to the hearth so he could take a better look.

He lifted the brass frame and studied the fair-haired man's image. He wished he could say that he recognized him, but he didn't.

"That's Dave," Chloe said.

Joe turned toward her voice. She stood in the doorway that led down the hall to the bedrooms. The moment their gazes met, he felt another stirring—one that was far more appealing than the scent of leather and hay that had provoked his senses in the barn.

"His mother never understood why he'd joined the service in the first place," Chloe said. "As the only child, the only son, he knew his father expected him to stay on the ranch and take over someday. But I've sensed there was more to it than that. I think he had a blowup with his dad, although he never said anything to me about it."

Joe took another gander at the photo in his hand.

"Does he look familiar?" Chloe asked.

"No, I'm afraid not." Joe returned the frame to the mantel.

"Well, you definitely knew him. In his letter, he mentioned that he'd given it to you and asked you to bring it to me."

"That's all he had to say?"

She bit down on her bottom lip, as though struggling with the answer. "About you? Yes, that's all."

What else had Dave written? The rest of his message had obviously been personal and something she wasn't eager to share.

Joe figured he didn't have a right to ask if he could read it himself, although his curiosity was mounting. And so was his interest in what made Chloe tick, an interest that threatened to turn into full-blown attraction if he'd let it.

And maybe it was morphing into that anyway.

Even today, with her white-blond hair pulled into a ponytail that hung down her back and no makeup other than the pink lipstick she had nearly worn off, he found her intriguing.

She wasn't wearing anything fancy—just faded jeans and a blue, lightweight sweater. Yet she couldn't hide her wholesome beauty behind a plain Jane facade. Not when those whiskey-colored eyes had zeroed in on him and set his libido on end.

As if unaware of his thoughts, she crossed the room, joined him near the fireplace and reached for the framed photograph he'd just replaced on the mantel. As she stood within touching distance, her faint, lemon-blossom scent aroused more than his interest.

She studied the marine in the photo for a moment. While she did so, Joe studied her—the thick dark lashes, the delicate features of her face, the fullness of her lips…

"After Dave joined the service and his father passed away, his mom was left to run the ranch on her own." Chloe took one last look at the photo, then returned the frame to its rightful place on the mantel. "When she got sick, I tried my best to help in any way I could, but I didn't know anything about working on a ranch—although I'm learning."

"So you'll wait here until Dave returns home?"

She bit down on her lip again, then gave a slight shrug of her left shoulder. "Since Teresa had provided a home for me when I needed one, I felt a certain obligation to her. So I promised her I'd stay until then."

Did she feel obligated to Teresa's son, as well?

Again, Joe shook off the curiosity that plagued him. Well, at least he tried to. There was a lot Chloe had left unsaid, a lot he wanted to know about her. And since his past wasn't readily available to him, he focused on learning more about hers.

"So where are you from?" he asked.

She smiled wistfully. "Here, there and everywhere."

He leaned against the mantel, crossed his arms and tossed her a grin to soften his line of questioning. "So you don't like to be tied down to one place?"

"No, it's not that at all. My parents are both in the military, so we moved around a lot when I was a kid. I also had to change schools more often than seemed fair. So now that I'm on my own, I want to settle down and create some stability in my life."

Since she'd mentioned that Mrs. Cummings had taken her in when she'd needed a place to stay, he suspected she'd had a few bad breaks—or trouble at home.

"Do you see your family very often?" he asked.

"I used to try and spend the bigger holidays with them, but I wasn't able to do that last Christmas because they were stationed in Hawaii. And it looks like I'll be staying in Brighton Valley again this year, too."

He had a feeling that she wasn't happy about it, so he said, "That's too bad."

"Do you…" She paused, and her cheeks turned a rosy hue. "I'm sorry. I was going to ask about your family and their holiday traditions."

He shrugged a single shoulder. "Don't worry about it. I wish I had an answer for you."

Chloe reached out and touched his arm, sending a pulsing shot of heat through his veins. He glanced down at the delicate fingers that rested on his sleeve and warmed him from the inside out.

She wasn't wearing any jewelry. But what about her other hand?

He fought the compulsion to check out her left ring finger—something he'd neglected to do earlier. But he didn't want her to catch him in the act. So he looked into her eyes instead, nearly losing himself in her intoxicating gaze.

"Christmas always makes me homesick," she said. "My mother really does things up big. Probably to make me and my brothers feel as though we had a real home and more stability in our lives. But I'm stuck here this year. And apparently, you are, too. So we'll just have to roll with that and create a down-home, country-style Christmas for the two of us. That way, maybe we can help each other make a brand-new memory."

Her suggestion caught him off guard, although he wasn't sure why. The fact that his brain was still healing, maybe. And that she'd removed her hand from his arm, stealing the warmth of her touch.

But as she continued to peer into his eyes, to search his expression, to silently plead her case, he gave in. "Sure. Why not?"

He'd been tempted to shake off her offer for more reasons than one. But as he thought about it, he realized that he actually liked the idea of making new memories with Chloe.

When the buzzer on the dryer sounded, Chloe retrieved the last load of laundry. After folding the small batch of towels and linens, she carried them down the hall to put them away.

Before placing them in the linen closet, she decided to make a quick check of the guest bathroom to make sure there were plenty of clean washcloths for Joe to use.

She reached for the doorknob and gave it a turn. The locking mechanism made a click-click sound, but the door swung right open, releasing a bit of steam.

And revealing Joe standing at the counter, his face lathered with shaving cream, his body bare other than a small white towel wrapped around his waist.

Her cheeks warmed. "Oh, my gosh. I'm so sorry. I—"

"It's okay. I'm practically dressed."

No, it wasn't all right. And he was naked underneath that towel. All it would take was one simple little tug at the waist…

Reining in her sexual thoughts, she gathered her wits. "The door. You didn't lock it."

"Actually, I did. But apparently it isn't working."

Yeah, well… She supposed she could cast the blame on the lock—or on everyone else, including the man in the moon, but that didn't cool her cheeks. Nor did it hide the handsome man who was a sight to behold.

She swallowed—hard. It was nearly impossible to

think, let alone speak, so she nodded, turned and shut the door.

As she put away the folded washcloths into the linen closet, she fought the urge to slip outside and find some chores to do in the yard so she wouldn't have to return to the house. But that wasn't feasible. She'd have to go back inside eventually. So she may as well deal with the embarrassment.

Still, just living with Joe here, knowing that he was sleeping down the hall, just two doors away from her bedroom, sent her thoughts scampering in an unexpected direction.

She blew out a ragged sigh. The flash of physical attraction she'd initially felt had magnified and left her feeling awkward and uneasy.

After placing the washcloths on the shelf where they belonged, she returned to the kitchen. It would be lunchtime soon, so she might as well whip up something to eat. She wondered if he'd like a tuna-salad sandwich.

She pulled the can opener from the drawer, a small mixing bowl from the cupboard, and mayonnaise, pickles and celery from the fridge. Then she searched the pantry for a can of tuna. She'd no more than shut the door when Joe said, "The bathroom is free now."

If she could have gotten away with pretending she hadn't heard him, she would have done it. As it was, she slowly turned to face him, her cheeks warming all over again.

She glanced down at her feet, willing herself to cool. When she looked back to his freshly shaven face and those striking blue eyes, her breath caught, her heart thumped and her cheeks warmed all over again.

"I'm sorry about walking in on you," she said. "I should have realized that you might have been in there."

"Like I said, it wasn't a big deal. I was covered up."

Yes, but just barely.

Fortunately, he was dressed now, although in Dave's clothing. The pants were at least an inch too short, and the T-shirt, which stretched across his broad chest, didn't hide the rippling muscles underneath.

"I promise to knock next time," she said.

Joe chuckled. "And I'll put 'Repair the Bathroom Lock' at the top of my to-do list."

"Good idea." She offered him an appreciative smile, then turned her back and continued her search for the canned tuna.

Now that she'd seen the handsome marine in the buff—or pretty close to it—fixing that door lock would only solve half her problem because the image of him wearing only a smile and a skimpy towel was engrained in her mind.

And that was one breath-stealing memory she wasn't likely to forget any time soon.

Joe couldn't help enjoying Chloe's obvious discomfort. In fact, ever since she'd walked in on him shaving—and up until the time they sat down to eat lunch—she seemed to avoid making eye contact with him.

A couple of times, he'd been tempted to tease her, but he decided to let it go. No need to stir up those kinds of sexual thoughts when he wasn't in any position to do anything about them.

As Chloe stood from her seat at the kitchen table and

picked up their empty plates, she asked, "Do you need anything in town?"

Some clothing that actually fit him would be nice. But since he didn't want to ask any more of her than he had already, he said, "I can't think of anything. Why?"

"I'm going to visit a friend who's living in a nursing home near the Brighton Valley Medical Center. Afterward I'm going to stop at the market and run a few errands. I thought, since the sheriff didn't want you to go into town that I could pick up anything you might need."

"I can make do with whatever is here." He just hoped that he and Dave actually were friends. If not, and the guy came home to find Joe staying in his house, wearing his clothes and using his shaving kit, things could become awkward.

"All right," she said. "I won't be gone too long. And when I get back, I'll fix dinner."

"Is there anything I can do for you while you're gone?"

"If you happen to see Tomas, will you ask him to bring in the plastic storage boxes filled with Christmas decorations? I think Teresa kept them in the hayloft."

"I can get them for you."

"No, I'd rather you took it easy and rested today. Believe me, there's still going to be plenty for you to do once you're feeling better."

"I feel better already."

"Is that right?" She crossed her arms and tossed him an impish grin. "Then why are you still taking that pain medication?"

"Okay. So I'm not quite back to fighting weight. But I'm definitely better."

"I have no doubt about that. Still, I'd rather have

Tomas bring in the decorations when he has time. I'll save you for bigger, more important things."

"Like what?"

She flushed again, and this time he couldn't resist teasing her. "What's the problem?"

"Excuse me?"

"Your cheeks are red, and you keep looking at everything except me. Are you that bothered about walking in on me in the bathroom?"

"You're wrong. It didn't faze me a bit."

He didn't believe her. In fact, he suspected she was still reeling from having seen him half-dressed. And since she seemed to be so flustered by it, he found it a bit flattering. But he didn't want her to feel awkward about it.

"Don't be embarrassed," he said. "Those things happen."

"I'm not." She stood a little taller and lifted her chin. "It's a hazard of being blonde and fair. I flush easily—and usually for no reason whatsoever. It's really no big deal."

"Good. I'm glad to hear that."

She might claim to be immune to him, but he wasn't buying it. Still, it was nice to know that her body easily displayed the effects of heating up.

Without any conscious effort on his part, a vision came to mind—her curvy, fair-skinned body stretched out on his bed sheets, pink and rosy from his caresses, her hair splayed on his pillow, her eyes glazed with passion.

"So," she said, her voice interrupting his erotic daydream, "since you don't need anything, I'll take off and run my own errands. Try and get some rest while I'm gone."

He'd try, but he doubted he'd get much rest at all, especially if he was plagued with any more sexy visions of her. But on top of that, he also had something that would keep him busy for a while.

"By the way," he said, "I noticed a computer in the den. Would it be okay if I used it while you were gone?"

Her movements stilled, and her eyes grew wide. "Do you remember how?"

Judging by the way his thoughts had veered off course a few seconds ago, he also remembered how to make love to a beautiful woman. But there was no point in making Chloe any more uncomfortable than she already was.

"I still have all my same abilities," he said. "The only thing I've forgotten is the past."

"What do you plan to use the computer for?"

Something told him that he was a man who kept his thoughts and tactics close to the vest. But Chloe didn't appear to be suspicious, just curious. So he would let her in on his plan. "I'm going to search for clues about who I really am—not that I even know the first place to start looking."

"Good idea. I'll get you logged in. Then, when I come home, maybe you can share some new information with me."

Sure, he thought. *I'll share with you, just as soon as you share that letter with me.* But he smiled and kept that thought to himself.

He followed her to the den, where she set him up on an old desktop device that looked as though it was about to give up the ghost. Joe had no reason to suspect that he was any big computer whiz, but he could easily see that the PC was out-of-date. He couldn't recall having any expertise in technology or electronics, but he'd seen the fancy Geekon laptops that the nursing staff had used at the medical center.

There'd been something about the brand name that had struck a chord and triggered a feeling of familiarity. But he hadn't said anything to anyone about that. Why get excited about something he still couldn't put his finger on?

When his sexy Florence Nightingale was satisfied that he could operate the machine and that he wouldn't stay on it for more than an hour before giving his mind and body another rest, she left him alone in the den to search for clues he didn't know how to find.

Outside, the engine of the old ranch pickup started up, letting him know he was on his own for a while. So he typed in his name, only to get eighty-two thousand hits. So he narrowed his search.

Okay, apparently he was somewhat computer literate. But even that tidbit of information didn't tell him squat. And even an hour later, he still hadn't found anything to go on. He suspected that he'd be out of luck until his brain sorted itself out—or until the sheriff came by with more information.

But he wasn't going to give up that easily. So he typed in Dave Cummings, Brighton Valley and the Rocking C Ranch. This time, the search yielded a better result.

He found an article about the Brighton Valley High School music club and spotted a black-and-white photo of Dave and several of his bandmates.

As he continued his search, he uncovered obituaries for both Mr. Cummings and his wife. As he read them, a heaviness filled his chest, but he'd be damned if he knew why. The fact that they'd died fairly young, he supposed.

He found quite a few articles about Brighton Valley, and so he spent the next fifteen minutes reading through the city's online newspaper in the hope that something about the small Texas town would jump out at him.

The only article that came close to triggering any sense of significance was a fairly recent one about Clay Jenkins, the founder of Geekon Enterprises and mastermind behind creating its computers and repair stores. Jenkins had gone to school in nearby Wexler, but apparently Brighton Valley had claimed him as a native son.

The brains behind all the impressive Geekon products had recently moved back to town and had married a woman who'd been working in the local Zorba the Geek computer repair shop.

As Joe studied the picture of the billionaire, another sense of familiarity settled over him.

Why was that? Did he know the man? They appeared to be close in age.

After looking up more information on the big shot in the software industry, Joe decided that Clay's popularity and fame led to what little recognition he'd sensed.

He glanced at the small antique brass clock on one of the bookshelves. It was getting close to three o'clock, well after the hour when he'd promised to shut down the computer and take an afternoon nap. But he wanted to run one more search.

So he typed in Chloe Dawson. It wasn't the most common name, but it still garnered several hits. She'd said she was an army brat and had moved around a lot, so Joe wasn't really sure where her hometown of record would be. But a picture of a homecoming queen at a small school just outside of Fort Hood, Texas, certainly resembled the lovely woman who'd volunteered to nurse a poor, unknown former marine back to health.

She stood next to a handsome jock wearing a crown and a sash over his football uniform. Like her, he was holding a bouquet of roses and flashing a happy smile.

Chloe had been a pretty teenager who'd blossomed into a stunning beauty—even when she'd traded in the fancy gown for a pair of faded jeans and a flannel shirt.

That's why Joe had a difficult time wrapping his head around the possibility that a popular homecoming queen could be attracted to a short, scrawny band geek like Dave. Of course, Dave must have grown up and filled out after joining the Marines. But still, something didn't compute.

Maybe the two weren't involved in any sort of intimate relationship. Chloe had said they were only friends. But if that were the case, then why would she stay here on the ranch, breaking her back to keep things running for a guy who couldn't even find time to call or otherwise check in?

It seemed like a waste, especially when her heart and talents should be pursuing her desired career in the nursing field.

Another question continued to nag him. Why would Dave task a buddy with a mission to hand deliver a letter to the beautiful Miss Dawson when a phone call or a certified letter could have done the same job—and been a whole lot easier?

Thc delivery method he'd chosen meant the message had to be personal. And as much as Joe would like to get his hands on that letter to find out what was so important that he'd come to Brighton Valley in the first place, he'd sure hate to find out that he was lusting after his buddy's girl.

Chapter Five

The Sheltering Arms Nursing Home was located just two blocks down from the Brighton Valley Medical Center and next door to a senior apartment complex that also offered assisted living for the residents who needed additional care.

On the outside, the two-story brick building didn't look much different from any of the other medical offices that had sprung up around the hospital. But on the inside, the staff and volunteers did their best to provide a warm, cozy environment so the patients would feel more at home.

That was one of the things Chloe liked about the place. Most of the staff cared about the elderly residents and went above and beyond when it came to their comfort and care. The other thing was the seniors themselves, two of whom she'd grown especially close to.

After stopping by the market and running a few errands, she pulled into the parking lot. She hadn't been back to the Sheltering Arms since the day she'd been fired, and while everything inside her urged her to stay away, she couldn't just abandon Sam Darnell, the elderly man who reminded her of her great-grandfather, a one-time rodeo cowboy who'd passed away just weeks after losing his wife of fifty-eight years.

Sam had been a cowboy, too, although he'd been a rancher and had never competed in rodeos. He and his wife, Nellie, had moved into the senior apartment complex just down the block, intending to live out their remaining years together. They hadn't wanted to be a burden on their nephew, an attorney who lived and worked in Los Angeles.

But Nellie had died in her sleep last winter, and Sam had taken her loss hard. By spring he'd moved into the assisted-living facility because he'd grown weak and unsteady on his feet. And he'd continued to decline physically to the point that he had to move into the nursing home.

Chloe had been assigned to his room, and the two of them had connected in a special way. Sam had actually begun to eat again, and she'd seen an improvement in both his attitude and his physical condition.

She'd written to him regularly since her termination, but that wasn't the same as a real visit. So she'd set aside her own uneasiness and had made the effort today.

While she'd been at the market, she'd seen a display of small potted Christmas trees. So she'd picked one up for him to keep near his bed. She'd also made a stop at Caroline's Diner, where she'd purchased blueberry muffins.

Sam and his wife had been big fans of Megan Adams, who not only had a popular booth at the Brighton Valley farmer's market, but who also supplied homemade jams and baked items for Caroline.

Megan had recently married Clay Jenkins, but she was still baking up a storm and canning her award-winning jams. From what Chloe had heard, she'd even struck a big deal to sell her products regionally through a supermarket chain.

Sam had always claimed that Megan's muffins were the best he'd ever eaten, so Chloe knew the unexpected treat would please him. She'd also picked up a muffin for Ethel Furman, another of her elderly friends.

Upon entering the lobby, which boasted a fully decorated, seven-foot noble fir with a variety of brightly wrapped presents underneath, Chloe carried the small potted tree and made her way to the elevator and rode it up to the third floor.

When the doors opened, Merrilee Turner, one of several aides who took turns manning the nurses' desk, looked up from her work. When she spotted Chloe, she offered a warm smile. "Hey, girl. It's good to see you. How's it going?"

"Fine. Thanks." Chloe wondered if Merrilee would realize she'd chosen to visit on the hospital administrator's day off. Not that the man would object to her being here. It's not as if she'd been banned from the nursing home. But she'd hoped to avoid running into him.

"I thought I'd stop in to see Mr. Darnell," Chloe said. "How's he been?"

"About the same as when you were working here. He sure brightens up when one of your cards arrives in the mail."

Then it was well worth the effort of sending them to him every few days.

Chloe scanned the corridors, hoping that Sarah Poston still worked the same split shift. No need to run into her if she didn't have to. Ever since Chloe had reported Sarah's unprofessional behavior to the administrator, a charge that hadn't been followed up on and which had resulted in Chloe being discharged, there'd been bad blood between them.

Relieved not to see the dark-haired nurse, Chloe lifted the bag that held the muffins she'd brought for her elderly friends. "I brought Sam a treat as well as something to brighten up his room."

"I'm sure he'll appreciate that."

Chloe returned Merrilee's smile, then made her way to Sam's room. When she approached his door, she could hear his television cranked up a bit too loud, something Sarah had always chided him for.

"Anyone home?" Chloe asked, as she entered the room.

The silver-haired cowboy, who'd been watching a John Wayne movie, tore his gaze from the television screen. When he saw Chloe, he broke into a full-on grin. "Well, look who's here. If it ain't my favorite gal. Where have you been keeping yourself?"

Chloe hadn't shared any of her work-related issues with him before and wasn't about to do it now. So she told him about Joe's accident, the resulting amnesia and how she'd taken him in to live with her at the Rocking C.

Sam furrowed his craggy brow and wagged an arthritic finger. "You let a stranger move in with you? That's plain foolish. You don't know anything about him."

"I know he's a friend of Dave's—and that when he served in the Marine Corps he had an impressive service record."

"Humph." Sam shook his head. "He's still a man. And you're a beautiful woman. Besides, consider your reputation."

The only reputation she was really concerned about was the one here at the Sheltering Arms, which her firing had tarnished, but she merely smiled. "I'm sure Joe will be heading back to wherever he calls home as soon as his memory returns. So there's not much chance of people talking."

"I hope you're right."

"So what does Dr. Crenshaw have to say these days? Has he been in to see you?"

"The dermatologist?" Sam clucked his tongue. "Not sure if he even graduated from medical school."

"He's definitely a real doctor—but for the record, his specialty is internal medicine, not dermatology."

"What difference does it make?" Sam's eyes twinkled. "If you ask me, they all try and skin you."

Chloe laughed. That's what she loved about Sam. He might be gruff and crotchety on the outside, but he had a dry wit that contributed to his awesome sense of humor.

They continued to chat for a while. Then, after she left him the blueberry muffin, which he set aside and promised to eat later, she gave him a hug. "I'll stop by to see you again next week."

"I hope so."

"You can count on it." She gave him one last smile, then headed down the hall to Ethel Furman's room. Ethel was another special patient—and one Chloe missed. Unlike Sam, Ethel didn't have any family to look after her. And even though she'd been a schoolteacher in Brighton Valley for more than forty years, her students rarely visited.

Chloe gave a little knock on the doorjamb, then slowly entered Ethel's room, where the frail, silver-haired lady dozed in her bed.

"Good afternoon," Chloe said.

Ethel's eyes flickered open, and she turned her head toward the doorway. A slow smile stretched across her face. "What a nice surprise. How are you, dear?"

"I'm doing well. How about you?"

"I can't complain, although I need new glasses. My eyesight isn't what it used to be, and I miss being able to read."

"Did you tell anyone?" Chloe asked, as she made her way to her friend's bedside.

"Yes, but it doesn't seem to help. Apparently, they're much too busy around here to worry about an old woman."

Chloe reached for Ethel's hand, noting the frailty of her wrist—and that it was bare. "What happened to your allergy alert bracelet?"

"The clasp is broken, so I took it off."

"But you're allergic to penicillin. It's important that you wear it."

"I mentioned something to Sarah. She said she would either get it fixed or order a new one for me."

Sarah, the incompetent nurse? Good luck with that.

"How long has it been broken?" Chloe asked.

"A week or two. I'm not sure. My memory isn't what it used to be, either."

And apparently, Sarah's wasn't any better.

"I'll talk to Merrilee," Chloe said. Sometimes it seemed that the third-floor aides were more responsive and reliant than the nurse in charge.

After giving Ethel the last muffin, Chloe promised to return for another visit. Then she gave her friend a hug and left the room. But before she could reach the safety of the elevator, she spotted the one woman she'd hoped to avoid.

Apparently, Sarah wasn't working her usual split shift today. Great. Chloe hated confrontations, and this was sure to be one.

"Well, I'll be," the dark-haired nurse said. "Look what the cat dragged in."

Chloe flinched—at least, on the inside. Then she scolded herself for letting the snide comment get to her.

Sarah crossed her arms. "I didn't expect you to come around again."

"Why not?" It wasn't as though she'd done anything wrong. "I have quite a few friends here."

Sarah made a noise that sounded like a muffled snicker.

"By the way," Chloe said, "Ethel isn't wearing her allergy alert bracelet. The clasp needs to be repaired—or she'll need a new one."

"It's been ordered."

"Maybe you should provide her with some kind of temporary—"

"That won't be necessary. Her allergy is noted in her medical record."

"Maybe so, but the bracelet serves as a reminder that would eliminate the risk of someone making a mistake."

"And that's why I ordered her a new one."

Maybe so, but Ethel had been without it for quite a while already. Chloe was about to suggest that Sarah check on it, but decided she'd said enough already. At least, about Ethel. "I hear that Sam Darnell hasn't been eating well."

"We can't force him to do something against his will. Nor do we have the time to spoon-feed him. However, we offer him a healthy plate of food at each meal. If he doesn't like the taste, it's not my fault. Besides, his family should bring him other options—just like you did with that muffin today."

So Sarah had talked to Merrilee, the aide at the desk. Or maybe she'd seen the muffin in Sam's room and he'd told her who'd brought it. Either way, she'd known that Chloe was here today. Had she come looking for her?

In the scheme of things, Chloe supposed it didn't matter. "Sam and his wife never had children. And his nephew lives out of state. Since Nellie died, he has no one nearby to worry about him. Maybe, if someone sat with him during meal-time—"

"He isn't the only patient on this floor."

No, he wasn't. But something told Chloe the old man was different from the others in the nursing facility. "Another thing you might consider is sending him back to his apartment. In a more homelike setting he might get better—and stronger."

Sarah clucked her tongue. "Aren't you full of helpful ideas. You're suggesting that we take a gamble that a move might help. And I can't do that. What if he fell and broke a hip? Besides, he can't very well return to the assisted-living complex when he's resistant to any kind of assistance."

Chloe was tempted to go over Sarah's head and report her to the administrator again for her lack of compassion and her complete disregard of the feelings and wishes of the patients. But a lot of good that had done last time. So she decided not to bother. After all, she only had the training of an aide—even though she felt more qualified than the third-floor nurse in charge of the patients she'd come to know and love.

Maybe, after she graduated from nursing school, she'd have more knowledge and would feel better about challenging the woman and facing the powers that be.

Still, that didn't mean she couldn't step up to the plate and be an advocate for both Sam and Ethel.

Especially when it seemed that Chloe was the only one they had.

The sun had begun to set by the time Chloe arrived home. After parking the old ranch pickup near the barn, she made her way to the porch. As she placed her hand on the railing, it wobbled. She made a mental note to ask Joe to fix it—if he knew how.

However, she hated to overload him with chores to do. She and Tomas might need the help, but she didn't want to ask too much of the man. Even if he didn't figure out who he was and hightail it out of here in the first rental car he came across, he was still recovering from a pretty serious head injury.

She reached for the doorknob and let herself inside. The moment she stepped into the living room, the spicy aroma of meat, tomatoes and cumin filled the air.

Apparently, Joe had been busy while she'd been gone. She wondered what he'd found to cook, especially when, after looking into the pantry earlier, she'd decided that she would have to go to the market in order to come up with an appealing menu for dinner tonight.

She placed her purse on the hutch near the front door, then scanned the living room, where several red and green plastic storage containers were stacked near the hearth.

Oh, good. He'd remembered to have Tomas bring in the Christmas decorations. Chloe might not be able to go home for the holidays, but she could at least make the best of it here on the Rocking C, just as her mother always had.

No matter where in the world her parents were stationed or who was gone on deployment, Chloe's mom, an army nurse, made sure that Christmas was a special time of the year and always did things up big. And because of her efforts and the decorations they'd transported from house to house, the spirit of the season, had always been magical and had brightened their home.

In fact, because of the transient nature of her and her husband's military careers, Captain Louella Dawson took great pains to always maintain their family traditions, including a passed down recipe for hot buttered cranberry and orange scones.

Granted, her mother's skill as a combat medic was more laudable than those of being a cook, but that didn't stop her. And those scones, which had been a family recipe for longer than anyone could remember, had become as much a part of the Dawsons' winter wonderland as Santa Claus himself.

When Chloe had talked to her parents last week, they'd been thrilled that two of their three children would be with them for the holidays. As much as Chloe would have liked to have been one of those kids, she didn't have the money for airfare to Fort Drum in New York, which was where her parents were currently assigned. And even though they would have gladly shelled out the money for her travel, Chloe needed to be independent and demonstrate that she was capable of managing her own life—as well as her diminishing bank account—even if that meant being alone during the most wonderful time of the year.

Well, maybe not *alone*.

"I'm back," she called.

Joe really ought to be in bed, resting, but the smell coming from the kitchen told her he'd kept himself busy—too busy—while she'd been gone.

"I'm in here," he said.

She followed the sound of his voice, as well as the mouthwatering aroma, and found him standing at the stove, peering into a pot.

She probably ought to chastise her patient for overdoing it, especially after he'd assured her that he wouldn't, but she was too hungry and too impressed with what he'd done to make a big deal about it.

"You obviously know how to cook," she said, as she entered the kitchen with the grocery bags in hand. "Maybe you worked in the mess hall when you were in the service."

He turned and flashed a handsome grin. "Marines call it the chow hall."

He certainly seemed to remember some things—like military terms.

"Is cooking another memory?" she asked.

He shrugged, then cocked his head as if he was thinking over the possibility. "No, just common knowledge, I guess."

"Nevertheless, something sure smells delicious."

He wiped his hands on a dish towel, then took the bags from her and placed them on the counter.

"What are you doing?" she asked.

"Just messing around."

"You're supposed to be resting."

"I must've rested too much this morning. I don't think I'm used to sitting around doing nothing all day."

Chloe looked at the way his biceps filled out the borrowed Future Farmers of America T-shirt she'd found in Dave's drawer.

Ever since she'd seen his bare chest, she'd found it impossible to stop thinking about his chiseled torso or the way his muscles rippled. He certainly looked like a man who was used to action and lots of it.

In fact, she could easily envision him lifting weights, running or kickboxing if he needed an outlet for his energy. But she never would have expected to see him in the kitchen, creating something that smelled so good that her stomach was growling.

"So you decided to do some cooking?" she asked.

"Well, I started to, but then I realized I didn't have all the ingredients I needed."

"You should have called me on my cell. I could've picked them up while I was at the market."

Joe turned off the fire on the stove. "I didn't want to bother you. Plus, I didn't know if the stores in Brighton Valley would carry what I needed. Besides, when Tomas and I brought in those Christmas decorations earlier, he mentioned that his wife had bought more than they needed last weekend. She was going to make some of the dough tonight, and he promised to bring some to me tomorrow."

The small town didn't boast a mega supermarket, but they usually kept most staples in stock. "What is Tomas supposed to bring you?"

"Masa. It's a corn dough made from hominy."

"What exactly are you trying to make?"

"Tamales," Joe said simply, as if he was making something as ordinary as a peanut butter and jelly sandwich.

"You actually know how to make tamales?"

"Strangely enough, that's another thing I know how to do. Don't ask me why because I doubt that I used to make Mexican food as a sergeant in the Marines. But when I saw all those ornaments and the nativity set, all I could think of was tamales. I must associate them with Christmas. So I decided to make some. We can eat a few tomorrow, then freeze whatever is left and have them as part of the holiday meal."

"That makes sense. I associate cranberry-orange scones with Christmas because it was a holiday tradition for my family. But…" Chloe trailed off, not wanting to risk offending her guest, who was eager to have at least a small tidbit of information from his past.

"But what?" he asked.

"Well, it's just that most of the families I know who make homemade tamales for Christmas are Hispanic. But Wilcox doesn't really strike me as a typical last name."

"That's something I thought of, too. But, let's face it. My coloring would indicate that there's some ethnic blood running through my family tree. Also, when Tomas was here earlier, he said something in Spanish. I not only understood him, but I responded."

"In Spanish?"

"Yes, so either I was adopted or my mother was a lovely little señorita who married Mr. Wilcox, which is what I'm leaning toward since I obviously grew up with that heritage."

Chloe bit her cheek so that she wouldn't reflect how sad she felt about him not having any idea who his family was, especially at this time of year. She might live far away from the Dawson clan, but at least she knew where she belonged. Joe didn't even have that.

Yet instead of blustering in frustration or sinking into a depression, the guy was in here, floating around her kitchen, trying to make the best of whatever miniscule detail he *could* recall.

She liked knowing that he was a glass-half-full kind of person. Kevin Boswell, her ex-boyfriend, had always been such a pessimist, thinking the world was out to get him. And Dave, even though he wasn't ever anything more than a friend, was always so melancholy and down that Chloe's spirits sank whenever she was around either of them.

"So, how does one make tamales?" she asked.

"I had to double-check on the internet, which brought up more recipes and instructions than you can believe. And although there are lots of different methods, the one that seemed the most familiar is a two-day process anyway. So tonight I cooked the filling with some pork I found in the freezer. We can eat some of that over the rice I made."

"Boy, you have been busy," Chloe said, her admiration growing.

"I hope you don't mind me making myself at home."

"Of course not." How could she when she saw the excitement in his eyes, something she hadn't noticed before? *"Mi casa es su casa."*

He chuckled at her attempt to speak Spanish. "Tomorrow, when Tomas brings me some masa and some corn husks, I'll be able to make the dough and assemble everything together." He replaced the lid on one of the pans he had on the stove.

She liked seeing him comfortable in the kitchen, but she was even happier to know that he'd be spending one more day in the house and not out on the ranch, trying to attempt more strenuous chores. This way, he felt useful, and they were both winners.

As she began to put away the groceries she'd purchased earlier, Joe zeroed in on the sugar, vanilla, oranges and dried cranberries.

"Is that for the scones you were talking about?" he asked.

"Yes, I thought I'd make them this evening."

"I don't suppose you'd be willing to make some cookies one of these days."

"Of course. I have some great family recipes. It wouldn't be Christmas without a variety of goodies."

At that, his eyes brightened like a child standing in front of a bakery display case.

"You must like sweets," she said.

"I think you're right."

Another memory, it seemed. But not one they could build upon.

"Do you like to bake?" he asked.

"Yes, especially at this time of year. That's why I wanted to make the scones tonight. We always used to eat them when we decorated the house for Christmas."

In all honesty, Chloe would much rather spend the day baking than making a holiday meal.

"You mentioned being hungry," he said, "and dinner is ready. Do you want to eat before you make the scones?"

"It won't take me long to whip up the dough—unless you're too hungry to wait."

"I'm okay. I ate the rest of the tuna salad for a late afternoon snack. Computer sleuthing is hard work."

"How did that go, by the way?" Chloe wished she would've thought of looking him up online yesterday, but living out at the Rocking C full-time was like being in a technological time warp.

She was usually so busy with the chores and managing the ranch that she rarely had a chance to use the old computer. She'd often thought of how getting a newer modem or laptop would help streamline the day-to-day management of the ranch, like paying bills, ordering merchandise, and cutting checks to vendors and their two employees. But at the end of the month, she couldn't justify the expense. So she was left with the antiquated system Teresa Cummings had set up at least a decade ago.

"My search went about as well as I expected," Joe said. "A big fat nada on any information about me, but I did learn some interesting things about Brighton Valley."

While she mixed the ingredients for the scones and Joe wiped down the countertops, he filled her in on what he'd discovered online.

She set the oven timer just as he finished washing the mixing bowl and the pots he'd used.

"By the way, I hope you don't mind that I got into the pantry and the freezer without asking if it was okay."

She laughed. "Even if I'd had plans to use that pork you found in the freezer or the rice and beans, I'm too hungry to object."

As he placed the bowls of food on the table, she set out the plates and silverware. Then they both took their seats.

After eating the first delicious bite and savoring the taste, she said, "You must be a chef or something in your real life. This is way too good to be chow-hall fare. What'd you put in the sauce?"

"I just threw in some seasonings I found in the spice cabinet."

He'd certainly made himself at home in what she'd once considered her domain, but if he could whip up meals like this, she'd be the last one to complain. Besides, it had been ages since someone had cooked for her. And if truth be told, she liked being a guest instead of the hostess.

As they dug into their meal and silence stretched between them, she couldn't help letting her thoughts drift to Sam, Ethel and the other patients on the third floor of the Sheltering Arms. And as she did, her worry grew.

She had to do something, but what? She no longer worked there, so her hands were tied.

"What's wrong?" Joe asked.

Had her heavy thoughts been so obvious? "Why do you ask?"

"You seem sad and preoccupied."

"I visited my friends at the nursing home today and…" She paused, wondering how much to divulge. If she confided too much in him, she'd have to tell him about being fired. And then she'd have to defend her actions, or risk having him think she was a flake or a screw up or worse. And she didn't like the idea of him questioning her abilities. So she finished the sentence she'd started. "It just makes me sad. That's all."

"I'm sorry."

"Me, too." Eager to change the subject, she added, "I picked up a Christmas tree while I was in town. Maybe, after dinner, you can help me bring it inside and decorate it."

"Sure, I'd be glad to."

As she dug back into the scrumptious meal Joe had

cooked, she pondered her usual holiday traditions. Yet for some reason, she didn't seem quite as lonely as before. Nor did she think she would miss the family Christmas in New York as much as she'd once thought she would.

She might have wanted to help Joe get through the holidays this year, but now it seemed that *he* was helping *her.*

And she looked forward to creating a few new Christmas memories—with him.

Chapter Six

The night sky provided a clear view of the stars as Joe went out to get the tree from the back of the ranch pickup.

He took a moment to study the constellations, noting both the Big and Little Dippers. Apparently he had at least some astronomical knowledge, which was another tidbit of information that hadn't been completely lost to him.

For some reason, he felt oddly at home on the Rocking C. He knew where to find things, like the mop he'd used earlier today and the ladder he'd needed so he and Tomas could climb into the hayloft for the Christmas decorations. He'd even walked right up to the container of oats and molasses, popped open the lid and scooped out a handful to feed as a treat to Lola, the mare.

In spite of the fact that Hernandez, the Rocking C foreman, hadn't given him any reason to believe he'd ever stepped foot on the ranch before, Joe still couldn't seem to kick that uncanny feeling that he had.

But if so, he didn't have a clue what the circumstances had been.

Had he worked here? Maybe even lived here? If not, he must have visited Dave and his family at least once.

As he walked out to the pickup Chloe had driven to

town earlier, a crisp winter breeze stirred up the ranch scents that seemed more and more familiar.

In spite of what Hernandez had said, somewhere along the line, Joe *had* been here.

His boots crunched along the graveled drive as he headed toward the faded green GMC Chloe had parked near the barn. Hell, even that weathered old truck looked familiar. Had he driven it before? Or had he just ridden in it?

"The tree is in the back of the pickup," Chloe had told him before heading to the kitchen to check on the scones baking in the oven.

Sure enough, there it was.

He reached in, grabbed the tree by the trunk and pulled it out. As he shook out the branches, he caught the scent of pine, which didn't provoke any memories.

He had to have celebrated Christmas before. He had a tamale recipe to prove it. He cursed the amnesia that plagued him while he carried the six-foot tree into the house. Then he placed it in the stand that had been stored in the loft with all the other holiday decorations.

Joe had no more than stepped back to check out his work when Chloe carried in a tray with two steaming cups of hot cocoa and a plate of scones.

"It's a bit crooked," she said.

"I can fix that." Joe made a few minor adjustments in the stand, then tilted the trunk slightly to the left.

"That's better," Chloe said as she set the tray on the coffee table. "I'll get some water to fill the reservoir. Then we can get started."

After she returned with a plastic pitcher, she knelt and watered the tree. When she finished, she stood and brushed her hands against her denim-clad hips. Then she began to unpack the red and green plastic storage boxes.

First they strung the lights, tiny, multicolored bulbs that blinked on and off. The ornaments came next. While they worked, they'd stop long enough to nibble on the warm, buttered scones and to sip the hot chocolate.

Joe couldn't say whether he'd ever decorated a tree before, but doing so with Chloe sure felt like a first.

"Oh, look," she said as she unwrapped the tissue from an angel. "This is the perfect tree topper. Don't you think?"

Actually, just hearing her ooh and aah over the various ornaments while her eyes lit up like a hopeful child made the entire evening seem perfect. And he couldn't help but smile. "You bet."

"Can you reach to put it up? Or should I get a chair?"

"I've got it." He took the angel from her hands and put it in place.

With that done, they both stood back and studied their handiwork.

"It's beautiful," she said, her eyes glistening.

She was beautiful—even in jeans. And he couldn't help thinking that she belonged here—on the ranch, decorating a tree and making a memory.

When it was all over—not just Christmas, but his amnesia—he'd have to ask her out, just to see her all dressed up. Maybe he'd take her to that Italian restaurant…

Wait. He could almost see an actual place in his mind, a quaint restaurant with a European flair—a mural of Venice hand-painted on a white plaster wall, dark wood tables covered with white linen, a bud vase with a single red rose, a flickering candle… Where was it? When had he seen it?

"What do you think?" she asked.

About *her?* About taking her out for a romantic evening on the town?

"I love Christmas," she said, drawing his thoughts back to reality and the subject at hand.

But he still couldn't help allowing his own musing to drift back to the romantic fantasy. "All we're missing is a little mistletoe to hang over the doorway." She flushed, and he was tempted to draw her to him anyway, to kiss her senseless. In fact, as she lifted her eyes to his, as their gazes locked, desire flared.

He had no business following through on it, though. He didn't even know where he'd been, let alone where he was going. But if she didn't stop looking at him like that…

Oh, what the hell.

"Then again, something tells me I've never needed any prompts." He stepped forward, placed his hands on her cheeks. He waited a moment, taking the time to study her eyes, her expression, checking for any sign of protest.

Instead, her chin lifted and her lips parted.

That was all the invitation he needed.

As Joe lowered his mouth to hers, Chloe's heart soared in anticipation. She really shouldn't kiss him, although for the life of her, she could no longer come up with a good reason to object. Instead, she slipped her hands around his neck and stepped into his embrace.

His lips brushed hers tentatively at first, then a second time. The whisper of his breath, the promise of what was to come, sent her senses reeling, and she was soon caught up in a swirl of heat and desire.

Goodness. The man might not recall a lot of things, but he certainly knew how to kiss.

As their tongues met and mated, she lost herself in his musky, mountain fresh scent and in his sweet, chocolate-laced taste.

Did she dare put a stop to it? Or take him by the hand and lead him to one of the bedrooms?

In truth, with her knees about to give out on her, she doubted whether she could urge her feet to take a single step.

When they finally came up for air, she had to hold on to him so she wouldn't collapse into a heap on the floor.

"I was curious," he said, his breath warm against her face. "So thanks for indulging me."

She'd been curious, too, but she was even more so now. Not about kissing, but about what other heart-spinning, soul-stirring talents Joe might have. Needless to say, he would make an incredible lover.

"Well," she said, "now you know."

"Yes, but it opened a whole other world of questions."

She released her grip on his shoulders and took a step back. "Maybe so, but I don't think we ought to ponder the answers right now."

"You're probably right." He let his own hands slip down her back, his fingers leaving a trail of heat, until he released her altogether. "You'll have to forgive me. I should have known better."

"There's nothing to be sorry for. I could have resisted."

Oh, yeah? a small voice asked. *That's not true.*

Okay, so she'd been a willing participant—and an active one at that.

Joe turned away and strode to the stone fireplace, where Dave's photo sat on the mantel. The young man in uniform seemed to be watching them.

Something told Chloe that Dave hadn't intended for his buddy and the woman he'd thought of as "his girl" to…

What? Kiss? Become involved?

Fat chance of that happening. Chloe was in no position to strike up a romance with anyone. Not until she moved on and established herself as a nursing student at the junior college in nearby Wexler.

And Joe had to feel the same way, since his future was even sketchier than hers—at least, until he could remember his past.

His gaze drifted to the other photos on the mantel, as if they could somehow provide him with his missing identity. She suspected that he was having some of the same thoughts she was, the same concerns.

"Would you like some more cocoa?" she asked, pretending as if the kiss hadn't happened, as if she wasn't confused by all the feelings and desires it had sparked.

"Sure," he said. "Why not?"

Why not indeed? They obviously needed a distraction or something to help them cool off. She offered him a smile. "I'll just be a minute."

"While you're gone, I'll see if there are any good movies on television."

She supposed that watching TV was as good an idea as any. Yet as she left Joe to surf the channels, her thoughts made a complete one-eighty.

Too bad she wasn't free to pursue the attraction that

raged between them. But only a fool would pin her hopes and dreams on a man who knew nothing about his past, very little about his present and had no idea where the future would take him.

A noise—either real or imagined—jolted Chloe from a sound sleep, and she shot up in bed, her heart pounding as though it might jump out of her chest. She scanned the room, her eyes desperately trying to adjust to the darkness.

She didn't hear anything but the tick-tock of the clock on the bureau, so she assumed all was well and that she'd only been dreaming. That, she supposed, was the result of being overly tired.

She and Joe had turned in just before eleven o'clock. Yet, try as she might, she couldn't find a comfortable spot on the mattress. At least, not while their blood-stirring kiss continued to haunt her thoughts.

As it was, she hadn't drifted off to sleep until well past midnight.

"No!" Joe yelled from the guestroom down the hall, setting Chloe's fight-or-flight response on high alert.

"Fall back!" he shouted.

He must be having a nightmare. She glanced at the clock on the bureau. It was 3:17.

"Don't!" Joe called out again.

She threw off her blankets, rolled out of bed and hurried down the lighted hallway to the room where he slept. She stood before the closed door for a moment, her escalated pulse throbbing, her fist lifted and prepared to knock.

A moan sounded from within, and she rapped lightly.

Instead of answering, Joe yelled, "Down, dammit. Get down!"

Was he dreaming? Or was he reliving a memory?

She opened his door, allowing the light from the hall to spill inside, and watched as he thrashed around on the bed.

"Medic," he groaned.

She crossed the hardwood floor in her bare feet, then touched his shoulder, felt the warmth of his skin, the bulk of his muscles.

"Joe?" she said softly, not wanting to startle him.

Still, he lurched up on the mattress, the blanket dropping to his waist. His chest was broad—and bare—his breathing ragged. He glanced around the room as if desperate to make sense of it all.

"It's okay," she said. "You were having a nightmare."

Although his eyes were open and she suspected he was awake, he couldn't seem to blink away the fear, the confusion.

Her hand lingered on his shoulder, then trailed down a bulging biceps—the one with the military insignia—until it rested on his forearm.

Finally, his gaze cleared and he zeroed in on her, snagging something deep inside and giving it a squeeze.

"Where am I?" he asked.

Her heart went out to him. "You're at the Cummings ranch. And you were…dreaming." She reached for the glass of water he must have placed on the bedside table before retiring this evening and handed it to him.

She watched him take a long swig, watched the muscles along his throat contract. "Do you want to talk about it?"

"Not really." He raked his hand through his hair.

"I can understand," she said. "But maybe if you do, I can help you to make sense of it."

He set the water glass on the nightstand, his fingers trembling a bit as he did. Then he reached for her hand and gripped it tightly in his. "Don't leave yet."

She wouldn't consider abandoning him in a strange house and an unfamiliar bed, especially after everything he'd been through. So she took a seat on the mattress.

With his free hand, the one she wasn't holding, he threw the covers off his left leg, which was the one farthest from her hip. Then he reached down and massaged his knee. Was he wearing briefs or boxers under the blanket that barely covered him now? She supposed it didn't matter. Yet she couldn't help wondering if he was naked.

She glanced down at the flimsy gown she wore, wishing she'd taken the time to throw on a robe. But she'd been so startled by his outburst, so concerned about him, that she'd rushed to his side without thinking. That shouldn't be a problem, though. Joe was probably so caught up in that frightening nightmare that he hadn't noticed. Or maybe he didn't care either way.

"What were you dreaming about?" she asked.

He stretched out his left leg, extending his knee. "About the day I got this injury, I think. Although I can't be sure."

"From the words you said, I gathered that you were on a battlefield. You even called for a medic."

"Yeah. I was in battle. And Dave was with me."

"So you were in the same platoon?"

"I'm not sure about that. Maybe. But I was looking at that photo of him on the mantel earlier and trying hard to remember his face. So it's possible that his image only infiltrated my dream. And that none of it had been real." He blew out a ragged sigh. "But as much as I hate living with amnesia, I hope it wasn't a memory. I'd rather not think that I actually lived through that."

She could understand how he felt. But in a way, she hoped he had. And that the other memories would soon follow.

Joe lay back on his pillow, but he didn't release her hand. "I suspect it was real, though. We were under attack. And I'm pretty sure it was Afghanistan. This may sound weird to you, but I remember several phrases in an Afghani dialect. How else would I know that?"

She had no idea, but she said, "It makes sense that you would."

Once he started to talk, the tension in his body eased and his breathing slowed. Yet he still didn't let go of her hand.

She felt a yawn coming on and tried to stifle it to no avail.

"I'm sorry," he said.

"About waking me up? Don't be. I'm sure that dream was troubling. And if it helps having someone to talk to, I'm happy to be here."

"It does help. But you're tired. Go on back to bed."

She couldn't do that. Not when she knew he hadn't wanted to be alone. She might be tired, but she'd feel pretty selfish if she left him. "Is it okay if I just lie down next to you for a while?"

He scooted to the side, making room for her. So she stretched out on the mattress, on top of the covers so that their bodies were separated by the bedding. He seemed to take comfort in having her near and in whatever emotional solace she was providing.

If truth be told, she found lying next to him to be a bit comforting, too. She liked holding his hand and breathing in his masculine scent.

She wished she could help him sort through the puzzle pieces, but she couldn't.

As he continued to drift off, his breathing low and deep, the masculine timbre lulled her, sending her off to dreamland. Only her nocturnal visions weren't the least bit frightening.

She dreamed of a handsome soldier who'd just returned from war, of joining him in bed, cuddling next to him.

And as his arm draped her waist, as he drew her close, she breathed in the scent of bath soap and musk and slept peacefully until dawn chased away the night.

A pounding on the front door jarred Joe from his sleep, although the petite blonde in his arms had already awakened everything below his waist.

If the damn knocking would stop, he could focus on sexy Chloe and the fact that she was all soft and warm and curled up beside him in bed. But he couldn't take advantage of the sleeping woman who'd only climbed in next to him last night to comfort him after his nightmare.

Besides, whoever was at the door was obviously on a mission and wasn't leaving any time soon.

He rolled to the side, slipped out of the bed and pulled on the jeans he'd worn yesterday. Then he grabbed a clean shirt from the stack of clothes Chloe had left for him. He didn't realize it until he was about to open the door that the writing on the front of the snug T read: BVHS Marching Band—Drummers Bring the Boom.

Great. Now someone would think that he was a band geek, too.

He made his way to the living room. When he pulled open the front door, he found Sheriff Hollister standing on the stoop.

Joe greeted him, then stepped aside and allowed the lawman to enter. "You want some coffee?"

"Only if you have some already made."

Chloe was still asleep, so there was no way she'd risen early to put on a pot. But Joe didn't want to give off the appearance that he and the lady of the house had been up lolling around in bed together until—he peered at the grandfather clock in the living room—0900 hours.

Damn. He never slept that late. But then again, once Chloe had climbed into his bed, he'd crashed.

"I'm sorry," Joe said. "I just woke up. But Chloe might have made some already. And if she didn't, I'll make a pot."

He hoped he'd convinced the sheriff that he had no idea where his benefactor was. The last thing he wanted to do was ruin her reputation. Assuming, of course, that she had one to ruin.

Wow. Where had that crazy thought come from? Why wouldn't she have a reputation to ruin?

As the two men filed into the kitchen, Joe got started on brewing a fresh pot while Hollister took a seat at the table.

"I take it you have more news," Joe said.

"I'm afraid so."

Joe expected the sheriff to expound on that, but he

held back when Chloe came into the kitchen wearing her standard jeans and a pink long-sleeved T-shirt. She looked far more rested and a lot less tousled than Joe felt.

Hopefully, Hollister wasn't so astute that he'd realize they'd woken up together.

"Good morning," Chloe said. "Did you uncover any more information, Sheriff?"

Hollister leaned back in his seat. "According to my friend at NCIS, Joe and Dave served in the same squad. They were both injured in the line of duty and sent to a hospital in Germany to recover. Since Dave was in worse shape than Joe, they were medically discharged at different times."

"So what's the bad news I'm sensing?" Joe asked.

Hollister took a deep breath, then slowly let it out. "Dave Cummings is dead."

The news hit Joe hard, but he turned to Chloe, who'd paled considerably. Her hand was on her chest, the fingers splayed over her heart. And her eyes glimmered with tears that threatened to spill out at any time. "What happened? Was it a result of his war injuries?"

"Not that I know of," Hollister said. "I'm still investigating that."

The coffee machine pinged, signaling it had finished brewing. Joe poured them each a cup. He laced one with cream and sugar, just the way Chloe drank hers yesterday morning, then handed it to her.

She thanked him before focusing her attention back on the sheriff.

What was she thinking? How was she really taking the news? Was she grieving for Dave, the man she'd claimed was a family friend?

"Joe, would you mind pouring the sheriff a cup of coffee?" Chloe asked.

Crap. He'd been so caught up in the news and in trying to jar his fragile memory that he'd forgotten to serve anyone other than Chloe.

"Don't bother," Hollister said. "Not unless you have a to-go cup. I have a lot going on today and need to head back to town."

"There are some disposable cups in the cupboard over the fridge," Chloe said.

Joe reached for one, then filled it with coffee for the lawman. "Cream or sugar?"

"Neither, thanks. Just black."

This time, as the sheriff headed for the door, Joe followed him out. "Thanks for coming by, even if the news was bad. I appreciate your efforts to help."

"You're welcome. It's part of the job. I just hope things work out for you. And sooner, rather than later."

"I'd been meaning to ask," Joe said. "Whatever happened to my rental car?"

"Last I heard, it was parked at the county impound lot. You'd paid two weeks in advance. You can pick it up whenever you want to. The rental company would probably be willing to send someone to collect it, though, if you're not up to driving yet."

Joe nodded, still trying to take it all in. What had he planned to do in town for so long? Or did he have other places to go?

"I think a trip to Houston is in order," Joe said. "I'd like to see what I can find out on my own. You think your buddy at NCIS would be willing to talk to me?"

"He said he's always willing to help out a fellow devil dog. But he said that he's only at liberty to divulge so much info." Hollister reached into his pocket, pulled out a couple of business cards. When he found the one he was looking for, he handed it to Joe. "Here's his office address. I'll call ahead and let him know you're coming by."

"Thanks." Joe studied the card for a moment, then added, "I doubt he'll be able to tell me anything more than he's already told you, but I'd still like to find out more about Dave—and what happened to him."

"So would I."

Joe stiffened. "You don't think his death had anything to do with me being hit by a car, do you?"

"I don't like to leave stones unturned. However, I doubt that the two incidents are related. In the meantime, we've contacted all the local companies who do bodywork on vehicles. If the driver who hit you was one of the locals and had been drinking at the bar, he might have left the scene so he could avoid getting slapped with a DWI. We might be able to find him that way."

"Him? It was a man?"

"The woman who placed the 9-1-1 call said she didn't see the driver or the vehicle. But there was another witness down the street who said the driver was a male in a Silverado pickup. So we're following up on that lead."

"So you'd still rather I didn't go into Brighton Valley?"

"Not yet. But I hope to have some solid answers soon."

Joe nodded, then thanked Hollister again and waited until he'd driven away.

Moments later, when Joe returned to the kitchen, he found Chloe seated at the table, deep in thought. He noted her stricken expression, the way she nibbled on her bottom lip.

What was wrong? Was she grieving for Dave?

"Are you okay?" Joe asked.

She glanced up and forced a smile. "Yes. I'm just feeling…sad. I hadn't even considered that Dave…" She blew out a sigh. "I'll be fine."

"I'm sorry," he said, wondering why he wasn't as grief stricken as she seemed to be. Probably because he still couldn't remember the guy who was supposed to be his buddy.

They said war was hell. But so was amnesia.

"Apparently," Chloe said, "that dream you had last night was real—and probably a flashback of some kind."

"I think you're right."

Her expression softened. "Maybe your memory will slowly return through your dreams."

"As much as I want to kick the brain fog, I'm not sure I want to be plagued with another nightmare."

She smiled, a rosy hue coloring her cheeks and brightening her eyes.

Was she thinking about how his arms had felt around her while they'd slept? If so, then another nightmare might be his undoing.

Especially if she spent another night in his bed.

Chapter Seven

Chloe studied the coffee mug in her hand, trying to gather her thoughts after the unexpected turn of events.

Just fifteen minutes earlier, when the morning sun filtering through the blinds had lit the guest room, she'd stretched and yawned. Then she'd rolled to the side and glanced across the mattress, only to find the spot where Joe slept empty, the sheets and blanket tousled.

She'd caught the scent of coffee in the air and assumed he was in the kitchen, fixing breakfast. So she'd climbed out of bed and padded down the hall to her own bedroom. Since she'd showered last night, before turning in, she'd dressed quickly and run a brush through her hair.

Sometime during the wee hours of the morning, Joe had slipped his arms around her and drawn her close. Well, as close as the blanket between them would allow. That intimacy—as well as the memory of the heated kiss they'd shared earlier—urged her to find him, to talk to him.

Would he feel better about sharing the details of that nightmare with her in the light of day? Had the dream triggered any of his memories?

She'd entered the kitchen with a spring in her step and a smile on her lips. And when she'd spotted Sheriff Hollister seated at the table, talking quietly to Joe, her mood had soared. Her hopes, too, as she'd waited to hear the news he'd brought.

But as he told them why he'd come, what he'd learned, a dark cloud of emotion hovered over her. Grief, doubt, worry and even a splash of guilt, all weighed her down.

Dave was *dead.*

She could hardly believe it. She grieved for him, of course—for the loss of his life. But learning that he was never coming home troubled her for more reasons than one.

What was she going to do about the ranch? The bills had been mounting, and last year's taxes had yet to be paid. She'd written to Dave, sharing her fears and hoping he'd offer some direction, telling her just what he wanted her to do in his absence.

But instead of an answer, her unopened letter had made its way back to the ranch. And now she knew why. The military must have assumed that Dave had gone home after his discharge. But somewhere along the way he'd died.

A nagging suspicion, a suffocating sense of remorse, threatened to drag her down even more. What if Dave had committed suicide? And what if Chloe's rejection had contributed to the despondence that had led him to end it all?

His letter to her, the one Joe had delivered, had been cryptic, his parting words so…final.

But if you're not interested in what we could have together, then I won't bother you again. Goodbye. Dave.

Had he hoped that she'd go looking for him? That

she'd tell him she'd changed her mind rather than risk losing him?

Chloe wouldn't have done that. She hadn't wanted to hurt Dave, but she would never marry a man she didn't love. Yet that didn't stop the grief—or the worry.

Maybe she should search the house to find a solution to the problems at hand. Had Teresa hidden money to use for a rainy day? If so, this would certainly be that day.

Teresa had also had a will. She'd told Chloe about it and had mentioned that her attorney, who had an office in Wexler, kept a copy of it in his files.

After her friend's funeral, Chloe had contacted the man, and he'd guided her and Dave through the process of transferring ownership of the ranch to Dave. He'd also drawn up the paperwork that had given Chloe power of attorney so she could keep the ranch going until Dave returned from deployment.

Did Dave have a will, too? If so, that would give Chloe some idea who should be notified, who would be able to look after the ranch now.

But unless she could find someone to hand the reins to, she couldn't very well leave. What would happen to Tomas and the other ranch hands? And what about the cattle and horses?

No, she needed to stay until the legalities were sorted out and settled. And while she really didn't have a place to go, she did have plans and dreams.

And sadly, as long as she stayed on the Rocking C she'd never be able to pursue her degree in nursing or to get on with her life. She may have wanted to settle down in one place, but she didn't want to be *stuck* there. And that's how she was beginning to feel.

"Will you excuse me?" she asked Joe without waiting for a reply.

Then she took her coffee mug and headed to the den to see what she could find.

Joe watched Chloe leave the kitchen in somber silence. She probably needed to grieve and wanted to do so alone. He couldn't blame her for that.

So he poured himself another cup of coffee and set about fixing breakfast—scrambled eggs and ham.

When it was ready and the table had been set, he went in search of her. He'd expected to find her holed up in her room, crying. But when he heard the sound of rustling papers in the den, he proceeded toward the open door.

He found her seated at the desk, where paperwork littered the polished oak surface. She had her back to him and was leaning to the side, digging through a drawer of files.

She didn't appear to be grieving, as he'd expected. Instead, she seemed to be looking for something.

"What's up?" he asked.

She stiffened, as though he'd caught her in the act of…well, hell, he didn't know what.

"Oh!" She lifted her head and glanced over her shoulder, her eyes wide, lips parted and cheeks flushed a pretty shade of pink. "I didn't hear you come in."

She'd been too intent in her search, he supposed.

"I fixed breakfast," he said. "It's ready whenever you are."

She glanced at the paperwork on the desk, then turned her gaze back on him. "I'll be there in a minute."

"Looking for something?"

She bit down on her bottom lip. Was she wondering if she could trust him with the answer? Or was she feeling guilty for sifting through the ranch files?

"Just some paperwork," she said.

"Need some help?"

"No, I've got it."

He nodded as though it made perfect sense. And in a way, he supposed it did. She'd been holding down the home front while Dave was away. And so she worked in here. Still, she'd looked a little sheepish when he'd found her.

Unable to quell his curiosity, he asked, "Does this have anything to do with the letter he wrote?"

"No. It's just ranch business."

He waited a moment, hoping she'd say something about the letter, about the contents. He wanted to know what was so important that he'd made a possible deathbed promise to deliver it.

When she didn't respond, his curiosity morphed into suspicion, although he couldn't exactly say why.

He nodded toward the doorway. "Well, since you're busy, I'll head back into the kitchen and leave you to your work."

"Thanks. I'm about done here."

As Joe turned to go, he couldn't quite shake his uneasiness. But then again, what did it matter? His amnesia had left him unsettled about a lot of things.

Joe had barely returned to the kitchen when Tomas arrived, bringing corn husks and the masa his wife had made. Joe thanked the foreman and paid him the cost of the needed items. Then he placed the dough in the refrigerator so he could make the tamales later in the day. Next, he fixed breakfast for two.

He'd just scooped out a heaping spoonful of scrambled eggs onto his plate when Chloe returned to the kitchen.

"That sure smells good," she said. "I still think you may have gone to culinary school."

Unfortunately, Joe had no clue about whether he had or hadn't. He took a slice of ham from the skillet, then carried his meal to the table. Chloe joined him and they ate in relative silence.

As she picked up their empty plates, Joe asked, "Do you mind if I borrow the ranch truck for the day?"

Her motions slowed to a stall. "The sheriff suggested that you stay on the ranch. And as far as I know, he didn't say anything about that changing. Where did you want to go?"

"To Houston. I'd like to do a little recon work on my identity."

"Did he provide you with any more to go on while the two of you were outside?"

"No. But I want to follow through on the military lead."

"That makes sense. And with Houston being nearly two hours from here, it's not likely anyone from Brighton Valley will see you. So sure. Go ahead."

"Thanks."

He turned to leave the room, but she reached for his arm and stopped him. "Would you like me to ride with you?"

He probably ought to tell her he'd rather be alone. But that wasn't true. For some reason, it seemed as though he'd spent the bulk of his life alone. And he wanted that—no, he needed that—to change.

So he offered her a smile. "Sure, why not?"

When she returned his smile and gave his arm a gentle squeeze, he realized that he was actually glad to have her come along.

Twenty minutes later, she'd changed into a pair of black slacks that rode low on her hips, a white blouse and a pale green sweater. She'd woven her long hair into a twist that was held by a silver clip and had applied lipstick.

Looked like the cowgirl had morphed into a stylish lady who'd blend in nicely with the city folk.

No, someone as pretty as Chloe would stand out in a crowd, no matter what she did to her appearance.

"Thanks for waiting," she said. "You ready to go?"

"Yep."

As she headed for the back door, he followed her and watched as she snagged the key ring off the hook on the mudroom wall. Once they were both outside, she led the way to the ranch pickup and opened the driver's door.

He could have asked her to let him drive, but he sat back and let her take the wheel. Being the passenger would give him a chance to check out the scenery and to see if something along the way would jog his memory.

He didn't like the idea of taking the old ranch truck such a long distance in case it broke down. He considered suggesting that they stop by the county impound lot to pick up his rental car, but on the outside chance that someone was actually looking for him, they'd be watching for a nondescript four-door sedan.

So it was Ol' Greenie that chugged along the county road, which would lead them to the interstate.

Wait. How had he known the pickup's nickname?

The answer came to him as quickly and as naturally as Ol' Greenie had. He'd remembered a distinct voice—*Dave's* voice?—referring to the beat-up ranch truck that way.

Joe stole a glance across the seat at Chloe, wondering if she could verify what had surely been a memory.

"Does this truck have a nickname?" he asked.

She shot a glance across the seat. "Why do you ask?"

"I think it does, and I want to check my memory."

"Dave used to call it Ol' Greenie."

Joe nodded. "That's what I thought."

As they continued on their way, they approached a park near Wexler. The playground was empty, yet Joe imagined—remembered?—a handful of barefoot kids wearing shorts and playing in those same fountains. He also envisioned a piñata hanging from the gazebo rafters. A birthday celebration, it seemed. But whose?

For some reason, he thought it might have been his.

He nearly mentioned that to Chloe, but why? One—or possibly two—little memory fragments certainly didn't mean much. He'd better wait until he had more to go on. But if he actually had played in that park as a kid, then he'd probably lived close by.

Had he and Dave been childhood friends? It would stand to reason. And if that was the case, then that would explain why Tomas, who'd come to work at the Rocking C four or five years ago, hadn't remembered ever seeing him. Maybe Joe and his family had moved away by that time.

Damn. He hated having to piece together bits and pieces of memory when he had no way of knowing how much—or if any of it—was right or wrong.

Chloe merged onto the interstate that would take them to Houston. They'd both kept pretty quiet since they'd driven off, instead letting Garth Brooks and Alan Jackson do the talking—or rather, the singing—for them.

When they finally pulled off the freeway, Joe checked the address on the business card Sheriff Hollister had given him.

"I know where that street is," Chloe said. Then she headed toward the NCIS office.

They parked and went inside the building. When they stopped by the reception desk, they asked for Agent Mike Danielson, the man who held more answers about Joe's identity than Joe did himself.

Moments later, Danielson greeted them in the lobby. The gray-haired agent had to be pushing sixty years old, but his appearance gave credence to that old adage, "Not as lean, not as mean, but still a marine."

"Nice to meet you," Danielson said before shaking hands with them both. "Shane called me and told me you were heading over here, so I got together as much information for you as I could. I even made some copies of the non-classified stuff in case you need that later on."

He escorted them to a cubicle office and pulled an extra chair over for Chloe. Then he handed a file to Joe. "Here's your discharge paperwork and some write-ups you had for your more recent medals."

Joe scanned the list of commendations he'd received during his years in the service, but he was more interested in his personal information than he was in his service record.

He'd joined the military six months after his eighteenth birthday, which was July 7, the same date that was listed on his California driver's license.

Danielson confirmed that Joe had never reported being married or otherwise having any dependents. "Of course, you could have gone AWOL and gotten married," the older man said. "But it seems like a soldier with your proven track record would have followed the rules and reported any changes to the appropriate channels. Besides, your emergency contact is listed as Stanley J. Conway in El Paso. His information is there if you want to take it, but I already tried to call him for you and his voice mailbox was full so we couldn't leave a message."

Joe wondered how he knew the man with a different last name. Didn't he have *any* relatives? He asked Danielson that same question.

"I did a little snooping and ran Conway's name through our database. I can't give you any information about a fellow marine, even though he's retired and has no listed relatives, either."

Joe understood immediately that the agent was letting him know that his next of kin was actually an older marine with no family to speak of. Clearly, Joe wasn't related to the man by blood, but apparently this guy was the closest thing he had to a family.

So where had the tamale recipe come from, not to mention that birthday party and the piñata memory, if Joe didn't have any relatives of his own? Had his family members died?

"What about David Cummings?" Chloe asked.

Joe wasn't surprised by her interest in finding out more information about her "family friend." He'd been watching her closely since she'd gotten the news of Dave's death. Granted, he didn't really know Chloe very well, but he could definitely spot a look of uneasiness on someone's face.

He'd seen her expression when she was sad, and he'd seen her confused. But up until this morning, he'd yet to see her look guilty.

Was that because she and Dave had been more than friends? And that before she'd known of his death, she'd kissed Joe?

Or did that have to do with whatever paperwork she'd been looking for today?

"I'm not at liberty to give you guys access to Corporal Cumming's file," Danielson said. "But off the record, he was injured by the same snipers who shot your knee."

Danielson told them that Joe and the men in his squad had been bunkered behind an overturned minibus in the middle of Helmand Province. They'd been under fire from Taliban insurgents carrying assault rifles and hiding in an abandoned apartment building. The communications specialist had radioed for backup.

"Before anyone arrived," Danielson said, "one of your men charged the snipers. He took down one of them, but was severely wounded. You followed him, grabbed him by the back of his pack and pulled him to safety—in spite of the fact that you took a bullet in the knee."

So that's how Joe had been wounded.

"Who was the man I went after?" Joe asked.

"David Cummings. His injuries were even more serious than yours, and by the looks of the report, you saved his life."

Too bad he didn't remain alive long enough to enjoy it.

"After you recovered in Germany," Danielson added, "you were medically discharged and returned to the States. Cummings was discharged later since his injuries were much more serious."

"So then he didn't die from his battle wounds?" Chloe asked.

"Negative. The coroner in San Diego notified us of his death and sent us the death certificate so that we could terminate disability benefits. My suggestion would be to contact them to get an autopsy report or death certificate for yourselves."

Joe could barely process what the agent had told them about Dave because he was still reading the incident report of what had happened in Afghanistan. Fragments of his dream began to make sense.

"That's all I've got for you," Danielson said as he politely extracted the confidential report from Joe's hand. "Good luck with that whole amnesia thing. If I hear anything else, I'll keep you posted."

Chloe thanked Danielson for his time and nudged Joe with her elbow. Apparently he'd been so wrapped up in his own thoughts that he hadn't noticed the NCIS agent trying to graciously end the meeting.

Danielson held out his hand, and Joe shook it.

"No matter what else you find out about your identity," Danielson said, "you're a hero, son."

Funny, but for some reason, Joe didn't feel like one.

As he and Chloe left the office and climbed back into Ol' Greenie, they both remained silent. He figured there was almost too much to say, but neither of them wanted to share their thoughts out loud.

Chloe started the engine and backed out of the parking space. Before she headed onto the street, she glanced across the seat at Joe. "Do you mind if we do a little shopping while we're here?"

"No, not at all." In fact, after talking to Danielson, he'd welcome a distraction. "What do you need to buy?"

"I already shipped gifts home to my parents, but I'd like to pick up a few last-minute presents for some of my friends."

He should have realized that she had a social life. A beautiful woman like her would.

"So what are we looking for? Clothes, perfume…?" He tossed her a grin as he dug for a little more information. "Aftershave?"

"Actually, I'm not sure what to get for them. They're both in a nursing home. Do you have any ideas?"

"Nope. Not a single one." Something told him he didn't usually get caught up in the Christmas spirit. "But I'm more than willing to help you shop. That is, as long as you don't make me carry your purse."

She laughed as she pulled out of the parking lot and headed toward the heart of downtown.

Now that he thought about it, Joe was glad they were going shopping. If he was going to spend Christmas with Chloe, he'd like to get her a gift.

As they chugged and rumbled along, he glanced at the discharge paperwork he still held and at the contact info for Stanley Conway. He'd have to call the guy who might be able to fill in even more details of his life.

Did he actually want to stick around in Brighton Valley? He knew enough about himself and had the means to leave and find his way home to California.

But when he stole a glance at the beautiful blonde humming along to a George Strait song on the old truck's FM dial, when he remembered the kiss they'd shared last night—and waking with her in his arms this morning—he realized that he wasn't quite ready to leave just yet.

By the time Chloe and Joe found the shopping district, it was early afternoon. She hadn't eaten much at breakfast and hunger pangs reminded her of that fact. Maybe she should suggest they eat while they were in town.

She snagged a parking space close to The Cowboy Connection, the store she'd wanted to visit, and shut off the ignition. As they climbed from the truck, she caught the aroma of grilled meat and barbecue sauce.

"Do you smell that?" Joe asked.

"I sure do." Chloe scanned the area and spotted Earl's Smokehouse, a restaurant across the street with a green door and a black, wrought iron railing around the outdoor curbside tables.

"Are you hungry?" he asked.

"Sounds like you are," she said with a smile. "And if you're talking about eating at Earl's, I'm game."

"You read my mind. The tables outside are empty, probably because of the chill. But look in the window. The place is packed. I'll bet it's really good."

"You're probably right. But then again, this is Texas. And we know good barbecue when we taste it."

"Then what are we waiting for?"

They crossed the street, and when they reached the green door, Joe opened it and stepped aside so Chloe could enter first.

They were greeted by a smiling, middle-aged brunette wearing a red-and white-checkered shirt and jeans. "Hey, y'all. Two for lunch?"

When Joe told her yes, she snagged the menus. "Come with me."

Once they were seated at a small booth in back, Joe said, "I think I grew up in Texas."

"Why is that?"

"Because I really have a hankering for barbecue beef, as if it's always been my favorite meal. Well, that and Mexican food."

"That's certainly possible," Chloe said. "But there has to be more reason for you to think that other than your food choices."

"There are, but it's more of a feeling right now. I can't explain it."

When the same waitress who'd seated them came by to take their orders, Chloe chose the chicken salad and a glass of sweet tea.

"I'll have tea, too," Joe said. "And for lunch, I'd like the sampler platter with potato salad, French fries and coleslaw. Plus a side of cornbread."

Chloe's jaw dropped. "Are you sure you want that sampler? I think it's meant for two or more people to share. It comes with three different kinds of meat."

Joe chuckled. "I guess I have a big appetite."

And he'd been right because, when the waitress brought the food on the large metal plates, he ate every last bite.

"How was it?" Chloe asked.

"Great. I'd come back."

When the bill came, Chloe reached for it, but Joe grabbed her wrist. "Oh, no, you don't." He continued to hold her arm while he used his free hand to pull out his wallet. "You drove, so I'm paying for lunch."

"Are you sure? You might need that money for something else."

"Like what?"

She laughed. "Like the ingredients to make a whole lot more tamales. With the way you can put away food, you must spend a fortune on groceries."

"Funny thing is, I still have room for dessert."

"I wouldn't be surprised to find out that you're a born Texan. Only someone from the Lone Star state can love brisket that much."

He smiled at her attempt at levity, then sobered. He supposed it was time to talk about the big white elephant sitting at the table with them. So he stroked her fingers softly, broaching that physical connection they'd had earlier and the attraction that had been brewing ever since they'd kissed last night. "How are you feeling about everything?"

"I'm sad about Dave," she said. "I'd expected him to come back to the ranch soon, and I'm in limbo."

"Why is that?"

Chloe pondered the question as well as her answer, since she didn't want to dump any more on Joe than she had to. "Because I don't want to move until the new owner is located."

"New owner?"

"Whoever stands to inherit the ranch now that Dave is gone." She figured that was enough of an explanation. "How about you? Are you feeling badly about Dave's death?"

"I don't know. I don't feel any differently than I did yesterday. If we were friends, and I'm beginning to believe that we were, I should be sad about his death.

But maybe because I don't remember him it hasn't really hit me yet."

"That's probably true."

"There might be another reason for it," he added. "If he gave me that letter before he died and I carried out his wish, it's possible I already knew about his death before coming here. And if that's the case, then maybe I've already done my grieving."

"Did Sheriff Hollister mention when Dave died?" Chloe asked, realizing she should have quizzed the sheriff.

"No. But that ought to be easy enough to figure out. We can check with the coroner in San Diego—or ask Hollister what they told him."

When the waitress returned with their change, Joe left a generous tip.

"Dr. Nielson was probably right," he said as he got to his feet. "I need to be patient and wait for my brain to heal and my memory to return. So let's enjoy our time in Houston and make the most of the rest of the day."

Chloe forced a smile, then stood. After they left the restaurant, they walked to The Cowboy Connection, a department store that catered to those who liked Western wardrobes and home decor.

The store had been adorned with wreaths and expensive ornaments, and Christmas music filled the air. Her mood continued to lift—no doubt due to the holiday spirit.

While they walked past displays that provided more than a few gift ideas, Joe helped her choose a bronze horse figurine for Sam Darnell.

Next she found a pair of pajamas for Ethel Furman. As she waited to pay the clerk for her purchase in the lingerie department, she glanced over to a display where Joe stood, fingering the silky fabric of a skimpy black nightie and studying it intently.

Had another memory returned? If so, Chloe couldn't find it in herself to be happy for him. She'd wanted him to remember the life he'd led before coming to Brighton Valley. But she certainly hadn't wanted him to remember a particular woman dressed in something so sexy.

When he turned toward the cash register where she stood, waiting in line to make her purchase, their gazes met and locked.

And for one magical moment, she wished she'd been the woman he was trying so hard to remember.

Chapter Eight

Joe hadn't expected Chloe to catch him looking at the sexy lingerie on display, let alone fondling them. So the moment their eyes met, he felt like a kid who'd been caught with his hand in the candy bowl.

Had she known that he'd been thinking of buying one of those skimpy nighties for her? That he'd envisioned her sitting on the side of his bed, like she had last night, only dressed in a whisper of black silk instead of a cotton gown? Not that the thin cotton hadn't been just as sweet and sensual to look at—just in a different sort of way.

He'd better put some distance between her and his lust-filled thoughts before he asked her to try on something for size. So he let the slinky fabric slip out of his hand and said, "If you don't mind, I'm going downstairs to check out the menswear. I need to buy some clothes that fit me better than jeans with a thirty-inch inseam and old high school T-shirts that make me look like a band geek." Then he headed for the escalator before she could answer.

She must have gotten sidetracked with another purchase, because by the time she found him in the shoe department, where he was trying on a pair of cowboy boots, he'd already bought three pairs of jeans and several work shirts. She took the seat next to him and glanced at the shopping bags on the floor. "I see you've been busy."

"It's easy when there's a good selection."

"That's why I love this store. Every time I come in here, I want a ranch of my own. I didn't grow up around horses, but I must be a cowgirl at heart."

"I thought you were a nurse at heart."

"Maybe I'm both."

He stopped wrestling with the second boot long enough to cast a glance her way and catch a glimmer in her eye. "If you had a ranch of your own, would you give up nursing?"

"I don't know. Maybe. I'd probably invite some friends to live with me, so I'm not sure how much time I'd have to study."

"Which friends?"

She bit down on that bottom lip again. Then she shrugged a single shoulder. "I'm not sure. I really haven't thought much about it."

He didn't believe her. She seemed too pensive. She must have given it more than a little consideration. But he let the remark pass and removed the first pair of boots from his feet and reached for the black Ropers.

As he tried those on, Chloe stood and wandered through the women's shoe section until she stopped at a table that displayed a pair of custom stitched red boots.

"Aren't these cool? I wonder if they have them in a size six." She turned them over and glanced at the sticker price on the sole. Then she put them right back where she'd found them.

She continued to study them a moment longer, though.

He figured she couldn't afford a new pair of anything, let alone expensive leather boots. Yet here she was, shopping for gifts for her elderly friends in the nursing home. She'd also been sharing her groceries with him and shelling out gas money to drive him into Houston.

When Chloe wandered off to check out a display of slippers, Joe asked the clerk if she had those red boots in a size six. When the woman said they did, he asked her to add them to his latest purchase—the black Roper boots.

Once he'd paid for both pairs, he hid hers at the bottom of the bag that held his clothing and headed for the slipper display to join her.

"Did you find something else to buy?" he asked.

"I was looking for something to go with the nightgown I bought for Ethel. But I don't think she'll like any of these." She shifted the shopping bag she held to her other hand. "Is there something else you need?"

"A hat," he said, "especially if I'll be working on the ranch with Tomas."

"I saw them near the escalators." She bumped his arm with hers. "Come on."

He followed her to the display and considered his options. Knowing he'd soon get it dirty, he reached for a straw hat and tried it on.

He'd no more than given it a proper tilt when Chloe snatched it from his head, replaced it with a black felt Stetson and smiled. "I've always been a sucker for a man in a black hat."

"Sold." He flashed her a boyish grin, then headed for the nearest register. After paying the clerk, he decided to wear it out of the store.

As Joe and Chloe strode toward the pickup, he inadvertently bumped her shoulder. Apparently she thought he'd done it on purpose, because she smiled and bumped him right back.

"I'm glad we came here today," she said. "It's been a nice break from everything, and I had fun."

"Me, too." He felt compelled to take her hand in his, but after considering the consequences of a move like that, the possible complications, he held back.

Besides, something still wasn't quite right, leaving him completely off stride. In spite of what he'd learned at the NCIS office, he felt undeserving, not only of medals, but of the beautiful blonde who walked beside him.

Why was that?

What memories was his mind still holding hostage?

Joe had been pretty quiet on the drive home, and his pensive mood hadn't lifted, even after dinner. He'd volunteered to do the dishes, then had insisted on making the tamales on his own, saying he wanted the quiet time, hoping it would trigger some memories.

If it had, Chloe had no way of knowing, because two hours later he excused himself and turned in for the night, leaving her to watch TV alone.

It had been a long day, and she was exhausted, so she turned off the television at ten. After setting the alarm for six so she'd be the first one up, she went to bed.

She slept fairly well and, just as she'd hoped, she beat Joe to the kitchen, where she put on the coffee, then fried some turkey sausage and whipped up the pancake batter. She'd just set the table, when Joe finally entered the room.

He was sporting his new clothes and holding his hat,

which he set on the table. As he sauntered to the coffeemaker and poured himself a cup of the fresh brew, he moved with a sexy swagger that scrambled her senses.

Dang. Joe Wilcox looked better than a cowboy had a right to.

If he knew she'd been ogling him, he didn't let on. Instead, when he looked at her, he blessed her with a heart-stopping grin.

"So what's on the agenda today?" he asked.

"What do you mean?" Did he think she had another shopping trip in store for him?

"Do you have a list of things you'd like me to do? Or should I go outside and look for Tomas?"

Oh, he meant work. Actually, having him busy and out of the house would allow her more time to search the files in the den and to decide what she was going to do now that Dave wasn't coming home.

She also wanted to contact the coroner's office in San Diego and find out how she could get a copy of Dave's death certificate. She didn't know a thing about estate planning or probate court, but she was pretty sure she'd need to file some official documents with somebody. But she kept those thoughts to herself.

It wasn't that she didn't want Joe to know what she was doing. She had nothing to hide. But after the troubling dream he'd had two nights ago and their visit to the NCIS office yesterday, she figured the poor man had been through enough and she didn't want to burden him with her financial woes.

"Tomas is probably already out and about," Chloe said. "As soon as I see him, I'll ask if he has any work that needs to be done. Do you know anything about cattle or horses?"

"I'm not sure. I guess we'll find out soon enough." He went back to eating, digging into that stack of hotcakes and syrup with the same gusto he'd shown yesterday at lunch and again last night at dinner.

Joe either had a hearty appetite or was just as anxious to get to work as she was. An active man like him had to be going stir-crazy by being cooped up indoors with no physical outlet.

Of course, if they spent any more time alone together, Chloe might lose her head and offer to provide him with a physical outlet of the bedroom variety.

Her cheeks warmed at the thought, and she turned away to avoid his gaze.

When a horse whinnied outside, she looked out the big bay window and spotted Tomas walking Lola to the paddock. The prize broodmare had been stabled in the barn and was expected to foal soon. He must be exercising her.

"There's Tomas now," she said. "Why don't we go out and ask him what needs to be done. I'll come back and wash the breakfast dishes later."

Joe's chair scraped the tile floor as he scooted away from the table. Then, after getting to his feet, he snatched his hat and followed her from the kitchen, through the mudroom and out the back door.

Once outside, he slipped on the new Stetson and gave it a little adjustment—just like a real live Texan.

Even though his stonewashed jeans and flannel work shirt were brand-new, they appeared to have been worn several times before. With the added boots and hat, he looked like the real McCoy—born and raised on the Rocking C—and not just a city slicker who wanted to play rancher.

Chloe hadn't meant to admire the sexy marine's transformation, but she'd always been a sucker for a handsome cowboy. And she was eager to see how he did on a horse.

She had a sneaking suspicion that he was no stranger to the ranch life. And with the way his backside filled out that denim, he was certainly no stranger to looking the part.

"Buenos dias," Joe said to Tomas.

The ranch foreman responded in Spanish. They spoke that way for a while, then lapsed into English.

If Chloe had been able to focus on more than two words at a time, she would have appreciated the switch to a language she could understand.

While they talked, she tried to get her lusty thoughts in check. Finally, she managed to tune in to the end of their conversation.

"That would be helpful," Tomas said, "if you're sure you're up for it."

Joe insisted that he was.

"Good." The foreman brightened. "Then I can stay here and work in the stables, just in case Lola needs me."

Tomas started toward the barn with Joe on his heels, and Chloe hurried to catch up—both physically and mentally. Apparently, the foreman had told Joe there'd been some damage to the fence after the last storm.

"I'll ride along the boundary of the ranch," Joe said. "If I see any damage, I'll fix it."

"If there's anything you and those tools you're carrying can't handle, just flag the spot. When you get done, I'll go back out with you."

The men made it sound like a simple task. And it

probably would be. Joe seemed hearty enough to stay in the saddle and not get lost.

"Make sure you take plenty of water with you," Chloe said, her nursing instincts finally kicking in. "Even though it's cold out, you can still get dehydrated."

Both men looked at her as though they didn't much welcome her ministrations, so she excused herself and told them she was going back inside to do the dishes.

Once that was out of the way, she went to the den. But instead of immediately dealing with the stack of bills on the desk, she stood at the window and watched Joe lead Dave's gelding out of the stable.

Fortunately, Firestorm had been named for his reddish color and not for his temperament. He was a strong and dependable horse, well-suited for ranch work. But was Joe?

Chloe knew she shouldn't worry, but as he mounted, as he threw his right leg over the saddle, she held her breath.

He settled into the saddle like a natural, then cantered around the yard, no doubt allowing the horse to get used to him—and vice versa.

When she realized that he was perfectly capable of handling the reins, she let out the breath she'd been holding. Her stance relaxed even more when Tomas handed Joe one of the ranch's walkie-talkies. At least, if he had a problem along the way, he could call for help.

Still, she stood at the window and watched until Joe and Firestorm were well out of sight. At that point, she turned back to the desk and finished the work that had piled up since Joe had arrived.

Next, she did an internet search to find contact information for the San Diego coroner's office. It was two hours earlier on the west coast, so she couldn't call yet. But fortunately she learned how to request the records she needed.

With that knowledge tucked under her belt, she searched Texas probate law. It didn't take long to realize she wasn't going to handle any of that on her own. She was in way over her head.

She checked the time—a couple of minutes after nine—and then placed a call to Jeffrey McDougall, the attorney who'd handled Teresa's estate.

Mr. McDougall was out of the office, but his secretary assured Chloe that he was familiar with the Rocking C and the Cummings family. The woman expressed her condolences over Dave's death and told Chloe that the attorney would call back the next afternoon.

After hanging up, she tackled the overdue invoices from some of the ranch's suppliers. Before mailing any payments, she would need to reconcile the Rocking C bank account and figure out how the ranch was going to pay its two employees after January rolled around.

A local rancher had offered to purchase a hundred head of cattle, but Chloe had been reluctant to accept it. She had a feeling the buyer was lowballing her—not only because she was a female, but because he knew she wasn't all that familiar with the going rate for cattle.

Unfortunately, Tomas, who'd been a ranch hand prior to stepping up to help run things when the previous foreman retired, wasn't up on fair prices, either.

But Chloe knew someone who was. The next time she stopped by the Sheltering Arms for a visit—which would be soon—she would talk to Sam Darnell about it. The old cattleman may not keep up on his food intake, but he definitely kept up on his agricultural knowledge.

By noon, Joe had crept back into her thoughts. He'd been gone for quite a while. Maybe he'd overdone it by repairing one of the fence posts that often came loose following an East Texas rainstorm.

Of course, she didn't want him to think that she doubted his ability, but she'd feel a lot better if she could check things out herself.

So she decided to fix some sandwiches and ride out to wherever he was working, under the pretext of bringing him lunch. The man never turned down food. And while he ate, his stomach would be too busy to allow his brain to question her intentions.

Ten minutes later, she delivered one of the thick ham sandwiches to Tomas, who was cleaning out the stalls in the barn. Then she saddled Rosabelle, the gentle mare she usually rode, and tied a rolled up quilt behind the saddle. When it was secure, she stowed the impromptu picnic lunch in the saddlebags.

Satisfied that she had everything she needed, she mounted Rosabelle and rode off to find Joe.

Joe had just finished restringing the lower line of barbed wire when he heard Firestorm whinny at an approaching rider. He looked up to see Chloe, her blond ponytail bouncing behind her as she trotted over to where he'd tied his horse.

He couldn't say that he was surprised. A natural caretaker like her was probably worried that he might overdo it.

"You come out to check on me?" he asked.

"No, I was more concerned about the time of day. It's been four hours since you had anything to eat. I figured your hunger pains would be out of control by now."

"Well, what do you know? The woman is not only beautiful, she's smart." He watched the blush creep up her face before she dismounted and turned to dig in the saddlebags.

Was she trying to hide her flush from him? Had she planned to bring more than lunch?

If so, that was a bad idea—although an intriguing one.

"I don't want to get in your way," she said. "I can just leave your food here."

"Did you already eat?" he asked, his gloved hand still gripping a strand of barbed wire.

"No, not yet."

"Then if you'll give me a few minutes, I'll be finished here, and we can have lunch together. That is, assuming you packed enough food for two."

"Are you kidding?" She shot him an impish grin. "I've seen you eat, so I packed enough food for six."

He liked watching her blush, but he enjoyed her witty banter even more.

As he finished pulling the wire around the post, he asked, "You get much done this morning?"

"Actually, I did. I called Teresa's attorney and left a message with him. Then I tackled some paperwork and paid some bills. I'm trying my best to hold everything together until I know what's going to happen with the ranch."

The stress of Dave's death and the pending what-ifs must have been bugging her. And he was glad she was finally opening up to him about it—even if he couldn't help her solve her problems. He wondered where she would go if she had to leave the Rocking C.

Before he could ask, she changed the subject. "It

looks like you know what you're doing." She nodded toward the repaired fence.

"Yeah, who would have known?" He straightened and checked over his work. Then he placed his tools in his saddlebags. "This is my third repair this morning, and each time, it was like second nature."

She stroked Firestorm's nose. "How're you doing on this valiant steed?"

"I must be doing all right. My legs haven't begun to bow. And I'm not sore yet."

She laughed. "That's sounds like a good sign to me."

"So where should we eat?" he asked.

"Up by that copse of trees. There's a little pond there. I believe ranch folk would call it a swimming hole."

Joe froze, and a vision of the pond burst forth in his mind, even though they'd yet to reach it.

As they led the horses around a big boulder, he said, "I've been here before."

"Where?"

"*Here*. This place," he said, unable to mask the awe in his voice.

When they reached a big tree near the water's edge and they tied the horses to one of the low branches, he was sure of it. "I've even swam in that pond."

"When?"

"I don't know. I'm guessing a while ago. Maybe when I was a kid." He scanned the pond that was surrounded by cottonwoods, as well as a tall eucalyptus. "Other things on this ranch have given me a slightly familiar feeling, but nothing like this. I remember this exact swimming hole."

"What else do you remember?"

Joe paced the water's edge as if that would help him go back in time, to relive the moment.

"There used to be a rope swing over there." He pointed at the huge eucalyptus. "It was sweltering hot that day. Dave and I were taking turns launching ourselves off the rope and into the water."

"So you remember Dave."

"Yes. Sort of. We'd been out riding and repairing fence lines, I think. Don't you see? I'd had this uncanny feeling that I'd done that before, too."

"That's great. What else?"

"Dave asked if I knew how to swim. He said, 'I've never seen your aunt or uncle take you guys to the community pool.'"

"Who were your aunt and uncle?"

"I have no idea. I can only remember him asking me that question."

"And he said 'you guys,' like maybe your siblings or cousins or someone else who lived with you."

Joe wanted to recall the exact memory before he examined every detail for clues. So he didn't answer as he walked closer to the eucalyptus. He looked up at the sturdy branch overhead. The swing was gone now, but the frayed end of the rope was still there. "I remember Dave tying the rope up there."

"How old were you?"

"High school age, I guess. Dave slipped and landed in that shallow part right there." Joe pointed to the spot, where reeds still grew out of the water. "He busted his arm, and Mr. Cummings flipped out because we were playing around when we were supposed to be working. So he cut the rope."

"As a punishment?"

"No, I think he cut it down because Dave got hurt on the swing. Dave yelled at his dad and accused him of being too protective."

"Teresa used to say that Dave had a sensitive nature, and that his father used to coddle him at times." Chloe stared off into the distance.

Joe suspected there was more to the story than that. Of course, judging by how secretive Chloe had been while digging around in the desk yesterday, he had a feeling there was a lot she hadn't shared with him about Dave, his parents and the ranch.

If she wasn't going to open up with him, then he wouldn't disclose the rest of his memory with her—including what Old Man Cummings had told Dave while scolding him. The words, the hurt they'd inflicted, rang clear in his mind now.

I knew letting that boy hang out on the ranch was a bad idea, Davey. Joey's a bad influence on you.

The father and son had argued some more, but the rest was too blurry to recall.

Yet the sharp pricks of shame cut just as deeply, the sting just as intense, as if the conversation had unfolded only seconds ago.

And that was the real reason Joe hadn't wanted to enlighten Chloe about that part of the memory. He didn't want her to think Mr. Cummings had been right.

As Chloe unbuckled a rolled up quilt from the back of Rosabelle's saddle and spread it out on the grass, Joe again looked up at the discarded remnant of rope still hanging in the tree and replayed the scene over again in his mind.

He'd been right. He knew Dave before the guy had ever enlisted, which meant they'd gone to high school together. Could Joe actually be from Brighton Valley? Was this small town his home?

No, it couldn't be. Not any longer. He had no dependents, no family. And his driver's license as well as his discharge papers said his home was in California.

He also had a friend in El Paso. Of course, a lot of good that contact information had been. Joe had called him yesterday after dinner. But the man hadn't answered his phone, and he'd let his messages pile up until there was no room left for another one.

Chloe must've been thinking along the same line because she said, "I wonder if we should call Sheriff Hollister and let him know about this breakthrough. Since you can't go into town yourself, maybe he can ask around and see if anyone remembers you."

"I would think that he already asked all the locals that question and came up blank." Joe helped her unpack the bags that held their lunch and carry them to the blanket.

She set out four sandwiches, some leftover scones, a thermos of lemonade and two apples. Then her motions stalled. "You know, if you went to high school with Dave, Sheriff Hollister might be able to talk to some of the other kids who were in your class."

"Sure, but Hollister seems like a smart guy. I'll bet he's already asked every person my age if they remember me. And he didn't have anything to report."

"You have a point. But he did say that he was still investigating."

Joe reached for a sandwich, removed it from the plastic baggie and took a bite, which would help to quench his hunger for lunch. But it wouldn't do much when he was starving for more details on his background.

The small flashback triggered a desperate need to find out more about who he'd been, where he'd been. Even though Chloe was keeping mum about her own business, Joe couldn't keep his memories locked up tight. He needed someone with whom he could bounce off his ideas and theories, and he suspected that the pretty blonde lounging next to him was eager to speculate with him.

"Maybe I was just hired help," Joe said, "like Tomas. That day that we went swimming was hot. And I was here working. So it's possible that the Cummings gave me a summer job, and that I'm not from around here."

"But Dave mentioned your aunt and uncle, so maybe he knew them. You might have only lived with them during summers."

"Then why didn't I list them as my next of kin on my enlistment paperwork?"

They went around and around, speculating and eating and speculating some more. But none of the scenarios they came up with felt right.

Joe was just about to reach for a scone when he decided not to ruin a nice day spent with Chloe by bringing up all the what-ifs. So he lay back on the quilt instead, letting his hat fall off and stacking his hands under his head.

"You know what?" he asked. "As much as I want all the answers right this second, they're not going to magically appear just because we've talked the possibilities to death. I'm just going to have to be patient and hope that something else comes along and jogs my memory."

"Dr. Nielson suggested you give your brain time to heal and let nature take its course. You might only get snippets of memory here and there, but with time, it should all come back to you."

"I hope so."

"It's amazing how you took one look at this pond and *poof*." She snapped her fingers. "A boyhood recollection reappeared. I wonder what else you can remember by experiencing something similar."

"I wouldn't mind remembering how it felt to lie down under the blue sky and kiss a beautiful woman."

She caught his gaze, and her smile faded. "Is that something you've experienced before?"

"I don't know. Come a little closer and help me find out."

He'd just been testing her, teasing her. But when she smiled, he turned to his side, reached for her and…just let nature take its course.

Chapter Nine

Chloe had no business kissing Joe again, but as those amazing blue eyes reached deep inside of her, as his arms slipped around her and he drew her close, she couldn't help leaning toward him and just…letting go.

She expected the kiss to start slowly—much like the first one had. But the moment their lips met, hers parted, and the kiss exploded with passion.

As their tongues touched, twisting and mating, their hands stroked, explored, caressed.

She knew she should pull back and stop things before they got out of hand, but it had been so long since she'd lost herself in a man's arms, in his kiss.

Then again, her only experience had never been like this. Before she was blinded by a haze of lust and found herself making love outdoors, she drew her mouth from his. She meant to explain her reason for stopping, but she didn't dare say a word until her breathing slowed to a normal rate and her heart stopped pounding.

"That was some kiss," he said.

It certainly was.

"I don't mean to be a tease," she finally said, "but I don't think we should jump into anything."

He ran his knuckles along her cheek. "Because of my amnesia?"

That was one reason to be cautious. She hardly knew the man as it was. And while her heart—not to mention, her body—seemed to insist it didn't matter, that she could easily fall for him anyway, she had to be reasonable.

"Don't you think we should take things slow until your memory returns?" she said.

"Probably."

She bit down on her bottom lip, pondering how much to share with him about the mistake she'd made, but there was a part of her that didn't want him to think she was flighty or that she didn't have any morals.

"I made a bad choice once, and I told myself I'd be more careful next time."

"What happened?"

She really hadn't told anyone before, other than Teresa, but it seemed as though Joe deserved an explanation. "I was lonely and got caught up in a relationship that wasn't right for me."

She'd met Mark Foster her first semester at the junior college in Wexler. She hadn't had a chance to make any friends in town yet, and he'd been funny and charming. She'd been flattered by his interest in her, thinking that he actually cared for her.

He'd pursued her, coming on pretty strong, and she hadn't been experienced in the ways of the world. She should have taken the time to think things through, to get to know his true character, but she hadn't. He'd taken advantage of her naivety by taking her out to an expensive dinner in Wexler, pulling out all the romantic stops and plying her with enough champagne to make her head spin.

She'd never in a million years thought that she'd have

sex in the back of a car—especially her first time. She'd cried afterward. And then she'd gotten sick. The whole thing was a disappointing and embarrassing experience she'd like to forget.

Apparently, Mark had more luck at forgetting than she had. He never called her again, while she couldn't get that awful night out of her mind.

"So what did he do to you?" Joe asked. "Did he break your heart?"

No, it was her self-respect that had suffered the most, which was why Chloe had never shared the embarrassing details with anyone.

"My heart was a little bruised," she said, "but not broken. Let's just say that things didn't work out the way I'd hoped."

She'd learned a hard lesson that night, one that didn't need repeating. From then on, she'd resolved not to drink on a date and not to have sex with someone she didn't love—or barely knew.

And even though she felt as though she could fall for Joe, he had amnesia, and she didn't know any more about him than he knew about himself.

After that heated kiss by the pond earlier that afternoon, Joe had been careful to respect Chloe's wishes, even though it had taken every ounce of his resolve to put some distance between them once he'd come in for dinner.

He was bone tired after a hard day's work, and the hot shower he'd taken upon entering the house had refreshed him only enough to eat the chicken and roasted potatoes Chloe had made for dinner. When his eyes began drifting closed at the table, his little Florence Nightingale returned and ordered him to bed.

Within minutes of his head hitting the pillow, he'd fallen into a deep sleep, and his dreams took him far away from horses and watering holes, from two laughing boys and an irate rancher.

As Dave's father's words grew dim, the vision's backdrop shifted from a green and fertile Texas ranch to a dry and dusty urban war zone in Afghanistan, where bullets flew and mortar boomed…

Three or four Taliban insurgents carrying assault rifles and strategically hiding in an abandoned apartment building fired on Joe and his men. And they took cover behind an overturned minibus.

"Hold your positions," Joe commanded.

His communications specialist had radioed for backup. He just needed to keep his troops in cover position a few more seconds until reinforcement arrived.

The metal tracks of the cavalry tank sounded, just a short distance away, providing a sense of relief. But the corporal beside him fidgeted with his rifle, clearly on edge from more than just the gunshots around them.

"I can't take this no more," the corporal said, tears streaming down his face. "If she doesn't want me, then what do I have left?"

"Hold tight, buddy. The armored tanks are almost—"

Before Joe could finish his order, the young marine was up and running, revealing their hid-

ing position and exposing the other members of their patrol squad.

"Fall back, Dave. Fall back!" Joe screamed. But the hotheaded corporal didn't listen. Instead, he charged toward the snipers, spraying bullets at no target in particular.

Dave only had so many rounds, and when he emptied his rifle, he'd be a sitting duck. As the squad commander, Joe was responsible for all of his men, even those who were hell-bent on disobeying direct orders and compromising the safety of fellow marines.

"I'm going after Corporal Cummings," Joe told the man beside him. "Cover me, but don't move until the armored vehicles set up a blockade. On three..."

Joe ran out to Dave, grabbed the crazed man by his pack and pulled his body back toward the safety of the minibus. But his friend swung his rifle around, clocking Joe in the face, allowing the snipers above them to get a free shot.

Dave, weighted down by his full gear and a rage of helplessness, fell onto Joe just as the first lumbering Humvee pulled in front of them. But not before Joe's knee exploded.

"Dammit," Joe yelled. "I told you to fall back, Dave."

A tap on his shoulder, followed by a gentle hand tugging at him, drew him out of the gunfire, the dust and the heat.

"Joe, wake up. You're having another nightmare."

At the sound of Chloe's voice, he almost lurched out

of bed, determined to dive over her body and protect her from enemy fire. But her calming strokes along his biceps told him that she was real, not just a figment of his nocturnal imagination.

"Here," she said, "have some water."

He sat up, letting the sheet drop to his waist, and took a deep drink from the glass she offered him.

"Sorry for being such a..." What? A head case? A nut job? He shook his head and sighed. "I'm sorry for waking you up. *Again.*"

"Don't worry about it," she said, her words coming out softly, soothing him.

Just having Chloe near helped. His racing pulse slowed, but his pounding heart wasn't so quick to respond.

"You went through a traumatic ordeal," she said, "and it's only natural that you'd dream about it."

Was she talking about the accident that had robbed him of his memory? Or the battle he'd just relived in his sleep?

He let out a deep breath and ran his hand through his hair before taking another gulp of water.

"Do you want to tell me about it?" she asked as her fingers continued their soothing caress along his upper arm.

She was wearing a thin cotton nightgown, the hem barely reaching her thighs when she sat beside him on the bed. She meant to comfort him, no doubt, but his decelerating heartbeat leaped back into action, quickening its tempo.

He'd tried so hard to be a gentleman earlier tonight. To keep his distance so he wouldn't be tempted to pull her into his arms for another heated kiss like the one they'd shared on that picnic blanket.

In the dim light filtering in from the hallway, he could see her expression and realized it was one of concern, not lust. So he didn't dare meet her eyes. Not when his thoughts had shifted from the war zone to the bedroom.

He lowered his gaze to her chest, where the clinging cotton gown she wore couldn't hide her rounded breasts. She wasn't wearing a bra, and as her arm moved up and down so she could rub his biceps, he could see the outline of her dusky nipples with each movement.

"Another dream?" she asked.

"It was the same as before, only more detailed. I think it was a memory of the battle I read about in Danielson's report."

Her hand shifted from his side to his back, and with each stroke of her fingers along his spine, his arousal grew. If he couldn't get his hormones under control, he'd have to get her off his bed and out the door before he did something they'd both regret later.

Amnesia or not, he was still a man. And if she kept touching his bare skin like that…

"I'm okay now," he said. "Go on back to bed. You need your rest, too."

"You're still shivering. I'm not going to leave until your body settles down."

Oh, yeah? If she kept stroking him like that, taunting him, his body would never calm down. He wasn't shivering because of his nightmare. Just looking at her tousled hair and sleepy eyes had riled him up.

Unable to take it anymore, he grabbed her hand, his fingers circling her wrist.

Her mouth opened slightly in surprise, but she didn't try to pull away.

"Listen, Chloe. If you don't get back to your room right this second, I'm going to do a lot more than kiss you."

The pulse in her wrist quickened, and her eyes dropped to the sheet barely covering his lap. His arousal had to be obvious.

She raised her gaze to his, but she didn't make a move to leave.

He continued to hold her wrist, his thumb tracing slow circles on her skin. Their gazes met and locked. He lifted his free hand and cupped her jaw. Yet she didn't seem to be the least bit worried about what might happen if she continued to stay with him.

He leaned forward and brushed his lips across hers—gently, just in case she came to her senses and decided to pull away.

Instead, she opened her mouth, allowing his tongue to explore her warm depths. She pressed in, her own tongue matching his with equal fervor. He pulled her closer, her breasts splayed against his bare torso.

He was tempted to tear the thin fabric so he could feel all of her warm fragrant skin against his. He needed the intimacy, the closeness of another person.

No, not just any person. He needed *Chloe*.

He drew back slightly, trying to read her expression, to gauge her thoughts.

Her eyes, glazed with passion, searched his face, too, as if trying to assess what he might be thinking, feeling.

"Are you sure?" he whispered, loud enough to appease his conscience, yet soft enough for her to realize she had the power to slow things down or bring them to a complete halt.

She reached for the back of his neck, drew his mouth to hers and whispered against his lips, "I'm sure."

They kissed again, long and deep. As his hands slid along the bare curve of her back and down the slope of her hips, a surge of desire shot clean through him. He lifted the hem of her nightgown and removed the barrier before laying her down beside him.

He paused a moment to drink in the angelic sight of pretty Chloe, lying on his bed. Her throat flushed, her lips plump from their kisses.

"You're beautiful," he said.

A slow smile stretched across her lips. "So are you."

He didn't know about that. He was beat up from a hard day's work and scarred from battle—and who knew what else. But her words pleased him.

Her nails skimmed across his chest, sending a shimmy of heat through his blood, and he kissed her again until they were both drowning in need.

She pulled her lips from his, yet she continued to hold him. "I want to feel you inside me, Joe."

Words he'd been hoping—maybe longing—to hear.

As she opened for him, he entered her. She raised her hips to meet him, and their bodies became one, taking and giving.

As they both reached a peak, he released with her, and their climax set off a sexual explosion that left him seeing stars.

The night stood still, and nothing mattered but the two of them and what they'd just experienced in each other's arms. That is, until reality settled over him.

He had nothing to offer her. At least, not until his

memory returned. So he hoped she wouldn't consider this another mistake she'd made, or him to be another bad choice.

While he was tempted to tell her that she was safe with him, another more pressing, more daunting reality slammed into him.

He'd been so caught up in desire that he'd neglected to even consider using any means of protection.

Did he dare mention that to her? Had the thought even crossed her mind?

He stroked the length of her arm, then took her hand in his. "As nice as that was, as much as I enjoyed it, we got a little carried away. We didn't use any protection."

"I know," she said a bit breathlessly. "I just realized that."

He gave her fingers a gentle squeeze. "I'm not an irresponsible lover. It's just that…"

"I know," she said again. Then she smiled. "I don't think we have to worry about pregnancy. It's not the right time of the month. But we'll need to plan ahead next time."

Thank goodness. He was relieved that she wasn't too worried. And glad that she'd said "next time."

He blew out the breath he'd been holding, then drew her close, wrapping his arms around her.

Still, his momentary relief and gladness couldn't block out the regret that began to settle over him.

His body was in the most relaxed state of bliss it had been in as long as he could…well, at least since he woke up in that hospital bed. But his mind was still reeling. And the dream Chloe's presence had chased away thirty minutes ago came back to haunt him once again.

In that nocturnal window to the past, Dave had been

talking about a woman right before he'd made a suicidal run straight into enemy fire. A woman Joe suspected was Chloe.

If she doesn't want me, then what do I have left?

Had Dave really said that? Or was Joe's spotty recollection once again playing tricks on him?

What exactly had been between Chloe and Dave? She said they were only family friends, but what if Dave had believed they were more than that?

The woman dozing softly beside him felt perfect in his arms. But nothing else felt right. Not even his name. Who in the hell was Joe Wilcox? And what was he doing on the Cummings ranch, living Dave's life?

Joe was staying in the man's house, sleeping in his bed, riding his horse. Had he just slept with Dave's lover, the blonde who'd driven him to risk death over life without her?

If so, Joe had no right to any of it.

As Chloe stretched her arms over her head, she listened to the sound of running water coming from the bathroom down the hall.

She should be mortified that she'd woken up naked in Joe's bed, but thinking about the way he'd brought her body to life last night, she felt nothing but contentment.

Still, she couldn't just lay here and bask in the memory. She should get up and get dressed before Tomas arrived for work.

Instead, she pulled the sheet tighter around her and snuggled deeper into the mattress.

Why didn't she feel any remorse for her behavior last night? For enjoying their lovemaking so much that she was hoping Joe would get out of the shower and come back to bed?

When she'd hurried into his room to waken him from his nightmare, he'd given her several opportunities to leave. Yet, despite what her mind had told her, she hadn't been able to get her traitorous body to follow suit.

She had no job and, once the attorney started probate on the ranch, she would have no home. In short, she had absolutely no future. On top of that, she had no idea who Joe really was or where he'd be going once he regained his memory.

So then why was she smiling and frolicking with a stranger in bed as though she had nothing to lose?

The sound of an approaching pickup—the foreman, no doubt—reminded her that there was work to be done today. And that she still had a reputation to uphold, even if her stay on the Rocking C was only temporary.

She sat up and spotted her nightgown on the floor across the room, lying right where Joe had tossed it.

Joe. How would he act toward her this morning? He was usually so lighthearted and playful—never taking things too seriously. Maybe some of his attitude was rubbing off on her because she didn't much feel like taking any of this seriously, either.

If she did, it might hurt too much when it was all over.

She crossed the hall to her bedroom, her steps faltering. Maybe there was plenty to regret. They'd made love without protection last night. And while it was a fairly safe time of the month, accidental pregnancies occurred.

While she showered and shampooed her hair, she tried to shake off the remote possibility—and the fact that she'd been reckless again last night. Not that she regretted what she'd shared with Joe. That part had been amazing. But she should have considered using a contraceptive.

After drying off with a fluffy towel, she slipped on a pair of jeans and a white blouse. She topped it off with the only Christmasy thing she could find—a red sweater. By the time she entered the kitchen, Joe already had the coffee made. He stood at the counter, cracking eggs into a bowl. A steaming cup of java rested within his reach.

She smiled to herself as she thought of the appetite he must've worked up last night.

"Good morning," she said, the softness in her voice revealing more vulnerability than she'd had when she woke this morning.

"Hey, you're up. Good. Breakfast is almost ready."

She told herself not to look too deeply into his eyes for hidden messages. But maybe she shouldn't bother. Reading men didn't seem to be her forte. At least, not in the past. So she decided to just go along with the flow.

"I see you're cooking again," she said.

"It's the least I can do after keeping you up so late last night."

A blush warmed her cheeks, and while she headed for the coffeepot, she avoided eye contact. She reached into the cupboard and removed a mug. Then she filled it with the fresh morning brew, adding a splash of cream and a spoonful of sugar.

"Just for the record, I didn't mind waking up in the middle of the night." She smiled, then lifted her cup and took a sip.

Their brief morning-after banter was cut off by a rapping on the back door.

It was Tomas standing on the porch, his hat off, his brow furrowed, his expression laden with worry. "Hurry, Miss Chloe. It's Lola. She's going to foal, but something's wrong."

"Did you call the vet?" Chloe asked, her mug quickly forgotten on the counter.

"Yes, but Dr. Peterson's answering service said he was on vacation. Another doctor is handling his patients while he's gone. They gave me his number."

Chloe followed the foreman to the barn, Joe close on their heels.

"Were they going to contact the other vet?" she asked. "Or should we do that?"

"He's just down the road at the Beecham ranch. The woman at the answering service said she would call him on his cell, but the reception isn't very good there. Maybe I should just drive over and get him myself. It'll be faster."

Poor Tomas. Chloe's heart went out to him. He was a good man and a hard worker, but he hadn't wanted the foreman position. He was good with the animals, though. And he was obviously worried about the mare he'd been babying for her entire pregnancy.

"Okay," Chloe said, "you go get the doctor. I'll stay out here with Lola and try to keep her calm."

Tomas nodded, then hurried from the barn, presumably to his own truck, which was more reliable than Ol' Greenie.

"You okay?" Joe asked.

Chloe hoped her own worry wasn't reflected in her eyes because Joe looked concerned enough for both of them. One thing she'd learned early on in her work with patients was to keep the family members calm.

"Yes, I'm fine. The Beecham ranch is only about ten minutes from here, so the vet should be here soon enough."

"Do you have much experience with horses and breech births?"

"Honestly, I don't have much practice with any type of births. Horse, breech or otherwise. I've always specialized in geriatric care. Not too many labors happen at the Sheltering Arms."

Joe stepped away from Lola and placed a hand on Chloe's shoulder. "Relax. I'm sure she'll be okay."

All the stress that Chloe should have been dealing with this morning as she lounged around in his bed rushed into her heart, and reality grew as big as Lola's belly.

"But what if Lola isn't all right? She's our prize mare. That foal she's carrying is worth thousands. We bred her with Night Wind, a stud from Houston who's sired plenty of prize cutting horses. The Rocking C has a lot riding on this birth being a healthy one."

"What happens to the ranch if Lola can't pay her way?"

"The whole place could go under." She blew out a ragged sigh, revealing the truth she struggled with each day. "I've tried my best to run things since Teresa died, but I'm a nurse, not a rancher. Now that Dave's gone, who knows what will happen to the place?"

And more worrisome of all, who knew what would happen to Chloe?

Chapter Ten

So the Rocking C was in limbo.

Joe suspected that Chloe wasn't only concerned with the bottom line or the ranch's finances. From the sound of things, he sensed that she was also concerned about herself. What would happen to her if she had to move?

He knew she wasn't selfish. Didn't he? At least, nothing she'd done up until now would make him think so. In fact, it was just the opposite. Yet something nagged at him, something he couldn't put his finger on.

It was probably a side effect of the amnesia.

"So what would you do if you could stay on the ranch?" He'd meant the question to distract her from worry. At least, that's what he told himself. But had he been fishing for ulterior motives?

And if so, why?

His question seemed to hang in the air for a moment, then she said, "I don't know. I've had a few ideas. But like I said, I'm not really a rancher, I'm a nurse. There aren't too many jobs that would incorporate the two."

"Tell me some of them."

She bit her bottom lip, but before she could answer, a pickup drove into the yard and parked.

"Oh, good," she said, her voice light as she shook

off his question altogether and strode toward the black Dodge Ram. "That must be the vet."

Joe watched a dark-haired man slide out of the driver's seat. The moment the vet looked up, his blue eyes zeroed in on Joe, and recognition dawned on him like the noonday sun.

Joe had a feeling he knew the guy, too. It wasn't a flashback coming to him in the same way one struck him out by the swimming hole. This was different.

Maybe it was the blue eyes, the dark hair and the olive complexion, because the vet was as familiar to Joe as the face he saw in the mirror each morning.

"Oh, my God," the vet said. "*Joey?* Is that you?"

Joe wasn't sure what to say. Nor did he know how much he wanted to divulge about who he thought he was or what his circumstances were. But Joe wanted answers more than anonymity.

As the vet eased closer, Joe said, "Yeah."

"It's me," the vet said. "Rick."

Joe was almost too stunned to speak. Had he recognized the guy because he'd actually known him in the past? Or because of their resemblance and the fact that Rick the vet had called him Joey?

"Do you know Joe Wilcox?" Chloe asked the vet.

He had to, Joe thought. They looked similar enough to be brothers.

Brothers? The moment the word crossed his mind, a flicker exploded in his brain, illuminating a couple of the dark corners that had been hidden.

This guy—or rather, Rick—had been a part of Joe's life at one time. But he'd be damned if he knew any more than that.

"I've been looking for you for almost ten years." Rick

started to reach out toward Joe, possibly to pull him in for a brotherly hug. But then his movements stalled, as if he thought better of it. He ran a hand through his hair instead and slowly shook his head. "Have you been on the Cummings ranch all this time? I never realized you and Dave were so tight."

Chloe coughed discreetly, and Rick glanced her way as if he'd forgotten she was standing there, watching the awkward, one-sided reunion.

"I'm sorry." Rick reached out to shake the extended hand Chloe offered. "I'm Rick Martinez, and I haven't seen my brother since we were teenagers."

Joe couldn't do much more than stand there, staring at the man who looked just like him and claimed to be his long lost brother. This amnesia crap was getting to be too damn much for him.

"But Joe's last name is Wilcox," Chloe said, looking only slightly less confused than Joe felt.

Rick turned to Joe, his brow furrowed, his head cocked slightly. "What'd you do? Change your name? Maybe that's why Clay Jenkins couldn't find you."

Clay Jenkins. The computer guru? Joe had been right. He really had recognized the billionaire's photo—and not necessarily because he'd seen his face in magazines or newspapers or online.

But those few little dots were the only ones his brain would let him connect.

Damn. Joe hated not having an answer to questions like that. And he was sick and tired of repeating the same mantra time and time again. But he didn't have any truthful options. "I'm afraid I don't know."

The furrow in Rick's brow deepened, and Chloe jumped to the rescue once again. "Joe was hit by a car outside the Stagecoach Inn and suffered a head injury. He has amnesia, so we're not exactly sure who he is."

Before Rick could respond, Tomas jogged out of the barn and interrupted. "Doctor, please. Lola is this way. She needs you."

"Of course." Rick squared his shoulders and grabbed a case out of the back of his truck before following Tomas into the stable.

Joe watched his brother walk away. He might have stood there gaping like an idiot, but Chloe elbowed him to get his attention.

When he glanced down at the petite blonde's upturned face, she arched a single brow and nodded toward the barn. "Do you remember him?"

"I…I don't know. I mean, he looks just like me. And even though we have different names, there definitely seemed to be something there when I saw him. Not necessarily an immediate fraternal bond, but *something*."

Chloe hesitated for a minute. "Let's go into the barn. Maybe seeing Dr. Martinez in action or spending some more time with him will trigger another memory."

Joe followed her, feeling like a lost little child who needed direction.

Up until this point, he hadn't let the amnesia render him helpless, and he wasn't about to start now. This was his first major opportunity to learn more about himself. And he needed to face it head on.

When they reached Lola's stall, Rick was already examining the mare. "You were right, Tomas. The foal is breech."

Lola whinnied, and Rick stroked her neck and made soft shushing sounds. "It's okay, mama. It's okay."

Joe could almost believe him. Maybe things would soon be "okay" with him, too.

Joe hung out in the barn until Lola had dropped a healthy foal—a filly. Then he'd gone to the kitchen to put on a pot of coffee. He figured Rick would want to talk to him, and it seemed like a better idea to do it while seated at the kitchen table and not out in the driveway.

The pot had just stopped percolating when Rick entered the kitchen from the mudroom.

"How's Lola doing?" Joe asked.

"Happy to have it all over, I'm sure. But she and her foal are bonding, so that's good. Tomas and Chloe are with her now."

"How about some coffee?" he asked.

"Sounds good. Thanks."

As Joe poured two cups of the fresh brew, he said, "So, you're my brother."

"It's been ten years, and you've grown up—and filled out. But I believe you are—unless you're an amazing lookalike."

"You believe it—or you *know* it? I mean, if you haven't seen me since I was sixteen, how can you be sure?"

The vet hooked his thumbs into the front pockets of his jeans and studied him quietly—and not at all defensive that Joe was calling him out to prove his claim.

"You have a three-inch scar on your right arm," Rick said. "A burn mark you got when you were eight. Tío Ramon, our uncle, came home, cocked and ready for a fight. When Tía Rosa didn't get dinner on the table fast enough, he grabbed the frying pan off the stove. It had hot oil in it because she was getting ready to fry corn tortillas, but Ramon didn't give that a second thought. He threw it at her, and you jumped in front of her to protect her and got hit instead."

Joe closed his eyes, the truth setting in, even if the memory hadn't surfaced. Then he rolled up his right sleeve and showed Rick the raised scar…

As Rick reached out and fingered the scar, another vision flashed in Joe's brain, this one involving a ten-year-old boy, a younger version of Rick, rubbing ice along the same strip of singed flesh on a smaller arm—Joe's arm?—and saying, *You'll be okay. But stay out of Tío's way next time he comes home drunk. You and me gotta stick together.*

"So," Rick said, intruding on Joe's flashback, "you joined the Marines. That would make sense. You were always trying to protect people—Tía Rosa, kids being bullied at school."

"You told me that the two of us had to stick together," Joe said, but not accusingly. He was just sharing a memory.

"I tried, Joey. I really did."

Maybe so, but they'd obviously had some kind of falling out. Otherwise, Joe would have given Rick's name and address as a contact number.

"So what happened?" he asked. "Why didn't we stay together?"

"After they arrested Tío Ramon and protective services got involved, we were sent to different foster homes. Then, about the time I turned eighteen, Mallory got pregnant, her grandparents sent her out of state and my life spiraled out of control for a while. You ran away and it was damn near impossible to find you—

even with the help of a private investigator and a computer whiz."

"Who's Mallory?" Joe had no more than asked the question when Chloe entered the kitchen, her hair falling loose around her shoulders, clearly worn out from the ordeal with Lola—and most likely, their own late night.

Rick glanced at her as though he wasn't sure how to answer any personal questions in front of a nonfamily member, then returned his focus on Joe.

But hell, Joe wasn't sure he wanted her to know all the details, either. It sounded as if they'd had a pretty crappy life. And from what Chloe had told him, her childhood had been picture-perfect.

Besides that, he had this inexplicable urge to keep some stuff private—between him and his brother.

Sure, Chloe had taken excellent care of him after the accident. He'd been completely dependent upon her and, after last night, their relationship had only gotten stronger.

So why did he feel the need to hide things from her? And why did he question whether he could fully trust her?

Judging by the questioning look Rick was directing at him, Joe didn't think his brother trusted her much, either. But when Joe didn't object, he said, "Mallory is my wife now. But back in high school, she was my girlfriend. She got pregnant, and…well, things got pretty complicated. Let's just say that I had a lot on my plate back then and was too young to do much about anything."

"You mentioned Clay Jenkins had been looking for me, too. Do I know him?"

"You, Clay and I ran around together in high school. He has a computer business now. And after I got my DVM degree and was in a position to find you and take care of you, I started looking for you. When I continued to run into walls, probably because of your name change, I finally called him and asked for his help."

"So I'm from Brighton Valley originally?"

"Wow, you really don't remember much of anything." Rick turned to Chloe, directing the question at her. "How long has he been like this?"

Joe bristled. It was almost as if Rick thought Joe was too simpleminded to answer for himself.

"Nearly a week." Chloe looked at Joe as if wanting to get his permission to continue.

He nodded, and she went on to tell Rick about the accident and everything else they'd found out from NCIS since then. But Joe tuned them out, as another flashback popped into his mind, one of a teenage Rick telling Joe he needed to get a hold of his temper. *Don't be such a hard-ass, Joey. If you get sent to juvie, I can't take care of you there.*

Joe was so absorbed in his own thoughts and flickering memories, he almost didn't catch the fact that Chloe hadn't mentioned Dave or his letter.

"So what were you doing in town in the first place?" Rick asked him. "Do you remember that?"

"No, they tell me that I had a letter from Dave Cummings in my pocket when they found me. According to military records, I served with him in the Marine Corps before we both got medically discharged."

Joe told Rick about Dave's death and hoped his brother didn't ask what was in the dying man's last letter. Because the truth was, Joe had no idea himself, since that was another thing that Chloe had yet to tell him.

Maybe that's why he didn't completely trust her.

Rick's cell phone rang, and Joe wanted to throw the offending object into the yard. Didn't the answering service realize that the vet had just found his long lost brother, and they had years to catch up on?

Rick looked at the screen and then silenced the phone before saying, "Listen, I know this is probably a lot for you to take in. And Lord knows that I want to spend the next two weeks out here with you catching up and helping you figure things out. But I don't want to overwhelm you, and I promised Doc Peterson that I'd take care of his emergency calls while he's on vacation. I'd like to stop back tomorrow so I can check on Lola anyway."

"I'd like that," Joe said.

"All right. I'll see you then."

Joe wasn't sure if he should shake Rick's hand, but his brother made the decision for him and pulled him into a tight squeeze, giving him a few solid thumps on the back. "Man, I missed you, Joey. We'll have to play catch-up tomorrow."

Joe was reluctant to let go, but he still had all his ranch chores to take care of and a lot of thinking to do. So he walked Rick out to his truck. All the while, he started a mental list of things to ask his brother.

As Rick got into his truck, Joe watched him drive away.

His life was finally coming together. He had a brother, a family. And his memory was slowly coming back, albeit in scattered pieces.

So why did he still feel unsettled—as if he still had unfinished business?

* * *

After Dr. Martinez left and Joe went to help Tomas with the chores, Chloe sat at the kitchen table, staring into her empty coffee mug. She didn't know what to make of it all. Joe's discovery that he'd grown up in Brighton Valley and that he had a brother had been mind-boggling. But what effect—if any—would that have on their budding relationship?

There hadn't been any of the awkwardness she would have expected after they'd slept together, since they'd barely had a chance to touch upon it this morning. The foal's birth had interrupted their conversation, making it easy to avoid asking him, "Now what? Where do we go from here?"

Then Dr. Martinez had provided another diversion when he'd arrived with his surprising revelation.

Chloe found the news almost overwhelming and couldn't begin to imagine how Joe must feel.

Just moments ago, he'd asked her to call Sheriff Hollister and relay the recent development, which was probably because he was still trying to wrap his mind around it and wasn't ready to talk about his thoughts.

So, using the kitchen phone, she dialed the sheriff's office. When he answered, Chloe filled him in.

"Well, what do you know," Sheriff Hollister said. "But I wonder why my deputy didn't find any links to that family tie of Joe's when he was going through high school yearbooks."

"From what Dr. Martinez said, Joe must have changed his name to Wilcox after he left town."

"Is that right? Hold on a sec." The sheriff's voice drifted when his mouth no longer spoke directly into the receiver. "Taylor, bring me those Brighton Valley High yearbooks you were looking through." After an unmistakable rustle of pages, the sheriff continued, "Yep, I found him. Joseph Martinez. He's a sophomore here, just a kid, but I'm sure that's him."

"Joe came to town to deliver Dave's letter," Chloe said. "But maybe he planned to get reacquainted with his brother while he was here."

"That would be my guess. He rented that car for two weeks, so that would certainly give him time for a visit."

She sure hoped that was the case. From what she'd gathered, Joe and Rick had been estranged after a falling-out—a bad one. Otherwise, Joe wouldn't have left town, changed his name and not contacted Rick for ten years.

The fact that he might be the kind of man to hold a grudge was a real possibility. And if so, that wasn't an admirable trait. Had she jumped into a sexual relationship too quickly? It certainly wouldn't be the first time.

But last night had been so very different from her only other experience. It had not only been amazing, but it had been special. And, at least on her part, it had been a decision of the heart.

"By the way," Sheriff Hollister said, "I was going to call him and let him know that we received an anonymous tip. One of the customers at the Stagecoach Inn drives a vehicle that matches the description of the one that hit him. We're still investigating, so we haven't made an arrest, but with that information, coupled with Joe's apparent connection to Brighton Valley, I seriously doubt that he was a targeted victim. So he doesn't need to keep hiding out on the ranch anymore."

"It's okay for him to go into town?"

"I'm sure it's fine."

"He'll be glad to hear that." And while Chloe took it as good news, too, she couldn't say that she was especially happy that Joe was free to leave. Sure, she was relieved to know that no one was out to get him. And it warmed her heart to know that he had at least one family member who obviously loved him—and a local, upstanding citizen at that. But still, at the same time, she found it unsettling.

She'd known there would come a time when he would go back to his old life, but what about the new one he'd just begun to create with her?

"If anything comes up," Sheriff Hollister said, "or if we make an arrest, I'll let you know."

"Thanks. Joe will appreciate that."

Chloe had no more than ended the call when the subject of her thoughts walked into the kitchen and provided her with a brand-new dilemma.

Should she tell him that he was free to leave, that there was no need for him to stay cooped up on the Rocking C any longer? Or did she dare to keep the new information to herself so she could hold on to him a little longer?

Was there really even a choice?

"I came to get some water to take with me out to the pasture," Joe said, as he hung his hat on the peg near the mudroom door.

She watched him proceed to the cupboard for an insulated jug. Then he carried it to the kitchen sink and turned on the spigot.

While he filled his container with water, she said, "I just got off the phone with Sheriff Hollister." She went on to relate everything the lawman had told her.

"So I'm free to venture off the ranch now and head into Brighton Valley? I can actually leave?"

"That's what he said. But if you're not feeling up to it—or if you like being here—you're welcome to stay as long as you want to." She bit down on her lower lip, hoping he'd tell her that he didn't want to go. That he'd come to…care for her. And, that after last night, he… might even love…

That possibility was almost too wild to imagine, although she'd felt her feelings drifting in that direction.

"I'd like to take a look around town," he said. "It might spark more memories. But if it's all the same to you, I'd feel more comfortable staying here on the ranch for a while."

Chloe released the breath she'd been holding, but she reined in her enthusiasm. "I think that's a good idea."

"So what do you have planned for this afternoon?" he asked.

"I'm going to drive out to the nursing home. I'd like to visit Sam Darnell and ask him a few questions about ranching. But I can wait until you're finished helping Tomas. That way, you can come with me—if you want to. And when we're done, we can drive down Main Street. Maybe we can even go to the ice-cream shop near town square."

He seemed to give the idea some thought before shaking his head. "I'd better pass. Tomas has a lot of work to do, and I know he'd appreciate my help. Maybe we can go into town next weekend."

Chloe wondered if Joe was trying to avoid being with her or if he was reluctant to bombard his brain with too many memories all at once. But she hated to confront the issue head-on right now. They'd probably both feel better about discussing it later this evening—before bed, when it would be impossible to avoid asking him what their next step should be.

Ten minutes later, after changing her clothes, she grabbed her purse, climbed into Ol' Greenie and drove to the Sheltering Arms.

She stopped in the lobby, where Christmas music played softly in the background—the toe-tapping tune of "Jingle Bell Rock." She took a moment to appreciate the holiday decor and the faint scent of pine. Then she continued on her way to the elevator, humming along with the spunky beat and thinking that December was, indeed, a "swell time."

When the doors opened, she rode up to the third floor, where Merrilee Turner was manning the nurse's desk again. She smiled when she spotted Chloe. "You're back. It's good to see you."

"Thanks. I stopped by to visit Sam and Ethel."

"Sam is in his room, watching TV. But Ethel is probably sleeping. At least, she was the last time I stopped by her room. She's picked up a cold and has a nasty cough."

"That's too bad. Does Sarah know?"

"I mentioned it to her, and she said she'd put a call in to the doctor."

"That's good." Chloe just hoped Sarah hadn't forgotten. The woman was often scattered and forgetful—not a good trait for the third-floor nurse to have. But she had other habits and traits that Chloe found even more troublesome.

When Chloe had worked at the Stagecoach Inn, she'd often seen Sarah partying with her friends and throwing back quite a few beers, keeping late hours on nights when she was supposed to be at work early the next day. It wasn't like she would call in sick, but she'd often come in late and hungover. And she had a tendency to snap at the aides, as well as the patients.

But since Merrilee was the one who'd picked up on Ethel's illness, at least it had been noted. So Chloe wouldn't stress too much about it.

"If Ethel is resting," Chloe said, "I'll let her have a few more minutes to sleep."

"Good idea."

Chloe's first stop was Sam Darnell's room, where the retired cowboy lay in bed, his head propped up with pillows, his lunch still on the portable bedside table.

"Hey," she said, peering at the food he'd yet to touch. "What are you doing? Having a late meal?"

"Nope. I'm done. They just haven't come in to haul the dishes away."

"But you've hardly eaten a thing."

"I wasn't hungry. A fella doesn't burn up too many calories when he's laid up in bed."

She glanced at an untouched slice of three-layer cake with gooey frosting. "I can't believe you didn't eat your dessert. You love chocolate. And you never sent sweets back to the kitchen when I worked here."

"That's because you used to force me to eat, and I didn't have the heart or the energy to wrestle with you."

Chloe laughed. "I did no such thing."

They made small talk for a while, then Chloe told him about the offer she'd received for the hundred head of cattle.

Sam clucked his tongue. "Don't take it. That price is way too low. The guy might as well come onto the ranch in the middle of the night and rustle the entire herd."

"I had a feeling he was trying to take advantage of me."

"A lot of folks will do just that if you don't stand up for yourself."

Sam had said as much to her before, so she gave him the same response. "You know that I don't really like confrontations."

"But sometimes you gotta stand up for what's right."

"I know. And I will." After a beat, she added, "I don't suppose you'd come out to the Rocking C with me and negotiate that deal."

Sam brightened. "I'd be happy to. But do you think you can spring me from this place?"

Chloe crossed her arms. "I'm not sure. Do you think you can eat your lunch?"

"You drive a hard bargain, missy. How 'bout I just eat that cake?"

Chloe laughed. "Are you sure you don't want to come out of retirement? The Rocking C could sure use your help. And I could, too."

Sam let out a harrumph, but his tired eyes sparked and glistened in a way she hadn't seen since his wife passed away.

"You don't want me," he said. "I'll be eighty-two on my next birthday. You'd be better off with a younger man."

"I already have one. But Tomas told me himself that he's not foreman material, and while I like him a lot, I'd have to agree. Besides, I need someone who's savvy about things like this, someone I can trust."

He seemed to consider her suggestion. "I couldn't give you a full day's work anymore, but I wouldn't mind coming out to the ranch and having a little look-see.

And I'd actually like to talk to that cattle buyer. I'd let him know that he ain't messing with a fool greenhorn."

Chloe smiled. "I'd like that, Sam. Let me see what I can do about getting you out of here in the next day or so."

"Call my nephew. He'll give the okay. He's also a fancy city lawyer who likes to throw his weight around."

"I'll do that." Chloe watched Sam dig into the cake. And when he'd swallowed the last bite, he chugged down his milk.

Maybe all he needed was to feel useful again. She'd have to keep that in mind.

After saying goodbye and promising to come back, she headed down the hall to check on Ethel, only to find the frail, silver-haired lady dozing, the blankets pulled up to her chest.

Her arms were uncovered, her hands at her side. She wore a long sleeve flannel gown, but her wrists were in plain sight—and completely bare.

Apparently her allergy alert bracelet, which was supposed to be on order, hadn't come in yet.

Not wanting to disturb her dear friend, especially if she was sick and needed her rest, Chloe remained in the doorway a minute longer. Then she turned away and left the room.

As she walked to the elevator, she spotted Sarah Poston at the nurse's desk, standing over Merrilee and complaining about something.

"I take it that Ethel's allergy alert bracelet hasn't come in," Chloe said.

Sarah crossed her arms and shifted her weight to one foot. "It should be here any day. Besides, like I told you, her allergy is noted in her chart."

If Chloe still worked here, she'd peek at Ethel's chart herself. But she'd been let go, terminated unfairly for speaking her mind about Sarah's disregard for protocol and her attitude toward certain patients.

Too bad Ethel didn't have a family to insist that she get the best quality care possible. For a couple of beats, Chloe considered her options at this point.

One came to the forefront. *Sometimes you gotta stand up for what's right.*

Yes, but how far did she want to go in challenging Sarah? Did she want to take it up with the administrator—again?

She really didn't have any solid evidence against the woman. Was she prepared for the fallout if her accusation didn't prove true?

Chloe hated confrontations, especially those she didn't think she could win. Besides, there was another confrontation awaiting her at home—one she was dreading, but one that had to be faced.

Because she and Joe needed to talk about the sexual turn their relationship had taken last night.

Chapter Eleven

Throughout the day, while working with Tomas, Joe's memories continued to return sporadically and in no particular order.

Sometimes he'd get a vision, a brief glimpse into the past. At other times a feeling would wash over him—a righteous anger or just plain sadness—which only frustrated him more.

At first, he'd assumed that he'd been angered or hurt by something his brother had done. And that's why he'd left town and never looked back. What else would have compelled him to change his name and lose contact with his family?

Yet each time he'd looked at Rick yesterday, he'd sensed a strong brotherly bond. And while he was more than okay with that, he couldn't just accept everything at face value.

Even more troubling was the fact that, in spite of his life slowly coming back to him, he still didn't have a handle on his true identity, either, and that left him more unsettled than ever.

For that reason, after dinner, he thanked Chloe for the meal and turned in early, giving himself a chance to sort through the mixed-up feelings alone.

She was so understanding about it, too. Which confused him all the more. Most women would want to know why the man they'd spent the previous night with all of a sudden wanted to sleep alone. But not Nurse Chloe.

He rose early the next morning, when he was sure she'd still be asleep. Then he went outside to check on Lola and her foal. There'd been plenty of chores to do, so he kept himself busy until Rick arrived.

Joe greeted his brother in the yard, then walked with him to the barn, where Rick examined Lola and the foal.

"They both look good," Rick said.

Joe thought so, too. "I checked on them earlier this morning. Lola sure seems to be a good mother."

Rick glanced at his boots, then back to Joe. "You and I weren't so lucky."

"Somehow, that doesn't surprise me."

"Do you remember any of it? That apartment complex where we lived? The fighting? Dad running off with that stripper? He'd said she was a professional dancer, but I didn't buy it. And neither did Mom."

"I have a vague recollection, but nothing solid."

"What about moving in with our aunt and uncle after Mom died and Dad took off? Do you remember that?"

"Last night, when I undressed for bed, I noticed that scar on my arm. You'd told me what happened, but I was able to remember it—the yelling and screaming. The huge sense of relief I felt when the police arrived before our uncle beat the crap out of her. The feeling that it hadn't been the first nor the last time something like that had happened."

"Things were pretty bad at times. I don't blame you for wanting to put it all behind you. I might have run off, too, but Mallory had been sent to Boston to finish out her pregnancy and have our baby. And I'd wanted to wait for her to come back. Then I met up with Hank Lazarro, who helped me turn my life around."

Joe wondered if he'd found a mentor of his own along the way. Had Conway, the retired marine, stepped in and befriended him? Had Joe gone on to find new friends and a family in the corps? The answers to his questions seemed to be yes.

"Hey," Rick said, placing a hand on Joe's shoulder. "Why don't you ride into town with me? I've been craving Caroline's hotcakes all week. And since I left home early this morning, I didn't get a chance to have breakfast. We can talk in my truck and at the diner. Maybe that will jostle your memory."

Joe had no idea who Caroline was or what diner his brother was talking about, but he'd slipped out of the house without eating, too. "That sounds good to me."

Twenty minutes later, they entered the small town eatery, where a middle-age waitress, a woman Rick addressed as Margie, greeted them with a smile. "Good mornin', Doc Martinez. Who have you got here? Don't tell me this is Joey, all grown up."

"Yep. It sure is."

"Where've you been, son? We haven't seen you in… well, it's been ages."

"He joined the Marines after he left town," Rick said. "And when I went off to college, we lost touch for a while."

Apparently, Rick hadn't told anyone Joe had run off.

"Isn't that nice? Y'all found each other. And just in time for Christmas." Margie grabbed a couple of menus and led them back to a corner booth, all the while chattering about how family should be together during the holidays.

When she offered them menus, Rick said, "I don't need one. I'll have the rancher's breakfast—eggs over easy, bacon and a stack of Caroline's hotcakes."

"I'll have the same thing," Joe said, "only with scrambled eggs and the country sausage."

"Coffee?" Margie asked, as she made a note of their orders on a small pad.

"You bet," Rick said. "Thanks."

When Margie walked away, leaving the brothers alone, Rick said, "Neither one of us had the kind of past I liked to talk about, so very few people around here know anything about where you went or why." He reached into his shirt pocket and pulled out some snapshots, one black-and-white, the others in color. "I brought some family pictures for you to see. I thought it might help."

When he handed them over, Joe looked at each one, then focused on the old Polaroid of a couple in their late twenties to early thirties.

"That's one of the only shots I have of our mom and dad," Rick said. "You can see that she's blonde. We obviously get one of our genes for blue eyes from the Norwegian side of the family."

Joe wished he could say that he remembered their parents, but he didn't. "How old were we when mom died?"

"You were six. I was eight."

At that age, Joe doubted that he'd have too many memories of them anyway. He flipped through the pictures and found one of a dark-haired couple in their mid-forties. He flashed it at Rick. "Is this Ramon and Rosa?"

"Yeah. Do you remember them?"

"Vaguely, but more than I remember our parents. I keep getting flashes of memory—bits and pieces I'm trying to put together. So keep talking. I think it's working."

"Tío Ramon was Dad's brother. He liked to stop by La Cantina, a little dive in Wexler, every night after work. He was a mean drunk and had some anger issues, especially when he was three sheets to the wind. I'm sure that had a lot to do with him not keeping a job. But for some reason, he always seemed to find a new one."

"You mentioned the abuse, the domestic violence. It must have been pretty bad."

"It was. Ramon and Rosa loved each other, but they fought something awful, especially when they'd both been drinking."

Margie stopped by with the carafe of coffee and filled both cups. Then she left a creamer and sugar.

Rick thanked her, and when she walked away, he continued. "We'd tried to talk Rosa into leaving him before it was too late, but she didn't listen. And one night, he nearly killed her. After Ramon went to prison and Rosa recovered from that last beating, she joined AA and turned her life around. She and I reestablished a relationship, although we weren't especially close at first. I've since reconciled with Tío Ramon, too. But that's been fairly recent. I wanted to be sure that he was serious about his sobriety. And I believe he is. He's due to get his two-year token next spring."

Joe lifted his mug and took a sip. "I'd think he could use some anger management classes."

"That was mandated by the court. He took them while he was in prison, but he took a refresher course after his release. He and Tía Rosa have reconciled and are attending church regularly. You'd hardly know them."

Joe hardly knew them as it was. And something told him he ought to be grateful that he'd forgotten those early years.

Rick took a sip of coffee. "Because Tío kept losing his job, it seemed as though we had to move each time he found a new one. We lived in several different apartments in Houston, a mobile home and a duplex in Wexler, and then a townhome in Brighton Valley. After I met Mallory in my junior year, I spent more and more time away from home. And that left you to deal with all the family dysfunction on your own. I think you felt abandoned, and I can see why you would. I'd like to say that I wasn't much more than a kid at that time, but I won't make excuses. I was all you really had, and I let you down."

Joe forgave him. At least, the man he'd become after the accident did. And maybe the old Joe did, too. After a ten-year separation, a tour of duty in a war zone, and an accident that damn near killed him and left him with amnesia…well, he was glad to have someone and something to hang on to. And that someone was sitting across the table from him, looking at him with eyes laden with emotion.

"I love you," Rick said. "And I missed you something awful. Now that we've both grown up and moved on, I'd like to establish a better relationship."

"I'd like that," Joe said. "I'd like it a lot."

Margie returned to the table and placed their meals in front of them. Just a whiff of the sausage triggered another memory. Joe paused, allowing it to unfold.

Seated at the kitchen table, Joe watched Tía frying breakfast meat, her bruised eyes nearly swollen shut, her bottom lip split. The words Joe said to her that morning. *You gotta leave him, Tía!*

I know, mijo. *But deep inside, your* tío *is a good man. And I love him.*

But next time, he could kill you. And me...

The memory faded. And while it really wasn't a whole lot for Joe to go on, it validated the things Rick had told him.

Yet that simple vision and the feelings it triggered stirred up even more bits and pieces, allowing him to cobble some of them together.

"You're right," Joe said. "I felt abandoned and left alone to weather the storms at home. I remember trying to talk some sense into Tía Rosa. I'd beg her to leave him, but she wouldn't listen. It used to make me so angry because it wasn't just her life she was ruining, it was mine. I'm not sure that she even cared that each time I stepped in to protect her, I'd get beat on myself."

"I should have been there to protect you."

Joe shrugged a single shoulder. "Maybe, but I wasn't looking for protection as much as a backup. If you'd have been home one of those nights, we could have stopped him and knocked some sense into him."

"You're probably right. But in retrospect, that might have landed you and me in juvenile hall—or worse."

Joe reached for his fork, only to have another memory kick in, one that he'd never forget again. And along with it, more emotions: anger, frustration, grief.

"What's the matter?" Rick asked. "Did you remember something else?"

"Yeah. Going home after what must have been their

last fight. Red lights were flashing all around the neighborhood. The sheriff was there. Not Hollister, but an older man—heavyset, graying hair. He had *Tío* cuffed and locked in the back of the squad car. *Tía* was already in an ambulance, and they wouldn't let me see her."

"She nearly died that night. She spent two weeks in ICU and nearly six months in rehab."

"I remember thinking that it was all my fault," Joe said.

"There's no way. You weren't even there when it happened. *Tío* was a brute when he drank."

"Yeah, but if I'd been home, I might have stopped it."

Rick reached across the table and placed his hand over Joe's. "You were only fifteen. And if you *had* been there, you would have tried to stop it. But then you might have been the one hauled off in the ambulance or the squad car."

"Maybe so."

Joe didn't bring it up because he didn't think it was necessary, but he also remembered that he and his brother had both been sent to different foster homes that night, separating them when Joe had needed him most.

"I can't fix what happened in the past," Rick said. "But I want you to know that I'm sorry for whatever I might have done to you—or whatever I failed to do for you. You're my brother, and I don't want you to leave town without knowing how I feel."

"Speaking of leaving Brighton Valley," Joe said, "do you have any idea why I might have changed my name after I left?"

"I can't be sure, but I think it was because you wanted to put our lousy past behind you. Ramon and Rosa made newspaper headlines for a while, and the whole mess was pretty embarrassing. I found it hard to deal with and didn't speak to either of them for years. But Ramon learned a hard lesson while he was incarcerated. You might find this hard to believe—I know I did—but now that he's quit drinking and gone through some intensive counseling, he's like a new person."

Joe wished he had something to say to that, some feelings to go along with it, but he dug into his breakfast and let his scattered thoughts and memories simmer.

By the time they'd finished eating, a lot of things had begun to come together for him.

The foster parents Joe had to live with weren't too bad, but Darrell, one of the other kids, used to bully the smaller boys. And since Joe had seen more than his share of abuse—and hated it—they butted heads more often than not.

One day, when Darrell began picking on one of the band geeks in the school cafeteria, Joe confronted him. A fight broke out, and even though Joe's reason for getting involved was noble, the principal suspended them both.

Rick hadn't been around that day, which led Joe to think he'd probably ditched school to spend time with his friends. And more than ever, Joe began to feel helpless and alone—with no one to care about him.

He had, however, earned the undying support of the band geek he'd stepped in to help—Dave Cummings.

Pieces of his ranch memories began to come together, and Joe soon realized when he'd been on the Rocking C before.

On several occasions, he'd run away from home and had ended up on the Cummings ranch. Just being around Dave and his parents had given him a glimpse of what a real family was supposed to be like, and he'd found himself drawn there.

"Do you need to go back to the ranch now?" Rick asked as he pushed his plate aside. "If not, I can take you to my place and you can meet Mallory and our son, Lucas. I can't wait to introduce you."

"I guess I should head back to the ranch. Maybe when my head is on a little straighter, I'll make a better impression on your wife and son." Joe really wasn't up to meeting anyone right now, especially with his thoughts and feelings still jumbled. But it was nice that Rick had asked.

Joe took one last look at the picture of his parents, trying to get another vision, another memory, but nothing came to mind.

He handed the photos back to his brother. "I'm glad I can't remember how crappy life was before our mom died."

"She had a prescription drug problem, which eventually killed her. She died of an overdose."

A vision slammed into Joe, striking him as hard and unexpected as the Silverado pickup that had hit him in the dead of night, causing his amnesia in the first place.

Overdose.

Dave, cold and lifeless, sprawled out on the kitchen floor. The pain meds he used to swallow—two and three at a time, washed down by whatever liquid was handy.

Bits and pieces of his memory merged with the disjointed dreams he'd had, unleashing a storm of emotion: Worry and disappointment, irritation and resentment.

And it all came back to him.

Well, not all of it. But the memories of a battlefield

will… Joe blinked, remembering Dave giving it to him, as well as the message Dave had asked Joe to deliver on his death and the reckless, suicidal rush at the Taliban insurgents… They were still a bit scattered, but they were clues enough.

He finally understood why he'd returned to Brighton Valley in the first place. He'd promised Dave he would deliver that letter, which Chloe hadn't let him read.

The annoyance he'd felt off and on since the accident rose up inside of him, bordering on anger. And a sense of betrayal lanced his heart.

Dave had loved that woman enough to give her everything. And she'd led him on, convincing him that she loved him, too. Then she'd dumped him, and Dave had chosen death over life without her.

Just like Joe's mom had done when she hadn't been able to cope after their dad abandoned his family for that stripper.

More distrust and suspicion crept over him as another vision, this one recent, flashed before him: Chloe in the Cummings den, digging through files and scanning papers.

She'd looked up and spotted him in the doorway, guilt splashed across her face.

Her reaction had left him uneasy at the time, and now he knew why. He hadn't trusted her.

But why? What clues had he missed? He racked his brain, trying to recall things she'd said to him when they'd talked about the Rocking C.

As the fragments of their conversations came back to him, he tried to make sense of them.

I'm trying my best to hold everything together until I know what's going to happen with the ranch.

Had she already known about Dave's death before the sheriff had notified her? Joe had, but that memory had been lost with all the rest.

I don't want to move until the new owner is located.

Joe had quizzed her about that at the time. *The new owner*?

Whoever stands to inherit the ranch now that Dave is gone.

Chloe had given him the impression that she planned to move on. Yet she seemed to have settled in at the Rocking C, even going so far as to decorate the house for Christmas.

Joe had asked if she'd like a ranch of her own, and if so, would she give up her plan to go to nursing school.

I don't know. Maybe. I'd probably invite some friends to live with me, so I'm not sure how much time I'd have to study.

Damn. Did she already have plans to take over the Rocking C? Would she fill it with friends and free-loaders?

I'd like to visit Sam Darnell, a retired cowboy I know, and ask him a few questions about ranching.

So she did mean to stay on and to make a go of the place. Apparently, she'd planned to all along. And when Joe had seen her in the den, rifling through the files, she must have been looking for a will or a deed or something that would secure her claim.

His gut twisted as suspicion settled over him. He shifted in his seat, but was unable to shake it.

What had that last letter said? Had Dave told her what he'd planned to do—and that he'd left her the ranch?

"Are you okay?" Rick asked. "You look a little shaken and confused."

Was it that obvious?

Joe blew out a sigh. "I've just had a major breakthrough, Rick. Things are still a little sketchy, but images and memories are slamming into me, along with a slew of emotions I'm trying to deal with. And the more I think about it, the less comfortable I feel about staying at the ranch. Would you mind taking me back for my things, then dropping me off at the Night Owl?"

"I'll take you anywhere you want to go. But if you're looking for a place to stay, come home with me. Mallory and I have a guest room, and you're more than welcome to stay with us as long as you'd like. Besides, I want you to meet Lucas. He's a great kid—and the spitting image of you."

Joe had been a loner most of his adult life, but he didn't want to be alone tonight. "If you're sure Mallory won't mind."

"She's eager to meet you—and she'll be glad to have you with us, especially for Christmas." Rick reached into his pocket and pulled out his car keys. "But why don't you just drop me off at the clinic and take my truck to pick up your stuff from the ranch?"

Joe took the keys, while Rick picked up the check. "Thanks. It won't take me long to pack."

"Keep the truck as long as you need it."

Joe didn't expect to be more than a few minutes at the ranch, just long enough to talk to Chloe. And to say the words he'd meant to have with her when he'd first crossed city limits.

Chloe was seated in the kitchen, staring out the bay window, when she saw Dr. Martinez's truck pull in the driveway. She knew Joe would be returning soon, but she hadn't expected to see him behind the wheel.

That was odd. She couldn't imagine a busy veterinarian like Rick not needing his vehicle, which meant Joe must not be planning to stay long.

Oh, for Pete's sake. What was wrong with her? The man hadn't even entered the house and she was already reading way too much into the situation. But one look at the scowl marring his face, and she knew something wasn't right before he even made it to the back porch.

She met him at the mudroom door, just as he let himself in. Before she could quiz him about driving his brother's truck, he said, "I came to pick up my stuff."

"What? Why?" She followed him to the guest room, hating herself for morphing into the kind of woman who got all clingy when a man was trying to leave. But she deserved to know just what in the heck was going on.

He pulled open the dresser drawers and piled his new pants and shirts on the bed.

"What are you doing?"

"I'm getting my things."

"Why?"

He turned to her, his eyes full of something she'd never seen in his expression before. Disgust? Blame? Anger?

"I had a major breakthrough while I was at Caroline's Diner with my brother."

That should have been a good thing, but why was he so…cold?

"A big chunk of my memory came flooding back almost all at once, and I finally remembered the real reason I came to Brighton Valley in the first place." He scanned the room, his gaze landing on the clothes he'd placed on the bed, then he raked his hand through his hair. "Dammit, I don't even have a freakin' suitcase."

"I can get you a bag—if you need it." She still didn't understand why he wanted to leave.

"I probably should have just left all of this here, anyway. It's not like I'm going to need any ranch clothes any time soon. Unlike you, who'll apparently get everything your scheming heart had hoped for."

What was he talking about?

And just who did he think he was talking to?

"Slow down, Joe. What in the world is going on?"

He tore his gaze from the folded clothing, from the bed where they'd so recently made love and zeroed in on her. "I'm talking about what you did to Dave. How you convinced the poor guy to leave everything to you. And then you dumped him, right when he needed you most."

"What?" Chloe crossed her arms. "I didn't convince Dave of anything."

"Right. Well, that's not how he figured it. He was crazy in love with you, and you broke his heart. Hell, the truth of the matter is, you broke *him*."

Chloe closed her eyes, Joe's words echoing the guilt that she felt since learning about Dave's death. For the briefest of moments she wanted to turn away in shame, but she shook off the misplaced feelings.

"Listen, Joe. It wasn't like that with me and Dave. We never had anything together. We certainly never had…" She waved her hand between the two of their bodies. "We never had this."

"This?" Joe gazed at her, his expression accusing her all over again.

But she held firm. Dave hadn't been emotionally stable, and she hadn't done anything wrong.

"What we had wasn't…" Joe's voice trailed off, and his expression softened. Then he sat on the bed, shoulders slumped.

The nurse in her was ready to forgive him for lashing out at her when his memories still had to be a jumbled up mess. But the woman who'd given him her heart was crushed.

"What we *had?*" she asked.

"Hell, I don't know. Had. Have. I won't deny that I fell for you, but I can't very well stay out here with you knowing now what I should have known all along."

"And what's that, Joe? What *do* you know? Please clue me in, because you seem to suddenly have all the answers, and I can't even begin to understand why you're so angry—especially at me."

"I don't know. Maybe because Dave was one of my men—and a buddy. And I knew how damn much he loved you, idolized you. And maybe because I crossed a code of honor between friends."

"Dave only *thought* he was in love with me. He was upset over his mom's illness and death and he latched on to me and mistook the friendship I offered him. But I assure you, it was only friendship on my side. I never lied to him or misled him. In fact, I even sent him a letter explaining as clearly as I could that nothing romantic would ever happen between us."

"Yeah." Joe leaned forward, placed his elbows on his knees and held his head as if to shake loose his thoughts—or maybe to hold them still. "I saw what that letter did to his psyche. Hell, what it did to his whole career. Crap, what it did to *my* whole career. Your so-called 'clear explanation' caused him to lose it when we were under attack." He looked up, caught her gaze. "You know my nightmare?"

Chloe said nothing, not wanting to be reminded of their passionate lovemaking that had followed that same frightening dream. Not when he'd just practically accused her of killing Dave herself.

"It all came back to me. Before running into the gunfire, Dave told me he couldn't go on without you. So, yes, I'm familiar with that carefully worded letter you sent him."

She felt compelled to ease closer, to sit next to him on the bed, but her wounded pride wouldn't have been able to recover if he got up or moved away. So she stood firm and tried to reason with him. "If you remember Dave's words and his recklessness, then surely you must know how sensitive he was. How he didn't handle things very well. I'm sorry that he's dead, and I'm sorry that your knee and your career are blown. But those were a result of Dave's actions, not mine."

He blew out a ragged breath, but he held his thoughts at bay.

"Was I supposed to lie to him and let him think there was something between us? Do you think I should have promised to be waiting for him when he came home from war?"

Joe gazed up at her, his eyes filled with accusation. "But you *were* waiting for him. You even told me that you were taking care of the place for him. Or maybe you were just taking care of your own investment, banking on Dave's fragile mental state to secure you a ranch of your own."

He couldn't have shocked her more, hurt her more, if he'd struck her with his fist.

"What are you talking about?" she asked. "I've wasted months of my life holding this place together because I promised his mom, not him, that I would. How would his death in any way benefit me?"

"Because Dave signed a battlefield will right before he died leaving the entire ranch to you."

Chloe almost sunk to the floor. Her hand, which trembled with indignation only seconds ago, flew to her mouth, which was incapable of speech anyway.

Joe's expression held no warmth, no familiarity. "That's why I came to Brighton Valley. To deliver my buddy's letter and to see for myself just what kind of woman would take a poor sucker like him for everything he had."

"Are you kidding me? I can't believe that you think me capable of that. How could I…? How could *you,* especially after we…?" She didn't know what she was trying to say, but she was too stunned to continue.

"If my memory had been intact, nothing would've happened two nights ago."

Now even the compassionate nurse in her let sympathy and understanding go by the wayside. His accusations were so far-fetched. But still, she could only handle so much confrontation, and it didn't look like there was anything she could say to change his mind. And right this minute, her pride didn't want her to even try. So she stayed silent, fuming with indignation.

"I'll be staying at my brother's house for a while, at least until I can wrap my head around everything." He got to his feet and reached for the folded clothes. "But don't worry. I won't interfere with the probate or bother you anymore."

And with his parting shot striking her heart dead

center, cracking it right in two, he walked out of the room, out of the house and out of her life.

She wasn't sure how long she continued to stand in the bedroom that had once held sweet memories of their lovemaking. She was too busy reeling from his hurtful words, from his false accusations, to form a solid game plan.

Yet in spite of her pain and disappointment, she felt a sense of peace, too. When Joe had blamed her for causing Dave's depression and, ultimately, his death—something for which she'd also blamed herself—she'd stood up to those charges, rejecting them and defending herself. And by doing so, she was able to release the guilt that had once tormented her and accept the truth.

Dave had been devastated by the loss of his mother and by his decision to join the Marines when he should have been home trying to mend his relationship with his father. He'd also felt somehow to blame for his dad's heart attack—or at least for the estrangement that had shortened what little time on earth they'd had together.

His guilt and conflicting duty to family and country, as well as the battlefield itself, must have taken a toll on him, and Chloe refused to accept responsibility for his death.

But that didn't mean she wasn't crushed by Joe's other allegations, by his lack of faith and trust in her.

It took every ounce of strength she possessed to not fall onto the bed, curl up into a ball and cry her eyes out. But once he was long gone, she gradually moved from the disbelief and bargaining stage to anger.

How dare he accuse her of setting her designs on Dave or on this ranch?

She might not like confrontations, but she wasn't

about to take this lying down. So she went to the den, plopped down in the desk chair and picked up the phone. Teresa's attorney hadn't returned her call yet, but she wasn't going to wait for him to find time to get back to her. If she had to track him down at his home or in the courthouse, she'd do it.

Luckily, Mr. McDougall's secretary said he was in the office and transferred her call right away.

"Hello, Ms. Dawson. I got your message, but things have been pretty hectic this morning. What can I do for you?"

She explained about Dave's death and about requesting the documents from the San Diego coroner's office.

"Okay. As soon as I get that report, we can get the ball rolling and settle the estate."

"That leads me to another issue, Mr. McDougall." Chloe didn't know how to word her question without sounding like the gold digger Joe had accused her of being. But there was no other way to get the answer she needed. "What exactly is going to happen to the estate?"

"Did Dave have a will?" the attorney asked. "I never made one for him."

Chloe told him about the handwritten will he'd made in Afghanistan, which may have listed her as the heir. "But I don't know if it's legal. Actually, I don't even know if it exists. I haven't seen it."

"Well, if he did have one—and you can find it—probate will go more smoothly. From what I remember, the Cummings family didn't have any other relatives or people who could lay claim to the ranch. So if the will exists—and if it's legit—then you'd be the owner of the Rocking C."

Great. Chloe didn't want the burden or the guilt

that would come along with that sort of unexpected inheritance.

"On a side note," the attorney said, "I do have a copy of Dave's life insurance policy—the one he took out before his last deployment. It names Joseph Wilcox as the beneficiary."

If Chloe hadn't already been seated in the old desk chair, she would have fallen to the floor. "Joe Wilcox is the beneficiary?"

"Yes. Do you know him?"

"Not as well as I thought I did. But I know where you can find him." Chloe provided the attorney with Rick Martinez's contact information.

They made an appointment to meet in person, then ended the call.

Chloe would sure like to see the look on Joe's face when he learned that Chloe wasn't the only person who benefitted from Dave's death. It would serve him right to have to eat his words.

She supposed that was cruel to think something like that at a time like this. But she was still furious with Joe for breaking her heart and crushing her dreams. And she was also angry at Dave for putting her in this situation to start with.

She'd never asked for any of this.

Yet, here she sat.

Out the window, she spotted a squad car pulling into the drive. So she headed for the front door, just as Sheriff Hollister knocked.

The sheriff stood on the porch, holding two green canvas duffel bags, both of which appeared to be military issued.

"Afternoon, Miss Dawson. The clerk over at the

Night Owl called us and let us know that they found these bags in the room Joe had checked into. Apparently, they were wedged under the bed. My deputy must have missed them in his initial search of the room."

"Why are there two?"

"One appears to be Joe's. The other is probably Dave's. Is Joe here?"

"Uh, no. He's at his brother's right now." Chloe should probably tell Sheriff Hollister that Joe had moved out, but she wasn't ready to explain why or what had happened between them.

"Should I bring them inside for you?"

No. She didn't want anything more to do with Joe, Dave or their stuff.

"Just leave them on the porch," she said. "I'll make sure that Joe gets them."

Chapter Twelve

Chloe didn't want to hold on to those duffel bags any longer than she had to. So after the sheriff left, she lugged them to Ol' Greenie, one at a time, then heaved them into the back.

After returning to the house to get her purse and to lock up, she climbed into the truck and drove to Rick's veterinary clinic since she had no idea where he lived.

But when she pulled into the parking lot, which was nearly empty, she spotted Rick's truck.

Apparently, this was where Joe had holed up. Well, she'd just leave the bags with him and be done with it.

Better yet, she'd tell him he could just come outside and get the fool things himself. So she headed for the entrance to the clinic and stepped into the waiting room.

The moment Joe spotted her, he got to his feet. She felt like lighting into him, but she didn't see the use. "Sheriff Hollister stopped by with two duffel bags. I told him that I'd give them to you. They're in the back of the pickup."

His expression softened a bit. "Listen, Chloe. I'm sorry if I might have come across a little harsh."

She stiffened. "A *little* harsh? You were a complete jerk."

He raked a hand through his hair. "I didn't mean to

jump you the moment I entered the house. It just happened. All the memories and bottled emotions erupted. And I should have at least thanked you for what you did for me. You didn't deserve to get reamed. I just need some time to think things through."

"Take all the time you want," she said. "But first come outside and get those duffel bags."

Before either of them could make a move, her cell phone rang. She glanced at the display. The Sheltering Arms?

"Excuse me. I need to take this."

When she answered, Merrilee said, "Chloe, I'm sorry to bother you, but I thought you'd want to know."

Her heart dropped to the pit of her tummy. Could this day get any worse? "What's wrong?"

"Ethel took a turn for the worse, so I called 9-1-1. Paramedics took her to the Brighton Valley Medical Center."

"Is she okay?"

"No, she's had a complication."

Chloe knew what her friend was going to say before she even said a word. Still, she asked, "What happened?"

"She was diagnosed with pneumonia and given an injection of penicillin. I'm afraid she had a serious allergic reaction, so they sent her to ICU."

"I'll head over to the hospital now. I'm going to ask the nursing staff to see if her allergy was noted in her chart. I bet it wasn't."

"What'll you do if you're right?"

Chloe left Joe standing in his brother's waiting room and headed for the door. "After I talk to Dr. Nielson at the hospital and check on Ethel, I'm going to the Sheltering Arms. It's time I took Sam's advice."

"What'd he say?"

"Sometimes you gotta stand up for what's right."

"What are you going to do? You don't even work here any longer."

"I don't care. If Sarah lied to me about Ethel's allergy being noted in her chart, or if she assumed that it was and didn't double-check to make sure, I'm going to blow the whistle on her, as well as the entire administration for not doing something about my initial complaint sooner."

"I was afraid of losing my job before," Merrilee said. "But I'm not going to stand by and let Sarah risk another patient's life. I'll back you up any way I can."

"Thanks. I'll let you know if there's anything you can do to help."

Chloe was unlocking the driver's door, sliding behind the wheel and turning on Ol' Greenie's ignition before she noticed that Joe had followed her outside.

He might want to talk, but she'd have to deal with him later. In fact, she probably ought to thank him for pumping her full of courage and spunk. Because right now, the normally mild-mannered, former nurse's aide who'd avoided confrontations at all costs was cocked and loaded for bear.

After Chloe drove away, Joe stood in the parking lot, trying to make sense of it all.

He was still standing there, staring in the direction Ol' Greenie had gone, when Rick came out of the clinic. If his brother noticed anything weird about the way Joe was gaping or at the confusion that had to be splashed on his face, he didn't say anything.

"I'm finished here," Rick said. "Let's go home."

"Okay." Joe nodded at the duffel bags resting on the ground. "Let's put these in the back of your truck."

Minutes later, Rick pulled into the drive of a white, two-story house on Chinaberry Lane. After grabbing both bags and the sack of Joe's clothes, they entered the front door.

"Honey," Rick called out, "I'm home."

The words had a nice ring to them, and Joe was happy for his brother.

When a beautiful blonde with an obvious baby bump entered the living room with a warm and welcoming smile, Joe reached out his hand in greeting.

Mallory took it and gave it a gentle squeeze, but instead of letting go, she blessed him with a smile. "Would you mind if I gave you a hug, Joey? You have no idea how happy your brother is to have you back in his life—and how excited I am to have you home in time for Christmas."

As weird and awkward as it might have once seemed to be reunited with people he'd once thought he'd never want to see again, the sincerity in Mallory's gaze made it pretty darn easy to...well, to lower his guard and step into her embrace.

"Thanks, Mallory. I appreciate...having a home where I can...spend the holiday."

"Where's Lucas?" Rick asked.

"He's at Jimmy's," Mallory said. "He'll be back at four. Do you want me to call and ask him to come home now?"

"No, let him play. There's plenty of time to introduce him to his uncle." Rick turned to Joe. "Why don't I show you to your room so you can put that stuff away?"

"Sure." Joe followed his brother upstairs and to the guest room.

"Would you like a soda or iced tea?" Rick asked.

"Maybe later. If you don't mind, I'd like to go through my bag and see what's inside."

"Take your time. I'll be downstairs." When Rick stepped back into the hall, he paused and glanced over his shoulder. "Want me to close the door and give you some privacy?"

"That's not necessary."

Rick had no more than left the room when Joe began to rummage through his bag. When he found a couple of photographs, he paused to look at them.

One was a picture of him, Rick and Clay shooting baskets at the park. That photo must have been taken right before he and Rick had been separated and placed in different foster homes.

The anger that had exploded inside him back at the ranch began to make sense. Only now, it was targeted at the people who'd hurt him the most—his uncle for being a mean drunk, his aunt for allowing her husband to abuse her and the system that had taken him away from the one person who'd always taken care of him.

But he was no longer angry at Rick, as he'd been when he'd first run away. Looking back, as an adult, Joe couldn't blame his brother for wanting to escape their childhood. Or for wanting to create a home with Mallory.

His thoughts drifted to Chloe, to the night he'd held her in his arms after making love. At the time, he'd wanted to create a home for himself, too, a place where he felt like decorating Christmas trees, eating scones and sipping hot cocoa.

But Joe had pretty much ruined any chance of a dream like that happening, especially with Chloe. It hadn't seemed to matter an hour ago, but he wasn't so sure about that now.

Was it Chloe who'd made him yearn for home and hearth? Or was it just being at the Rocking C itself?

When things had escalated at his foster home and then again at school, Joe had made up his mind to run away for good. He'd had enough and wanted to put it all behind him—the embarrassment following his uncle's arrest for domestic violence, the trouble with the principal, the perceived abandonment of his brother.

He had a little money from working on the Rocking C that summer and, instead of purchasing a ticket all the way to L.A., where someone might find him—if anyone cared to look—he purchased tickets for the trek in segments. He traveled first to San Antonio, then to El Paso and on to Albuquerque. He'd intended to end up in Los Angeles.

The only person who knew of his plan—and the only one he'd told goodbye—was Dave, who'd kept his secret as promised.

So at sixteen, Joe left town—and his past—behind him. And he never—well, he rarely—looked back.

He set the photo aside and picked up another, this one taken somewhere in Arizona with the marines who'd become his friends and family.

There'd been a bad accident on the interstate on the final leg of his trip. The marines had been on leave and were returning to their duty assignment in Yuma when they'd pulled up alongside his bus and immediately jumped out and became heroes that day.

Joe had always helped the underdogs, like Dave Cummings and Clay Jenkins, when they'd been bullied in high school. He'd also tried to protect his aunt, only to get battered for his efforts. But when Red Conway, an older marine, actually asked for Joe's assistance, he'd stepped up, of course, gaining respect and hero status in the process.

After the accident, the sergeants were in a hurry to get back to Yuma so they wouldn't be AWOL. But instead of riding with the other passengers on a different bus to Los Angeles, Joe hitched a ride with his new friends. Red offered him a place to stay, and they all took him under wing, each one replacing the big brother he'd once had.

The day he turned eighteen, in an attempt to embrace his future by shedding his past and everything that reminded him of the lost boy he'd once been, Joe began the process to legally change his name. His marine buddies encouraged him to get his GED and to join the corps, helping him set a goal and find a purpose.

Joe set the picture aside and picked up one of him and Dave outfitted in matching camouflage. Dave had followed in Joe's footsteps and enlisted a few years ago.

But in spite of getting through boot camp, Dave had a tough time making the transition from the coddled only son of an overbearing rancher to a marine. So like his buddies had done for him, Joe took Dave under his wing, doing his best to coach him and help when he could.

When he found out that Dave had been assigned to his battalion, he asked Red to pull a few strings, and they managed to get him transferred to the same squad, where Joe could look out for him.

But Dave had never been cut out to be a devil dog. Or a grunt. Chloe had been right when she'd said he was too sensitive.

Joe had always liked the guy, but he could become needy and emotional when things got tough. In fact, Joe remembered wondering what a pretty girl like Chloe saw in Dave. He'd figured money or property had interested her more. And that might have been where his angry, suspicious vibes had originated.

Sure, Dave's family owned a ranch, but if a woman who looked like Chloe had wanted to get her hands on some quick cash, she certainly could have set her sights a lot higher than Dave.

Joe's stomach flopped and his face heated as he thought of the insults he'd flung at her. Had he been so angry at Dave's senseless death, the loss of his career and his promise to return to the one place on earth he'd vowed to never step foot in again that he'd lashed out at the only person he could find to blame?

It seemed that way.

As he recalled how his words had hurt her, his gut twisted hard and tight.

Chloe had taken him in when he was a complete stranger. She'd befriended the elderly patients in the nursing home. And, from what he'd gathered after listening to her side of a telephone conversation, she'd just sped off to become a voice for them.

How had he forgotten all she'd done? How she'd made it fun to trim the tree, decorate the house, eat scones and drink hot cocoa?

And then, when he'd been caught in the throes of a

nightmare that had been more real than imagined, she'd sat on the bed, whispered soothing words, stroked his arm…

He'd fallen for her that night—for the woman she really was and not the woman he'd imagined her to be.

What a heartless fool he'd been.

Joe put his stuff back in his duffel and proceeded to empty out Dave's bag on the guest room bed. Uniforms and street clothes toppled out, as well as a few pieces of mail and a folder. He recognized Chloe's handwriting on one envelope. Joe had seen that letter when he'd packed up Dave's effects and set out on his Brighton Valley trip. But he hadn't wanted to read it then.

He pulled out the folded stationery to see what she'd had to say.

Dear Dave,

I'm sorry that you're far away from home and feeling so lonely. And while I appreciate your kind words, I have no idea where you got the idea that we were even dating, let alone engaged. You're a good man, and I pray each night for your safe return home.

I've taken a break from nursing school so that I can look after the ranch until you get here. I'd promised your mother that I'd do that, and when I make a commitment to someone I care about, I keep it.

But that's the only commitment I've made—to your mother. Once you get home, I'll move into a studio apartment near the junior college in Wexler. I considered waiting to tell you these things to your face, but it seemed that with each letter you wrote, your dream of a future with me grew. And I don't want to give you false hope.

Someday you'll find a woman who truly loves you—and one who deserves you and all you have to offer her.

I hope you understand. In the meantime, please take care of yourself.

Your friend, Chloe

She'd been right. Her letter had been direct, but gentle and kind. And Dave had made a reckless choice.

What had Joe done?

Chloe hadn't wanted the ranch. Or anything from Dave—certainly not the guilt from his suicide, if that's what he'd actually done. Yet, Joe had accused her of all of that and so much worse.

He needed to see her, talk to her and apologize. How could he have been such an ass?

Before he could shove Dave's stuff back into the bag and head downstairs, Mallory knocked on the doorjamb and poked her head in. "There's a call for you. It's a Mr. McDougall."

She handed him the cordless phone, and he took the call.

"Is this Joe Wilcox?" the man asked.

Joe wondered how he knew where to find him. "Yes, it is."

"I'm the attorney handling David Cummings's estate. I'm not sure if Chloe Dawson mentioned me or told you I would call, but she gave me your contact number."

Chloe had said something about talking to an attorney. At the time, he'd thought that she'd been trying to stake her claim. But in reality, she'd probably been as overwhelmed with the situation as he'd been. And she'd merely wanted to hand over the reins to the ranch and get on with her life.

"She mentioned it," Joe said, "but I don't really know the details."

The attorney spoke of the probate process and filing paperwork as Joe's mind drifted to how he could apologize to Chloe for all of the horrible things he'd said.

What would he do if she refused to forgive him?

"So," McDougall said, "as dual beneficiaries, you might want to consider working together to make a go of the ranch."

"Excuse me?" Joe didn't want to admit that he hadn't been paying attention, but it was the truth. "I missed the last part."

"I said, if the will you told Chloe about holds up, she'll inherit the ranch. It's in debt, but it has a lot of potential, and I know that the Cummings family would have wanted Dave's legacy to continue on. So you might want to consider using a portion of the life insurance benefits you're going to receive and offer her a loan so she can make a go of it."

"I'm sorry. Did you say benefits *I* would receive?"

"Yes, Mr. Wilcox. You're the sole beneficiary of Dave Cummings's five-hundred-thousand-dollar life insurance policy."

Joe almost collapsed on top of the stuff littering the bed. "But his death was… I mean, won't you need a death certificate?"

"I've already checked into that. The coroner ruled it an accidental overdose, which is a real shame." McDougall went on to explain that it would take some time to file everything properly and again suggested Joe work with Chloe to get the ranch back up and running.

"But does she even want the ranch?" Joe asked.

"Who's to say? I don't know many people who would take on that kind of responsibility even if it was forced on them. But Chloe Dawson is a sweet girl, and Teresa thought the world of her. It'll be hard for her to keep it, though. You definitely got the better end of the deal."

After the call ended, Joe's mind reeled with everything the attorney had disclosed. He reached for the picture of him and Dave, a somewhat goofy-looking guy who'd never stood a chance with Chloe.

Yet just hours ago, Joe had stood a damn good chance with the most kindhearted and beautiful woman in the world, and he'd thrown it away.

But he wasn't about to let her go without a fight. And he wasn't going to waste another minute in preparing for battle.

After checking on Ethel at the Brighton Valley Medical Center and having a chat with Dr. Nielson, Chloe had pulled into the parking lot of the Sheltering Arms and braced herself for a confrontation with the administrator. She was done hiding from arguments and was going to give him a piece of her mind.

So she marched right into Anthony J. Peabody's office and demanded to speak to him.

The slightly balding man looked up from his desk, rolled back his chair and crossed his arms. "Is this about losing your job?"

"No, it's about yours, Mr. Peabody—and Sarah Poston's. I warned you about her unprofessional behavior and her disregard for most of the patients, but you wouldn't listen to me. Instead, you got rid of me for being a squeaky wheel. But you won't get rid of me so easily this time."

"Is that a threat?"

"No, it's a promise. Ethel Furman is in the ICU right now, and it's all Sarah's fault."

"That's a pretty strong accusation. Ethel has pneumonia."

"Yes, and she also had a severe allergic reaction to the penicillin they gave her in the E.R. I warned Sarah about Ethel's allergy on several occasions and insisted that she order a new medical alert bracelet and that she note it in the chart."

"What did she say?" Mr. Peabody asked.

"That the bracelet was on order. And that her allergy was already noted in her chart. But rather than double-check to make sure, she refused to do so."

"Maybe someone in the E.R. didn't look at the chart that accompanied her in the ambulance."

Chloe crossed her arms. "I'm not sure what relationship you have with Sarah—familial or romantic—but you'd better stop trying to defend her without checking the facts. I spoke to Dr. Betsy Nielson just a few minutes ago, and she told me her allergy to penicillin definitely *wasn't* noted in the chart. Then she showed me herself. Sarah is guilty of lying or negligence. I suggest you figure out which one it is and deal with it—before Ethel's attorney contacts you about a lawsuit."

Mr. Peabody blanched, then swallowed—hard. "Ms. Poston and I aren't related in any way, shape or form. And I assure you that I'll check into your allegation."

"See that you do." Then Chloe turned on her heel and strode out of the admin office. Her steps didn't slow until she reached the lobby and spotted Joe chatting with several of the elderly patients who'd gathered near the Christmas tree in their wheelchairs or seated with their canes and walkers nearby.

She had no idea what Joe was doing here, but he'd better duck for cover because she was feeling pretty cocky after her last confrontation. And she wasn't the least bit concerned about having another blowup—even here in the lobby.

As she neared the older men, all of whom were military vets, she realized Joe was holding court and sharing war stories. Or so it seemed.

Sam Darnell was one of them, and while he looked especially lively seated with the other vets, she couldn't help her snippy tone when she addressed Joe. "What are you doing here?"

He got to his feet, but not with any of the bluster he'd had earlier. "I came to find you and apologize."

The wind should have died in her sails, but she was too angry and primed for battle to back down now. No simple apology would be enough to assuage the hurt she'd felt at being called a gold digger and being blamed for Dave's suicide.

"You're going to need to do a lot more than hang out with some of my friends, trading battlefield gossip to make up for the things you said."

"Battlefield gossip?" Sam swore under his breath. "I'll have you know that a war zone is no beauty parlor, missy."

She turned to the old cowboy, arms crossed. "I realize that. But Sergeant Wilcox shot a bazooka through my heart. Did he tell you about that?"

Sam aimed a furrowed gaze at Joe. "That true, son?"

Oh, how the tide was shifting. While these silver-haired vets might want to support a fellow marine, Chloe was the one who brought them their magazines and their favorite bakery treats.

Semper fi or not, if Joe didn't watch his step, he'd be facing a possible mutiny from his new cohorts.

"Yes," he admitted. "It's true. I said things out of misplaced anger and an emotion I'd never had to deal with before."

Ralph Mason, who refused to wash his WWII hat or replace it with a new one, leaned toward Joe. "You know, son, they have those PTSD programs over at the VA clinic. My nephew runs one of the support groups. You'd probably get a lot out of it."

"Thanks," Joe told him. "But I'm not talking about PTSD emotions, Ralph. I'm talking about love."

Chloe sucked in her breath. Did he just say what she thought he did?

Cliff Hawkins, a Korean War vet, chimed in. "My daughter joined one of those dating websites when her cheating ex-husband left her for that waitress over at that new cafeteria in Wexler. I'll bet they could help you find the right match."

Joe patted the wheelchair-bound vet on the knee. "That won't be necessary, Cliff. I already found the woman I love, although I have a whole lot of apologizing to do."

As he made his way toward Chloe, those amazing blue eyes zeroing in on her, turning her spine to mush and setting her heart on end, her anger dissolved. Only her wobbly knees supported her now.

Joe was within arm's reach when he said, "I just have

to convince her that she needs me just as much as I need her. And if she'll just give me a chance, I'll prove it."

"Ah hell," Ralph said. "Women don't need a man these days, son. What you gotta do is convince her that you'll love her no matter what and always buy her new dresses and promise to let her mother live with you, even when you hate the old biddy."

As much as Chloe wanted to scowl, she couldn't help smiling at the advice Joe's new cronies were giving him.

Nor could she tear her eyes away from the intensity and sincerity in his gaze.

He took her by the hand, and while her damaged ego and frail heart urged her to pull away, she didn't move a muscle.

"I love you," he said. "And I was a fool to think those awful things about you. And I was a real ass for saying them out loud. My amnesia was no excuse, but when all those memories came rushing back to me, I was overcome with all those old emotions I'd kept locked away. I didn't know who I was, but I do now. And I want to share that man with you—and let you know that he'll always stand beside you and always have your back."

Emotion clogged Chloe's throat, and she wasn't sure she could get the words out, even if she tried.

But the truth was, she'd seen the man Joe was talking about. She'd known he was there all along. And she wanted to trust him, to believe him.

But could she?

"Okay," Sam said, "Don't make the devil dog grovel, missy. Can't you just give him a second chance? If he lets you down again, he'll have to answer to me."

"He'll have to answer to all of us," Ralph said.

She almost choked on a laugh before George Eggleston added, "If Joe says he's sorry, you can believe it. Now go on and prove it to her, boy."

Before Chloe could respond, Joe followed the old man's advice and did just that, lifting her in his arms and kissing her with all the love he'd said he felt.

When they came up for air, she asked, "What about the ranch?"

"What about it? You can sell it or keep it—whatever you want. I now realize that you never really wanted it. Just know that I'll stand by whatever you decide to do. If you want to go back to nursing school, I'll even volunteer to let you practice poking me with hypodermic needles. I just want to be with you. I love you, Chloe Dawson."

Then he kissed her a second time while the men behind him erupted in cheers as if it was V-day all over again.

And that gave her pause—and the courage to broach the dream she'd kept hidden from him before.

"What about these guys?" she asked. "What if I wanted them to all come home and live on the ranch with us?"

Joe merely smiled, his eyes bright. "I've got the money to make that dream happen for you. Come to find out, I got an inheritance, too. So all you have to do is say the word."

"The word is I love you, too, Joe Martinez Wilcox." Then she kissed him again with all the love in her heart.

Epilogue

When Joe and Chloe arrived at Rick and Mallory's house for Christmas, their hosts opened the front door before they could even get out of the new truck Joe purchased to replace Ol' Greenie.

Just two weeks ago, he didn't even know he had a family. And now he was spending the holidays with his brother and sister-in-law, his nephew, and his soon-to-be fiancée—assuming Chloe said yes when she opened her Christmas gift.

As Joe reached into the back of the truck for their presents, Chloe carried a foil-covered pan up the sidewalk.

"What do you have there?" Mallory asked. "You didn't need to bring anything."

"Rick will want these," Joe said. "I used Tía Rosa's recipe. It won't be Christmas without them."

"You brought tamales?" Rick asked as he ushered them inside. His eyes lit up as he breathed in the spicy scent from the still-warm pan.

"I sure did."

Neither man mentioned the fact that most Christmases after their parents died hadn't been merry or bright. They'd often been ruined by their uncle's drunken escapades or alcoholic rants. But one thing they could always count on having were *Tía*'s tamales.

From what Joe had heard, their aunt and uncle's home was a happy one these days. So he planned to visit them sometime next week.

"I'd planned to bring some of my cranberry orange scones," Chloe told Mallory, "But Joe ate them all."

"Don't worry. Megan, Clay's wife, has been baking up a storm and brought a ton of desserts. Come on, I'll show you. She's in the kitchen, setting them out."

Joe had been looking forward to seeing Clay, his old high school buddy. He was also eager to meet Megan. He'd heard she was not only a fabulous cook, but had just launched her own line of homemade jams and preserves. There was talk of her opening a bakery, too.

"Did you hear what happened to drunk Larry?" Rick asked.

That was the driver of the Silverado that had hit Joe outside the Stagecoach Inn. "I knew his wife talked him into turning himself in right before Sheriff Hollister was going to make an arrest. And that he's out on bail."

"Apparently he decided to celebrate his freedom at a bar in Wexler two nights ago and was involved in another accident."

"No kidding? You'd think he would have learned his lesson."

"This time he hit a squad car driven by one of Wexler's finest," Rick said. "So it looks like he won't be driving or drinking for a while."

Joe was glad to hear that.

"Come on." Rick placed a hand on Joe's back. "Let's go find Clay."

"Good idea."

The reunion between the men—once three of Brighton Valley's most notorious outcasts—was soon filled with good-natured teasing and laughter. They didn't do much reminiscing, since none of them had the kind of past that had made Christmas special. But in true holiday spirit, they focused on the new blessings life had brought their way.

As Joe glanced around the crowded house, he saw that the kids were having a good time, too. His nephew Lucas, who actually did look a whole lot like him, had hit it off with Tyler, Clay and Megan's son. The boys sat near the tree, checking out their new video games and trying to decide which one to play first. And Lisa, Tyler's sister, was begging to go outside and try out her new soccer ball.

As Mallory passed out the eggnog, Rick stopped her long enough to pat her baby bump. A warm and tender moment passed between the obviously happy couple, which was enough to make Joe both grateful and envious at the same time. Maybe, if things went the way he hoped they would, he and Chloe would be adding to the Martinez clan one of these days.

"With the way the family is growing," Rick said, "we may have to move this party to the ranch next Christmas."

"I'd love that," Chloe said as she joined Rick near the hearth.

"Speaking of the ranch," Mallory said, "is the probate going okay?"

"Mr. McDougall seems to think it should move along without any snags. And once that's done, we should be able to start making changes to the ranch house and open the Brighton Valley Retired Cowboys' Home. We hope to welcome our first residents by spring."

"Actually," Joe said, "Sam Darnell, our first cowboy, will be moving in next week. He's a great guy. You'll have to come meet him. He'll be helping me learn the ins and outs of ranching."

"I never expected you to grow up to be a cowboy, Joey." Rick chuckled and gave him a brotherly nudge. "Of course, I never expected you to be a soldier, either."

"Why's that?" Joe asked.

"Because I wouldn't have thought you'd make it through boot camp."

"Well, I did. And if you think that was unbelievable, you're about to see a real miracle." He grabbed the wrapped box from beneath the tree and headed toward Chloe, who was seated on the sofa, talking to both Megan and Mallory.

Joe handed her the large gift with a bright red bow. "Merry Christmas, Chloe."

She looked at it in confusion, probably wondering when he'd had a chance to buy her anything. Then her gaze lifted to his. "But, Joe, I thought we weren't exchanging gifts until tomorrow morning."

Well, some of the things he'd bought her, like the black lace nightie he'd picked up at The Cowboy Connection in Houston, would have to wait until they were alone. But this was one he wanted to give her in front of his family and friends.

"I know," he said, "but indulge me and open this tonight." He stood before her and waited as she slowly removed the ribbon and unwrapped the box.

When she lifted the lid and spotted the red cowboy

boots she'd admired, her breath caught and a smile burst across her pretty face. "Joe, you remembered!"

He grinned, his heart swelling until he felt like the hero the military claimed he was.

"Try them on," he said.

"I'm sure they'll fit. Besides, I'd rather try them on at home."

"Please. Do it for me. I'd like to see how they look on you."

She balked one more time, but at his gentle urging, she removed her shoes. Then she slipped her foot partway into the right boot and frowned. "There must be cardboard or something shoved in there to keep the shape."

After removing her foot, she reached into the boot to retrieve whatever was stuffed inside, only to find a small, black velvet box. She gasped, then studied it in awe before realizing Joe had placed it there and had intended for her to find it.

By the time she flipped open the lid and spotted the sparkling diamond ring, Joe was down on one knee. "I love you, Chloe Dawson. Will you marry me?"

Her eyes sparkled, and she broke into a happy smile. "Yes!"

Then she wrapped her arms around his neck and kissed him, making a Christmas memory neither of them would ever forget.

* * * * *

MAVERICK CHRISTMAS SURPRISE

BRENDA HARLEN

To my MAC girls – Stacy, Freda, Elena & Jen – with
thanks for so many fabulous memories
(and in anticipation of many, many more!).

Prologue

Dallas, Texas
Christmas Eve

Beth Ames couldn't help but sing along with the holiday song on the radio. Christmas had always been her favorite time of the year, and she was even more excited this holiday season because it was her nephew's first. Four-month-old Cody was the love of her life, and she was grateful—if a little surprised—that her sister had invited her to celebrate the milestone occasion with them.

Over the years, the relationship between Beth and Leighton had been strained more often than not. While Beth might wish it wasn't so, she couldn't change the dynamic on her own, and her sister had always rebuffed her efforts to get closer. That had finally changed when Leighton confided to Beth that she was pregnant.

No doubt Leighton had been scared about the prospect of having and raising a child on her own, now that the baby's father was no longer a part of her life. Of course, Beth had questions about the man, but Leighton refused to answer them. And the more she pushed, the more her sister resisted.

"I appreciate your support, but I don't need your lectures," she'd said. "So if you want to be there with me when the baby is born, you'll stop asking about a guy who, I can assure you, has less than zero interest in being a dad."

Beth wondered how her sister could be so certain of his disinterest if she hadn't told him about her condition, but she bit her tongue. Because as much as she believed the father-to-be had a right to know, she didn't want to do anything to jeopardize their tentative truce.

Instead, Beth had focused on doing what she could to support Leighton throughout her pregnancy. She'd coached her during sixteen hours of labor, and she'd spent every free minute with the new mom and her baby during the first few weeks—until Leighton had recovered enough to demand some space.

Still, she understood that motherhood was a big adjustment for her usually vivacious and fun-loving sister, and she tried to help without stepping on the new mom's toes. But as the weeks turned into months, Leighton seemed increasingly worn out and unhappy.

Thankfully the onset of the Christmas season had revived her sister's good spirits. She'd been so genuinely filled with holiday spirit that she'd invited Beth to spend Christmas Eve at her apartment and even stay over to share in the morning celebration.

So now here she was, with her back seat full of festively wrapped presents and a box of groceries to prepare the holiday meal.

She didn't see her sister's car in its assigned parking spot, but it wouldn't be out of character for her to have forgotten something she needed to have before the stores closed. And since Leighton had given her a spare key, Beth didn't hesitate to let herself in so that she could put the perishables in the fridge.

After the groceries were away, she plugged in the Christmas tree lights and turned on the radio, tuning it to her favorite station that had been playing "all holiday music, all the time" since the first of December.

Feeling excited, and a little impatient, Beth decided to

call her sister to find out when she'd be home. She was surprised, when the phone started to ring, to hear an echo of the sound coming from the bedroom—where she discovered Leighton's cell plugged into the charger on the bedside table.

Shaking her head over her sister's forgetfulness, she started to turn away when she saw a note beside the charger with her name on it.

Beth,
Change of plans—sorry. I'll explain when I can.
Merry Christmas.
XO
L

Change of plans?

What the heck was *that* supposed to mean?

Where had her sister gone?

And, more important, *where was Cody*?

Chapter One

Rust Creek Falls, Montana
Christmas Day

And another one bites the dust, Wilder thought, listening to the excited chatter of conversation around the table as everyone congratulated Hunter and Merry on their engagement.

But he kept a smile on his face, because his brother was grinning, the bride-to-be was glowing and six-year-old Wren was ecstatic that her Christmas wish for a new mommy had come true. He was happy for Hunter and Merry and the new family they were making together, but he was also grateful that he wasn't shackled with the responsibilities of a wife or child.

Not that any of his siblings acted as if they were constrained by their relationships. In fact, his brothers Logan, Xander, Knox, Finn and now Hunter, too, seemed sincerely happy to have found a special someone to share their lives. But Wilder wasn't in any hurry to follow in their footsteps. He was perfectly happy with his life the way it was right now. As the old saying went, "if it ain't broke, don't fix it."

"I'm a lucky woman," Merry said, responding to a comment from one of her future brothers-in-law.

"And Hunter's a lucky man," Max said, about his newly engaged son.

Wilder couldn't help but notice that, in addition to the paternal pride on his father's face, there was a look of smug satisfaction. When the family had moved from Dallas to Rust Creek Falls six months earlier, Max had set out to find romantic matches for all of his sons—even going so far as to enlist the services of a local wedding planner to act as a matchmaker and offering her a million-dollar bonus if she succeeded. With the announcement of Hunter and Merry's engagement, he obviously felt as if he was well on his way to accomplishing his goal.

Five out of six was a pretty impressive success rate, Wilder acknowledged to himself. But his dad was doomed to disappointment if he expected to go six-for-six, because, at this point in his life, Wilder would rather be dead than wed.

"I'm lucky, too," Wren piped up, eager to be part of the conversation.

"You certainly are," Max agreed, and winked at his granddaughter before turning his attention back to the little girl's father and Hunter's fiancée. "And if there was any doubt about what was going on between you two, your daughter took care of that when she spilled the beans as soon as she ran into the house."

Wren's brow furrowed. "I didn't spill anything, Gramps," she said, obviously interpreting his remark literally. "I just said that Daddy's gonna marry Merry, and I get to be in the wedding and then she's gonna be my mom."

Yep, five out of six was impressive.

And now that five of his sons were happily settled, Max would no doubt focus all his attention on the sole remaining holdout.

Oh, hell.

Wilder didn't realize he'd spoken aloud until Hunter sternly admonished him with a single word: "Language."

"Sorry," he said, his apology automatic and sincere as he looked at each of the couples around the table.

"But I just realized that I'm the last Crawford bachelor standing."

His announcement of this uncomfortable truth was followed by several chuckles and teasing warnings from his siblings and their partners.

"I'm right there with you," Max pointed out to his youngest son.

"Says the man paying to get us all married off," Wilder noted dryly.

"Suck it up, kid," Finn said, with absolutely no sympathy in his tone. Because why should he feel sorry for his little brother? Finn was happily married to Avery and anticipating the birth of his first child with his bride of two months.

Then Finn shifted his attention to Hunter and Merry. "I guess this means that you two will be the next Crawford couple to take on the mysterious diary."

The book he was referring to had been discovered beneath a loose floorboard shortly after they'd moved into the two-story log home on the Ambling A Ranch. Apparently the "A" was for "Abernathy"—the name of the family who'd originally owned the property. A jewel-encrusted "A" was also on the front cover of the diary, suggesting the book had belonged to a member of the family.

Merry looked at her fiancé. "With everything going on, I almost forgot to tell you what I found out the night of Wren's play."

But whatever she'd learned would remain unknown to the rest of them a while longer, as an unexpected knock at the door interrupted her announcement.

Wilder's gaze moved around the table again, confirming that everyone who was supposed to be there for the family meal was present and accounted for.

So who the heck would be visiting on Christmas Day?

He pushed his chair away from the table to find out. Hunter stood at the same time, and the brothers made their way through the kitchen toward the source of the summons.

As Hunter opened the door, Wilder's attention was snagged by a blur of color on the driveway. By the time he registered that it was a red car, he was staring at taillights as the vehicle drove off. Fast. He squinted, trying to decipher the license plate, but the car was already too far away. The best he could do was to note that the plate was from Texas.

"I guess whoever knocked must have realized they were at the wrong place," he decided, despite a niggling feeling that he should have recognized the departing car.

"Or they did what they came here to do," his brother suggested.

Wilder glanced questioningly at Hunter, then followed the direction he was pointing and discovered an infant car seat on the porch—with a baby inside!

"What the—"

"There's a note." Hunter bent down to fish out a piece of paper pinned to the blue blanket wrapped around the sleeping baby.

He unfolded the page to reveal a handwritten message in a distinctly feminine scrawl and began to read aloud:

"'Wilder—'" he glanced up from the page to give his brother a quizzical look before continuing "'—this is your baby. I've done the best I could for four months and I can't do it anymore. A boy needs a dad and you're Cody's, so it's your turn now. Please take good care of him.' It's signed 'L.'"

He looked at Wilder again. "Well, little brother, looks like you got a baby for Christmas."

Wilder snatched the paper out of Hunter's hand to read it for himself.

His brother said something else, but Wilder didn't hear him.

He stared at the writing on the page, as if he could will the words to change—or at least make sense of them. But none of this made any sense to him. It simply wasn't possible that he was the father of this kid.

Was it?

"What's going on out here?" Max wanted to know, pushing his way between his sons. "Good Lord…it's a baby."

"Wilder's baby," Hunter said and, miming the act of washing his hands, retreated into the house where the rest of the family was gathered.

His father pinned Wilder with his gaze. "You want to explain this?"

"I wish I could," he said. "But I've never seen the kid before. I'm as shocked by this as you are."

"But it's yours," his father remarked.

It wasn't a question.

"That's what the note says," Wilder acknowledged.

"You don't believe it?" Max asked him.

"I don't know what to believe. What to think." He scrubbed a hand over his face, sincerely baffled by this turn of events. He wanted to believe it was a joke, though he wasn't the least bit amused. "Who would abandon their kid on somebody's doorstep in the middle of winter?"

"Not just *somebody's* doorstep," his father argued. "The baby's father's doorstep."

He shook his head. "It's not possible."

"You've never been intimate with a woman?" Max challenged.

It was, of course, a rhetorical question. Though Wilder didn't share details of his romantic encounters, he'd been caught—more than once—sneaking into the house the morning after he'd spent the night in a woman's bed.

"I'm careful," he assured his father. *"Always."*

"Accidents happen," Max said matter-of-factly.

It was a terrifying thought.

"The note says he's four months old," his father continued. "Adding nine months to that is thirteen, which means the baby would have been conceived sometime around November last year."

"Okay," Wilder said hesitantly.

"So who were you with last November?" Max pressed.

Last November? *Seriously?*

He shrugged. "How am I supposed to remember something that happened that far back?"

Which he immediately realized was *not* the right thing to say to his father under the circumstances.

"You should darn well remember a woman who shared your bed," Max said, the low tone of his voice doing nothing to disguise the underlying anger and disappointment. "I don't expect you to be in love with every woman you sleep with, but you should know and respect her enough to remember her name."

"Give me a break," Wilder pleaded. "My head's spinning so fast, it's a wonder I know my own name right now."

"Well, there's no doubt the baby looks like a Crawford."

"The baby looks like a baby," Wilder said. Because in his admittedly limited experience with infants, they all looked like bald, chubby-cheeked, squalling little monsters.

As if on cue, the one buckled into the car seat started to squirm and squall.

Wilder stepped back, an instinctive retreat.

"Pick him up and bring him inside," Max said.

"Me?" Wilder was horrified by the very thought.

With a sigh, his father reached down and grabbed the

car seat with one hand and the enormous diaper bag with the other.

"Hunter said there was a baby on the doorstep," Avery said, entering the kitchen from the dining room at the same time that Wilder and Max came in from the porch.

Then she spotted the carrier in Max's hand and her expression softened. "Ohmygod—it *is* a baby." Her gaze shifted to Wilder. "Why didn't you tell anyone you're a daddy?"

"Because I'm *not*," Wilder insisted. "There's no way that kid's mine."

"He's in denial," Genevieve, his brother Knox's wife, said. Because apparently Hunter's announcement had drawn everyone away from the table.

"I think the baby's hungry," Lily said worriedly.

"You just want to feed everyone," her husband Xander teased.

"He is gnawing on his fist," Hunter noted. "And that's a telltale sign of hunger."

As Hunter was the only one of his brothers with significant daddy experience, Wilder was willing to defer to his expertise. But having the problem identified didn't give him the first clue about how to solve it.

So when his brothers and their partners—and Wren—huddled around the baby, pushing Wilder and Max out of the way, Wilder didn't object.

"He's definitely hungry," Sarah said, as the baby's unhappy cries turned to sobs.

"Let's see if there's a bottle in the bag," Merry suggested.

There were, in fact, two bottles—one premixed and one empty, plus a can of powdered formula.

Avery unbuckled the harness and lifted the infant out of his seat. His plaintive cries immediately ceased.

Everyone seemed to be talking at once, speculating

about the note as they fussed over the little guy. Wilder took advantage of their preoccupation to study the baby—who didn't seem quite so intimidating now that he was quiet—and realized, a little uneasily, that the baby was staring back at him.

Is it possible? he wondered. *Can he be mine?*

"Where'd the baby come from?" Wren wanted to know.

"Someone left him on the doorstep," her dad explained.

"Maybe he's a gift from Santa," she suggested.

Hunter chuckled. "Unfortunately for Uncle Wilder, I don't think the baby came with a gift receipt."

"He does look a lot like Wilder's old baby photos," Logan, the eldest Crawford brother, noted.

"He does not," Wilder denied, though without much conviction.

But no one was paying any attention to him, anyway.

Except his father, who sidled closer. "The note was signed with the letter 'L,'" Max noted. "Does that jog your memory at all?"

He automatically started to shake his head, because he didn't want his memory jogged. And if he was in denial—well, he was quite happy to stay there. Because in denial, his life was easy and carefree and he didn't have the responsibility of an infant who'd been dumped into his lap—or, to be more precise, on his doorstep.

But somehow, in the midst of all the chaos going on around him, hazy memories slowly came into focus in Wilder's mind. Memories of an early holiday party at Reunion Tower in Dallas, a few too many cocktails and a pretty—and very adventurous—blonde named Leighton Ames. And no, he wasn't oblivious to the fact that her name started with the same letter that had been scrawled on the bottom of the note.

They'd had a good time together, not just that night, but

for several weeks afterward. And then, just as suddenly as their relationship had started, it ended.

Her decision, Wilder remembered now.

Just after the New Year, she'd abruptly called things off. He'd been a little disappointed at first, but there were plenty of other women in the world. And truthfully, he hadn't thought of her again—until now.

Was Leighton the baby's mother?

Was it possible that he *was* the father of this baby who'd been abandoned on the doorstep?

But if she believed that to be true, why hadn't she ever told him that she was pregnant?

Well, he could probably guess the answer to that one. Either Leighton wasn't sure about the baby's paternity, or she didn't trust him to step up.

He would have, of course. He would have undoubtedly felt panicked and trapped, but he would have done the right thing. Not that she could have known that, because they hadn't had the type of relationship where they talked about their future hopes and dreams. Their conversations had been more along the lines of "your place or mine?" And after that question had been answered, there had been even less talking.

But if she hadn't trusted him to step up, why would she dump the baby on him now?

And how did she even know where to find him?

He'd had no communication with her in almost a year. And the last time they were together, he didn't know that he'd be moving to Rust Creek Falls, so it was unlikely she could have tracked him down here.

Reassured by his own reasoning that it couldn't have been Leighton who dropped the baby off—and conveniently ignoring the fact that his name was on the note—Wilder breathed a sigh of relief, confident that he was off the hook. But his father would require additional proof, so as the rest of the family went back into the dining room, he scrolled through the contacts in his phone to see if he still had her number.

Amazingly, he did, and tapped it to initiate the call.

"Hello?"

The female voice that immediately answered sounded frantic.

"Um...hi," he said. "I'm trying to reach Leighton Ames."

"You and me both," she replied, sounding as if she was fighting tears.

He frowned at that. "Is this still her number?"

"Yes, but she forgot her phone when she left." The woman on the other end of the line sighed. "Or maybe she didn't forget it."

Which didn't make any sense to him, but all he said was: "Well, if you hear from her, can you ask her to call Wilder Crawford?"

"Why?" She sounded both curious and wary. "What business do you have with my sister?"

Sister?

He couldn't recall Leighton mentioning a sister, but surely a sister would know if Leighton had had a baby. And if this was Leighton's baby, that meant the woman on the phone was the baby's aunt.

Before he could ask, she spoke again. "Wait a minute—did you say Wilder Crawford?"

"I did," he confirmed.

"I found your name and a Montana address scrawled on a Post-it note in Leighton's apartment," she said. "I think she might be on her way to see you."

The knots in his stomach tightened. "She might have been here already...and left something."

He heard a sharp intake of breath. "What kind of something?"

"A baby," he admitted. "Did she—"

"Cody!" she immediately interjected, not giving him a chance to finish. "You have Cody?"

"That's the name in the note," he confirmed.

"Note?" she echoed.

"The baby was left on my doorstep with a note."

"I don't understand. Why would she leave her baby?"

"I wish I knew," he told her.

"Are you Cody's father?" she guessed.

"Obviously your sister thinks so."

"You haven't seen her or talked to her?"

"Not in the past year."

"But Cody's with you? At the Ambling A Ranch in Montana?"

"That's right," he confirmed.

"Okay. I'll be there as soon as I can," she promised.

"Wait—"

But she'd already disconnected the call.

"What did you find out?" Max asked, when Wilder returned to the table where Lily had resumed serving dessert and Avery rocked the now quiet baby.

"The kid's mom is Leighton Ames," he said. "I spoke to her sister, but she doesn't know where she is or why she left the baby here."

"Because she wanted him to be with his dad," Max suggested as an answer to the latter question.

Wilder hoped like hell his father was wrong.

"Do you want ice cream with your pie?" Merry asked him.

Because for the rest of the family gathered together, today was still a celebration—and it was time for dessert.

"Sure," he said.

Though he wasn't even sure he wanted the pie now, he didn't want his family to know how freaked out he was about the arrival of the baby they were all happy enough to assume was his and turning down dessert would be a definite red flag.

"I want ice cream," Wren piped up, pushing her bowl toward her soon-to-be-stepmother who was scooping it.

"You already had ice cream," her dad reminded her, pulling the bowl back again before Merry could indulge the little girl's request.

Wren pouted and dragged her spoon around the inside of the empty vessel.

Wilder took the plate Merry passed to him and murmured his thanks. Then he halved the scoop of ice cream with the side of his fork and slid half into his niece's bowl.

Wren beamed at him; Hunter scowled.

"There's a reason I'm the favorite uncle," he said, and winked at the little girl.

"I'm finished with my dessert," Finn said to his wife then, "if you want me to take the baby."

"I can manage the baby," Avery assured him. "If you want to be helpful, you can start clearing the table."

As Finn began gathering empty plates and glasses, Wilder dug his fork into his pie, giving up the pretense of an appetite.

"Did you ask for a baby for Christmas, Uncle Wilder?" his niece asked, around a mouthful of ice cream.

"No." His response was immediate and definitive.

"I guess you're just lucky then," Wren decided.

Lucky?

Oh yeah, he had a horseshoe so far up his butt he couldn't swallow the pie that was stuck in his throat.

The house emptied quickly after dessert was finished and the cleanup complete, leaving Wilder and his father alone with the baby. Then Max took off, too, to pick up a crib he'd arranged to borrow from one of their many Crawford relatives in town.

Wilder had offered to make the trip, but his dad had insisted that he stay at the Ambling A to watch the baby. For the first half hour, there weren't any major snags—because the kid slept. But when he woke up, he was not in a very good mood.

The baby didn't cry. Not really. But his face was all scrunched up and he was squirming in his seat, and Wilder braced himself for the crying to start.

"Avery promised that you would sleep for a few hours," Wilder said, trying to reason with the infant. "That was barely more than an hour ago."

His words got the kid's attention, though, and he fixed his big, blue eyes on Wilder.

"You can't be hungry already," he continued, in the same logical tone. "You sucked back a whole bottle before she left."

The baby continued to fuss, clearly unconvinced and unhappy.

And his lower lip was starting to do that quivering thing that warned Wilder real tears and sobs likely weren't too far behind.

"I'm sorry," he said. "But I don't know what to do."

"You could try picking him up."

Wilder turned to see Hunter standing in the doorway. "I thought you'd gone home."

"I did," his brother confirmed. "And then I came back."

"Why?"

"Because I thought you might want to talk to someone who's been where you are."

On another day, Wilder might have made a snarky comment about not remembering when a baby had been left on Hunter's doorstep, but right now, he was too grateful for his presence to risk saying anything that might prompt him to leave again.

"I think I need a manual more than a sounding board," he confided.

"A manual would be useless," Hunter said. "Because every baby is different."

"So how am I supposed to know what's wrong with this one?"

"He's probably out of sorts because he doesn't know where his mama is."

"That makes two of us," Wilder said.

"And when babies are out of sorts, they need to be comforted."

He gestured to the infant in his carrier. "Feel free."

But his brother shook his head. "You need to step up."

"I would have stepped up months ago if Leighton had told me she was pregnant," he said in his defense.

"So why are you hesitating now?" his brother challenged.

"Because I don't have the first clue what to do with a baby."

"No first-time parent has a clue in the beginning."

His brother's matter-of-fact statement was hardly reassuring.

And while they were talking, the baby was growing more distressed.

With a sigh of resignation, Wilder unhooked the strap and lifted him out of the seat.

The baby stopped fussing for a moment to stare at him, as if waiting for something else.

Something more.

Wilder looked at his brother. "I'm doing this wrong, aren't I?"

"Babies generally like to be held closer than arm's length," Hunter told him.

Wilder pulled his arms toward his chest, so that he was almost nose-to-nose with the kid.

Hunter started to chuckle, but quickly covered it with a cough when Wilder glared at him.

"Closer," he urged. "But to the side, with his head about level with your shoulder so he can see behind you. With newborns, you need to keep one hand on the bottom and the other on the head and neck, for support, but he's obviously strong enough to hold his head up just fine."

Wilder did his best to follow his brother's instructions.

"That's it," Hunter assured him.

"He feels so tiny." His whispered remark was filled with awe and wonder—and just a hint of the nerves that were tangled up inside him. "So fragile."

"It's normal to be scared. I was terrified the first time I held Wren in my arms," his brother confided. "And she was a lot smaller than Cody is."

"But you had nine months to prepare yourself for her arrival," Wilder pointed out, though he wasn't sure anything could have prepared him for this moment.

Hunter nodded. "True."

Wilder patted the baby's back gently, as he'd watched Sarah do, and was rewarded with a shockingly loud belch.

"Gas might have been another cause of his distress," Hunter noted then.

"You think?" Wilder asked dryly.

"And now that it's out of his system, you can try the cradle hold," he said, and talked him through shifting the baby's position so that he was tucked in the crook of Wilder's arm. "Now sit down and relax."

Relax? He wasn't sure he'd be able to relax so long as there was a baby under his roof.

And though Leighton's note had given no indication that she was planning to come back for the little guy, he had to believe that she would. After all, what kind of mom just left her kid?

Mine, he thought, then shoved the unpleasant twinge from his mind.

Hunter took another seat at the table, leaning back in the chair and stretching his legs out in front.

Obviously relaxing wasn't a problem for him.

"Where'd Dad go?" he asked.

"To pick up a crib," Wilder told him.

"Ah, right. He said he was going to try to rustle up some of the stuff you'd need from local relatives," his brother recalled.

"Unfortunately, I don't think one of those things is a nanny."

Hunter chuckled. "No, he's been pretty clear that your baby is your responsibility."

"But we don't even know for sure that he is my baby," Wilder felt compelled to point out again.

"Obviously his mom is sure. Though I have to wonder, if you haven't kept in touch with her, how did she know where to find you?"

"I've been wondering the same thing. My best guess is Malcolm," Wilder said, naming a close buddy from Dallas. "When I talked to him a few weeks back, he'd mentioned that one of the girls we'd met at the holiday party before Christmas last year had shown up at his office to ask about me. But he told me that before Thanksgiving, and since nothing came of it..."

"Until now," Hunter remarked.

"Until now," he agreed.

"So the who and the how have been answered," his brother noted. "But we still don't know the why—beyond the obvious, of course."

"What's the obvious?" Wilder wondered.

"What 'L' wrote in her note—a boy needs a dad."

"Which proves she doesn't know me at all, or she'd know I'm not dad material."

"Or maybe she knows you better than you know yourself," Hunter suggested. "But since I'm not completely without sympathy, I'll give you a crash course in diapering and feeding."

"I can hardly wait," he said dryly.

"Or I can let you figure it out on your own," his brother suggested as an alternative.

"Please don't," he said, immediately remorseful. "I need all the help I can get."

"You're doing okay so far," Hunter assured him.

"Because I'm not doing anything."

"You've managed to relax," his brother pointed out. "And that's allowed Cody to relax, too."

Wilder looked down at the little guy tucked in the crook of his arm, close to his body.

He did look relaxed. Content even, his eyelids heavy, as if he might—fingers crossed—drift off to sleep again. And Wilder felt a small measure of satisfaction that he'd been the one to put that look on his face, though the satisfaction wasn't nearly strong enough to quell the rising tide of panic within him.

"I'm not ready for this," he confided. "I figured I had another ten years of footloose and fancy-free living before I even thought about getting serious with a woman—and then a few more after that before I had to worry about becoming a dad."

"There's nothing more serious than parenthood, or more amazing and awe-inspiring," Hunter told him.

The baby turned his head then, rubbing his cheek against the soft plaid of Wilder's shirt, just about where he felt his heart swell inside his chest.

And Wilder knew that whatever happened next, he and the kid were in this together.

Chapter Two

Beth turned up the radio and lowered the window a couple of inches, just far enough to allow the icy December air to sweep through the interior of her car and jolt her weary brain and sleepy body awake. Eager to get to Rust Creek Falls, she'd left Dallas almost immediately after ending her telephone conversation with Wilder Crawford, making only brief stops to fill her gas tank and use the bathroom. Now, after almost twenty-eight hours on the road, she was tired and hungry but refused to give in to either before she reached her final destination—and Cody.

She'd looked into flights to Montana, but the last-minute airfares and required connections made it more logical to drive. And now her journey was finally nearing its end.

She couldn't wait to see Cody again, to hold his chubby little body in her arms and breathe in his sweet baby powder scent. She'd been so worried when she found Leighton's note, but after talking to Wilder Crawford, she had reason to believe the baby was okay. She had no clue about her sister. Though Leighton had always been adept at taking care of herself, she hadn't quite been herself since the baby was born. Maybe it wasn't Beth's place to worry about her sister, but of course she *was* worried. And she was concerned that her sweet and innocent nephew was being used as a pawn in whatever game his mother was playing.

When Beth realized her sister was gone—likely headed

to Montana, where one of the previously unidentified potential fathers of her baby apparently now resided—she'd considered that Leighton might want to reconcile with her ex. And she'd hoped, for Cody's sake, that was her sister's plan.

But if what Wilder Crawford had told her was true, Leighton hadn't even spoken to the man in almost a year. So why would her sister travel all this way and then not see him? And why would she abandon her baby on his doorstep without any warning?

Maybe Leighton had decided that she needed a break from the day-to-day responsibilities of caring for Cody. But why not leave him in Dallas with his aunt? Why drive all the way to Middle-of-Nowhere, Montana—in the middle of winter, no less—and leave him with a stranger?

Even more than those questions baffled Beth's brain, the insult wounded her heart. She'd made every effort to be there for Leighton since she'd learned of her sister's pregnancy. She'd tried to offer support without judgment, help without expectation. And she'd cried tears of joy along with her sister when Cody drew his first breath—and let it out again as an indignant wail.

Beth would do anything for her nephew—including driving through the night and all the next day to get to him. Unfortunately she hadn't considered the changes in weather that she would encounter en route, and the tires on her fuel-efficient hatchback had been slipping and sliding in protest against the snow and ice that had been her near constant companion since Colorado Springs.

But according to the faded "Welcome to Rust Creek Falls" sign posted at the side the highway, she had finally arrived. She checked her speed as she drove down Cedar Street, noting that the storefronts were all decked out for the holidays with boughs of evergreen and big red bows and twinkling lights. Of course, it was late on the day after

Christmas, so the stores were closed, the roads mostly empty. No doubt all the town's residents were huddled comfortably in their homes, basking in the holiday afterglow and enjoying time with family and friends.

Certainly that was how she'd anticipated spending her holiday—not driving 1700 miles on her own, worry growing with each tick of the odometer. But missing out on the holiday didn't matter right now. All that mattered was Cody.

Once she was reunited with her nephew, she would think about how to track down her sister. Or maybe—fingers crossed—Leighton had already decided to return to Rust Creek Falls to pick up her baby and Beth would find her sister at the Ambling A when she arrived.

Continuing to follow the directions on her phone, she finally pulled into a long, winding drive that would supposedly lead her to the Ambling A. Assuming, of course, that her GPS wasn't sending her into the middle of a field where she'd get stuck in the snow and find herself surrounded by angry cows.

The drive had been plowed, but it was still snow-covered, making everything appear blindingly white when her headlights cut through the blackness of the night. She drove slowly, carefully, following the tire tracks to ensure she didn't veer off the road and end up in a ditch.

The dash clock read 10:14 when she finally saw the two-story log home. Parking behind a dark pickup, she felt a slight twinge of disappointment that she didn't see Leighton's car, but right now her main focus was Cody.

Still, she gave herself a moment to close her eyes that were burning with strain and fatigue. But only a moment, because any longer than that and she wasn't sure she'd manage to open them again. And anyway, as exhausted as she was, her nephew was inside that house, and she couldn't wait a minute longer to see him.

Grabbing her purse, she pushed open the door. The blast of frigid air was a stark reminder that she wasn't in Dallas anymore. Stepping out of the car, she nearly lost her footing on the snow-covered ground as the short-heeled boots that were perfectly suitable for winter in Texas proved to be no match for the ice and snow of Montana.

She blinked in the sudden brightness as a floodlight activated. A motion sensor, she guessed, grateful for the illumination as she moved carefully over the frozen ground.

There were no lights on inside the house, but she wasn't going to let that stop her now.

She noted the pine boughs draped over the railing of the porch and an enormous evergreen wreath decorated with a fancy velvet bow on the door—more reminders of the holiday she'd missed celebrating. She climbed the porch steps and, after a moment's hesitation, bypassed the bell to knock on the door instead.

When there was no response, she knocked a little harder.

Then harder again.

Finally, a light came on overhead, the door was wrenched open from the other side, and Beth found herself face-to-face with an obviously irritated man.

Actually, she was face-to-chest with his gray T-shirt, so she didn't see the scowl that furrowed his brow until she took an instinctive step back and lifted her gaze to his face.

In addition to the scowl, he was wearing a pair of flannel pajama bottoms low on his hips and the previously noted T-shirt that stretched across his muscular torso. He folded strong arms over his broad chest now and pinned her with a dark, piercing gaze, causing her to belatedly question the wisdom of showing up at a stranger's door on an isolated ranch in the middle of the night.

Because she was certain that the sudden dryness of her throat and pounding of her heart were signs of fear and not an immediate and instinctive attraction to the prime male specimen in front of her.

"I don't know where you're from, honey, but 'round here, people don't come visiting in the middle of the night," he said.

The growly timbre of his voice made her shiver.

Or maybe it was just the frigid air temperature.

"Dallas," Beth heard herself respond to what was obviously a rhetorical question. "And I'm not visiting—I'm here for my nephew."

"You're the woman who answered Leighton's phone," he concluded.

"Lisbeth," she said. "But most people call me Beth. And you must be Wilder."

He nodded and, after only a moment's hesitation, stepped away from the door to allow her to enter.

She had a vague impression of a kitchen beyond the entranceway, though the interior was only dimly illuminated by the light that filtered through the window from the porch. She kicked off her boots and left them on the mat by the door and unbuttoned her thin coat as she followed Wilder further into a house that was toasty warm in contrast to the frigid air outside. "Where's Cody?"

She sensed more than saw his frown this time. "Did your sister send you to get him?"

In retrospect, Beth would acknowledge that she should have answered his question with a firm and decisive *yes*. But in her agitated and sleep-deprived state, she wasn't thinking clearly enough to see the obvious solution to her dilemma.

"No, I still haven't heard from Leighton," she admitted instead. "And I'm starting to worry that something might have happened to her."

"I think what happened is that she got tired of being

tied down by a baby," he said, and handed her a piece of paper that he'd retrieved from the table.

As she unfolded the page, he turned on the light over the stove so that she'd be able to read it. Beth immediately recognized her sister's handwriting, and her heart sank as she skimmed the brief words. Then she read them more carefully.

"I don't understand," she said, after she'd scanned the note a third time.

"That makes two of us."

She looked at him again, noting the stubble that darkened his jaw and the overlong and tousled hair that suggested he'd just crawled out of bed. He was undeniably sexy with a slightly dangerous edge—exactly her sister's type.

None of which explained why she felt a quiver low in her belly when she found him looking back at her. Of course, it was probably just that she was overtired and overwhelmed and worried about her nephew. It certainly wasn't a visceral response to his nearness. It couldn't be.

She cleared her throat as she refolded the note and handed it back to Wilder. "I want to see Cody now. Please."

He hesitated, and for a moment, she thought he might refuse. But maybe he sensed that she wouldn't be put off—and that, if he even tried, she'd raise enough ruckus to wake the whole house—because he finally nodded.

She followed him through the darkness, up a set of stairs, then down a hall until he finally paused in an open doorway. She glanced past him, into a room dimly illuminated by a nightlight plugged in beside a crib.

"It looks like maybe you were expecting him," she noted.

He shook his head. "Maggie and Jesse—distant but local relatives—loaned us the crib. And the rocking chair."

Beth tiptoed to the crib, exhaling a long, quiet sigh of relief when she gazed down at the sleeping baby.

"It's okay, Cody. I'm here to take you home now." She murmured the words softly as she reached down to lift him into her arms and cuddle him against her chest. He squirmed a little at first, but settled quickly again without making a sound of protest.

Wilder stepped in front of the door, as if to block her path, and crossed those strong arms over his impressive chest again. "What are you talking about?" Though he kept his volume low so as not to disturb the sleeping infant, there was no mistaking the steel in his words. "You're not going anywhere with that baby."

"Of course, I am," she said. "I'm his aunt. He belongs with me."

"If his mother believed that, why'd she drive halfway across the country to bring him to me?" he challenged.

Beth faltered. "I don't know. But my sister's done a lot of things in her life that I can't begin to fathom."

"Well, it seems obvious to me that there must be a reason Leighton didn't want you caring for her baby."

"*Her* baby?" she echoed. "You don't think he's your baby, too?"

"I don't know what to think," he admitted. "But I know that it's late and this conversation should be tabled until the morning."

"Morning?" she echoed. "I expected to be halfway back to Dallas by morning."

"When was the last time you slept, Lisbeth?"

"It's Beth," she corrected automatically. "And…I'm not sure."

He nodded. "That's what I figured." He pointed to the rocking chair beside the crib. "Sit there with the baby for a few minutes while I make up the bed in the spare room across the hall."

"Oh. Um…thank you."

She hadn't expected an invitation to stay. Of course,

his words had been more in the nature of a command than an offer, but still, she was grateful. So she lowered herself into the rocking chair and snuggled with her nephew.

There were no words to express how happy she was to have Cody in her arms again, how grateful she was to know that he was safe. Worry and desperation had fueled her throughout the trip from Dallas—along with regular infusions of caffeine. But now that she was here, she felt completely drained—physically and emotionally.

She was also relieved that she didn't have to drive any further tonight, even if it was just back into town to rent a room at a local motel. Assuming there was a motel in this town.

In any event, it probably wasn't a bad idea for her to catch some shut-eye before embarking on the return journey.

It didn't take Wilder long to put sheets on the bed in the guest room. And yet, he wasn't surprised to return to the spare room that had been turned into a temporary nursery to find Beth fast asleep in the rocking chair, her nephew still in her arms.

Though he had no reason to doubt her claim that she was Leighton's sister, he couldn't see any obvious family resemblance. Leighton was a spirited blonde, and his first impression of Lisbeth was of a solemn brunette. With her messy ponytail and shapeless coat, Beth bore no physical resemblance to her curvy sister with the infectious laugh and lust for life.

And yet, there was something about Beth that sparked an unexpected—and unwanted—awareness inside him. Or maybe it was her obvious connection to her nephew that tugged at him. She'd wasted no time in making the trip from Dallas to Rust Creek Falls when she learned that he was there, which made him wonder again why Leighton had made the same trip to leave her baby with him when she had a sister who obviously would have been happy to care for the kid.

Unfortunately, he wasn't going to get an answer to that question—or any other questions—tonight. So he reached for the baby, intending to return him to the crib. Beth's arms instinctively tightened around the baby and her eyes flew open—a warrior ready to battle.

"I'm just putting him back in his bed so that you can go to yours," he told her.

She blinked, and he noticed then that she had really pretty eyes—the color of dark chocolate and fringed by a sweep of long, dark lashes.

Those lashes fluttered again as the confusion slowly cleared from her gaze. "Oh. Okay." She whispered her response as she finally relinquished her hold. "I guess I'm more tired than I realized."

"You can sleep now," he said, as she rose from the chair.

She nodded. "Thank you. For letting me stay here tonight."

He didn't point out that the offer had been born of necessity rather than kindness, because he couldn't have her knocking on the door of Strickland's Boarding House at this late hour. And the only other option nearby was Maverick Manor, but he'd heard the owner proudly remark that the hotel was fully booked through the holidays.

"Go." He steered her toward the open doorway across the hall. "There's an unopened toothbrush and toothpaste in the adjoining bathroom, if you need them."

"Thank you," she said again.

He turned back to peek at the baby again, exhaling a weary sigh of relief that the little guy was still sleeping soundly—at least for the moment—before starting toward his own room.

Thanks to the attention and efforts of his family, the baby had been well cared for the previous day. But eventually they'd all headed back to their own homes, leaving Wilder and his dad alone with the infant.

As a father of six boys, Max had had more than his fair share of experience with diapers and bottles, but he'd insisted that this baby was his youngest son's responsibility. Wilder didn't think it was fair that his father was willing to assume that he was the kid's dad just because some woman had scrawled his name at the top of the note.

"And because you admitted that you had a relationship with the mother," Max had explained, when Wilder challenged the assumption of paternity.

He couldn't deny that argument had some merit. That it wasn't entirely outside the realm of possibility that he could be the father.

And that possibility scared the bejeezus out of him.

And if Leighton had paused long enough to consider the implications of that possibility before depositing her child at his door, it would have scared the bejeezus out of her, too.

What had she been thinking?

Unfortunately, the answer to that question was probably that she *hadn't* been thinking.

By her own admission, she wasn't much of a planner. It was more fun, she'd once told him, to live in the moment and embrace whatever surprises life had in store for her.

When Wilder had confided that he wasn't a big fan of surprises, she'd surprised the heck out of him by inviting him back to her place.

And yeah, he'd liked *that* surprise.

This "surprise, you're a daddy" thing—not so much.

And if he really was the kid's dad…well, he couldn't help but feel sorry for the little guy, because there was no chance Wilder was ever going to win a "Father of the Year" award.

Chapter Three

Beth didn't remember her head hitting the pillow.

She fell asleep quickly and slept deeply, and when she opened her eyes again, the clock on the bedside table read 12:48 p.m.

Certain that number couldn't be accurate, she pressed the button on the side of her watch to illuminate its face.

12:48.

She jolted upright, shocked to realize that she'd slept for almost fourteen hours!

Her first thought after that: *Cody.*

She immediately pushed back the covers and hurried across the hall. Her heart, which had been pounding furiously against her ribs, settled into a more normal rhythm when she found her nephew in the crib, sleeping soundly.

She didn't believe for a minute that he was *still* sleeping. More likely, Cody had been up at 6 a.m.—as was his habit—and was now down for his second nap of the day. And because he was napping, she decided to steal a few more minutes for herself and indulge in a hot shower.

And it was an indulgence. She had no idea how old or new the house was, but it was apparent that the bathroom had been recently renovated with a mosaic tile floor and glass-walled shower. She stood for a long time beneath the rainfall shower head, letting the warm water wash over her body, easing the tension and aches in her muscles.

She used the shampoo and bodywash in the enclosure, as her own toiletries were in the duffel bag that she'd left in her car. Which meant that the change of clothes she'd packed for her overnight stay at her sister's apartment was still in the car, too.

As she wrapped herself in a thick, fluffy towel from the heated rack, she considered that ranching was obviously a much more lucrative profession than teaching. Not that she'd ever trade her class of kindergarteners for a field of cows, but she suspected that her sister might not have been so quick to discount the idea of spending her life with a cowboy if she'd known Wilder was a wealthy cowboy.

Of course, thinking about Leighton led to worrying about Leighton, even though Beth knew it was an exercise in futility. She had no way of getting in touch with her sister, so all she could do was monitor her social media accounts, check in with her friends and wait for Leighton to contact her—and ensure that Cody was taken care of while he waited for his mom to come back.

Because Leighton *would* come back. Notwithstanding what she'd written in the note she'd left with Cody, Beth knew that her sister wouldn't abandon her baby. She loved him too much.

Reassured by this internal pep talk, Beth toweled off and got dressed in her old clothes. As she finished towel-drying her hair, she heard voices across the hall in her nephew's temporary bedroom.

No, only one voice, she realized.

Deep and masculine, murmuring in a quiet tone.

Wilder's voice.

Her heart skipped a beat then, as it had the night before when he'd appeared in the door: six-feet-plus of rugged masculinity that, even in her worried and sleep-deprived state, she couldn't help but respond to.

She'd had two brief conversations with him: the first on the telephone, when he'd called looking for Leighton, and the second last night, when she'd arrived at the ranch, unannounced and uninvited. Although she should have been expected, as she'd told him she'd be on her way to Rust Creek Falls to get her nephew as soon as possible. Regardless, Wilder had been more hospitable than she'd had any right to expect.

Or maybe he'd been relieved to see her. Because standing in the doorway of the room across the hall, it was obvious to Beth that this cowboy had absolutely no clue how to take care of a baby.

"I know you can't do this on your own," Wilder said to the baby. "But is it too much to ask for just a little bit of cooperation?"

Of course Cody didn't respond, and Beth stayed quiet, too, watching as Wilder struggled to get the baby's legs out of his sleeper, opting to stretch the fabric rather than attempt to bend his limbs.

When that was finally done, he unsnapped the fasteners of the onesie and peeled it back to reveal the diaper.

"Or maybe this is some kind of test that only someone worthy of being called Mommy or Daddy can figure out," Wilder considered, as he opened the Velcro tabs. "And I think it's pretty obvious to both of us by now that I'm not worthy."

Beth wanted to say something then, to reassure the handsome cowboy that everyone struggled with parenting tasks in the beginning. But before she could find the right words, he pulled the diaper away and reached down to retrieve a clean one from the bag on the floor.

Cody responded as most baby boys would when his private parts were exposed to the fresh air, and Wilder yelped in surprise at the stream that fountained into the air.

Beth couldn't help it—she laughed.

The sound caught the attention of Cody and Wilder, and they both turned to the doorway. But while the baby smiled in recognition, the man looked so miserably unhappy she couldn't help but feel sorry for him, at least a little.

She swallowed another chuckle as she stepped into the room. "Is this your first time changing a diaper?"

"No," he denied, and blew out a breath. "I just don't expect him to do that every single time."

"You need to keep baby boys covered," she told him.

"How am I supposed to keep him covered *and* change his diaper?" Wilder grumbled, rummaging through the bag again.

"It isn't that difficult," she said. "You just don't remove the wet diaper until you have a dry one ready."

He sighed wearily and shoved the diaper bag aside. "And apparently that was the last clean undershirt thing."

"I packed some things for Cody before I left Leighton's apartment," Beth said. "But the bag's still on the passenger seat in my car."

"If you don't mind keeping an eye on him for a few minutes, I'll go get it for you," Wilder said.

"The keys are in my coat pocket," she told him.

He nodded. "I'll be right back."

While he was gone, she stripped Cody out of his damp clothes and put a clean diaper on him, chatting with him the whole while. Or chatting *to* him, as her nephew didn't respond except with happy gurgles and excited kicks. But those were enough for Beth to know that he was glad to see her.

After wrapping Cody in a blanket to keep him warm until Wilder returned, she sat with him in the rocking chair and rummaged through the diaper bag.

"It doesn't look like your mama thought to pack you any toys or books," she remarked. "Hopefully that's because she doesn't plan on being gone for too long."

Although the note Leighton had written suggested otherwise, Beth refused to believe that her sister would leave

Cody for more than a few days. It was more likely, she reasoned, that her sister had made the trip to Montana so that Cody could meet his dad, and the long journey with the baby had pushed her beyond the limits of her patience.

But Beth still didn't understand what had compelled her sister to contact the man now. Or why she hadn't mentioned her plans to Beth. Especially when they'd made arrangements to celebrate Cody's first Christmas together.

"I couldn't imagine any reason she would want to bring you to Montana," Beth admitted. "But now that I've met the very handsome cowboy who might be your daddy, I think I'm beginning to understand."

"So you *do* think I'm handsome."

Beth glanced up then to see Wilder in the doorway, a cocky grin on his face, and felt her cheeks burn.

"It's not my opinion so much as a simple fact," she said, furiously attempting to backpedal from her own admission.

"But attraction is very much subjective," he pointed out.

"I didn't say I was attracted to you," she denied hotly. "I was merely commenting that I could understand why *my sister* was attracted to you."

"Sure. We'll go with that," he said, as he dropped the duffel bag on the floor beside the rocking chair. But the playful wink that followed his words told a different story.

She looked away to unzip the bag, then frowned as she rifled through the contents. "Everything is ice-cold."

"The bag was in your car, overnight, in the middle of winter," he pointed out reasonably.

"And, as I discovered yesterday, winter in Montana is a lot different than winter in Texas," she acknowledged, as she pulled out a onesie, a pair of socks and a two-piece outfit. "Can you put these in the clothes dryer for a few minutes?"

He took the items from her hand. "They're not wet."

"No, but they're cold," she said again. "And a quick tumble in the dryer will warm them up to a more comfortable temperature for Cody."

He shrugged but headed out to do her bidding. Or maybe he was grateful for any excuse to leave her with the baby that he didn't believe was his.

Maybe he was right to be skeptical.

Maybe Leighton had been mistaken.

And maybe, after having spent a couple of days with Cody, he understood now how much time and attention a baby needed and would willingly accede to her request to take her nephew back to Dallas.

When Wilder returned with the warm garments, Beth quickly dressed the baby in a red top that had an appliqué reindeer head with Christmas lights looped around its antlers and a pair of dark brown corduroy pants.

"Very festive," Wilder noted.

"He has a lot of holiday outfits," she confided. "Every time I was out shopping, I seemed to find another one that I just couldn't resist."

"And all those Christmas gifts in the back seat of your car—more things you couldn't resist?" he guessed.

"He's my only nephew," she said, by way of explanation. "And it's his first Christmas."

"Do you want me to bring the presents inside?"

She shook her head. "Thanks, but I'd rather celebrate with Cody at home. And since I'm rested now, thanks to you and your kind hospitality, we can be on our way."

Now it was Wilder who shook his head. "I don't think that's a good idea."

"You can't want us to stay here," she said.

"Nothing has been about what I want since Leighton left her baby on my doorstep," he acknowledged.

"And considering what an inconvenience that's obviously been for you, why would you object to us leaving?" she asked coolly.

"Because I still don't know why your sister brought her baby to Rust Creek Falls instead of leaving him in Dallas with you," he said.

"No one but Leighton knows what she was thinking," Beth said.

"Maybe you don't know, but you can probably guess," he suggested.

Beth didn't respond to that. Because yes, she probably could guess. But she had no intention of sharing her suppositions with this man who might or might not be Cody's father and who, in any event, had no right to pry into the painful details of her often difficult relationship with her sister.

A relationship that she'd been certain was turning a corner—before recent events proved otherwise.

"And until you can answer that question to my satisfaction, the baby isn't going anywhere," Wilder said.

An assertion that, of course, put her back up.

"Who put you—a cowboy who clearly doesn't have the first clue about parenting and might not even be Cody's biological father—in charge?" she demanded.

"Your sister," he answered. "When she left her kid with me."

"My sister obviously wasn't thinking clearly," Beth said.

"I don't disagree, but that doesn't change the fact that she brought the baby here."

She hated that he was right. Even more, she hated that Leighton hadn't trusted her enough to talk to her about her plans. Instead, she'd snuck away, leaving only a cryptic note that did nothing to alleviate Beth's worries. And thinking about it now only made her head hurt. She lifted a hand and pressed her fingertips to her temple, as if that might assuage the ache.

"You're probably hungry," Wilder said, his tone more conciliatory than confrontational now.

She frowned. "What?"

"I'm guessing that your head hurts because you haven't eaten," he clarified.

"How do you…oh." She dropped her hand away.

"When did you last have a meal?"

"I grabbed a burger last night when I fueled up my car outside of Bozeman." But she'd only managed to choke down a few bites of the tasteless patty before she'd wrapped it up again and tossed it back into the bag.

"Well, according to the schedule I was given, it's time for the baby to have a bottle, so let's get you something to eat, too," he suggested.

"I'll be down in a minute," she said, reaching for the duffel bag. "I just want to change my clothes first."

"Did you want me to warm yours in the dryer, too?"

Though she didn't relish the idea of wriggling into cold undergarments, it was preferable to handing her bra and panties to a stranger. Especially a sexy stranger who had undoubtedly removed sexier undergarments from her sister's body.

"Thanks, but I'll be fine," she told him.

"Okay, I'll get started fixing the bottle."

She didn't ask him to take Cody and he didn't offer. She did wonder if his reticence was a result of not knowing what to do to take care of a baby or not wanting to acknowledge that Cody might be his.

And she had no intention of pushing him outside of his comfort zone. As far as she was concerned, the sooner he realized that he couldn't handle taking care of an infant, the sooner she could be on her way back to Dallas with her nephew.

When she was changed, she retraced her steps—as best she could recall—from the night before. But it had been dark then, and she'd been focused on Wilder's form moving ahead of her, unable to see much of anything else. In the light of day, she could appreciate the warmth and design of the home that Wilder lived in with…well, she had no idea who else lived in this house. Obviously she had more questions about the man than answers, but hopefully that would change over lunch.

Her stomach growled in support of that plan.

She reached the bottom step and turned—apparently in the wrong direction. Because she found herself in a family room with a grouping of leather furniture around a stone fireplace and a towering Christmas tree that almost touched the vaulted beam ceiling.

"Look at that," she said to Cody, her voice a reverent whisper as she moved closer. "It's almost as big as the tree at the mall where we saw Santa."

Of course, Cody didn't understand what she was talking about and would have no memory of the event even if he did. By the time they'd got to the front of the line and it was his turn to see the jolly man in the red suit, he was fast asleep. Beth hadn't wanted to wake him and risk ending up with a photo of an unhappy or crying baby. Instead, she had a beautiful photo of her nephew, decked out in a red velvet Santa sleeper and matching hat, peacefully tucked into the crook of Santa's arm.

She'd bought two copies of the photo and had framed and wrapped the second one as a Christmas gift for her sister. Of course, she'd invited Leighton to go to the mall with them, but her sister had waved off the suggestion, insisting that Cody was too young to even care. It was undoubtedly true, and yet, Beth couldn't let the occasion of his first Christmas pass without a visit to Santa.

She pushed the memory aside to focus on the tree in

front of her now. It wasn't just big, it was beautifully decorated in what she would call "country chic," with burlap ribbon, handcrafted wooden ornaments, home-sewn felt shapes, crocheted snowflakes, tied clusters of dried fruit, sprigs of berries and striped candy canes.

And unlike the plastic tree in the mall, this one was real. She could smell the rich, fragrant scent of pine in the air.

"Did you get lost?"

She started, turned. "What?"

A smile twitched at the corners of Wilder's mouth, somehow making him look even more unbelievably handsome, and making her wonder what was wrong with her that she could be so immediately and undeniably attracted to the man who might very well be her nephew's father.

"I asked if you got lost," he said.

"Oh, no. I mean, I took a wrong turn, and then..." She shrugged. "I got distracted. You have a beautiful home."

"It's got good bones," he said, turning to exit the room, no doubt expecting her to follow. Which, of course, she did. "But it's also been a lot of work to renovate and update."

"Have you done the work yourself?" she asked, glancing at the framed photos on the sideboard as they passed through the dining room. She was tempted to pause and examine the pictures more closely, but her empty stomach growled to remind her that she had other priorities at the moment.

"Me, my brothers and our dad," he said, handing her a ready-made bottle for the baby.

"Thanks," she said. "But I would have mixed up his formula."

"I just followed the instructions on the label."

She nibbled on her bottom lip, not wanting to appear ungrateful but needing to ask, "Did you use previously boiled water?"

"That's what the instructions said to do," he pointed out. "Plus Hunter, one of my brothers, gave me a crash course on basic childcare."

"He has kids?" Beth guessed, testing the temperature of the formula by shaking a few drops onto the inside of her wrist.

"One. A six-and-a-half-year-old daughter."

"There's no better teacher than experience," Beth said. "But in the absence of experience, there are some good childcare books that help. Leighton had about half a dozen beside her bed when she was pregnant."

She didn't tell him that she'd bought the books for her sister, or admit that Leighton hadn't cracked the covers on most of them. Because her sister had never been a fan of book learning—preferring to figure things out as she went along.

"I have to admit, that surprises me a little," he told her. "The Leighton I knew wasn't really the maternal type."

"I wouldn't have thought so, either," she admitted, as she settled into a chair at the table to give Cody his bottle. "But everything changed when she found out she was pregnant."

Wilder grabbed a mug from the cupboard and filled it from the carafe on a warming burner. "Are you a coffee drinker?" he asked.

"Only on days ending in a 'y,'" she told him.

He chuckled at that as he reached for another mug, then filled it with the steaming brew.

"Cream? Sugar?"

"Cream, please."

He opened the fridge to retrieve the carton, then added a splash to her cup and set it in front of her.

"Thanks." She lifted the mug to her lips and sipped. "That's good and strong."

"It's the only way my dad knows how to make it."

"So this is his house?" she guessed.

Wilder nodded. "When we first moved to Rust Creek Falls, in the summer, Xander and Finn lived here, too. But Xander and Lily have their own place closer to town now, and Finn and Avery renovated a cabin on the far side of the property, so it's just me and my dad left."

"So you've got three brothers?" She wasn't just making conversation; she was genuinely curious to learn more about his family, who might prove to be her nephew's family, too.

"No, I've got five brothers."

"Five?"

He nodded.

"Wow. Six boys. Your mom obviously had her hands full," she remarked.

"Maybe that's why she took off before my first birthday," he noted.

Chapter Four

Beth winced. "I'm sorry."

Wilder immediately waved off her apology. "No reason to be. You couldn't know."

"All the more reason not to speak without thinking." Then, in an apparent effort to smooth over the awkwardness, she quickly changed the subject. "Tell me about your brothers."

He responded readily, happy not to delve any deeper into the details of his mother's abandonment—especially when he honestly didn't know most of them. "Logan, the oldest, is married to Sarah. Hunter's a year younger, the one with the six-and-a-half-year-old daughter, and now engaged to Merry—that's with a capital 'M' followed by an 'e,'" he clarified. "Although I suppose it's also accurate the other way, too.

"Anyway, next after Hunter is Xander, who's married to Lily. Then there's Finn, who's married to Avery and expecting a baby in the spring, and finally Knox, who's married to Gen."

"So all of your brothers are married or engaged," she mused.

He nodded.

"You're not feeling any pressure to follow in their footsteps?"

"Not at all. I'm perfectly happy with my life the way it is," he assured her.

Then his gaze slid in Cody's direction, and when it

shifted back again, the look on Beth's face told him she knew that what he really meant was that he'd been perfectly happy with his life the way it *was*.

He turned to the fridge, away from her knowing expression. "I promised you food," he said. "What are you in the mood for?"

"Oh, um, just some toast would be fine," she said, as she settled into a chair at the table and positioned the bottle close to the baby's mouth. Cody immediately latched onto the nipple and began sucking.

"How about a sandwich?" he suggested.

"That sounds even better," she agreed.

"Do you like turkey?"

"Almost as much as coffee."

He pulled a cellophane-covered platter from the refrigerator.

"That's a lot of turkey," she noted.

"We had a full house for the Christmas meal, so my dad insisted on two birds to ensure we'd have leftover for sandwiches," he explained.

"I'd love a turkey sandwich—if you're sure he wouldn't mind sharing," Beth said.

"There's plenty." He pulled the plastic wrap off the meat. "I guess you didn't get to enjoy Christmas dinner, did you?"

She shook her head. "I mostly fueled myself on coffee and doughnuts."

More coffee than doughnuts, Wilder guessed, with a glance at her thin frame. He generally preferred the women he dated to look like women, with curves rather than angles. Beth was all angles, and yet, there was something about her—an innate warmth and sweetness that appealed to him.

The observation made him frown. Because while he appreciated the female form in various shapes and sizes,

Beth wasn't a female to be ogled—she was Cody's aunt. Leighton's sister.

And definitely not his type.

"White or dark meat?" he asked, turning his attention back to his task.

"Either or," she said. "And I can make my own sandwich."

"You're feeding the baby," he noted. "And that's something I'm not so good at."

"Your brother didn't give you a tutorial?" she teased.

"Apparently I'm not a very quick learner."

Beth smiled at that. "You're lucky your family is so supportive."

"Is 'supportive' another word for 'nosy and interfering?'"

"When it comes to family relationships, there's often some overlap," she acknowledged.

"Is your family supportive?"

"There's just me and Leighton—and Cody—now," she told him. "Our parents were killed during a bank robbery gone wrong almost ten years ago. Innocent bystanders."

Though the words were spoken matter-of-factly, the flatness of her tone suggested that the passage of time had done little to dull the heartache. As someone who'd grown up without a mother, he understood how the pain of loss could linger and wished he could take back the question.

"I'm sorry," he said instead, sounding and feeling awkward.

"Thanks." She eased the nipple of the already empty bottle from the baby's mouth and turned him onto her shoulder, gently rubbing his back.

Was it a maternal instinct that allowed women to anticipate and respond to an infant's needs? Or was it, as his brother had suggested, a parenting instinct? In which case, it was an instinct that Wilder obviously lacked.

"He was hungry," he noted.

"He always is," Beth remarked.

"And so are you," he remembered, refocusing on his task. "Cranberry or mayo?"

"Both."

Wilder made a face but retrieved the condiments from the fridge.

"Coleslaw?" he asked, when he'd cut the sandwiches and set them on two plates.

Her stomach grumbled a response before she did. "Sure."

He spooned some onto the plate beside her sandwich and set it on the table. After Cody had burped, she put him in his car seat and picked up her sandwich.

Wilder expected her to nibble around the crust, pretending more than eating, so he was surprised to see her take a hearty bite. And even more so when she closed her eyes and let out a blissful sigh that he was more accustomed to hearing in the bedroom than the kitchen.

"Oh. My. Goodness." She chewed slowly, swallowed. "You make a really good turkey sandwich."

It wasn't the only thing he did really well. In fact, sandwich-making didn't even crack the top ten list of things he did to please a woman, but he'd be happy to show her—

No. He immediately cut off his wayward thought, unwilling to go there with Beth, who wasn't just a guest under his roof but the baby's aunt.

He cleared his throat along with his mind. "I only assembled the ingredients," he told her. "Lily worked her magic with the bird."

"Lily is...married to Knox?"

He shook his head. "Xander. She runs her own business—Lily's Home Cookin'—now, but she used to be a cook at Maverick Manor."

"What's Maverick Manor?"

"The only decent hotel between here and Kalispell. It was originally an enormous house, nicknamed Bledsoe's Folly in honor of the man who built it. When he died, it stood dark and empty for a lot of years until Nate Crawford bought it and turned it into a hotel."

"A relative of yours?" she guessed.

"Apparently."

"Do you have a lot of family in Rust Creek Falls?" she asked.

"You can't walk down Sawmill Street without bumping into a Crawford—or two or three," he told her. "I thought I'd miss the anonymity of living in a big city, but there's something about this place that makes it feel like home already."

"Maybe the fact that you can't walk down Sawmill Street without bumping into a Crawford," she said, echoing his own words.

He chuckled. "That might be part of it."

She picked up the second half of her sandwich. "I honestly can't remember the last time I had turkey," she told him. "But I'm sure I don't remember it tasting this good."

He popped the last bite of his own sandwich into his mouth. "Last Christmas?"

"What?"

"You said you couldn't remember the last time you had turkey," he reminded her. "I suggested that it was probably last Christmas."

She shook her head. "I cooked a ham. Leighton isn't a fan of turkey."

"Do you always cater to your sister's preferences?"

"Not always," she denied. "But I probably do give in to her more often than I should."

"And I'll bet the more you indulge her, the more she takes advantage."

Beth frowned at his blunt assessment, but she didn't contradict it.

Aware that he was edging toward sensitive territory, he shifted the topic of conversation again. "Do you want anything else to eat?"

She shook her head as she pushed her now empty plate aside. "No, that was more than enough, thanks."

"Are you sure? Because I'm going to have a piece of leftover apple pie."

"I'm sure," she said. "Although if you'd said pumpkin, I might have been tempted."

"We have that, too," he told her. "And bourbon whipped cream."

"You're the devil, aren't you?"

"'A handsome devil' is what the ladies usually say," he replied, with a flirtatious wink.

Beth didn't respond to Wilder's comment, not even with a hint of a smile. If anything, she looked…disapproving.

Well, perhaps his teasing remark hadn't been entirely appropriate considering that she was the sister of one of his former lovers who believed that he was the father of her nephew.

"Was that a 'yes' to the bourbon whipped cream?" he asked, as he plated a slice of pumpkin pie.

"That was a 'yes, please,'" she confirmed, rising from the table to retrieve the coffee carafe from the warmer.

He opened the lid of the container and scooped a generous spoonful of the creamy topping onto the pie. Then he cut a wedge of apple for himself, grabbed two forks from the drawer and carried the plates and cutlery to the table.

"Thanks," she said, topping up his mug with coffee before refilling her own.

He nodded and straddled the seat across from her.

"Are you older or younger than Leighton?" he asked, when she sat down again.

"Older, by twenty-two months," she said, picking up her fork.

His lips curved as he popped the first bite of pie into his mouth.

"What?" she asked, though he hadn't spoken a single word.

"Just the way you said 'twenty-two months,'" he remarked. "I'll bet you held that over her head when you were growing up together."

"I did not," she immediately denied, dipping her fork into her pie.

"Yes, you did," he said. "As the older sibling, you probably couldn't help yourself. I know my brothers always held their maturity over me."

She seemed to consider this comment as she chewed, then slowly nodded. "Maybe I did," she acknowledged. "Of course, that completely backfired on me a few years ago, after my twenty-fifth birthday, when she started to take pleasure in pointing out that she was twenty-two months younger."

He chuckled. "Just like I refer to my brothers as 'old men' now. 'Old' *and* 'married' if I'm talking about Logan, Finn, Xander or Knox—because that's two nails in the coffin."

She frowned at that. "Not everyone looks at marriage as a death sentence."

"It was a joke," he told her.

"Was it?" she countered.

"You know, now that I've had some time to think about it, I do recall Leighton mentioning a sister…and referring to her as a stick-in-the-mud."

"That would be me," Beth agreed.

Now *he* frowned. "It's no fun to take a shot at someone who doesn't shoot back."

"Why would you expect anything different from a stick-in-the-mud?" she asked him. "And, for the record, she's also referred to me as a worrywart, a spoilsport and a killjoy."

"And the one who always does the right thing," he added.

"What?"

"I forgot that," he said, speaking almost to himself. "I guess she talked about you more than I realized, because I can remember her telling me that you were the one who always did the right thing. 'Little Miss Perfect'—cleaning up the messes she made."

"Not a term of endearment," she acknowledged wryly.

"I'm not so sure," he mused. "I think she really looks up to you, her older-by-twenty-two-months sister."

That earned him a hint of a smile. And he couldn't help noticing how pretty she was when she smiled.

But apparently she'd said everything she intended to on the subject of her sister, because the next time Beth spoke, it was to ask a completely random question.

"Aren't you supposed to be ranching?"

The vagueness and broadness of the question proved to Wilder that she was as unfamiliar with the responsibilities of a rancher as he was those of a parent.

"I wish," he said.

At her lifted brow, he shrugged. "Although ranching is a year-round job, things slow down a little in winter. Aside from feeding the cattle and livestock every day, we mostly focus on maintenance of buildings and equipment and perimeter fence checks, cutting and collecting firewood, and clearing snow."

"That sounds busy enough to me," she remarked.

"It is," he agreed. "But my dad assured me that he had plenty of hands to do the chores that needed to be done and that my hands should be taking care of the baby."

"Obviously he hasn't seen you try to change a diaper," she teased.

"Kids aren't really my thing," he acknowledged. Not that there was any chance she might have assumed otherwise.

"You know there's an easy way out of your dilemma," she said. "You could let me take Cody back to Dallas and pretend the last forty-eight hours never happened."

"Don't think I'm not tempted, but I don't walk away from my mistakes."

Beth bristled. "Cody is *not* a mistake."

"I didn't mean that the way it sounded," he said, immediately regretting his unthinking response.

"Then what did you mean?" she challenged.

"Let me just say that I wasn't thrilled to learn that I might be a father to a baby I didn't know anything about," Wilder told her. "And your questions about his paternity make me wonder how many other men Leighton was dating while we were together."

"I don't know," Beth admitted. "She didn't share those kinds of details with me."

Except to point out that Leighton, unlike Beth, had a personal life. Or remark that Beth was such a killjoy no one would ever be interested in her.

Beth never let her sister know how much those comments hurt. Because as much as Leighton could be kind and generous at times, she could also be hard and cruel, and—like a shark scenting blood—any sign of weakness could escalate her attack.

Beth pushed those uncomfortable memories aside to refocus on her conversation with Wilder. "And I didn't mean to suggest that there were others…during the time that she was with you. She didn't juggle men like that."

"That's a relief, I guess," he noted.

But the glance he sent in the direction of the now sleeping baby suggested to Beth that he was still more wary than reassured.

"My dad seems convinced that he's a Crawford, but I'm not quite willing to let myself be put on the hook on the basis of his gut feeling."

"If that's your attitude, then I really hope you're not Cody's father," she said.

"You don't think I should want proof?"

"Of course you should want proof," she said. "But instead of worrying about whether you're 'on the hook,' you might consider fatherhood as an opportunity rather than an obligation."

"I guess there's only one way to decide our next step," he said, and reached for his cell phone.

"Who are you calling?" Beth asked, as she dipped her fork into her pie again.

"The medical clinic—as soon as I can find the number," he said, searching for the listing.

"For a paternity test?" she guessed.

He nodded.

She chewed as Wilder connected the call, but her attention was no longer on the pie.

"Okay," Wilder said, when he'd set his phone aside again. "We've got an appointment at eleven o'clock tomorrow morning."

"That was quick," she said, surprised.

"The sooner we get the test done, the sooner we can get the results," he pointed out.

She nodded her agreement, eager to know the truth and still a little bit worried about what that truth might be.

"If it turns out that the baby isn't mine, I won't object to you taking him back to Dallas," Wilder continued. "Until then, however, he isn't going anywhere."

"But…the results will probably take several days. Maybe even longer."

"I guess that's possible," he acknowledged.

"You can't expect me to stay in Rust Creek Falls that long," she protested.

"You can leave anytime you want," he said. "But you'll leave without the baby."

Chapter Five

Wilder could tell his statement had surprised her. It had surprised him, too. If Beth had shown up immediately after Leighton had left the baby on his doorstep, he would have happily turned the infant over to his aunt. But somehow, over the past forty-eight hours, he'd started to get attached to the little guy.

He wasn't quite ready to accept that the kid was his, and truthfully—for Cody's sake—he still hoped Leighton had been wrong in identifying him as the dad. But he was invested in discovering the truth now, and determined to have it before making any decisions about his future.

"But my job is in Dallas," Beth protested. "My *life* is in Dallas."

"What is your job?" Wilder asked.

"I teach kindergarten."

"Then it's your winter break right now, isn't it?" he pointed out logically.

"It is," she acknowledged. "And I didn't plan on spending my holidays in Montana."

He shrugged. "As I said, you can go anytime you want."

"But you won't let me take Cody with me."

"Nope," he confirmed.

She sighed. "Is there a hotel in town?"

"Only Maverick Manor, just off the highway. But it's booked through to the New Year."

"Motel, then? Or bed-and-breakfast?"

"There's Strickland's Boarding House in town," he told

her. "But if you plan on staying in Rust Creek Falls, there's no reason you can't stay here. The room you slept in last night has been empty since Finn moved out."

"Are you sure the rest of your family wouldn't mind?"

"It's just me and my dad here now," he said. "And truthfully, I wouldn't object to some help with the baby."

"Cody," she said.

He scowled. "What?"

"His name is Cody."

"I know his name."

"Do you? Because I haven't heard you say it—not even once."

His scowl deepened at that.

"It's only four letters. Just two short syllables. *Co-dy*," she said again, deliberately emphasizing each syllable.

"I know his name," Wilder repeated.

"But you won't get attached if you don't use it," she guessed. "If you continue to refer to him as 'the baby,' and it turns out that he's not *your* baby, it'll be easier for you to walk away."

Annoyed by her insightful assessment—though not necessarily willing to believe it was true—he hit back. "I think I'm beginning to see why Leighton brought her baby here rather than leaving him with you."

Surprise and hurt were clearly reflected in her eyes before she sucked in a breath and quickly looked away.

Wilder winced. "I'm sorry."

"Are you?" she challenged, her eyes shiny with what he suspected were tears.

"I sometimes lash out when I'm feeling defensive, and you got caught in the crossfire," he explained.

"And I can be overprotective of those I love," she said. "I want what's best for Cody, and apparently Leighton thought that was you, so you need to step up and act like his father."

"*If* I am his father," Wilder said, still not quite ready to believe it was possible.

Because in the brief time that he'd been with Leighton, there'd been no forgotten or broken condoms, no reason at all for him to suspect she might have been pregnant with his child when they parted ways.

Yet somehow, in the short time that the baby—*Cody,* he mentally amended—had been at the ranch, Wilder had started to accept that fatherhood might not be the worst thing that could happen to him. That maybe it was time for him to not just step up but grow up.

Beth nodded in acknowledgement of his point as a knock sounded.

Before he could get up to answer the summons, the door opened and Avery stepped inside, kicking snow off her boots.

"No babies on your doorstep today?" his sister-in-law teased in lieu of a greeting.

"No," he said. "And not funny."

"I don't know," Beth said, maybe trying to prove that she wasn't a complete stick-in-the-mud. "I thought it was pretty funny."

Avery grinned. "That's because you have a better sense of humor than my grumpy brother-in-law."

"I have reason to be grumpy," he told her. "I was up I-don't-know-how-many times in the night with the baby."

His brother's wife was immediately sympathetic. "I'm not surprised the little guy had a restless night, in an unfamiliar place with people he doesn't know."

"And, as a result of his restless night, *I* had a restless night," Wilder felt compelled to point out.

"Actually, that's why I stopped by," she said. "To see if you were managing okay with the baby. I wished we could have stayed later the other night, but we had to get back to Pumpkin."

"Pumpkin is a goat," Wilder explained to Beth.

"Goat?" she echoed, as if uncertain she'd heard him correctly.

"Don't ask," he warned. "Because if you do, she'll never stop talking about it."

Avery's narrowed gaze promised retribution for what she perceived as the slight of her beloved pet, but she refocused on the purpose of her visit to ask again, "So how are you managing with Cody?"

"Lucky for the kid, I've got some help now," he said.

His sister-in-law's attention shifted back to Beth. "You must be the owner of the car in the driveway with the Texas plates."

She nodded and offered her hand. "Beth Ames. I'm Cody's aunt."

"It's nice to meet you. I'm Avery, one of Wilder's sisters-in-law," she introduced herself. "And since I'm obviously not needed here, I'm going to head back to my place. The furniture for the nursery was delivered this morning, and I can't wait to get it set up."

"You mean you can't wait to nag Finn to set it up," Wilder said firmly, concerned that his sister-in-law might attempt to tackle the chore on her own.

"Finn's busy trying to rebuild the engine of some piece of equipment."

"The baler?" Wilder suggested.

"Maybe. I sometimes tune out when he's grumbling about stuff like that," she admitted. "And anyway, the point is that I know my way around a toolbox well enough to put the furniture together."

"You should wait for Finn to do it," Wilder insisted.

"I don't want to wait," Avery told him.

He sighed. "Fine. If Beth doesn't mind me leaving Cody in her capable hands, I'll go put your furniture together."

"Of course I don't mind taking care of *my nephew*," she said pointedly.

"And I'd be happy to keep Beth company while you're gone," Avery said.

"Why does that *not* reassure me?" he wondered aloud.

His sister-in-law grinned. "I won't spill all of your deepest, darkest secrets," she promised. "But only because I don't know them all."

"Lucky me," he said dryly.

"But Finn has shared enough stories that I can probably keep Beth entertained until you're back."

"I'm glad you stopped by," Beth said to Avery when Wilder had gone. "Because I wanted to thank you personally for helping take care of Cody. Wilder said you've been a big help."

"It was my pleasure," Avery said. "Your nephew is a real sweetie."

"I think so," she agreed, with a smile.

"Plus—" Avery rubbed a hand over her rounded belly "—it was good practice for my own little bundle of joy."

"Wilder said you're due in the spring?"

"Early March," the other woman confirmed. "I feel as if I've been pregnant forever, but now I can finally almost see the light at the end of the tunnel." Then she sighed. "What I can't see are my feet. But maybe that's a good thing, because I haven't had a pedicure in…forever."

"You should treat yourself," Beth said. "Because you'll have even less time for those kinds of indulgences once your baby comes."

"I'd love to treat myself," Avery agreed. "Unfortunately, there isn't a spa in Rust Creek Falls. It's one of the things I miss about living in Dallas."

"You're from Texas, too?"

"Born and raised," the expectant mom confirmed.

"So what brought you to Montana?"

"Finn," she said. "We'd known each other in Dallas, and when I heard he'd moved to Rust Creek Falls, I came here to see him and decided to stay."

"You know it's love when," Beth said.

Avery chuckled. "Yeah, it was a pretty big change," she acknowledged. "But Rust Creek Falls isn't so bad, once you get used to it."

"I don't plan on being here long enough to get used to it," Beth said.

"That's too bad. Because Wilder's going to need some help learning how to be a dad to Cody."

"Do you really think he's interested in being a dad?" she asked dubiously.

"I *know* he is," Avery said. "Even if *he* doesn't know it yet."

Beth frowned at that.

"He just needs some time to get used to the idea, especially considering how the happy news was delivered."

"I encouraged Leighton to get in touch with the father, as soon as she told me she was pregnant, but she insisted he wouldn't want to know," Beth confided.

"I'm not judging your sister," the other woman hastened to assure her. "I walked more than a few miles in her shoes."

Beth's confusion must have shown on her face, because Avery said, "You didn't know that I was pregnant with Finn's baby before we got married?"

She shook her head.

"Well, I was," Avery said. "And although I came to Rust Creek Falls specifically to tell him that we were going to have a baby, it still took me a long time to find the right words—or any words, really."

"But you did it," Beth noted.

"I did it," the other woman confirmed. "And then, as if I

wasn't freaked out enough about being pregnant, I freaked out even more when Finn suggested we get married."

"You didn't want to get married?"

"I didn't know what I wanted. I was scared and confused and everything just seemed to be happening so fast. We had a one-night stand, I got pregnant, I told him about the baby, he proposed, we got married—" she paused then, a smile curving her lips "—and then we fell in love."

Beth sighed, a little wistfully. "It sounds like a romance novel."

Avery chuckled. "There was enough drama between our families to fill a lot of pages, that's for sure."

"And now you're one big happy family."

"Or faking it," Avery said. "But I don't care if our respective fathers are just going through the motions, because I know that Finn loves me as much as I love him."

"I'm glad things worked out for you."

Avery rubbed her belly again. "Me, too."

And maybe Beth was guilty of reading too many fairy tales to her kindergarten class, but one of the reasons she'd continued to encourage—Leighton would probably say "nag"—her sister to reach out to Cody's father was that she wanted a happy ending for them, too.

Though leaving the baby at his door wasn't quite what she'd had in mind, Beth wanted to believe it was the first step toward a possible reconciliation of Cody's parents.

Assuming that Wilder was the little boy's father.

Of course, she had no reason to doubt the claim in her sister's letter. No reason except Leighton's confession that she wasn't 100 percent certain.

But if she was being honest, she'd suspected, even at the time, that her sister had only been pretending to be uncertain so that Beth would stop nagging. Because she couldn't be expected to contact the father if she wasn't sure who was the father. And the fact that Leighton had brought Cody here proved she wasn't uncertain at all.

But if Beth acknowledged that the hunky cowboy was her nephew's father, and if Wilder was willing to step up and be his father, where would that leave her?

On her way back to Dallas, alone.

And that scenario wasn't one she wanted to contemplate.

When Avery had gone, Beth took Cody into the family room with the giant Christmas tree for some playtime. The ranch house was so warm and homey, she'd been taken aback to learn that Max was an unmarried rancher with six sons.

Of course, it was possible that he'd had the house professionally furnished. Or maybe one or more of his daughters-in-law had helped with the finishing touches. In any event, Beth felt comfortable in the house, despite being an uninvited guest.

She sat Cody in her lap on the floor and played patty-cake with him, then she entertained him with "Itsy Bitsy Spider" and used his favorite blanket as a curtain for peekaboo.

As much as she always enjoyed playful interaction with her nephew, she understood the importance of alone time, too, to teach him independence. But considering that Cody hadn't seen his mother since Christmas Day, she opted to focus on play today so he wouldn't worry that she'd left him, too.

"How about some tummy time?" she suggested, spreading his blanket out on the carpet.

"This is supposed to help you build strength for sitting up and rolling over," she said, laying him down on his belly on top of the blanket.

Then she stretched out on the carpet facing him, her chin propped up on her folded arms.

Cody lifted his head to look at her, a wide, toothless smile spreading across his face.

"You're already such a strong boy, aren't you?" she said, wiping his drooly chin with the corner of the blanket. "You're going to be rolling over before we know it, then I won't be able to put you down for fear of losing you."

Cody pushed himself up higher, as if to prove he was ready to move on to bigger and better things.

"I lost track of the number of times I had to tell my kids to get their feet off the furniture," a deep voice said from behind her. "But I never objected to anyone sitting on it."

Embarrassed to have been caught in such an undignified position, Beth immediately rolled over and rose to her feet. If his reference to "kids" hadn't already identified him as Wilder's father, she would have guessed the relationship just from looking at him.

She gauged him to be in his midsixties. His handsome face, deeply tanned and lined, attesting to a life spent outdoors. Though she knew him to be a rancher and he was dressed in the cattleman's usual uniform of jeans and plaid shirt, his clothes looked more Rodeo Drive than rodeo.

"Um, hi," she said, scooping Cody up off the floor. "We were just having some tummy time."

He nodded. "I heard."

"Oh." Her cheeks flushed hotter as she wondered how long he'd been standing there, watching them, and if she'd said anything she shouldn't have. She tended to think out loud when she was with Cody, to help build his listening and vocabulary skills, and often didn't even realize she was doing it.

"To build strength for sitting up and rolling over," he noted.

She nodded. "It also reduces the risk of developing a flat spot on the back of the head as a result of spending too much time on his back."

"We didn't worry about that when my boys were babies," Max told her. "Because the conventional wisdom of the time was to put babies to sleep on their tummies."

"Now 'back to sleep' is the recommendation," Beth said.

"I learned that when my first granddaughter was born," he acknowledged. "She's six and a half now—and a total princess."

"Is this hers?" Beth asked, reaching under the sofa to retrieve the Princess Aurora doll she'd spotted earlier.

"It is," Max confirmed. "Hunter called last night, asking me to look for it, and I insisted it wasn't here. Obviously I was wrong."

She gave him the doll. "A fringe benefit of tummy time is finding things you didn't even know you'd lost."

"Well, Wren will certainly be happy that it was found."

"By the way, I'm Beth," she said.

"I guessed as much," he said. "Wilder said you arrived late last night."

Beth nodded. "I'm sorry for showing up unannounced and uninvited," she said. "When Wilder called and said that Cody was here, all I could think about was getting to him."

"You don't need to apologize for caring about your nephew," Max told her. "The kind of love and devotion that compelled you to drive straight through from Dallas is admirable."

"I'd do anything for Cody," she said sincerely.

"But you don't know why his mother left him here with his father?"

She frowned at his ready acceptance of the paternity claim. "You believe Wilder is Cody's dad?"

"Don't you?" he countered.

"I don't know what to believe," she confided.

"Well, having raised six sons of my own, I have no doubt that little boy is a Crawford."

"I'm afraid I'm going to need something a little more scientific than that to be convinced," she told him.

His lips twitched, as if he was fighting a smile. "You're a skeptic, are you?"

"I'd say cautious."

"Is that why you're not married with a family yet?" Max asked.

She was taken aback by both his assumption and the personal nature of the question. "How do you know I'm not?"

"You left Texas on Christmas Day to drive halfway across the country for your sister's son. That suggests to me that you weren't celebrating with your own family."

A valid point, she acknowledged. "I guess I'm still waiting to meet the right person," she said. "And anyway, my focus right now is on Cody—and finding my sister."

"You don't have any idea where she might have gone?"

"I had no idea even that she was coming here," Beth confided.

"You're not close."

It was more a statement than a question, but she responded anyway.

"Not as close as I'd like us to be," she acknowledged, and wondered why she felt guilty for something that wasn't her fault. Or at least not entirely her fault.

But she'd only just met this man and had no intention of opening up her heart—or family history—to him. She definitely wasn't going to say anything that might cause him to view her sister in a negative light. Of course, Leighton's abandonment of her child on his doorstep had likely taken care of that already.

"I had six kids," Max said again. "You don't need to tell me about sibling relationships."

"But we've grown closer since she told me she was

pregnant with Cody. And especially in the past four and a half months."

"And yet she still left Dallas without telling you where she was going," he noted.

She nodded, because yeah, there was no denying that. And no pretending that it didn't hurt.

"Well, you're here now," Max said. "And it's obvious that your nephew is happy to see you, so can I assume you're planning to stay a while?"

"It's looking that way at the moment," she acknowledged. "I offered to go to the boarding house in town, but Wilder was kind enough to invite me to stay here. Assuming it's okay with you."

Max's lips twitched, as if he was fighting a smile. "I'm not sure it was kindness that motivated his offer. But we have plenty of space," he confirmed, before Beth could question his first statement. "And you're welcome to stay as long as you need to."

"I appreciate it," she said. "But if I'm going to stay, I'd like to help out in some way."

"That isn't necessary," Max said.

"I'm not a bad cook," she told him.

The rancher tilted his head, considering her offer. "Do you by any chance know how to make meatloaf?" he asked, with a twinkle in his eye.

"I've got my mother's recipe stored right here," she said, tapping a finger to her head. "And it's the best I've ever tasted."

"In that case, there's a package of ground beef in the fridge."

She smiled, grateful for the opportunity to repay him in some small way for his hospitality. "What time do you like to eat?"

Chapter Six

Wilder felt a little guilty about abandoning the baby in Beth's care while he went to his brother's cabin to put together the nursery furniture. A little guilty and a lot grateful, because the more time he spent with Cody, the more doubts he had that he'd ever figure out this daddy stuff.

He'd been making a sincere effort, but he didn't seem to have any kind of instincts when it came to interpreting the baby's needs. Logan claimed he could tell if Sophia was hungry or wet or tired by the sound of her cry. Wilder only wanted to stop the baby from crying, but his attempts weren't always successful.

He had made some progress, though. The baby had only peed on Wilder once. And he was getting pretty good at mixing formula and giving the baby a bottle. But feeding him cereal? He'd swear the kid spit out more than he took in. And when that stuff dried, it was like trying to wash off hardened cement.

Despite his incompetence and missteps, Cody was a pretty good sport about everything. And just last night—in the middle of the night, when he'd been summoned by the baby's cries and tried to rock him back to sleep, the little guy had stared at him for a long time and then, finally, he'd smiled at him.

And Wilder's heart had completely melted.

The reaction had both surprised and unnerved him. Because while he'd figured he would probably become a dad one day, that day was supposed to be in the distant future. So far down the road he couldn't even see a speck of it on the horizon. It wasn't supposed to be now. And it definitely wasn't supposed to happen without any warning or preparation.

So maybe he took his time with the furniture, checking and double-checking that every bolt and screw was securely fastened. Then he moved it into position in the room—or at least as he thought it should be positioned—and tidied up all the packaging. Only when he'd run out of tasks and couldn't imagine any more, did he leave his brother's cabin to return to the main house.

He hung his coat up on a hook inside the door, beside Beth's. Because of course she was still there—where would she have gone while he was out?

And even if she did want to go out, she shouldn't venture far in the lightweight coat and useless boots she'd brought from Dallas. If she planned to stay in Rust Creek Falls for any length of time—and apparently she did—she was going to need some proper winter clothing.

He wandered through the house until he found her, sitting in the rocking chair beside the crib, watching Cody sleep. He paused there for a moment, wondering why the image of woman and child suddenly seemed so appealing to him—and maybe wishing the smart and sexy woman wasn't completely off-limits to him.

"Why are you hiding up here?" he asked. Then, as a thought occurred to him, "Did my father scare you off?"

"I'm not hiding," she denied. "And your father isn't scary. A little opinionated and outspoken, perhaps, but not scary."

"So you did meet him?"

She nodded. "We had a brief but pleasant chat."

"Do you have any idea where he is now?"

"I think he went to… Hunter's house?"

"Are you telling me or asking me?"

"Which one of your brothers has the little girl who likes princesses?"

"Hunter," he confirmed.

She nodded. "Then I'm telling you. He went to Hunter's house to return the doll that Wren left here at Christmas."

"And if my father's not home, why are you hiding up here?"

"I'm not hiding," she said again. "I just wanted to be close when Cody wakes up."

"Trust me, you don't need to be close to hear him," Wilder said.

"I didn't hear him during the night," she noted, but rose from the chair to follow him out of the room now.

"Yeah, you were pretty dead to the world when you crashed."

She frowned. "How do you know?"

"Because I walked by the door and saw you passed out on top of the covers."

Apparently she didn't want to venture any further down that path, because she asked instead, "Did you get the crib put together for your sister-in-law?"

"The crib *and* the changing table *and* two dressers." He shook his head. "I don't have enough clothes to fill two dressers. I can't imagine an infant's going to need all that space."

"Your brother and sister-in-law are obviously excited about their first baby."

"You mean their first human baby," he remarked. "Because Avery babies that goat like it *is* a baby."

"They really do have a pet goat?"

"I would not make that up," he assured her.

"Do they keep it in the house?"

"No," he said. "And don't give Avery any ideas, or she'll be after Finn to build another addition."

"Or sweet-talk her brother-in-law into doing it," Beth remarked, tongue in cheek.

"You think she sweet-talked me into putting her furniture together?" he asked, reaching into the cupboard for a mug.

She lifted one slender shoulder in a half shrug, and he couldn't help but notice how her breast rose and fell with the motion.

Off-limits, he reminded himself.

"All I know is Avery got to hang out here with me and then go home to a nursery full of baby furniture without breaking a sweat," Beth said.

"She's almost seven months pregnant. She shouldn't be breaking a sweat," he said, reaching for the coffeepot.

"Are you really going to drink that?" Beth asked, as he filled his mug.

"What else would I do with it?"

"It's been on the warmer for hours. Let me make a fresh pot."

"It's fine," he said, and lifted the mug to his mouth to prove it.

Okay, it was a little stale and slightly burnt, but the hot liquid warmed his body and the caffeine jolted his brain, and that was what mattered. Or maybe it was the interaction with Cody's aunt that revved up his system.

Beth shuddered as she watched him swallow another mouthful.

"I'm guessing you don't want any?"

She shook her head. "I'm coffeed out."

"There are tea bags around here somewhere, if you prefer that. Or juice and soda in the fridge, if you want something cold."

"No, I'm fine, thanks."

He swallowed another mouthful of coffee, then lifted his head and sniffed the air. "What do I smell?"

"Burnt coffee?" she guessed.

"No. Something smells good."

"Oh, your dad wanted meatloaf for dinner."

He opened the oven door to peer inside.

"You're letting the heat out," Beth admonished.

He closed the door. "My dad wanted meatloaf?"

"Why do you sound surprised?"

"Because meatloaf isn't his favorite meal," Wilder admitted.

But it was one of Wilder's favorites, a fact of which his father was well aware. And the fact that Max had asked Beth to prepare one of Wilder's favorite meals started his internal alarms clanging.

Was it possible that his father was attempting to make a match between his youngest son and Cody's aunt? Would he dare?

Of course, the answer to both those questions was "yes." With Max, anything was possible, and he would dare almost anything.

It was also possible that Wilder was being a little bit paranoid.

Except that it wasn't paranoia if it was true, and there was no doubt that Max was on a quest to see each of his sons happily married—or that he would never be satisfied with five out of six.

"So…you know how to cook," he mused, remembering that Leighton had claimed she couldn't boil water without a recipe.

"I'm not a gourmet chef, but my mom taught me the basics."

"She taught you but not your sister?"

Beth shrugged. "Leighton wasn't interested in learning."

"Or maybe she was happier to let other people take care of her."

"That's a possibility," Beth acknowledged. "Although

not one that reflects favorably upon the woman who might be the mother of your child."

"I liked your sister well enough, but I wasn't blind to her ability to manipulate people."

"I didn't think you knew her for very long—or very well."

"The Leighton I knew wasn't big on subtlety."

"Fair enough," she decided.

He sensed that Beth, though aware of her sister's faults, would defend Leighton against anyone else's criticism, and decided to shift the focus of their conversation. "I'm curious to know how two sisters, born of the same parents, could grow up to be so different," he told her.

"You have five brothers," she noted. "Are you all cut from the same cloth?"

"Of course not," he acknowledged. "But we all share similar traits—one of which is that women find us irresistible."

Beth rolled her eyes at that.

Most women, he mentally amended.

"Leighton and I share similar traits, too," she said. "Although she was labeled 'the pretty one' and I was 'the smart one,' she's just as smart as me—maybe even smarter."

Wilder had some doubts about that. Not because he questioned Leighton's intelligence, but because Beth was pretty, too. Maybe she didn't play up her attributes the way her sister had done, but her unenhanced beauty was even more alluring because there was no doubt she was real.

"And I think that was part of the problem," Beth continued, drawing his focus back to their conversation. "No one knew she struggled to read because she so quickly memorized the books she was being tested on. She was also good at mental math, so when she transposed numbers on tests, her teachers accused her of not paying attention to what she was doing. It wasn't until she was in high school that her dyslexia was discovered."

"Better late than never," he said.

"You'd think," Beth agreed. "But Leighton balked at being labeled. She wasn't interested in strategies to deal with her learning disability—she preferred to pretend she didn't care."

"Maybe she wasn't pretending," he suggested.

She frowned, as if that was a possibility she'd never considered. "Anyway, I suspect one of the reasons she never learned to cook is that she works at a bar in a restaurant and eats there most of the time."

"Well, I'm definitely glad you learned to cook, because that meatloaf smells really good," he told her, his mouth already watering.

In fact, he was starting to understand how a man could get used to coming in from a hard day's work on the ranch to a homecooked meal every night. Especially if that hot meal was prepared by a hot wife.

Wait! Where the heck had *that* come from?

He frowned at the dregs left in the bottom of his mug, as if the stale coffee was somehow responsible for the wayward idea. Yeah, a lot of things seemed to be changing in his life, but his readiness to put his neck in the marriage noose was *not* one of them.

Pushing the uneasy thought aside, he asked Beth: "So when do we get to eat it?"

They ate forty-five minutes later.

And it *was* good.

If Beth had any doubts about that, they were assuaged when both Wilder and his father refilled their plates. Max even insisted that the men would do the dishes to show their appreciation for "the delicious meal." Of course, Beth had already washed up all the bowls and equipment she'd used in the prep process, so they really only had to put the plates, cutlery and empty baking pan in the dishwasher. Still she was pleased to note that, despite his apparent wealth and status, the Crawford patriarch didn't expect to be waited on hand and foot.

When the men had finished cleaning up, Max headed into town to meet another rancher at the Ace in the Hole for a beer and a discussion about the potential sale of a piece of equipment, leaving Beth alone with Wilder and Cody.

"I forgot to ask earlier—do you have a bathtub?" She posed the question to Wilder after his father had gone.

"You want to take a bath?"

"Not for me," she said. "For Cody."

"There's one in my dad's bathroom," he told her.

"Do you think he'd mind if we used it?"

"Of course not."

"Great," she said. "If you can grab a couple of towels and a washcloth, I'll get Cody's baby shampoo and bodywash."

He went to get the requested towels while she retrieved the toiletries. Wilder had pointed out the door to Max's room earlier, but despite his assurance that his father wouldn't mind her making use of his en suite bath, she still hesitated to enter the Crawford patriarch's personal space.

"You can knock, if you want," he teased, when he found her hovering outside his father's room. "But he's not home, so he won't answer."

"I know," she admitted. "But it seems like a violation of his privacy to just walk right in."

"I'll go first," he said. "And kick aside any clothes he's left on the floor."

She followed in his wake, trying not to be too nosy but unable to resist a quick peek at Max's inner sanctum—which was furnished in a simple and masculine style and neat as a pin.

"You knew there wouldn't be any clothes lying around, didn't you?"

"Yeah," he admitted, leading the way to the en suite bath. "My dad has never tolerated messiness or clutter—which is inevitable with six kids under one roof. Not even the full-time housekeeper we had in Dallas could keep up with us."

"I can't imagine any one woman being able to keep up with six kids," she said sincerely. "But kudos to her for trying."

He grinned at that and hit the light switch on the wall, illuminating a bathroom that was half the size of the enormous bedroom and twice as luxurious.

"Wow," she said softly, grateful that he seemed to assume she was reacting to the revelation of the facilities rather than the curve of his lips.

"My dad spared no expense in here," he confirmed. "But his two priorities were a shower with body jets and a tub big enough for his horse."

She stared down at the oversize soaker tub and imagined sinking into steamy water filled with mountains of bubbles. Of course, the tub was more than big enough for two, and her traitorous imagination immediately invited Wilder's big, hard body to join her—

She blinked and quickly dispelled the tantalizing image.

"I wouldn't be surprised if you could get a horse in there," she agreed, not looking at him. "Because it's definitely too big for a baby."

"So what are you going to do?" he asked.

Since turning her bubble bath fantasy into a reality wasn't ever going to happen, she suggested, "Plan B."

"I thought you were joking when you said the kitchen sink," Wilder admitted.

Beth shook her head as she put the stopper in and

turned on the faucet, testing the water temperature with the inside of her wrist. When there was about six inches of water, she took one of the folded towels and set it in the bottom of the sink.

"I thought the towels were for drying the baby."

"The second towel is for drying the baby," she said. "This one is so he doesn't slip."

"Why do I think you've done this before?"

"Because I have." She rolled up the sleeves of her shirt. "One weekend when Cody stayed with me, I forgot to pack his baby tub along with the rest of his things, so...Plan B."

"*You* forgot to pack his tub?"

"That's what I said." She stripped the baby down to his diaper, then tested the temperature of the water again with her elbow before removing that final barrier and easing the little guy into the water.

"His mom didn't pack his stuff?" Wilder asked.

"Sometimes," Beth said.

It was a surprisingly vague response from a woman who usually seemed happy to talk about her nephew—and extol Leighton's maternal virtues. And though Wilder was tempted to press for more details, or at least inquire as to how many weekends she'd looked after a baby who was only four months old, he decided to let the topic slide—at least for now.

"What do you need me to do?" he asked instead.

"Why don't you wash him while I hold him?" she suggested.

"Because washing seems a lot more complicated than holding," he replied honestly.

She smiled but didn't offer to reassign tasks.

Of course, she was already up to her elbows in the water, holding the baby upright so he didn't topple over.

"Wet the washcloth, wring out the excess water and

gently clean his face and neck. And don't forget behind his ears," she said.

He followed her directions, feeling awkward and inept—and far too aware of the scent of his shampoo in her hair as he huddled close to her by the sink.

"Now squeeze a drop of bodywash onto the cloth and work up a lather," she said.

She patiently talked him through the process of washing and rinsing the baby's body, then his hair, while she held Cody in place.

"This will be a lot easier once he's able to sit up on his own," she promised.

"And a lot easier with help," he acknowledged. "I don't think I could have tackled this on my own."

"Sponge baths work in a pinch," she said. "But it's good to get babies accustomed to the water, and Cody always seems to enjoy his bath."

It was obvious to Wilder that she'd performed the same task dozens of times before, and he was grateful for her help and guidance. But her obvious ease with and affection for her nephew caused him to question again why Leighton, wanting a break from the demands of parenthood, hadn't chosen to leave the baby with Beth.

While he was mulling over these questions, she'd toweled off, diapered and dressed the baby.

"There's my sweet-smelling boy," she said, nuzzling him for a moment before setting him in his car seat.

"Only until he fills his diaper again," Wilder noted.

Beth shook her head as she turned back to the sink to drain the water.

It was then Wilder noticed that the front of her shirt was wet—and plastered against her like a second skin.

Though he knew he shouldn't stare, he couldn't tear his gaze away from the delicate lace pattern of her bra, clearly visible through the now-transparent fabric, and he couldn't help but admire the nicely rounded shape of the breasts inside the lace cups.

She lifted the sodden towel from the sink and twisted it in her hands to squeeze out the excess water, causing her breasts to lift and strain against the fabric, making his mouth go dry.

"—in the washing machine?"

He turned quickly, so that she wouldn't catch him staring. "I'm sorry, what did you say?"

"I asked if you could keep an eye on Cody while I go toss these towels in the washing machine," she said.

"I'll do it," he said, grabbing the towels from her and beating a hasty retreat, grateful for the opportunity to escape the temptation of her nearness.

Max found Beth waiting for the kettle to boil when he walked into the kitchen later that night.

"You couldn't sleep, either?" he guessed.

She shook her head. "I hope I didn't disturb you by moving around in here."

"I didn't hear anything but the leftover pumpkin pie calling my name," Max assured her.

"Are you sure it was pumpkin pie talking?" she asked. "Maybe it was apple."

"It was definitely pumpkin," he told her. "And bourbon whipped cream."

"I finished the pumpkin earlier," she confessed guiltily. "But I didn't know it was the last slice until I saw the empty pie plate after I'd eaten it."

"Was it good?"

"*Really* good," she admitted.

"Eva Stockton makes the best pies in Rust Creek Falls—maybe all of Montana," Max said, opening the door of the pantry. "Which is why I always order an extra one from

Daisy's Donuts in town." He winked at her then as he pulled a baker's box out of the back of the cupboard. "Or two."

She exhaled a sigh, apparently relieved to know that she hadn't deprived him of his coveted late-night snack.

"Do you want a cup of tea with your pie?" she asked, as the boiling kettle automatically shut off.

He cut a generous wedge and transferred it to a plate. "Thanks, but I prefer milk near bedtime."

She opened the fridge to retrieve the milk—and the container of bourbon whipped cream he craved.

"You should put a dollop of this in your tea," Max suggested, as he scooped up a mound of the alcohol-infused topping. "It might help you sleep."

"Maybe too well," she said. "I want to be able to hear Cody when he wakes up."

"Wilder will hear him," he said. "I had the crib set up in the room adjacent to his to ensure it."

"Clever," Beth acknowledged, as she carried her cup of tea to the table.

Max took a seat across from her with his pie and his glass of milk. "Wilder told me that he made an appointment at the clinic for a paternity test."

She nodded as she dunked her tea bag in the hot water. "Eleven o'clock tomorrow morning."

"Waste of time if you ask me," he said.

"I'd never heard your son's name before I saw it written on a sticky note in my sister's apartment." Beth admitted. "So when I did, I googled it."

"And?" Max prompted.

"And I'd think, considering your family's vast wealth, you'd want DNA proof before welcoming a random child into your home."

"Cody isn't a random child," Max said. "He's a Crawford."

"Well, if it's all the same to you, I'd like proof of that before I leave my nephew here."

"Ahh," Max said, and nodded. "This isn't really about Cody, it's about you."

She sipped her tea, perhaps considering his remark, before she responded. "I made a promise to my sister to always be there for him."

"And yet, she brought him here," he pointed out. "Abandoning him and abdicating her own responsibilities."

"She didn't abandon him," Beth denied. "She left Cody with the man she believes is his father."

Though Max could appreciate her wanting to defend her sister, facts were facts.

"She left him on the doorstep," he pointed out. "And I'm sorry if it seems as if I'm judging her too harshly, but I'd argue that a woman who can walk away from her children doesn't deserve to have them."

"Them?" Beth echoed.

"Him." Max cleared his throat. "She doesn't deserve *him*."

She nodded slowly, as if she understood that they were no longer talking about her sister—or not just her sister.

He scowled, none too pleased to realize that his son had spoken to this woman—a virtual stranger—about their painful family history. But of course he had. There was no other reason for her to have picked up on the slip of his tongue except if she knew about Sheila's defection.

And though Beth had admitted to googling Wilder's name, Max wasn't worried that a cursory online search might turn up details of his marriage or divorce. Especially when he'd paid good money to ensure they stayed buried.

"Leighton made a mistake," Beth said now, as she put her empty mug in the dishwasher. "But she'll come back for Cody. You'll see."

Max hoped she was right.

But he sat at the kitchen table with only his disquieting thoughts for company for a long time after Beth had gone upstairs to bed.

He should hit the sack, too. Morning came early and there was a lot of work to be done—especially as he'd directed Wilder to take a break from his usual chores to spend time with Cody. Of course, now that Beth was staying at the Ambling A, Max suspected that she'd assumed primary responsibility for her nephew. But it was good for Wilder to watch and learn, even if he was still in denial about his relationship to the child.

A certain amount of denial was to be expected under the circumstances, but Max anticipated that it would be followed soon by a whole gamut of other emotions. He hoped one of those emotions was anger. Because Wilder should be mad. He should feel ripped off of all the experiences he'd missed because Cody's mother hadn't bothered to tell him that she was going to have his child. He should be furious he'd missed the first four months of the little boy's life. That Leighton had deprived him of the opportunity to be there for his son from the beginning.

Just as Max had deprived Sheila of the opportunity to be there for her children.

He remembered the night of their final confrontation as clearly as if it had just happened.

"I could never love anyone more than I love my children," she insisted, when he accused her of choosing her lover over her family.

"And yet you left here and went to him," he pointed out, his tone dripping with anger and bitterness—but not hurt. He wouldn't let her see the hurt. He would never admit how her betrayal had gutted him.

"You told me to leave. I had nowhere else to go."

He had told her to leave—to get out. But only after she'd confessed that she'd fallen in love with another man.

"You chose him," he said again, confident that he was

on the moral high ground. Maybe he hadn't been the perfect husband, but he hadn't cheated.

"No," she protested. "I didn't choose him. Not over my children. I couldn't. Please, Max, try to understand—"

But Max had been too hurt and angry to understand.

Maybe there had been a tiny part of him that wondered if he was making a mistake, but he didn't allow himself to show any hesitation or doubt. It wasn't in his nature to back down. And it sure as hell wasn't in his nature to give a second chance to the woman who'd betrayed not just him but their family.

But in the end, he was the one who'd been deprived of a second chance to make things right. Because Sheila had signed the divorce papers he sent to her, then died of a broken heart.

A myocardial infarction, actually.

The autopsy would later reveal a previously undiagnosed condition that explained how a thirty-two-year-old woman in otherwise good health could suffer such a tragic event.

But Max knew the truth—he'd killed her.

Chapter Seven

Beth was up early the next morning and feeding Cody his cereal when Wilder came into the kitchen for his first cup of coffee.

"And I thought ranchers were early risers," he remarked, rubbing a hand over his raspy cheek.

The handsome cowboy was dressed in a similar fashion to what he'd been wearing when she first showed up at the ranch—flannel pajama bottoms and a soft cotton T-shirt over hard muscles. His jaw was similarly stubbled, his hair equally tousled. And just like then, her blood hummed in response to his raw masculinity.

"Ranchers have nothing on babies," she told him, pointedly ignoring her body's totally inappropriate reaction.

"Yeah, I learned that yesterday. And the day before," he acknowledged, stifling a yawn. "But I didn't hear him this morning."

"I managed to get to him before he made too much noise," she said.

"I'm pretty sure my father put him in the room next to mine so that I'd have to deal with middle-of-the-night feedings and diaper changes," Wilder remarked.

"And you did all of that the night before," she pointed out. "So it only seemed fair that last night was my turn."

"Do you always try to be fair, Lisbeth?"

"Maybe," she said, wondering how he managed to make fairness sound like a character flaw.

Or maybe she was being overly sensitive—which was definitely one of her character flaws.

"Do you want me to make you some eggs?" she asked, when Wilder opened the refrigerator door and stood for a long moment staring at its contents.

He took out the carton and slammed the fridge door shut again before turning back to face her. "If I want eggs, I can make my own eggs," he snapped at her.

"O-kay," she said, and dipped the plastic spoon into Cody's cereal again.

Because if she was guilty of being overly sensitive, he was just as guilty of being an arrogant jerk.

And apparently he wasn't done being an arrogant jerk, because after pulling a frying pan out of the cupboard he said, "I don't know what you think is happening here, but I have no interest in playing house with you."

"Playing house?" she echoed, torn between bafflement and outrage. "Is that what you think I'm doing—*playing?* Do you honestly think any of this has been *fun* for me?"

Though she kept her voice low so as not to upset her nephew, she made no effort to disguise the fury beneath her words. And when she stood to carry Cody's now empty bowl and spoon to the sink, she felt a grim sense of satisfaction that Wilder actually took a step back, out of her path.

"Let's revisit the most fun parts," she suggested. "Maybe showing up at my sister's apartment and discovering she'd left town without telling me?" She unbuckled the harness that held Cody in his seat, then lifted the baby into her arms. "Or answering her phone and finding out that my infant nephew was in the care of a stranger almost seventeen hundred miles away? And then driving for twenty-eight hours through the darkness of night and all kinds of weather to make sure he was okay—but essentially being held hostage by a man who doesn't even want to believe he's his father?

"You know what? You're right—it's been *so much fun* I almost wish I was back in grade school so I could write an essay on how I spent my Christmas holidays."

And with that parting shot, she turned on her heel and walked out.

He could be a complete ass at times.

Today was apparently one of those times.

Wilder had no defense for his behavior. Sure, he could make excuses—and having a baby dumped on his doorstep would probably be at the top of the list—but his actions and accusations were indefensible.

And if he was truthful, he'd admit that his questions about Cody and his relationship to the kid weren't all that had kept him awake last night or caused his pissy mood today.

He'd been thinking about Leighton, too, as he'd tossed and turned. Wondering why she'd never told him that she was pregnant. Even if she'd had valid reasons then, why had she never reached out after the baby was born? And, if not then, how about when she decided to undertake the drive from Dallas to Rust Creek Falls with the baby in the back seat of her car? Because a phone call at any of those times would have been preferable to no phone call at all.

And though he'd been thinking about Leighton and all the reasons he had to be furious with her as he'd finally drifted off the sleep, he'd dreamed about her sister.

And how screwed up was that?

Sure, Beth was an attractive woman, but she wasn't at all his type.

Not to mention that she was the kid's aunt, and since there was a possibility that he might be the kid's father, imagining her naked just seemed wrong. Because yes, he hadn't just dreamed about her, he'd had a sex dream about her—and woken up with a raging hard-on.

And then, as if that wasn't awkward enough, he'd walked into the kitchen and she was there. All soft eyes and warm smiles and "Do you want me to make you some eggs?"

So of course he'd responded by acting like a complete ass.

Her anger had been completely justified.

And ass that he was, he couldn't help but notice how pretty her eyes were when they flashed with fire, how kissable her lips seemed even while they were berating him.

But now that the caffeine had started to work its way through his system, he at least had the wherewithal to recognize the inappropriateness of his behavior and acknowledge that he owed her an apology.

He looked at the eggs on the counter and wondered if scrambled or fried would taste better with a side of crow.

Then he rummaged through the fridge for bacon. Because everything was better with bacon.

By the time Beth had Cody changed and dressed, ready for his trip to the clinic, she was ready to acknowledge that she may have overreacted.

Not that she wasn't in the right to be mad at Wilder—because she was—but perhaps she could have expressed her feelings a little less forcefully. No doubt it was the uncertainty of the situation that had them both on edge. But they had an appointment at the clinic today, and though she knew they wouldn't get any immediate answers, it was at least a step in the right direction.

"Just to be clear," she said, when she ventured back into the kitchen as Wilder was finishing his breakfast, "I don't want to be here any more than you want me here."

"I know." He cleared his empty plate then pulled a chair away from the table. "Sit down. Please."

She strapped Cody into his car seat first, and then she sat. Her puzzled gaze shifted from the folded napkin and cutlery to the steaming mug of fresh coffee with a splash of cream—and finally the plate of food he set in front of her.

"What's this?" she asked warily, as if the crisp bacon and scrambled eggs might, in fact, be something else.

"An apology," he said, proving her suspicion was correct.

She lifted the fork and poked at the eggs, as if she didn't quite trust that his culinary offering was a sincere effort to make amends.

"We don't keep any arsenic in the kitchen," he assured her.

"Why are you apologizing?" she asked, after she'd nipped the end off a slice of bacon.

"Because I was mad at your sister and I took it out on you."

His honesty was as surprising as his apparent contrition, and equally appreciated. Beth sampled the eggs, then nodded. "Apology accepted."

"Really?" Now it was his turn to sound skeptical. "Just like that?"

"I'm not too happy with Leighton right now myself," she acknowledged, still unable to understand why, if her sister was finding parenting such a challenge, she hadn't reached out to Beth.

But even as the question formed in her mind, she ruefully acknowledged the answer. Because Leighton had always viewed Beth as the favorite child, a rule follower who did everything right, even following in their mother's footsteps and becoming a kindergarten teacher. Leighton, on the other hand, liked to break the rules and had even dropped out of high school when she was sixteen to sing in a band.

They'd traveled across the country, en route to Seattle, playing in bars that paid them in free drinks, not caring that most of the band members were underage. Leighton had made it as far as Twin Falls, Idaho, before deciding that she'd had enough of eating fast food and sleeping in a rusty van.

Of course, she didn't come home with her tail between her legs. Regret and remorse had never been her style. Instead, she'd regaled Beth with outrageous stories about the things she'd seen and done, taking pleasure in shocking her straitlaced sister.

Their parents had only heard about half of the stories, but that had been enough to shock them, too. Eager to create some distance between their younger daughter and her so-called friends, Alfred and Lucy Ames had encouraged Leighton to spend a few months traveling in Europe.

Such a trip was a luxury beyond the means of their solidly middle-class lifestyle, but they made it work by cashing in Leighton's college fund. Since she'd given no indication that she was interested in even graduating from high school at the time, it seemed a better use of the money.

As Beth had mentioned to Wilder, Leighton eventually got her GED but she was still happy to work as a bartender, boasting that she could make more money in tips in one night than Beth made in a week working with "snotty-nosed little kids."

And wasn't it ironic that Beth, who'd always dreamed of marrying and having a family, was still single and alone, while Leighton, who never wanted to be tied down, had been blessed with a beautiful, perfect baby?

"So we're good?" Wilder prompted, drawing her attention back to the present.

"We're good," she said. "But if we don't get a move on, we're going to be late."

She was a little nervous about taking the baby into a clinic potentially full of sick people. Though Cody was as up-to-date with his immunizations as he could be at four and a half months, Beth still worried about unnecessary exposure to germs and viruses.

The Rust Creek Falls Clinic was bright and clean with friendly and efficient staff. While Wilder filled out the necessary paperwork, Beth sat Cody on her knee, gently jiggling her leg to keep him moving so he wouldn't fuss while they waited.

Thankfully, they didn't have to wait long. When the doctor came in to the exam room, he explained how the test worked, asked if they had any questions, then completed the procedure.

Wilder volunteered to go first, so that Cody could see how it was done. He showed no outward hesitation, but Beth sensed his wariness, though she suspected it was related to the potential results rather than the requirements of the test itself.

The doctor opened the sterile package, the potential daddy opened his mouth, and the inside of his cheek was swabbed. The swab with the collected sample was then deposited in a tube and sealed up again.

Cody was less cooperative on his turn. He didn't understand the concept of keeping his mouth open for the doctor to complete his task, and he didn't seem to approve of either the taste or the texture of what was in his mouth. Several times he clamped his jaw down on the wooden stick, prompting the doctor to remark that it was a good thing the baby didn't yet have any teeth. Still, it didn't take long for the doctor to be satisfied that he had an adequate sample, and less than half an hour after entering the clinic, they were exiting again.

"That was almost anticlimactic," Beth remarked, as she walked beside Wilder to his truck.

"Now we just have to wait for some computer to analyze the spit on those sticks and decide whether or not I'm the kid's father."

"Something like that," she agreed.

"Doesn't seem like it should take seven to ten days," he grumbled.

"The doctor said it's usually less than a week, but the lab might be backed up because of the holidays."

"I guess that puts a snag in your plans."

She shrugged. "I can't really complain about spending the holidays with my favorite guy."

"I'm flattered," he said.

She shook her head. "You know I wasn't talking about you."

"Yeah," he admitted with a grin. "But I do like to see you blush."

"Am I blushing?" she asked. "I can't tell, because my whole face is frozen."

He chuckled as he opened the passenger-side door of his truck for her.

Of course, she didn't immediately buckle up, because she had to wait for him to set Cody's baby seat in place and double-check that it was securely locked in the base.

"Are you hungry?" he asked, when he slid behind the wheel.

"It seems as if breakfast wasn't that long ago," she said. "But actually, I am hungry."

"You want to grab a bite at the Gold Rush Diner?"

"Sure," she said.

The restaurant wasn't far from the clinic—but according to Wilder, nothing in Rust Creek Falls was too far from anything else. A cowbell rang overhead as they entered, no doubt intended to alert restaurant employees to the comings and goings of customers. Though she would have thought they were ahead of the lunch crowd, several booths and tables were occupied by diners already eating or even finishing their meals.

Beth decided on a booth because she knew Cody's seat

would fit snugly on the red vinyl bench. She wrangled the carrier into place, then unzipped the fleece cover-over top so the baby—who'd been lulled to sleep on the short drive—wouldn't get overheated while they were in the restaurant.

Menus were tucked against the wall, propped up by a tray of condiments. Wilder handed one across the table to her, then took one for himself.

She quickly scanned the offerings, then set the menu aside.

"That was fast," he noted.

"I've had a craving for a spicy chicken sandwich, so I was happy to see it on the menu."

"Sounds good," he decided, and tucked his menu away, too.

A server appeared almost right away. She introduced herself as Raina and started to relay the lunch specials, then she spotted the baby seat and completely lost track of what she was saying in favor of cooing over the sleeping infant.

"See?" Wilder said to Beth, after Raina had finally managed to pull herself together and take their orders.

"What am I supposed to see?"

"The way she oohed and aahed over the baby."

"It happens all the time," Beth said matter-of-factly. "Because he's too adorable for real words."

"Well, my dad would say that's just more proof he's a Crawford," he said immodestly.

"What do you think?"

He shrugged. "I guess we'll know for sure in seven to ten days, won't we?"

"I guess we will," she agreed, as Raina delivered their drinks to the table.

As she sipped her diet cola, she noted interesting details about the decor. But while she looked around the restaurant, she got the uneasy feeling that others were looking at her. Not that anyone was blatantly or obviously staring, but a couple of times, she caught a gaze being quickly averted before connecting with her own.

"Why do I get the feeling people are staring at me?" she asked, whispering across the table to Wilder.

He turned his head so that he had a view of the seating area. "Because they probably are."

"Thanks for the reassurance," she said dryly.

"Or they could be staring at me," he suggested as an alternative, shifting his attention back to her. "Rust Creek Falls is a small town, and newcomers and strangers are equally rare sightings. And there's been a fair amount of talk and speculation about the Texas Crawfords—as we've been dubbed by some members of the community—who plunked down a boatload of cash for the Ambling A."

"How much is a boatload?" she wondered aloud.

"Are you looking for the specific number?" Wilder asked.

Beth immediately shook her head. "No, I'm only pointing out that 'boatload' is an incredibly imprecise measure," she told him. "I mean, a boat filled with singles wouldn't necessarily be a lot of money—unless it was a really big boat. On the other hand, a smaller boat filled with C-notes could be a significant amount."

He chuckled at that. "Fair point."

"But if the other diners are staring at you—Wilder Crawford from Texas with boatloads of money—they're probably also speculating about your relationship to the baby that your father insists looks so much like a Crawford no one would guess he was anything else."

"No doubt the gossip is spreading like wildfire," he agreed.

"That doesn't bother you?"

He shrugged. "I try not to be bothered by things that are out of my control."

"That's a very Zen attitude," she noted.

"Plus, there is a silver lining," he said.

"What's that?"

"Rumors that I knocked up an old flame in Dallas and moved away to shirk the responsibility of fatherhood might discourage the local women who have set their sights on snagging the last Crawford bachelor from Texas."

"Are such rumors going around?" she asked, immediately concerned for his reputation.

"No," he admitted. "But I haven't given up hope yet."

She shook her head despairingly. "Is it really such a trial to be sought after by a few young ladies in the community?"

"It is when 'sought after' becomes 'hunted'—which is what happened when my father put a bounty on my head."

"A bounty?" she echoed dubiously.

He nodded. "Max offered a ridiculous sum of money to a local matchmaker to find marriageable women for each of his sons."

She couldn't imagine that any of the Crawford brothers had ever needed help snagging a woman's attention. Though she hadn't yet met all of Wilder's siblings, there were enough photos around the house to prove they were a good-looking group. In her opinion, Wilder was the most handsome of the bunch, but none of them was hard on the eyes. And according to Avery, each one was as charming as he was good looking.

But her curiosity was piqued by his revelation, prompting her to ask, "An honest-to-goodness matchmaker?"

"Well, technically she's a wedding planner, but that didn't stop her from embracing the challenge. And though she hasn't had much success, every one of my brothers has gotten engaged or married since we moved to Rust Creek Falls."

"How long ago did you move here?" she asked him.

"Six months."

"You're kidding."

This time he shook his head. "Barely more than a month after a chance meeting at the matchmaker's office, Logan married Sarah at the Ace in the Hole and became an instant daddy to baby Sophia. Then Xander fell in love with Lily, though she was originally identified as a prospective match for Knox."

"Lily and Knox didn't hit it off?" she guessed.

"They never had a chance to hit it off. Knox decided to be a no-show for the blind date Vivienne had arranged, so Xander went in his place and the rest, as they say, is history. Very recent history, in this case."

"What happened next?" Beth wanted to know.

"Well, our dad was starting to feel pretty smug about two of his sons finding their matches in short order, so Knox married Gen to teach him a lesson about interfering in his life."

"That seems like an extreme response," she noted.

"And one with very unexpected consequences."

She held her breath, waiting for the reveal.

"They fell in love," he concluded.

"Unexpected but happy consequences," she decided.

"Maybe. Depending on your point of view."

"You don't think they're happy?"

"No, they are happy," he confirmed. "I just don't think falling in love is always a happy consequence."

"Have you ever been in love?"

"I'm too steady on my feet to fall," he told her, adding a cocky wink for good measure.

She rolled her eyes at that as she sipped her diet cola. "Okay, so that's three of your brothers."

He nodded before continuing his narrative. "Finn was the next—or maybe he was the first, because he'd actually hooked up with Avery in Dallas before we moved to Montana, but they only got married a couple months ago.

Their second wedding—after they'd already eloped—was a big, splashy affair in Rustler's Notch, Colorado. We convinced Hunter to bring a nanny along to help out with his daughter so he could have some grown-up fun, and now he's engaged to the nanny."

"But going back to Logan and Sarah, it all started with the visit to the matchmaker," Beth pointed out. "So maybe she's done a better job than you're giving her credit for."

And though it wasn't something she'd ever considered before, it occurred to her now that enlisting a professional to help her find a life partner might not be such a bad idea. Because as much as she wanted to believe that her perfect match was out there waiting for her, she was twenty-eight years old and starting to doubt her ability to find him on her own.

"Or she's secretly serving Homer Gilmore's spiked wedding punch to her clients," Wilder muttered.

"What?"

He waved a hand dismissively. "Never mind. That's another long story."

"So has this matchmaker turned her attention to finding a match for you now?"

"If she has, she's destined for failure there," he said. "Because I have no interest in being matched by her—and even less in being manipulated by my father."

"Leighton always balked at being told what to do, too," Beth noted. "Which is why I was so surprised to learn that she'd brought Cody to Montana, because from day one, I'd been urging her to contact his father."

"Why do you think she decided to listen to you now?"

"I don't know," Beth admitted. "But I don't doubt that she was doing what she thought was best for Cody."

"Do you really think she'll come back?" he asked, as Raina approached with their meals.

"I know she will," Beth said, attempting to project more

confidence in her voice than she actually felt. Because she wanted to believe it was true, though after five of days with no communication from her sister, she was beginning to have some doubts of her own.

Cody woke up when the server set their plates on the table, almost as if he expected there to be food for him, too. Instead, Beth gave him a pacifier to keep him busy—and quiet.

Still, his eyes followed her hand as she picked up a fry and moved it toward her mouth. Watching him, she chuckled softly. "Yeah, I bet you'd like to try these, wouldn't you? But you need a couple of teeth before you'll be ready to tackle something like this—although the way you've been gnawing on that pacifier, I wouldn't be surprised if the first ones aren't too far in the distance."

"When do babies usually get teeth?" Wilder asked.

"Usually around the six-month mark, but first teeth can show up as early as three months or as late as the first birthday."

"How do you know so much about these things?" he wondered.

"I read a lot."

"All those books you bought for Leighton?" he guessed.

She frowned. "Why do you assume I bought them?"

"Am I wrong?"

"No," she admitted. "I just wondered why you leaped to that conclusion."

"I won't pretend that I knew your sister very well, but based on what I did know about her, she wasn't the type to read about something if she could do it."

"I think that's why she asked me to be her birthing partner," Beth said. "Because she knew I'd study the course materials and take notes in childbirth classes, so it wouldn't matter if she didn't pay attention because I'd be there to talk her through it."

"So you were there—when she had the baby?"

"Yeah." She looked at Cody and smiled at the memory of his face all scrunched up and red as he screamed at the indignity of being born. "I was there."

He picked up his burger, bit into it.

She didn't offer any more detailed information, because she wasn't sure how much he'd want to know.

But when he'd finished chewing and swallowed, he asked, "What was it like?"

"The birth?"

He nodded.

"Long and sweaty and messy." She smiled again. "And the most amazing thing I've ever seen."

"How long?" he wondered.

"Sixteen hours," she said. "Leighton was a trouper through it all. There were a few scary moments when labor stalled and they considered a C-section, but she pushed through."

She'd thought her sister was afraid of being cut open—a not unreasonable fear—and only found out after the fact that what her sister had feared most was the possibility of a scar that might prevent her from wearing a bikini at the beach.

And though a lot of people might think it a shallow rationale, Beth understood the root of her sister's insecurities. Because while Leighton had struggled in school, she'd quickly learned that being "such a beautiful child" had a certain intrinsic value—and she'd capitalized on it. She wasn't just pretty, she was popular. While Lisbeth spent her evenings at home with her head stuck in a book, Leighton was usually out with friends.

Because she had been known as "Lisbeth" back then. After all, it was what her parents had always called her and the name they'd put on her birth certificate. But the summer before Lisbeth started high school, Leighton had suddenly started calling her "Beth."

The reason, she explained without apology, was that she didn't want it to be so obvious to her friends and the other popular kids at school that they were sisters. Even though Lisbeth would be in her junior year by the time her sister was a freshman, Leighton had no doubt that she'd be immediately accepted by the in-crowd and didn't want anyone to connect her with "Little Miss Perfect."

Beth could have protested, but dropping the first syllable of her name seemed like a small thing to help her sister. Or maybe she felt as if she owed her something, because learning had always come so easily to Beth while Leighton had struggled to attain good grades.

As a result, her sister had learned to exploit her other attributes. Unfortunately, those attributes were superficial, so that even when she was laboring to bring new life into the world, she wasn't able to embrace and celebrate that miracle without worrying about stretch marks and scars that might diminish her sense of self-worth.

"But Leighton battled through," Beth said, continuing her explanation of her sister's labor to Wilder. "And, a few hours later, Cody was born weighing seven pounds ten ounces and measuring nineteen and a half inches. He also had a sprinkling of dark hair and a very healthy set of lungs." She smiled at the memory of those lungs announcing his arrival to everyone in the maternity wing of the hospital, then her smile faded as she looked at Wilder across the table. "I'm sorry you weren't given the option to be there."

"So am I," he said.

"Would you have wanted to be there?" she asked, surprised by the sincere regret she heard in his tone.

"I would have stepped up," he assured her.

"That's not what I asked."

He took a long sip of his cola, then he nodded. "Yeah," he said. "I would have wanted to be there."

Before she could say anything else, Raina appeared to clear away their empty plates.

"Can I get you anything for dessert?" the server asked.

Wilder looked at Beth, who shook her head.

"No, thanks," he said. "Just the check."

He reached into his back pocket for his wallet as the server returned with the requested check.

But Beth was quicker, having already slid her credit card out of her wallet, and she immediately offered it as payment.

"What are you doing?" Wilder protested.

"Buying you lunch," she told him. "It's the least I can do, considering that I'm not paying to stay at your place."

"Fine, I'll let you buy lunch," he relented. "But you can't take out your wallet again for the rest of the day."

Chapter Eight

"You said you wanted to go to *the* General Store," Beth remarked as they entered. "You didn't mention that it was *Crawford's* General Store."

"But I did warn you about walking down Sawmill Street and bumping into my relatives," he reminded her, as they approached a pretty blonde at the checkout counter. "And this one is my third cousin twice removed, or something like that."

"But you can call me Natalie," the clerk said, with a warm smile.

"And this is Beth," Wilder said, continuing the introductions.

"It's nice to meet you," Beth said automatically.

But the other woman had already turned her attention to the car seat in Wilder's hand. "And I'm guessing this is Cody," she said, crouching for a closer look at the baby. "Maggie told me there was a new baby at the Ambling A."

Beth looked questioningly at Wilder.

"Maggie's married to Natalie's brother Jesse," he told her. "Maggie and Jesse loaned us the crib and rocking chair."

Beth nodded, recognizing the names now that she had a context.

"So what brings you in today?" Natalie asked. "Just making the rounds through town to meet the family?"

"Beth's having enough trouble adjusting to the Montana weather. I don't think she needs the shock of being subjected to our family."

"The Crawfords aren't so bad," Natalie said, then winked at Beth. "Although I've heard some rumors about the Dallas branch of the family tree."

Her warm smile and easy manner immediately put Beth at ease.

Wilder ignored Natalie's teasing remark. "We're here because Beth needs some underwear," he said.

And that quickly, Beth's feeling of ease vanished.

"What?" She squawked the question as her cheeks grew hot. She'd only had one extra pair of panties in her duffel bag, because she'd only planned on spending one night at her sister's, but how could Wilder know that?

"Long underwear," he clarified.

But Beth still couldn't look at him. Couldn't believe that this cowboy she'd known all of two days had brought her here to shop for underwear—even if only the thermal kind.

"Beth's from Dallas," he continued his explanation. "So she's ill-prepared for our winter."

"You're the little guy's mom?" the other woman guessed.

"His aunt," Beth clarified.

"Oooh, plot twist," Natalie said gleefully.

Wilder rolled his eyes.

"How long are you going to be in Rust Creek Falls?" Natalie asked Beth.

"Seven to ten days, apparently."

"Then you're going to need a real coat," the clerk told her. "And some decent footwear, too."

Beth's frigid toes automatically curled inside her unlined boots.

"Avery said she's got a down-filled jacket that Beth can borrow," Wilder said. "Since she can't get it zipped up over her belly right now, anyway."

"She's probably got a dozen pairs of boots, too," Natalie guessed.

"But her feet are bigger than Beth's."

"And how do you know that?" Beth demanded.

"Because I asked."

"You didn't ask me."

"No, I looked at the label inside your boots," he acknowledged. "You wear a seven, Avery's a nine. But Sarah said she's got a pair of size eights you can borrow."

"A pair of thick socks would make those work," Natalie noted.

"She's going to want some of those, too," Wilder said.

"*She* would very much appreciate being able to decide what she does and doesn't need," Beth said pointedly.

"I'm only trying to help."

"A coffee run would be helpful," Natalie said.

"I don't want coffee," he said.

"Well, I do," the clerk said. "More importantly, I don't think Beth wants you hovering while she picks out underwear."

"Thank you," Beth said when Wilder had finally gone.

The other woman smiled. "Sometimes men are so clueless, blunt is the only option."

"It was kind of Wilder to consider what I might need," Beth allowed. "But it is a little awkward to discuss undergarments with a man I barely know."

"Agreed," Natalie said. "Now the key to surviving a Montana winter is layers. Long underwear refers to thermal undergarments that you wear over your usual underwear and under your clothes."

"I know what long underwear is," Beth said. "I just—"

"Got flustered by a handsome cowboy talking about your underwear?" Natalie teased.

Beth's cheeks burned hotter. "Apparently."

The other woman grinned. "So you *do* think he's handsome?"

"I also need regular underwear," she confided, ignoring Natalie's question. She did not want to discuss Wilder's handsomeness or acknowledge—even to herself—that her knees turned to jelly every time he stood a little too close. "I didn't plan on being gone more than a single night, so I've only got one spare."

"We don't have a great selection," Natalie confided. "Anyone who wants sexy stuff either goes shopping in Kalispell or orders online from Victoria's Secret, but we do have some cotton bikinis with lace trim."

"I'm not looking for sexy," Beth hastened to assure her. "No one's going to see my underwear but me."

"Well, that's unfortunate," Natalie teased.

And Beth realized that she was right.

In fact, it wasn't just unfortunate but a little sad that she had no concerns about a man seeing her intimate apparel, because it meant that she had no prospects on the horizon for a relationship. But until she sorted out the situation with Cody, that was the way it was going to have to be.

Beth was standing at the checkout counter when Wilder returned to the store with Natalie's requested macchiato.

"What do you think you're doing?" he demanded, as she started to hand her credit card across the counter.

"Paying for my clothes," she said.

He shook his head. "You agreed to put your wallet away for the rest of the day."

"That was before I knew we were coming here."

"A deal's a deal," he insisted, handing the to-go cup to Natalie along with his platinum credit card.

"I wouldn't have agreed to get half this stuff if I'd known you were going to insist on paying for it," Beth felt compelled to protest.

"He can afford it," Natalie said, with a dismissive wave of her hand, obviously aware he had boatloads of money. "All of this and a lot more. In fact, you should get that other pair of jeans you tried on."

Beth shook her head. "I don't need more than one pair."

But Wilder vetoed her decision. "Add the other pair of jeans," he said to Natalie.

"I don't need them," Beth said again, even as they were added to the pile.

"At least this proves you're different from the other women Wilder has been seen with around town," Natalie said, processing the transaction.

"How so?" she asked, a little warily.

"Because he's buying clothes for you instead of taking them off you."

"Thanks for your help, Nat," Wilder said dryly, snatching his receipt out of her hand.

She winked. "Anytime."

When they got back to the Ambling A, Wilder mixed up a bottle of formula while Beth took her new clothes up to the guest room. She did feel a little strange, letting a man she barely knew—and a former lover of her sister—buy her clothes, but, as he'd argued on the drive, what he'd paid for today didn't begin to repay her for everything she'd done for Cody.

Not that she wanted repayment. Everything she'd done for her nephew had been done out of love. But equating the shopping trip today to packages of diapers and cans of formula, she felt a little less guilty about the money he'd spent.

When her new clothes were stored away, she crossed the hall to the makeshift nursery to ask Wilder a question. The query slipped from her mind, forgotten, as her gaze settled on the handsome cowboy giving a bottle to the baby cuddled against his chest.

She saw it then—not just the physical resemblance between the man and the child that Max kept insisting was obvious, but how right they looked together.

Father and son.

Wilder might be quick to point out that the familial relationship was yet unproven, but looking at them now, seeing how the baby was carefully cradled in the crook of his arm, seeing the earnestness of his expression, she no longer doubted that the man cared about her nephew. And in that moment, though she was still frustrated with her sister for the way she'd handled things, she had to consider that maybe Leighton had done the right thing in bringing Cody here.

She watched Wilder ease the bottle from the baby's mouth before shifting Cody to his shoulder, his big hand gently rubbing the tiny back, and her heart swelled inside her chest.

But even if Leighton had done the right thing, where was she now? And why hadn't she been in touch?

Because it was one thing for Leighton to invoke radio silence with respect to her sister, but she should want to reach out to the man with whom she'd left her baby.

Wasn't she the least bit worried about Cody?

And if she wasn't, she should be.

Because as Beth had discovered when she showed up at the Ambling A, the handsome cowboy could barely manage a diaper change.

Of course, he'd come a long way since then, but Leighton had no way of knowing that.

Leighton had no way of knowing anything because she hadn't been in communication with anyone.

Which Beth knew because she'd kept a close eye on her sister's social media accounts, messaged her friends and reached out to her boss—to no avail. She'd even contacted the authorities in Dallas to inquire about filing a missing person's report. But after summarizing the situation, she'd been told that since her sister had have left of her own free will, Beth should hire a private investigator if she really wanted to track her down—an idea that she was keeping in her back pocket for now.

Desperate for a distraction, she retreated to the kitchen to figure out something for the evening meal.

She'd been a little surprised to discover that the obviously wealthy family didn't have a full-time housekeeper-slash-cook. When she'd asked Wilder about it, he told her that the woman who'd filled those roles in Dallas had declined to make the move to Rust Creek Falls with them. Although she'd worked for Max for almost thirty years and had been like a surrogate mother to his six sons, she had children and grandchildren of her own in Texas and no desire to move so far away from them.

Max had promised to advertise for a cook when they moved into the Ambling A, but during the summer months, it had been easy enough to throw some meat on the grill. So while there was a housekeeper who came in twice a week to tidy up, the men of the Ambling A had mostly fended for themselves when it came to meals—or gone into town to eat.

Of course, now that five of his sons were married or headed in that direction, the responsibility for meals in the main house fell to the patriarch and his youngest son. As a result, they'd eaten a lot of steaks, burgers and pasta over the past several months—unless they were fortunate enough to have Lily prepare a meal for them.

With that thought in mind, Beth rummaged through the freezer looking for some inspiration.

She was chopping carrots and celery when Wilder came down to the kitchen with Cody's empty bottle in one hand

and the baby monitor he'd borrowed from another of his relatives in the other.

"We didn't have lunch all that long ago," he noted. "Are you hungry already?"

"Ha ha," she said. "I'm making stew for dinner."

"You know you don't have to cook for us, don't you?"

"I know," she agreed. "But I'm sleeping in your house and eating your food, so it seems the least I can do is put a meal on the table."

"You made meatloaf last night," he reminded her.

"Are you suggesting that because you had dinner last night you won't want to eat tonight?"

"Of course not," he said.

"Is it that you don't like stew?"

"Stew's basically meat and potatoes in gravy, right? What's not to like?"

"Good," she said, and gestured to the bag on the counter. "You can peel the potatoes."

Max came in a few hours later, stomping to knock the snow off his boots. "Forecast says we could get another four to six inches of the white stuff tonight," he remarked.

"Oh, goody," Beth said dryly.

The old man chuckled as he removed his boots. "Missing Dallas yet?"

"I was missing Dallas by the time I hit Colorado Springs."

"What's cooking?" Max asked, hanging his coat and hat on a hook by the door.

"Beef stew."

"It sure does smell good," he said.

"Hopefully it tastes as good."

"It does," Wilder said. At her questioning look, he shrugged. "I had to sample it for quality control purposes."

"Well, don't sample till it's done," Max said. "I'm hoping there will be some left over for my lunch tomorrow."

"You're not going to be here for dinner?" Beth guessed.

"No," he confirmed. "I've got other plans."

"What kind of plans?" his son wanted to know.

A hint of pink crept into Max's weathered cheeks. "I've got…a thing…in Kalispell."

"A thing?" Wilder echoed dubiously.

"I'm meeting someone for a bite to eat."

"A woman?"

"What's with the third degree?" his father challenged.

"A woman," Wilder said again, but it wasn't a question this time.

Max huffed out a breath. "Okay, fine. Yes. I'm meeting a woman."

"So you've got a date?"

"It's not a date," his father denied. "It's just…a thing."

"Dinner with a woman in Kalispell sounds like a date to me," Wilder remarked.

"I'm going to shower," was all Max said in response to that.

"You shouldn't tease him," Beth chided, when Wilder's father had gone.

"I wasn't really," he denied. "I was just…surprised to hear of his plans."

"He doesn't date very much?"

"It seemed like he had a new girlfriend every few months when we lived in Dallas, but since we moved to Rust Creek Falls, he's been so focused on getting the ranch up and running, I didn't think he'd had a chance to meet anyone."

"Maybe seeing his sons find love has made him want the same thing," she suggested.

"Maybe," he allowed, though his tone was doubtful.

"Does it bother you—your dad dating?" she asked.

He shrugged. "It's his life."

"So why do you seem worried?"

"Because it's not like him to be so secretive about his plans."

"Ah, so it's not really the dating but the possibility he might have met a woman he could really care about."

"Beneath that gruff exterior is a fragile heart," Wilder confided. "My mom leaving did a real number on him."

"Just on him?" she asked gently.

He shrugged. "I can't say that it really affected me, because I was just a baby when she left and honestly don't remember her ever being around."

Beth didn't know what to say to that, and she suspected any effort to delve deeper into the subject would only be brushed aside, so she remained silent.

"Is it just a strange coincidence, do you think, that Cody's mom took off when he was too young to remember her—like my mom did?"

"It's hardly the same situation," she said.

"It seems like the same situation to me," he argued.

She shook her head. "Leighton isn't gone forever."

He shrugged again. "I guess time will tell."

Before their conversation could devolve into another argument about her sister, Beth said, "Why don't you go check on Cody while I serve up dinner?"

As she opened the oven to take out the bread, his words about playing house from earlier that morning echoed in the back of her mind. And while she still maintained that nothing about the current situation was fun, all things considered, being here with Wilder and Cody wasn't so bad, either.

Wilder took a thick slice of warm bread from the basket and slathered it with butter.

"You know, most people run out to the store if they want bread," he said, still marveling over the fact that she'd made it. From scratch.

"Why would I venture outside in this ridiculous weather to buy something I could make right here?" she countered.

"It took me some time to adjust to the cold, too," he acknowledged. "But a rancher doesn't have the option of sheltering inside when there are animals to be tended to."

"Then it's a good thing I'm not a rancher."

"We'll get you out enjoying the snow yet," he said.

"Don't count on it," she said.

"Have you ever taken a ride in a horse-drawn sleigh?"

"No," she said. "And if your next question is, 'Have you ever wanted to ride in a horse-drawn sleigh?'—the answer would be 'no' again."

"I bet Cody would get a kick out of it," he said.

Her gaze narrowed. "Oh, now you're fighting dirty."

"I'm not fighting at all," he denied. "But I am surprised that you'd let your nephew miss out on an enjoyable activity just so that you can stay warm."

She huffed out a breath. "Fine," she relented. "We'll go tomorrow."

He grinned. "Don't forget your thermal underwear."

Chapter Nine

Beth stood at the window, looking out at the pristine landscape. The promised four to six inches had arrived overnight, so that everything was covered in a fresh blanket of white.

"It does look pretty," Beth said to Cody.

She was holding him with his back to her front, so he could see what she was seeing. He reached out to put his hand on the glass, then quickly pulled it back again.

"That's the problem," she said. "As pretty as it looks, it has to be cold for that white stuff not to melt."

"It's not that cold out today," Wilder said, joining their conversation as he entered the room.

"I don't see the snow melting," she remarked.

He smiled. "No, the snow's not melting," he agreed. "So go put on your coat and boots while I get Cody bundled up for his first sleigh ride."

She appreciated the way the words "first sleigh ride" rolled off his tongue. As if he anticipated there would be a second and a third. As if he wanted the little boy to spend more winters here in Rust Creek Falls with him. Maybe all the other seasons, too.

For herself, she expected that this would be her first and her last sleigh ride. And though she suspected she'd be too preoccupied with her frozen fingers and toes to enjoy it, a promise was a promise.

She'd put on a pair of thermal underwear that morning, as instructed, then added a long-sleeved shirt and a thick sweater, blue jeans and two pairs of socks. Cody was similarly dressed in layers, and Wilder had borrowed a down-filled bunting bag with built-in mittens and a faux fur-trimmed hood for the little guy.

In the foyer, she shoved her feet into the boots she'd borrowed from Sarah, wrapped herself in Avery's jacket, pulled a knitted hat over her head, wound a scarf around her neck, and slid her hands into fleece-lined mittens, all accessories courtesy of Lily.

Wilder chuckled. "You really are a tenderfoot, aren't you?"

"And not ashamed to admit it," she told him, her voice muffled through the scarf already pulled up to cover her mouth.

"Let's get out of here before you overheat," he suggested.

She nodded and followed Wilder and Cody out the door.

Though she braced herself for the cold air, she forgot about the weather altogether for a brief moment when she spotted the pair of enormous black horses harnessed to a fancy black sleigh with glossy-painted red runners, a tufted red velvet seat and collapsible roof.

"Did you steal Santa's ride?" she asked Wilder.

"I'm pretty sure that would get my name on the naughty list, so no," he said. "This is actually an antique doctor's sleigh."

"So you stole it from an old doctor?"

He chuckled. "That would be another no. My dad bought it, restored, at an auction."

"It's beautiful," she said, stroking a mittened hand over the curved side.

"And it rides incredibly smooth," he promised. "Of course, you have to actually get in the sleigh before we can go anywhere."

He offered his hand, and she stepped up into the sleigh.

"There aren't any seat belts," she realized, as she lowered herself onto the seat.

"Seat belts hadn't been invented when this sleigh was made," he pointed out, passing her the bundled baby. "But it's perfectly safe, I promise."

She nibbled on her lower lip as she hugged Cody close to her body, uneasy with the idea of taking her nephew for any kind of ride without him being secured in an NHTSA-approved child restraint system.

"You're not convinced?" he guessed.

"I'm a worrywart," she reminded him.

"There's nothing wrong with being cautious," he said. "But trust me, I wouldn't have suggested this ride if I wasn't one hundred percent certain that Cody would be safe. Although I can try to rig up some kind of anchor system for his car seat, if that would make you feel better."

It would make her feel better. But she couldn't imagine how they'd both fit in the sleigh with the baby's bulky car seat between them. And maybe she needed to learn to be a little less rigid all the time.

"You're one hundred percent certain?" she asked, seeking reassurance.

"One hundred percent," he confirmed.

"And you won't go too fast?"

"I'll go as slow as you need me to go," he said, with a teasing wink.

"Okay, then." She decided to ignore his double entendre as she tightened her arms around the baby. "Let's go for a ride."

He settled beside her and picked up the reins, and she felt a little niggle of fear as she shifted forward in her seat when the animals began to move. But their gait was slow and steady, the ride as smooth as Wilder had promised, and she soon relaxed again.

As the sleigh traveled over the snow-covered ground,

he identified the other buildings on the property and described their specific uses, pointed out the cabins belonging to his brothers, and answered her curious and numerous questions about raising the cattle she could see in the distance.

"Now are you willing to admit that this was worth leaving the house for?" he asked, as he paused the horses at the top of a hill for an overview of the sprawling property.

"More than," she agreed, as she turned her head to admire the pristine beauty of the land in every direction. "Is all of this really yours?"

He chuckled. "Not mine, but everything you can see, all the way to that fence—" he pointed to a barrier in the distance "—is the Ambling A."

"You really like it here, don't you?"

"I thought I'd miss being close to the city when we moved," Wilder confided. "And I did, at first. But it's amazing how quickly I adjusted to being out here."

"'Out here' being the middle of nowhere?" she guessed.

He grinned. "It's not so bad."

"There's not even a movie theater in town."

"They show movies in the high school gym on Friday and Saturday nights—so long as one of the sports teams isn't playing."

"Oh, well, I had no idea," she said. "Movies in the high school gym? This town is practically a booming metropolis."

"And for anyone who can't live without a real movie theater experience, Kalispell is only half an hour away."

"Kalispell isn't Dallas," she pointed out. "It isn't a quarter the size of Dallas."

"Life's about choices,' he said. "My dad chose to come here and, as much as he drives me crazy sometimes, I wanted to support that choice."

"You're a good son, Wilder Crawford."

"That's kind of you to say. Of course, being a good son doesn't necessarily equate to being a good father, does it?"

"Not necessarily," she agreed. "But it never hurts to have a positive role model."

"It couldn't have been easy for my dad, having to parent six rowdy sons on his own, but he did it," Wilder acknowledged. "I respect and admire that, but I wish he'd accept that we're grown-ups now and let us live our own lives."

"Is this about the matchmaker again?" she guessed.

"Among other things."

The cryptic response didn't invite further discussion, so she only said, "Well, thank you for bringing me and Cody out here. It really was an unforgettable experience."

"It was my pleasure," he said, then smiled as he glanced at the sleeping baby. "But I don't know that Cody got much out of it."

"If nothing else, he got some fresh air."

"One of my favorite things about being a rancher is working outdoors," Wilder confided. "I could never imagine myself stuck in an office from nine to five."

"But as a rancher, you often work longer hours than that, don't you?"

"And seven days a week," he agreed.

"So if it turns out that you are Cody's father, how would you juggle that schedule with the demands of parenting?" she asked.

"I don't know," he admitted. "But I know my family will help. And Cody's only one baby. There's another rancher in town—Jamie Stockton—who was widowed with infant triplets."

"That must have been overwhelming," she acknowledged.

"You'd think so," he agreed. "But that's the thing about a town like Rust Creek Falls—the community comes together to take care of its own."

"Didn't you just move here six months ago?"

"Yeah," he confirmed. "But I already feel as if I've lived here forever."

"Of course, that might have something to do with the fact that you share a last name with half the town's residents."

He chuckled. "Not quite half, but that's a valid point."

"So you don't have any doubts that you'd be able to handle it?"

"Are you kidding? I've got a ton of doubts. But I've never backed down in the face of a challenge."

Then, because he didn't want to think about all those doubts, he reached over and gently nudged her chin up. "Look."

"Oh." Her eyes sparkled with childlike excitement and her lips curved. "It's snowing again."

He studied her as she watched the big, fluffy flakes that seemed to be floating on the air rather than falling from the sky.

"I've never seen snow like this." She smiled again as a flake landed on her cheek. "It's so pretty."

Looking at her, watching her surprised joy at something as simple as a snowfall, he couldn't deny that she was right. It was pretty. And so was she.

"It's pretty—until you have to shovel it," he said.

"Now who's being a spoilsport?" she teased.

And the curve of those perfectly-shaped lips tempted him to taste them, to discover if they were as soft and sweet as they looked.

But, of course, he didn't. He couldn't.

Because she was Cody's aunt and completely off limits.

"Guilty," he acknowledged, and turned the horses back toward the house.

"Though white Christmases are an anomaly back home,

for some reason snow always makes me think of the holiday."

"'Tis the season."

"And since it doesn't look like Cody and I are going to be heading back to Texas anytime soon, would it be okay if I put his presents under the tree when we get back?"

"Of course," he agreed. "And while you're doing that, I'll make the hot chocolate."

Wilder stacked logs and built a fire in the hearth while Beth arranged Cody's presents under the tree, then he went to the kitchen to make the hot chocolate.

He returned to the family room with two steaming mugs topped with marshmallows just in time to catch her brushing an errant tear from her cheek.

"Everything okay?" he asked.

"Under the circumstances, everything is better than okay," she told him.

"So why are you crying?"

"I'm not," she denied, as she accepted the proffered mug.

"You just wiped away a tear."

"A single tear isn't crying," she said.

"So what is it?" he pressed.

"Proof that the holidays make me a little emotional," she confided. "Christmas is my favorite time of year, but it's a bittersweet time, too, because I can't help but remember all the happy Christmases of my childhood, which makes me think about my parents, and then I find myself missing them and—" she cut herself off then. "Oh, Wilder, I'm sorry."

"Why?"

"Because I know you lost your mom, too."

"I didn't lose her—she left," he reminded her.

"And she didn't stay in touch after the divorce?" she asked curiously.

"She died only a few months after the papers were signed."

She wanted to apologize again for bringing up such a difficult subject, but he would only deny it was difficult. Instead she said, "I'm sorry you don't have any memories of her."

He shrugged. "And since I don't, there's nothing for me to miss."

To Beth, that was just as sad.

"So what were your Christmases like?" she asked, hoping he might share some happy memories.

"Nothing out of the ordinary. Presents under the tree, a big turkey dinner. Christmas cookies," he said, and smiled then. "Our housekeeper made these amazing cookies decorated with icing and colored sugars.

"I thought we'd miss out this year, but she sent a box in the mail. There must have been six dozen cookies, and they were gone within two days."

"Not just between you and your dad?"

"No," he admitted. "The note said we had to share, so we did."

She smiled at the obvious regret in his tone. "What about your tree—have you always had a real one?"

"Is there another kind?"

She tapped a finger against one of the branches, watched the tip bob. "They do smell good," she confided.

"You don't get a real tree?" he guessed.

She shook her head. "My apartment's on the sixth floor, and it just seems like too much hassle to drag one into the building, cram it into an elevator, then haul it down the hall and into my apartment, leaving a path of needles along the way."

"A path of needles would make it easy for Santa to find you," he pointed out.

"Instead, I have a sign that goes in the window that says Santa, Please Stop Here!"

"You don't think Saint Nick knows where he's supposed to stop?"

"I don't like leaving some things to chance."

"And what was on your wish list for Santa this year?" Wilder asked her.

"Oh, um, just…you know…the usual stuff."

"You didn't make a list for Santa, did you?"

"Not exactly."

His gaze narrowed thoughtfully. "But there was something specific you wanted," he guessed.

"I just wanted to spend Christmas with Leighton and Cody—to be part of the happy memories of his first Christmas."

"You do know he's not going to remember his first Christmas when he's older?"

"I know," she admitted. "But I've been taking pictures of every event and milestone, to make a scrapbook of his first year, so that he'll be able to look back and know, even if he can't remember."

"You should have asked me to take a picture of the two of you in the sleigh," he told her.

"I was so mesmerized by the sleigh and the horses, I didn't even think about it," she confided.

"Next time," he promised.

But they both knew there might not be a next time, because Beth's days at the Ambling A were numbered—seven to ten—and the countdown was on.

She carefully sipped her hot chocolate and wondered why she didn't seem as excited to anticipate her return to Dallas as she'd been only three days earlier. Goodness knows, she would be happy enough to get back to a place where she didn't need long underwear to step out the front door. But when she did, she might actually miss interacting with Wilder and Max and the various other Crawfords who'd been in and out of the main house at the Ambling A during her brief time there.

She pushed the uncomfortable thought aside and sipped her drink again, savoring the warm sweetness as it slid down her throat. "This is really good," she told Wilder.

"The key ingredients are real cream and dark chocolate," he confided. "And marshmallows on top, of course."

"Of course," she agreed.

"Speaking of marshmallows, you've got some right here," he said, and indicated the location on his own lip.

"Oh." She instinctively sought out the sticky spot with the tip of her tongue. "Did I get it?"

Instead of answering, he reached over and brushed his thumb over the curve of her bottom lip. The callused pad scraped against her soft skin, causing her breath to back up in her lungs and sending tingles through her veins.

She lifted her gaze to find his fixed on her mouth, his head tilted toward her, and for the space of a single heartbeat, she actually thought he was going to kiss her.

And, oh, how she yearned for his kiss. Just the thought of his lips pressed against hers made her tummy feel tingly and her knees grow weak.

But instead of shifting closer, he abruptly pulled away.

"It's gone now," he told her.

And then Cody was awake, allowing her to focus on the baby and ignore the twinge of what might have been disappointment.

After she'd snapped a few pictures of Cody propped up against the pile of presents, Wilder took her cell phone and assumed photographer duties while she helped her nephew open his gifts.

There were sleepers and outfits, a pair of high-top running shoes (and of course Wilder questioned the purpose of running shoes for a kid who couldn't even walk), board books and bath books, wooden puzzles and cuddly toys, learning toys and silly toys.

"Let's try these on you," Beth said, tugging off Cody's socks and replacing them with the foot rattles he'd just opened.

One was red-and-orange and decorated to look like a giraffe; the other was black-and-white like a zebra; both had noisemakers sewn into their ears. She put them on his feet and helped him kick his legs to demonstrate how they could make sound.

Cody rewarded her with a gummy smile.

"What's this one?" Wilder asked, picking up a smallish square box wrapped in Santa paper with a red bow.

She took the box from his hand and glanced at the tag that read: To Mommy Love Cody.

"Oh." She managed a smile. "It's a 'Mommy' Christmas ornament, dated for the year Cody was born."

She set it aside and reached for a bigger and flatter package. After carefully prying the tag off the wrapping, she handed the gift to Wilder.

"What's this?"

"A present."

"I know you didn't buy this for me."

"No, I didn't," she acknowledged. "But it's something I'd like you to have."

Curious, he slid a finger beneath the fold of paper to break the tape. The flat, unmarked box didn't give anything away, so he lifted the lid and peeled back the tissue inside to reveal a beautiful brushed silver-tone frame engraved with the words "Cody's First Christmas." Inside the frame was a photo of the baby, asleep in the crook of Santa's arm.

"What a great picture," he said, sincerely touched by her gesture. "This was another gift for your sister?"

"Yeah, but I can get another one made for her," Beth said.

"Is this because you now believe I'm Cody's father?" he asked.

"Do *you* believe it?" she countered.

He looked at the little guy now sitting between his outstretched legs.

Did he believe it?

Were his residual doubts simply a manifestation of his reluctance to take on the responsibilities of fatherhood? Responsibilities that he wouldn't be able to duck if and when he was confirmed to be the baby's father. Not that he'd had much success ducking anything since the baby had appeared on the doorstep and his father had made his own determination about paternity. But doubts aside, the more time he spent with Cody, the less terrifying he found the idea of being his father.

"Well," she said with a shrug, obviously having given up on waiting for an answer. "If it turns out you're not his dad, you can give the picture back to me."

"For now, I'm going to put it right here," he said, propping the frame up on the side table.

Beth looked at the picture there and smiled. "Good choice."

Then she stood up and began gathering the discarded wrapping.

"Somebody lost a sock," Wilder noted, tickling the baby's bare toes as he reached to pick up the giraffe.

Cody giggled.

Beth gasped and spun around, clutching an armload of crumpled paper against her chest. "What did you do?" she asked Wilder.

"Me?" Had he done something wrong? "I just tickled his toes." Then he did it again, to demonstrate for her.

Cody responded with more giggles.

"Oh." The word was barely a whisper from her lips as

her eyes filled with tears. "That's the first time I've heard him laugh."

"Really?" Wilder asked, surprised.

She nodded.

Wilder brushed his fingertips over the bottom of the baby's foot, to see if he was ticklish there. The baby answered with another giggle.

Beth sighed. "Is there anything as sweet as that sound?"

Though she probably wasn't expecting an answer to her question, he heard himself responding, "It's pretty great."

"It makes me happy to know he's happy," she said.

"Of course, he's four months old, so his biggest concerns are a hungry belly or wet diaper," Wilder pointed out.

"And sore gums," she reminded him.

"Still, he's not lying awake at night worrying about the market price of beef," he said, as he worked the sock onto the baby's foot, stroking his fingertip along his sole and sending the little guy into a fresh wave of giggles.

Beth laughed, too, and their gazes met and held for a long moment of shared understanding and unexpected connection.

Then Cody kicked his feet again, shaking the rattles, and the moment was broken.

Chapter Ten

Wilder lay awake in bed for a long time that night, thinking about the day he'd spent with Cody and Beth. He couldn't help but admire Beth's devotion to her nephew and the way she overcame her own reservations to embrace opportunities and new experiences for the little boy. Everything she did seemed to be motivated by his best interests, even before her own wants and needs, her actions a stark contrast to those of her sister, who'd apparently had no qualms about abandoning her child.

Of course, Wilder knew from experience that maternal instincts weren't really instincts in the true sense of the word. They weren't as universal as the compulsion of birds to build nests. While a lot of parents might instinctively bond with, nurture and protect their children, giving birth to a child didn't automatically create or foster such instincts. If it did, his mother never would have walked away, leaving Max to raise their six sons on his own.

Had his father had stronger instincts to care for his children? Or had he only done what needed to be done because his wife's abandonment had left him with no other option?

More important, would Wilder be able to learn everything he needed to know to raise his son—if it turned out that Cody was his son? And why didn't he share Max's conviction that the baby was a Crawford? Was it because he didn't want to be a father to the little guy? Or was he afraid that he would fail in his efforts to be what Cody needed?

"Fatherhood changes everything," Max had told Wilder, when they were alone at the Ambling A after everyone else had gone on Christmas night.

Apparently that was true whether he wanted anything to change or not. And even without any confirmation that he was a father.

At first, he'd been panicked at the idea the kid was his. Now, after spending only a few days with Cody...well, he wasn't quite ready to start handing out cigars with blue bands that proclaimed "It's a Boy," but he wasn't quite so terrified anymore, either. Of course, cigars might be premature, anyway, as he was still waiting on the results of the DNA test.

Maybe he'd feel more of a connection to the kid if he'd known that he existed before he was four months old. If he'd had the opportunity to help Leighton prepare for his arrival. If he'd been there when their baby was born.

He was angry that she'd taken that opportunity away from him. That *she'd* chosen not to tell him about the pregnancy, to cut him out of the life of his child—*if* Cody was his child.

And he was still angry the next morning, and continuing to mull over these thoughts, as he sipped his coffee.

"Are you okay?" Beth asked.

"Sure. Why?"

"Because you're gripping the handle of that mug so tight it's a wonder it hasn't snapped off in your hand."

He uncurled his fist and set the mug on the counter.

"Wilder?" she prompted.

"I guess I'm just realizing how much I missed out on, not knowing that Leighton was pregnant."

"I think, in the beginning, she didn't reach out to you because she wasn't sure she was going to keep the baby," she admitted.

He swallowed. "She considered ending her pregnancy?"

"No." Beth immediately shook her head. "*Never.* She always planned to have the baby, but she didn't know if she would keep him."

"You're talking about adoption," he realized.

Now she nodded.

"But…why?" he wondered.

"Because she wanted her baby to have a better life than she could give him as a single mother. She wanted him to have a family."

"She didn't have to be a single mother. If Leighton had told me she was pregnant, I would have offered to do the right thing."

"Because getting married for the sake of a baby is the right thing?" she asked dubiously.

"Sometimes it is," he said.

"Maybe that's why she didn't tell you," Beth remarked.

"What does that mean?" he challenged.

"I can't imagine any woman being swept off her feet by such an offer, and it definitely wouldn't have swayed my sister."

He scowled at that. "You think she would have said *no*?"

"I wouldn't presume to know how she might have responded," Beth said. "But I think the fact that she didn't tell you she was pregnant proves she didn't trust you would support her choices."

"But she trusted you?" he challenged.

"I did support her," she said.

"And yet, when she got to the point where she felt overwhelmed by her responsibilities, she brought the baby to me," he pointed out.

He was right, and that truth was like a slap to Beth's face.

She'd thought she was doing what was best for hcr sister. She'd offered her a sympathetic ear and a strong shoulder; she'd listened and counseled and encouraged. And all the while she'd been promising her support, she'd also been pushing her sister in the direction Beth wanted her to go. *Of course it's your choice if you want to give your baby up for adoption. But if you decide to keep him, I'll be there for you. Whatever you need. Whatever he needs.*

Leighton had been honest in expressing her reservations about working as a bartender and raising a child on her own. She'd wanted to do the best thing for her baby—to give him a real family. But Beth had pointed out that they were a family; she'd assured her that they could be everything he'd ever need. And so Leighton had been persuaded to keep her baby.

But sometime during the past four months, she'd apparently had a change of heart.

Or maybe she'd begun to suspect her sister was wrong.

Either way, there was one fact that Beth could no longer deny: it was *her* fault Cody had been left on a ranch in Montana.

"We were just talking about the big New Year's Eve party at Maverick Manor," Max said, when Beth returned to the main level after putting Cody down for his nap. "It's the fancy hotel off the highway owned by Nate Crawford—you might have seen it on your way into Rust Creek Falls."

"Isn't everything in this town owned by a Crawford?" Beth asked.

"Not quite everything," Max said. Then he winked. "At least, not yet."

Beth smiled, though she suspected he wasn't entirely joking. The Crawford patriarch struck her as a man capable of world—or at least small-town—domination.

"So what do you think?" he asked.

"About what?"

"The party."

She looked at Wilder, as if he might be able to give her a clue as to why his father was asking, but he only shrugged.

"Sounds like fun?" she said.

"Great. I'll tell Nate to add your name to the guest list."

"Oh," she said, startled by the suggestion. "I meant it would be fun for you—not for me."

"You don't like parties?" Max challenged.

"She doesn't know how to have fun," Wilder said.

And though the twinkle in his eye assured Beth that he was only teasing, the remark too closely echoed her sister's oft-repeated criticism for her to slough it off.

"That's true," she said, aware that her tone was as stiff as her smile. "So while it's thoughtful of you to invite me, I have to decline."

"Don't say no," Max protested.

But she didn't stick around to discuss the matter any further. There was no point, when she knew she wouldn't change her mind.

She instinctively headed toward the guest room, just as she'd retreated to her bedroom when she was a child, as if closing the door could shut out the taunting voices that called her names.

"Worrywart."

"Spoilsport."

"Killjoy."

"Little Miss Perfect."

Sticks and stones may break my bones...

The childhood rhyme echoed in her head as Beth reached the top of the stairs.

Maybe names didn't leave physical scars, but they did hurt. The barbs stung even more when they were tossed by her sister. For as long as she could remember, Beth had adored her little sister, but she'd also been aware that her affection wasn't returned. So she'd tried harder to be liked by her sibling, to be included in her activities, to be part of her life.

Every once in a while, Leighton would invite her into her inner circle, allow her to be included in her plans. It didn't take Beth long to realize that her sister wasn't trying to befriend her so much as she was testing her. But it wasn't in Beth's nature to go along with the crowd when what the crowd was doing was questionable, dangerous or illegal. And Leighton had stopped inviting her, further cementing her status as an outcast, widening the gap between the sisters' lives.

Wilder caught up to her in the hall, before she even reached her room.

"I'm sorry," he said.

She shook her head. "You didn't say anything that wasn't true."

"But I didn't mean it."

"Yes, you did. And it's true. Leighton's the fun sister. I'm the responsible one.

"And normally that wouldn't bother me so much, except that her latest actions have been beyond irresponsible."

"You're worried about her," Wilder guessed.

"Of course, I'm worried about her. And I'm worried about Cody. And I'm mad that she doesn't seem to be worried about Cody."

She stalked back and forth in the hall. "I mean—she just left him here without telling anyone where she was going or when she would be back," Beth continued her rant. "How could she do that? And what if something were to happen to his mom? Where would that leave him?"

"I can understand your concerns," Wilder said. "But even in such a worst-case scenario, I'm confident that Cody would be just fine."

She frowned. "How can you say that?"

"Because he'd still have his Aunt Beth," he pointed out

to her. "And she's a force to be reckoned with. Brave and strong. Loving and loyal."

Inexplicably, her eyes filled.

"Oh, crap," Wilder said. "What did I say wrong now?"

She shook her head, but she couldn't stop the tears from spilling onto her cheeks. And though Wilder looked as if he'd rather be anywhere else in that moment, he drew her close and held her while she cried.

Of course he was only trying to offer her comfort, but with her face pressed against his shirt, she couldn't help but notice how the soft flannel contrasted to his hard muscles. And that he smelled really good.

"You want to tell me now what caused you to go from spitting nails to a complete meltdown in the blink of an eye?" he asked, when her tears had finally dried up.

She shook her head again.

"You don't know?" he queried.

"I don't want to tell you," she admitted.

"Why not?"

"Because you'll think I'm ridiculous."

"I won't think you're ridiculous," he promised.

"The things you said…about me being strong and loving…they were nice."

"And?" he prompted.

"No one's ever said such nice things about me before."

"You need to get some better friends," he told her.

She managed to smile at that. "I have wonderful friends," she assured him. "But I don't tend to open up and dump my emotional baggage on them."

"So why me?" he wondered.

"I guess you're just lucky."

He chuckled at that. "Yeah, that's what my niece said when a baby was left on my doorstep. And though I was skeptical at first, I'm beginning to think maybe she was right."

In only four days, Beth had seen it—he'd not just grown more comfortable with the daily responsibilities of taking care of a baby, but he'd learned to interpret Cody's cries and anticipate his needs. She'd heard it, too, in the warmth in his voice when he talked not just to Cody but about him. Forcing Beth to acknowledge that this was one more thing her sister had lied about.

Or maybe Leighton hadn't been able to guess how he would respond to the news of her unexpected pregnancy. Maybe she really hadn't known him well enough to anticipate that he would step up.

"So...will you reconsider coming to the party?" he asked.

Beth appreciated the invitation. She was even a little tempted. She couldn't remember the last time she'd gone out to celebrate the arrival of a new year, and the idea held a certain appeal. But she had nothing appropriate in her wardrobe for a night out, and no intention of trekking into town to spend money on an outfit she'd probably never wear again. Not to mention that she had no desire to see Wilder live up to his reputation, flirting with all the pretty girls in town.

"Truthfully, I'm not keen on the idea of hanging out with a bunch of people I don't know."

"You know me and my brothers," he pointed out.

Yes, and they were all—aside from Wilder and his father—engaged or married. In other words, if she went, she'd be surrounded by happy couples. And when the clock counted down to midnight, they'd instinctively turn to their significant others to embrace and kiss, reminding her once again that she was alone in the world—as she'd always been.

"I do appreciate the invitation," she said. "But I want to stay home with Cody."

Not only was that kind of celebration much more her

speed, but she sincerely wanted to spend the time with her nephew. Because she was beginning to suspect that, if Wilder was the little boy's father, he would want Cody to stay in Rust Creek Falls, which meant that her days and nights with her nephew were numbered.

"Did you convince Beth to come to the party?" Max asked, when Wilder made his way back downstairs.

"It's not my place to try to change her mind," he said, conveniently ignoring the fact that he'd attempted to do just that.

"I'm sure if you used some of your legendary charm, she'd reconsider," his father said.

Wilder narrowed his gaze. "What are you up to?"

"I'm not up to anything," Max denied.

"Then why do you care whether or not Beth goes to the party?"

"I just think she deserves a night out," his father said.

"That's the only reason?"

"What other reason could there be?"

Wilder didn't buy his father's innocent act for a minute. "Just as long as you don't have any crazy ideas in your head about matchmaking," he said.

"Why would I waste my time when I paid good money to Vivienne Dalton to take care of that?" Max countered.

"I didn't think you'd paid her anything yet."

His father waved a hand dismissively. "You know what I mean."

"I know that you've avoided giving a direct answer to the question," Wilder pointed out.

"How's this for direct? You don't need to worry that I've got any illusions about you and our houseguest from Dallas," Max assured him. "It's obvious that Cody's aunt isn't at all your type."

"I'm glad you can see that," Wilder said, even as a part of him wondered if his father—and his own instincts—might be wrong.

When Wilder walked into the kitchen while Beth was preparing a bottle for Cody on New Year's Eve, her heart actually bumped against her ribs. Because as good as Wilder looked in his usual jeans and flannel, decked out in a suit and tie and dress boots, he was even more mouthwateringly delicious. And looking at him now, she had absolutely no difficulty understanding why her sister had been so eager to fall into bed with him.

Not that Beth would ever do the same thing.

Of course, she'd never have the chance.

Because she and Leighton were complete opposites, and though her heart might act a little crazy whenever Wilder was near, the handsome cowboy had given her absolutely no indication that the unwelcome attraction she felt was reciprocated.

Well, except for that one time, when he'd brushed the remnants of gooey marshmallow off her lip and looked at her in a way that made her feel all gooey inside. But again, that was probably only her overreaction to a casual gesture not intended to be anything else.

"You clean up good, cowboy." She kept her tone light, as if she was unaffected by his appearance and merely making an observation.

He took a moment to peruse her outfit in turn: a chunky knit sweater, black leggings and wool socks. "And you look comfortable and warm," he said, with a wink.

"Because I am," she agreed.

"It's not too late to change your mind and come with us," Max said, entering the room.

He was dressed in a similar fashion to his son, and looking at him now, Beth could easily imagine what Wilder would look like in another thirty-five years—and it was a good look.

"Hunter and Merry are staying home with Wren tonight and said they'd be happy to watch Cody if you wanted to go out," he explained.

"I don't want to go out," Beth said. "But thank you again."

"Well, Happy New Year then," Max said, nudging his son toward the door.

She wished both men a happy new year in return, then locked the door behind them and settled in for a quiet night with her nephew.

As always, the advent of a new year caused her to look back and reflect on all the wonderful things that had happened in the past twelve months—the most notable event being Cody's arrival. She wondered if Leighton was thinking about him today, too. Maybe even missing him a little.

Six days had passed since she'd left Cody at the Ambling A Ranch. Seven since Beth had arrived at her sister's apartment on Christmas Eve in eager anticipation of celebrating the holiday together. And in all that time, she hadn't heard anything from Leighton. Not a single word aside from that brief and cryptic message left by her phone.

Maybe she could understand her sister not reaching out to her—especially if Leighton didn't want to answer the questions she knew Beth would ask—but she couldn't understand her not being in communication with her friends. Or her boss. And a full week's absence from social media was unprecedented.

Beth picked up her cell now, as if she could will her sister to call, but it remained silent, the screen blank. Of course, wherever Leighton was—unless she'd left the country—it was December 31, so she was probably out celebrating. There was nothing Leighton loved more than a party. The wilder the better. And yes, it had crossed Beth's mind, when she found Wilder's name and address in her sister's apartment, that Leighton would have found his name as appealing as the rest of him.

Beth had always been attracted to a different kind of man. The kind who would prefer a simple "dinner and a movie" date over loud music and fancy cocktails in a trendy nightclub. The kind who aspired to obtain a wife and a family rather than fast cars and faster women. She wanted a simple man with simple dreams.

Which was why her attraction to Wilder wasn't just unexpected but unwelcome. Because if he was her sister's type, he was definitely *not* hers. Unfortunately that knowledge didn't stop her pulse from racing when he was near, or prevent butterflies from swirling in her belly when he smiled at her, or cool the blood that heated when he touched her.

Aside from the fact that he wasn't her type, he was quite possibly her nephew's father. And regardless of whether or not the DNA results proved he was Cody's dad, there was no denying that he'd had an intimate physical relationship with her sister. Yes, that relationship had ended a long time ago, but it still felt as if she was violating some kind of unwritten code.

Or maybe a written code, she acknowledged, as coveting thy sister's lover was undoubtedly the moral equivalent of coveting thy neighbor's spouse.

Thou shall not, she reminded herself sternly.

But even if she did covet, nothing would ever come of her desires, because Wilder would never be attracted to someone like her. His history with her sister proved that he preferred a very different kind of woman.

So really, any fantasies that played out in her head—or in her dreams—were just that. And fantasies aside, she was happy with her life. She had a great job, a nice apartment, good friends and friendly neighbors, and now she had Cody, too.

The birth of her nephew had filled her life in ways she couldn't have imagined. But now she had to face the very real possibility that, if Leighton didn't come back and the DNA test proved that Wilder was Cody's father, she could lose him.

She no longer had any doubts that the cowboy would pursue legal custody of his child. And the courts, taking into consideration the biological connection and Leighton's apparent abandonment of her child, would likely rubber-stamp his application.

Sure, Beth could put in a claim for guardianship and argue that she had a stronger bond with her nephew, who'd never even met Wilder until he was four months old. But the courts tended to favor placement of a child with a parent, and they certainly wouldn't hold it against Wilder that he'd had no contact with a child he'd known nothing about.

Even if she believed she was better equipped to deal with Cody's day-to-day needs, she couldn't deny that Wilder had a lot of family support in Montana. And though she'd had limited interactions with his siblings and their spouses, it was evident that they'd readily accepted Cody as part of the family.

So the most likely scenario was that Cody would stay in Rust Creek Falls and she would go back to Dallas, and maybe she'd get to see her nephew a few times a year. The prospect made her heart ache unbearably.

Of course, if Leighton came back to reclaim her baby and Wilder consented to her returning with him to Dallas, then the status quo of Beth's life would be restored. Or maybe Leighton would return and decide to give her relationship with the cowboy another chance—to give Cody a family. Which was what Beth wanted more than anything for her nephew, even if it meant she'd be left on the outside looking in.

But perhaps this was a lesson to her. A reminder that she needed to live her own life and let Leighton live hers. Whether or not she agreed with her sister's choices, she had to accept that they were hers to make. And if Leighton made mistakes, she would have to own them and learn from them.

And maybe it was time for Beth to make some mistakes, too. Or at least take some chances. She'd mostly given up on dating, having grown tired of putting herself out there in an effort to meet "the right guy" only to find that she didn't click with anyone. Or, when she thought she clicked, to realize she'd been duped by someone who'd only said and done the right things to get her into bed and then totally ghosted on her.

Maybe she should put herself out there again—say "yes" the next time Barry Kendrick asked her to go out with him. So what if the fifth-grade science teacher didn't make her heart race or her belly quiver? It was time to grow up and accept that those physiological reactions didn't exist outside the pages of the romance novels that she loved to read.

Except that her body's responses to Wilder Crawford proved otherwise.

Chapter Eleven

Looking around the festively decorated ballroom of Maverick Manor, it seemed to Wilder that after a lot of years and a lot of parties, they all started to look and feel the same. The glittery venues and beautiful women mixed with champagne bubbles and blurred together in his mind.

His memories of last year's celebration, being the most recent, were perhaps a little clearer. He and Leighton had been seeing each other for a few weeks by then, and he easily pictured the sparkly green dress that hugged her curves and the sexy skyscraper heels that put her mouth within easy reach of his. But the rest of the details remained fuzzy.

He knew she had pale blond hair and moss green eyes, but the image that teased his mind now was of dark hair and dark eyes. And as the features came more fully into focus, he noticed other inconsistencies: the lush mouth was a little too full, and instead of being painted glossy red, the lips were naturally pink. Naked. And somehow even more tempting.

Beth's lips.

The realization was as startling to Wilder as it was unsettling.

Scowling, he escaped to the outdoor terrace to get some air and clear his head.

Looking around at the crowd, everyone decked out in their holiday finest, it belatedly occurred to him that Beth might not have wanted to come to the party because she didn't have anything appropriate to wear. He would have been happy to take her shopping, if she'd asked, though the way she'd balked at shopping with him the last time, he wasn't surprised that she didn't. Which was too bad. He wouldn't mind seeing her in something other than the jeans or leggings and bulky sweaters she seemed to favor. Or maybe in nothing at all.

Uneasy with the direction of his thoughts—and uncomfortable outside without a coat—he returned to the gathering. After a quick stop at the bar, he stood on the periphery of the crowd and spotted his father in conversation with an older, petite blonde he didn't recognize.

Could this be the mystery woman his father had gone into Kalispell to have dinner with? Max had been uncharacteristically tight-lipped the day after his date, volunteering no details and refusing to respond to his son's questions. But whoever this woman was with the platinum curls and four-inch heels, she seemed to have Max's complete and undivided attention.

And because Wilder was watching them, he didn't notice the pretty brunette who'd sidled up to him until she spoke. "Can I buy you a drink?"

His smile was automatic as he turned. She had dark hair pinned up in some kind of fancy twist, with a few strands pulled loose to frame her heart-shaped face. Her eyes were as blue as the sapphires in her ears and sparkled with wicked promise.

She was beautiful and confident and not at all subtle about what she wanted—the type of woman who usually made his blood hum in his veins. And yet, when he looked at her, he felt nothing but a vague appreciation for her obvious attributes.

In response to her question, he held up the bottle of beer in his hand. "I've already got one."

"Then I guess you should buy me one," she said.

Even if he wasn't interested, it wasn't in his nature to be rude. So he put his hand on her back and led her to the bar, where she ordered some kind of froufrou cocktail that set him back twenty bucks. A small price to pay for a man interested in what she was obviously offering. But he wasn't that man. Not tonight.

She introduced herself as Simone and told him that she lived in Billings but had come to Rust Creek Falls to visit a friend from college who'd recently split from a longtime boyfriend. Except that the longtime boyfriend had apparently seen the error of his ways and showed up with an engagement ring in hand, leaving Simone to celebrate on her own.

"Or maybe not entirely alone," she said hopefully.

"You're never really alone in a crowd like this," he remarked, looking around for one of his brothers in the vague and futile hope someone might come to his rescue.

He caught a glimpse of Logan, snuggled up with Sarah, oblivious to the world around them. Of course, even if he managed to snag Logan's attention, his brother would never guess that Wilder wanted to be rescued.

"Is something wrong?" Simone asked, licking her lips to remove the pink sugar that had transferred from the rim of her glass.

"What?"

"You're frowning," she told him.

"Sorry." He smoothed his brow. "I guess my mind was wandering."

"Not something a woman wants to hear when she's flirting with a handsome man," she chided, stroking a long, painted fingernail down his arm.

"Sorry," he said again. "It's not you, it's me."

The warmth in those blue eyes immediately chilled. "Yeah, I've heard that one before. Too many times." She stepped back then. "Thanks for the drink."

Then she turned and walked away.

He could have called her back. He knew how to turn on the charm and, with a wink and a smile, he could have smoothed her ruffled feathers and been kissing her at the stroke of midnight.

But he didn't want her to come back. He had no interest in yet another meaningless encounter with a virtual stranger.

A movement caught the corner of his eye, and he glanced over to see his brother Knox flying his hand through the air like a makeshift plane, then tipping his fingers to dive down and spreading them apart.

Wilder lifted a brow. "Are you having fun?"

"As a matter of fact, I am," Knox said. "Because not only am I here with the sexiest woman in all of Rust Creek Falls, but I just watched my little brother—the one that no woman can apparently resist—crash and burn."

"I didn't crash and burn," he denied.

"What are you guys talking about?" Xander asked, unapologetically shoving his way into their conversation.

"Our baby brother just crashed and burned," Knox said.

"You wish," Wilder retorted.

"So the sexy brunette with the mile-long legs in the skintight dress didn't just walk away from you?" Knox challenged.

"She walked away," he confirmed. "But only because I didn't want her to stay."

Xander frowned, feigning concern. "Did you hit your head when you crashed?"

"I didn't—" Wilder huffed out a breath. "You know what? I don't care. If you want to believe I crashed and burned, fine."

His brothers exchanged a glance.

"Okay, now I'm seriously starting to worry that there's something wrong with you," Knox said.

"There's nothing wrong," Wilder assured them. "I'm just not in the mood to spend the night with a woman who doesn't mean anything to me."

"But isn't that your whole MO?" Xander asked.

"If you stop having sex with women who don't mean anything, you won't be having sex with anyone," Knox warned.

"Unless he's met a woman who could actually mean something," Xander mused thoughtfully.

"Wilder?" Knox snorted. "As if."

"If you'd focus your attention on your own woman, you might realize that she's trying to snag your attention before she waves her arm right out of its socket," he replied.

Thankfully, the distraction worked in shifting the topic of conversation, but his brothers flanked him and maneuvered him over to the big table occupied by his siblings and their partners.

"What's going on?" Knox asked, when he'd lowered himself into the vacant seat beside Gen.

"Lily was just telling us the most recent news about the mystery lover in the Abernathy diary," she said, referring to the jewel-encrusted book they'd found hidden in the floorboards shortly after moving to the Ambling A.

"Am I the only one who feels uncomfortable about reading someone's diary?" Avery wondered aloud.

"Yes," Lily said. "I mean, a person's privacy should be respected, of course, but this diary is practically a historical document. And I believe Josiah Abernathy put his innermost thoughts on paper because he expected—or maybe even hoped—that someone else would read his words someday."

"Maybe the mysterious 'W,'" Sarah chimed in.

"Plus, there are some really steamy passages," Xander noted.

"Not trashy," his wife hastened to clarify. "But definitely passionate."

"I think he really loved her," Knox said.

"Who?" Logan asked.

Knox shrugged. "Whoever 'W' is."

"Are there any clues about her identity?"

"Asks the person who didn't think we should be reading the diary," Finn noted dryly.

Avery shrugged. "But since it is being read, are there any clues?" she pressed.

"Actually, there *is* something," Lily said. "Whoever she was, she was apparently pregnant with Josiah's baby."

Avery gasped. "He had a child with his mystery lady?"

Lily shook her head. "Apparently the baby was stillborn."

"Oh." The expectant mom instinctively touched a hand to the slight curve of her belly, as if to protect her own unborn child from such a tragic fate. "That's so sad."

Lily winced. "I'm sorry. I wasn't thinking—"

Avery shook her head. "There's no need to apologize. And I am as curious as everyone else about Josiah and the history of the Ambling A."

"Well, apparently 'W' was so devastated by the loss of her child that she went crazy."

"Literally or figuratively crazy?" Sarah asked curiously.

Her friend and sister-in-law shrugged. "I can only tell you what's written in the book."

"I asked because I'd heard that Winona Cobbs apparently spent some time in an asylum after the Abernathys left town," Logan's wife explained.

"The definitely eccentric and questionably clairvoyant Winona Cobbs?"

"The one and only," Sarah confirmed.

"But I've lived in Rust Creek Falls my whole life and I've never heard so much as a whisper of a rumor that Winona Cobbs was ever pregnant," Gen said.

"She wouldn't be the first woman to keep an out-of-wedlock baby a secret," Sarah remarked. "Especially so many years ago."

"Except that Winona isn't exactly known for her ability to keep secrets," Lily commented.

"And if the diary is as old as we think, she would have been a teenager at the time," Knox chimed in.

"On the other hand, if she did lose a child, well, that might explain why she's always been a little...odd," Gen acknowledged.

The mystery was admittedly intriguing, but as Wilder had nothing to add to the conversation, he decided to abandon the party and return to the place where it all started.

Max watched his youngest son slip away from the gathering and head out alone. Though Wilder had always enjoyed a party, he wasn't surprised to see him go. His life had been turned upside down since he'd found Cody on the doorstep, and though he'd yet to acknowledge the child as his own, over the past week, Wilder's denials of paternity had become less frequent and less adamant.

Max didn't blame him for not embracing the baby with open arms, because he knew it wasn't just the responsibilities of fatherhood that Wilder found daunting. It was the memories that had been stirred up by the realization that Cody's mother had walked out on him. Just like Sheila had walked out on her children when Wilder wasn't much older than Cody was now.

Of course, his youngest son had no real recollection of Sheila leaving, but he'd grown up believing that she'd chosen a life with another man over her children. Because that was what Max had wanted him to believe. What he'd wanted all his children to believe. Because admitting the truth would mean admitting that it was his fault his six sons had grown up without their mother.

"That's gotta be one of your boys," his female companion said, following the direction of his gaze.

Max nodded. "My youngest."

"He's a lucky boy," she remarked, with a bold wink. "Because he's almost as handsome as his daddy."

He smiled, appreciating her company and her flattery.

Of course, Max had always appreciated beautiful women, and Estelle fit the bill well enough. Blond curls framed a flawless face with thickly lashed blue eyes, a pert nose and slickly painted lips. He suspected she'd paid a price to retain—or maybe even enhance—her natural attributes, but he had no objections to hair dyes or face paint or even a little nip and tuck. Not when the results were so appealing.

Though she was barely five feet tall without the skinny heels that added several inches to her height, and probably not more than ninety pounds, she would never be described as diminutive. She was bossy and opinionated and didn't know the meaning of the word *quit*.

Some eighteen months earlier, she'd sold her wedding planning business to Vivienne Dalton—the same woman he'd hired as a matchmaker for his sons, though she'd been Vivienne Shuster at the time and the business had been located in Kalispell. Then Estelle had moved down to Phoenix to work with her sister in the funeral business. Six months later, she'd decided that the Grand Canyon State wasn't for her and returned to Kalispell.

"I'm not overly fond of cowboys," she'd said at their first meeting—set up by Vivienne Dalton—at a bar in her neighborhood. "But you don't look like the kind who buys his jeans at the same place he gets feed for his horses."

"I'm not overly fond of outspoken women," he'd replied, more amused than insulted by her blunt assessment. "And you do look like the kind who has an opinion about everything and not enough sense to know when to keep it to herself."

She'd smiled then. "You going to buy me a drink?"

"You going to order something ridiculously girly?"

She asked the bartender for Jack Daniel's Single Barrel Select, straight up. He'd had the same, and they'd chatted some more while they'd sipped the smooth whiskey.

Tonight, she was drinking champagne, as most of the other guests in attendance were doing. She lifted her glass to her lips now and swallowed the last mouthful of bubbly, then opened the clasp of her handbag and frowned as she examined its contents.

"Did you lose something?" he asked.

"I keep forgetting that I don't smoke anymore," she confided.

"Smoking's a bad habit," he said.

"My doctor spent years telling me the same thing," she confided. "But it wasn't until my sister lost her husband to lung cancer that I finally managed to kick it."

He nodded, only half listening to what she was saying.

But apparently Estelle was more intuitive than he'd given her credit for, because she stopped rambling about the treatments that had taken as much of a toll on her brother-in-law as the disease and asked, "What's got you so worried about your son?"

"He's going through some stuff right now," Max answered vaguely.

"In other words, none of my business," she guessed.

"More that it's not my place to tell," he said.

"Well, then, why don't we take ourselves to my place where I'll be better able to help you forget your worries?"

Max wasn't convinced anything could make him forget his worries, but he was willing to let her try.

The house was quiet after Wilder and Max had gone.

Too quiet.

Or maybe it was the isolation of the ranch that made Beth a little uneasy.

She was a city girl born and bred, accustomed to the lights and noises of an urban setting. Here, it was so quiet she'd be able to hear crickets if the insects hadn't entered into a state of complete dormancy to survive the frigid winter season.

She turned on the television to provide some background noise. Because being alone with the baby, she found herself jumping at every creak and groan of the big old house. She wouldn't be so uneasy if there was a dog around—and wasn't having a dog a prerequisite of being a rancher?

They'd had a German shepherd named Rowdy for almost thirteen years, Wilder had confided when she'd asked him the question. But they'd had to put him down only a few months before making the move from Dallas, and Max had vowed that he'd never get another dog. Wilder didn't really believe it was true, especially considering how Max fussed over Harry and Dobby—the two dachshunds that belonged to Xander and Lily, but for now, he was without a canine companion.

And Beth was a great big fraidycat, she acknowledged to herself as she plugged in the lights of the Christmas tree to enjoy the holiday display—and because she hoped more lights would make her less likely to jump at shadows.

Wilder had told her that they always went out to cut down a tree two weeks before Christmas and took it out of the house again on New Year's Day. Which reminded her that she'd have to deal with her own holiday decorations when she got home. So maybe it was fortunate that she didn't have a real tree. If she did, it would likely be nothing more than a bare trunk surrounded by a pile of dry needles by the time she returned.

After Cody had his cereal and his bath, Beth read him a couple of the books he'd got for Christmas. She guided his fingertips over the textured pages so he could feel soft and rough, bumpy and slippery, scaly and furry. By the time she closed the cover, his eyes were drifting shut.

"Look, Cody, they're having a big party in New York City. See all the people?" She pointed to the TV screen to direct his attention.

Though she knew television wasn't recommended for babies so young, she wasn't yet ready to take him upstairs and face the reality of spending yet another New Year's Eve alone. But Cody's eyes were closed before the ball dropped in Times Square, so she finally put him in his crib and turned on the baby monitor.

When she returned to the company of the television in the family room, she scrolled through the channels until she found another station that was counting down to the New Year, this time in Chicago. She'd just started to relax on the sofa when she heard what sounded like footsteps on the porch.

She froze, straining to hear over the thundering of her heart, even as she tried to assure herself it was nothing but her own overactive imagination.

But then she heard it again. A sound like feet stomping outside the door. Definitely *not* her imagination.

It might have occurred to her that an intruder wouldn't likely make so much noise, but at the moment, the rational part of her brain didn't seem to be communicating with the rest of her.

She pressed the mute button on the remote and strained her ears. It was a click this time, like the dead bolt being released, then a creak, as if the door had opened.

She dropped the remote to grab for her cell phone, ready to dial 9-1-1 and trying not to speculate about the length of time it would take the local police to arrive at her isolated location.

"Beth?"

All the air trapped in her lungs whooshed out in a single breath as she recognized Wilder's voice. She set her phone aside and willed her heart rate to return to something approximating normal.

"In the family room," she said, picking up the remote again to unmute the television so that she could pretend his unexpected early return hadn't scared ten years off her life.

"What are you doing home already?" she asked, when he appeared in the doorway.

He shrugged. "The party was a little too noisy and crowded for my liking."

"Aren't those the usual prerequisites of a party?" she asked.

"I guess so," he acknowledged. "But tonight I just wanted to be home."

"I'm not judging," she assured him.

He glanced at the baby monitor on the table beside her. "Cody asleep?"

She nodded. "He just went down."

He checked his watch. "It's a little late for him, isn't it?"

"Yeah, but it's New Year's Eve and he wanted to watch some of the celebration in New York City with me," she explained.

One side of his mouth tipped up in a half smile that never failed to do crazy things to her insides. "He did, did he?"

"He did," she confirmed, unwilling to admit that she'd deliberately tried to keep her nephew awake because she hadn't wanted to be alone.

But now she was alone *with* Wilder, and she wasn't sure if that was better or worse.

Then he loosened his tie and opened the top button of his shirt, and she decided it was both better *and* worse.

Chapter Twelve

As Beth watched Wilder unbutton his shirt, all rational thoughts slipped from her brain, her mouth went dry and her body got warm. His fingers deftly unfastened the second button and, imagining how those strong, calloused hands might feel against her skin, she felt a quiver low in her belly.

She wondered if he would open a third button, and then a fourth, so that she could discover if his broad chest and flat stomach were as chiseled in real life as they were in her imagination. Because yes, she'd imagined and fantasized about the handsome cowboy undressed. Dreamed about him—about his naked body entwined with her own. And woken up embarrassed and ashamed to realize that she could harbor such wanton feelings for a man who'd been her sister's lover—and was very likely the father of Leighton's baby.

Beth swallowed hard and tried to quash the lustful thoughts that teased her body and her brain.

"What?" she asked, when she realized he'd spoken but she hadn't heard a single word.

"I asked if it was okay for me to hang out here with you."

"It's your house," she reminded him.

"But you've got the remote."

"That means I'm in charge?"

He smiled at her dubious tone. "At least in charge of the TV."

She handed the controller to him. "I should probably head up to bed, anyway."

"It's not even ten thirty," he pointed out, his voice tinged with amusement.

"Oh," she said, feeling foolish. Because even a killjoy like her knew that going to bed at ten thirty on New Year's Eve was beyond lame. "I guess I could stay up a little longer. But I'm going to apologize in advance."

"For what?"

"The fact that I'll probably fall asleep before the clock strikes midnight."

He gasped, feigning shock. "On New Year's Eve?"

"Cody was up three times last night," she told him. "I'm convinced, by the way he's been gnawing and drooling, that a couple of teeth will be breaking through soon."

"Is that what the book says to watch for—gnawing and drooling?"

"There isn't one book that's the authority on everything, and every baby is different," she chided. "But yes, those are generally recognized as common signs of teething."

"If you don't think you'll make it to midnight, maybe we should crack open a bottle of champagne now and toast the New Year along with Chicago," he suggested.

"Sounds good to me," she said.

He retrieved a bottle of bubbly and a couple of glasses, popping the cork with an ease that attested to experience. And didn't that immediately highlight the differences in their lifestyles, that he could make an offhand suggestion and know the fancy wine would be chilling? If she ever expressed a spontaneous desire for champagne, the spontaneity would invariably be lost as she made a hurried trip to buy it, with her fingers crossed that the local store sold it already chilled.

He could have chosen to sit anywhere. There were plenty of options in the spacious room: the love seat adjacent to the couch she occupied, one of a trio of armchairs, or even the other end of the big sofa. For some reason, he chose to sit right beside her, so close that their thighs were touching.

He handed her a flute of champagne, tapped the rim of his own glass to hers and said, “Happy Almost New Year.”

“Happy Almost New Year,” she echoed, and took a tentative sip of the bubbly.

The cool and crisp liquid tickled as it slid down her throat, causing an almost irresistible urge to giggle. She swallowed the urge along with another sip of champagne.

“So how does this year compare to your last New Year’s Eve?” Wilder asked her.

“It’s almost a carbon copy,” she admitted. “But with a much better bottle of wine.” And the unexpected company of a very handsome cowboy—though she wisely kept that part to herself.

“You mean you sat at home watching other people celebrate the occasion?”

“I wasn’t lying when I said parties aren’t really my thing.”

“Why not?”

She shrugged. “I’ve just never felt comfortable around a lot of people. I prefer more intimate gatherings.” Then, realizing how her words might be misconstrued, she hastened to clarify, “I didn’t mean *intimate* intimate. I only meant that I prefer smaller groups and quieter settings.”

And then, to stop herself from babbling even more, she lifted her glass to her lips again.

“Intimate should definitely involve a smaller number,” he agreed, with a wink. “My preference has always been two.”

She couldn’t agree, because he might interpret that as flirting. And she couldn’t disagree, because if she suggested “or three or four,” he might think she was advertising an adventurous spirit she did not have.

"Or one," she said, deciding that was a safe option and also a truer reflection of her status.

It wasn't until his lips curved that she realized her mistake.

"You like to go it alone sometimes, Beth?"

She could really use a blast of Montana wind to cool her cheeks right now. In the absence of that, she sipped more of the chilled wine.

"I'm going to stop talking now," she decided.

His warm chuckle skimmed over her like a caress. "I didn't mean to embarrass you," he said.

"I think I embarrassed myself," she acknowledged, and was grateful when Wilder steered the conversation to more neutral topics.

They talked about books and movies and the successes or failures of books turned into movies. Then they debated the merits of favorite sports teams, with Wilder insisting that the Cowboys would win another Super Bowl before the Stars took another run at the Stanley Cup and Beth confiding that she'd rather watch the Rangers over the Mavericks any day of the week.

He shook his head. "Clearly you know nothing about basketball."

She narrowed her gaze. "What's your foundation for that claim? The fact that I prefer baseball?"

"And that watching baseball is about as exciting as watching paint dry."

"Clearly you know nothing about baseball," she told him.

"What I do know is that it's almost midnight and you're still awake," he noted, tipping the bottle to pour more champagne into her glass.

"I'm as surprised as you are," she said.

"I'm glad I didn't bore you to sleep."

"You didn't bore me at all. In fact, I quite enjoyed your company tonight."

"Who would have guessed that we could spend an evening together without sniping at one another?" he mused.

"We've spent a lot of time together over the past few days without sniping at each other," she pointed out.

"Yeah, it turns out that you're not quite as uptight as I originally thought."

"And I've been pleasantly surprised to discover that you're not as immature and irresponsible as my first impressions led me to believe."

He smiled. "There it is."

Her brows drew together. "I think I missed something."

"Because you haven't been paying attention," he chided.

"To what?"

"You've got passion and spirit, Lisbeth Ames. But—one early-morning outburst aside—I usually only see it in defense of your sister or your nephew. I'm happy to know that you're also capable of fighting back in defense of yourself."

"I thought we were trying not to fight."

"It turns out I enjoy our verbal sparring," he admitted.

"Given the choice, I'd rather be a lover than a fighter," she said.

Wilder's brows lifted. "Is that so?"

"I didn't mean—" She huffed out a breath. "I always seem to be putting my foot in my mouth around you."

"Let's see if we can find a better use for your mouth," Wilder suggested, as he set both of their champagne glasses aside.

And then he kissed her.

It wasn't a deep or passionate kiss—more a tentative exploration. And yet, when his lips brushed over hers, a jolt of arousal surged through her body, leaving hot tingles in its wake.

She lifted her eyes and saw that he was looking as shaken by the chemistry as she felt. Then his gaze shifted to her mouth, as if he maybe wanted to try that again.

Because she wanted the same thing, she took the initiative this time and leaned forward to kiss him. And he responded. His arm snaked around her waist, pulling her onto his lap so that her knees straddled his hips and her breasts tingled where they touched his chest, her nipples stiffening to tight peaks.

She pressed herself closer, relishing the feel of his rock-hard body. She slid her hands over his taut, sculpted shoulders to link them behind his head, her fingertips tangling in the ends of his hair.

He opened her mouth to deepen the kiss, exploring the sensitive inner recesses with his oh-so-talented tongue. She rocked against him, subconsciously mimicking the rhythm of mating, until he clamped his hands on her hips, stifling her moments.

"I'm going to embarrass myself if you don't stop that," he warned.

"I don't want to stop," she said. "But—"

"Shh." He brushed his lips gently over hers now. "Let's not analyze all the reasons this might be a mistake."

Then he nuzzled her throat, and the erotic scrape of his stubble against her skin made her shiver.

"But it would be, wouldn't it? Getting naked together would further complicate an already complicated situation."

"Or maybe it would simplify it," he suggested.

"How do you figure?"

"Sex is simple—the most primal and essential connection between a man and a woman," he explained, as he slid his hands under her sweater and up her torso to cup her breasts.

And the feel of those calloused palms moving over her skin was even more delicious than she'd imagined.

She moaned softly.

"I really like those noises you make when I touch you," he told her.

"Then keep touching me," she suggested.

"I don't think I can stop."

He rose to his feet then, effortlessly lifting her with him. She wrapped her legs around his waist, hooking her ankles as he carried her toward the stairs.

She felt like a fairy-tale princess in the arms of her Prince Charming.

Except that Wilder wasn't *her* anything and there was no happily-ever-after with him in her future.

But would it be so wrong to enjoy this one magical night? A stolen moment in time before the realities of the world descended upon them once more?

He carried her to the guest room, then set her on her feet beside the bed to whisk her sweater over her head and strip away her leggings.

"You, too," she said, unfastening the remaining buttons of his shirt to reveal a strong chest and rippling abs. *Definitely as chiseled as I'd imagined.* She touched her lips to his taut, warm skin, then flicked out her tongue. *And every bit as delicious.*

While she explored his chest, he discarded the rest of his clothes, then eased her onto the mattress, bracing himself over her and capturing her mouth with his again.

He seemed to know just where and how to touch her to heighten her desire, maximize her pleasure. Eager to reciprocate, she tentatively reached between their bodies to wrap her hand around his hard, velvety length. He pulsed in her hand; a groan rumbled in his chest. Emboldened by his response, she stroked her hand toward the tip, then back down again.

He unclasped her bra, releasing her breasts from the restraint of the lacy cups. Her already peaked nipples drew tighter when the cool air whispered over her skin.

He drew one of the aching tips into his mouth, tugging gently with his teeth, until she moaned and arched beneath him. His mouth moved to her other breast, affording it the same attention as his hands stroked over her body in a teasing exploration that made her quiver and yearn.

He gently parted her thighs, opening her to a more intimate investigation. His fingertips skimmed the sensitive skin of her inner thighs and traced the lacy edge of her panties, making her muscles tremble. Then his thumb brushed over the aching nub at her center, through the thin fabric barrier, making her whimper.

His mouth moved lower, skimming over her torso, then he caught the narrow band of lace at her side in his teeth and dragged it down over her hip before switching to the other side. He continued to alternate from side to side, inching her panties downward until they were dangling around one ankle. Then he spread her legs wide and lowered his head between them.

She felt the scrape of his stubble against the sensitive skin of her thighs, a surprisingly erotic sensation. When he touched her with his tongue, she gasped, shocked by the unexpected intimacy. And again, because the pleasure was more than she'd anticipated. More than she'd imagined.

He nibbled and licked, tasting and teasing, driving her ever closer to the pinnacle of pleasure. Then holding her there, right on the edge, until she was desperate for release. She could hear herself whimpering, pleading.

Stop. Please. More.

She didn't seem to know what she wanted, what she needed.

But Wilder knew, and he gave it to her. More and more,

until she couldn't take it anymore. Until she was no longer on the edge, but falling, falling, falling...

Her body was still quivering with the aftereffects of her climax when Wilder retrieved a condom from his wallet, then tore open the foil packet and covered himself. Only then did he position himself over her again, and finally bury himself between her thighs.

She wrapped herself around him, her hands gripping his shoulders, her legs anchored around his torso, pulling him even deeper inside. He began to move, and she met him thrust for thrust, urging him to find the same release he'd given her.

As their bodies merged and mated, she found her own desire escalating again. He picked up the pace, driving faster, harder, deeper. Pushing her to new and even loftier heights. But this time, when she took the plunge, he went with her.

Wilder was jolted awake—and jarred out of a tantalizingly explicit and erotic dream—by the sound of a baby crying. It took him a moment to get his bearings, for his eyes to adjust to the darkness and recognize that he was in the guest room, where he'd fallen asleep after making love with Beth.

He closed his eyes again and swore quietly as the memories washed over him.

It never should have happened.

But it had happened—and it had been amazing.

He'd always preferred the company of women who were looking for short-term companionship rather than long-term commitment. Beth was all about hearth and home right down to the marrow of her bones. She was the type of woman a man would choose to marry, and Wilder had no intention of being that man—for any woman.

But, as usual last night, he'd been thinking about his

own desires, selfishly taking what he wanted with little regard for the consequences.

And now…

A soft murmur joined the sound of the baby's cries. He realized the sounds were coming through the baby monitor on the table beside the bed and that Beth was already up and tending to Cody.

Cody.

He swore again as a fresh wave of guilt washed over him.

Barely a week earlier, he'd been reflecting on how great his life was, how lucky he was that he wasn't tied down in any kind of relationship, and how he had no interest in being saddled with a kid at this point in his life.

Because a week earlier, he hadn't known of Cody's existence. Now that he did, his intentions and interests were irrelevant. The fact was, if Cody was his child, he was going to step up and be the best father that he could be to him.

But it didn't really matter whether or not the kid was his. He should never have seduced his aunt. Because the intimacies they'd shared added a whole other layer of complications to an already complicated situation. Which, now that he thought about it, was almost exactly what she'd warned him about the night before.

Asserting his parental rights and applying for legal custody would deal a devastating blow to Beth, who'd been helping to care for her nephew since his birth.

But there was no way Wilder could let the child go. He wouldn't ever abandon his son, as his mother had abandoned hers. He wouldn't let anything matter more than his child.

But wasn't that exactly what he'd done last night?

Selfishly, and not surprisingly, he'd been thinking only

about himself. About what *he* wanted. And last night, he'd wanted Beth.

Maybe the realization had surprised him a little.

Being intimate with Beth had surprised him even more.

Despite her rigid expectations and uptight manner, she was a surprisingly passionate and gloriously uninhibited woman. And if he was the type of man who did relationships, he might be willing to take a chance with her. But he wasn't, and he couldn't.

Because everything else aside, he had a history with her sister. And yes, that was probably something he should have thought about last night before he'd removed Beth's lace panties with his teeth. It didn't matter that Leighton had made it clear she was done with him. He doubted she'd be pleased to discover that he'd picked up with her sister.

But had he picked up with her sister?

Or had last night been the beginning and end?

Frustrated that all he had were questions without answers, he pushed back the covers and gathered his discarded clothes. He dressed quickly in the dark, intending to go across the hall to help with the baby.

But he paused in the hallway, watching Beth, silhouetted by the dim light, as she tended to the baby. She continued to murmur softly, soothing the child as she dealt with the wet diaper that was likely the cause of his distress. After she'd finished with that task, she'd go downstairs to prepare a bottle to fill his tummy so that he might sleep comfortably for a few more hours.

Or Wilder could take care of that for her. He'd mixed the formula enough times now that he didn't even have to read the label anymore. But as much as they took turns with feedings and diaper changes during the day, sharing such duties in the darkness of the night felt like something else. Something more.

Like something a dad and mom might do—if they were a family.

And since he didn't even know for sure if he was Cody's dad, and she for sure wasn't his mom, it would be a mistake—even bigger than the one they'd made last night—to pretend they were a family.

So instead of offering to help, he retreated to his own room like the coward that he was.

Chapter Thirteen

"Hey, big guy." Beth crooned the words softly as she unfastened the tabs of her nephew's diaper, hoping to soothe the baby but not wake the sexy cowboy asleep across the hall. "What's going on in here?"

Cody's big blue eyes were swimming with tears, his long, dark lashes wet and spikey. But his quivering lips curved, just a little.

"I bet you're not just wet but hungry," she said, as she slid a dry diaper under his bottom. "Because you've been down for almost six hours." She stifled a yawn as she wiped his bottom. "Unfortunately, I've only slept about half that amount of time, so if you could go back to sleep without too much fuss, I'd appreciate it."

Cody shoved a fist into his mouth.

"Yes, of course, I'll give you a snack first," she promised, as she fastened the new diaper, then snapped up his diaper shirt and sleeper again. "There. That's better, isn't it?"

Cody continued to gnaw on his fist as she carried him downstairs. Though she'd only been at the ranch five full days, she'd quickly learned her way around the house in the dark—a necessary skill considering the number of times she was up and down with her nephew each night.

She blinked at the light when she opened the refrigerator to retrieve one of the bottles she'd prepared earlier. She turned on the kettle to heat the water to warm the formula, then turned it off again as she recalled Sharleesa—

a colleague from work and mother of three—mentioning that her kids all preferred a cold bottle when they were teething.

"Okay, we're going to try something different tonight," she said to Cody, uncapping the bottle and lowering the nipple toward his mouth. "Let's see what you think of this."

Cody thought it was just fine, apparently, as he latched on and immediately began sucking.

"Apparently you're not afraid to try new things," Beth mused as she headed back up the stairs again. "Which proves you inherited your mama's adventurous spirit."

As usual, thinking about Leighton led to worrying about Leighton. She wished she could adopt Wilder's philosophy and not worry about things she couldn't control, but she didn't think that would ever apply to her sister.

"I didn't make any resolutions this year," she said, continuing to talk softly to Cody. "But maybe it's not too late. Maybe this year, if I make more of an effort, your mama and I will learn to communicate better and grow closer."

Of course, if she really wanted a better relationship with Leighton, she probably shouldn't have slept with her ex, Beth acknowledged ruefully.

But maybe her sister wouldn't ever find out what she'd done. Certainly Beth had no intention of telling her, and she couldn't imagine that Wilder would volunteer the information. And since she was pretty sure their impulsive lovemaking had been the result of proximity and champagne, she was confident it wouldn't ever happen again.

And that was for the best, because when Leighton came back and saw how good Wilder was with Cody, maybe she'd decide to give their relationship another chance—to give their son a real family.

It was what Beth had always wanted for Cody. So why,

then, did the idea of her sister sharing Wilder's life—and his bed—make her heart ache?

Was it somehow possible that, over the course of only five days, she'd developed real feelings for the cowboy?

Thinking about it now, she knew it wasn't just possible but true. Because during that time, she'd had plenty of opportunities to interact with him and discover his true character.

Maybe he didn't instinctively know how to be a father, but he'd proven that he was open to learning and willing to make the effort. And though she knew he had a reputation with the ladies, since she'd been at the ranch, he appeared to have made the little boy his priority over all else.

Even tonight, when he'd gone out to celebrate the New Year with his family, he'd come home early. He'd said he wasn't in the mood for the crowds, but she suspected he'd really wanted to check on Cody. Because she knew, even if Wilder wasn't ready to admit it, that the baby had already worked his way into his heart.

There was so much more to him than the picture of the wild and aimless cowboy her sister had painted. He was undeniably the most handsome man she'd ever met, but aside from his striking good looks and mouthwatering muscles, he was intelligent and charming, insightful and compassionate. He also had a good sense of humor and a strong sense of family loyalty.

And after only five days at the Ambling A and one night in Wilder's arms, she was in serious danger of losing her heart.

"Why didn't you tell me that Cody's teeth had come in?" Wilder demanded, when he returned to the house following an early ride with his brother—and after hearing the news from his father, who'd puffed up like a proud grandpa as he delivered it.

"You didn't stick around long enough for me to say anything," Beth said, pointedly referencing his quick exit earlier that morning.

"I had to ride out with Hunter to check the fence."

"I'm sure you did." She dipped the spoon into the cereal bowl again and moved it toward the baby's mouth.

When Cody opened up, she let him swallow the cereal, then used the rubber tip of the spoon to gently pull down his lower lip and reveal the bumpy ridges of white poking through his gums so that Wilder could see what all the fuss was about.

"Look at that," he said, feeling his own chest puff up with pride, as if he was somehow responsible for the baby's milestone. "He's got teeth."

"They've still got a way to go, but now that they've broken through the gums, he should be a little less cranky," she said.

"That's good," he agreed.

Now if only he could figure out why Beth seemed so cranky this morning. Or maybe he already knew—which her next words confirmed.

"Should we talk about what happened last night?" she asked.

"If you want to," he agreed cautiously.

"What I want is for things to not be awkward between us," she said.

"Do things seem awkward to you?"

"It's hard to tell when we haven't been in the same room together for more than five minutes. Or maybe that is the tell," she decided.

"I haven't been avoiding you," he promised. "Hunter texted this morning and asked me to ride out to the eastern boundary with him."

"Why you?" she wondered aloud.

"Probably because he knew all our other brothers would be snuggled up with their wives."

"Oh." She blew out a breath. "So I may have overreacted," she acknowledged. "I'm not very good at this. I don't have a lot of experience with mornings after."

"Just say whatever it is you want to say," he suggested.

"Okay," she agreed. "I think last night was a mistake. I mean, it was great, but it shouldn't have happened. We shouldn't have…gotten carried away."

"Is that what happened? We got carried away?" he asked, wondering why her dismissal of their lovemaking bothered him when he'd arrived at the same conclusion.

"Isn't it?"

"Sure," he finally agreed. "We got carried away, it never should have happened, it won't happen again."

"Okay, then," she said.

"If that's all, I'm going to make myself a sandwich and then head back out to help my brothers fix the fence."

"Of course," she agreed.

He nodded brusquely and walked out, leaving Beth to wonder why, after he'd said everything she wanted him to say, she was so unhappy.

"What's going on with you and Beth?" Max asked the following morning, when Wilder returned to the supply shed for the box of screws Knox had left behind.

"What do you mean?" Wilder asked cautiously.

"She put on boots and a coat to go out to the barn and ask Hunter to put Cody's car seat in her vehicle."

"And?"

"Why didn't she ask you?"

He shrugged. "Maybe she figured Hunter has more experience with such things."

His father acknowledged that possibility with a slow

nod. "It would have been even easier to ask you to give her a lift into town."

"She knows I'm still working with Xander and Knox to fix the fence," Wilder told him, reminding his father of the barrier that had been destroyed when someone skidded off the road and crashed through it.

They didn't know what kind of vehicle or who was responsible, as the driver hadn't contacted Max to own up to the incident. But considering the damage to the fence and the fact that the vehicle had driven away, they suspected Butch Ferrell, who owned a jacked-up Escalade and had been known to get behind the wheel after a few too many drinks at the Ace in the Hole.

"Logan or Finn could've taken your place," Max pointed out.

"And then accused me of skipping out on the hard work." Wilder shook his head. "I don't think so."

"You'd rather skip out on spending time with your son," his father remarked with obvious disapproval. "Or maybe it's Beth that you don't want to spend time with."

"If I had a choice between fixing fence and shopping, I'd go with the fence every time," he told his father.

"Are you sure that's all it is?"

"Why do you think it's anything more?"

"Because recently it seems that every time one of you walks into a room, the other one walks out."

"You ever consider that maybe we each have our own stuff to do in different places?" he suggested, because he couldn't deny the accuracy of his father's observation.

Or that, despite Beth's claim that she didn't want things to be awkward between them, they were.

His father sighed. "I thought the two of you were finally starting to get along."

"We were. We *are*," he corrected.

"Really?" Max challenged. "Because it doesn't look like it from where I'm standing."

"There's no reason for you to worry, Dad," he said, grabbing the box of nails.

"Has Beth mentioned when she plans to go back to Dallas?" Max asked, apparently not yet ready to let his son return to his duties.

Wilder shook his head. "Not before the DNA results are in. Why? Do you suddenly have an objection to her being here?"

"I don't," his dad assured him. "We've got plenty of space, and I've eaten more home-cooked meals in the past week than in the six weeks prior to her showing up."

"Which only proves that we need to hire a cook," Wilder said. "Because she's not going to be here forever."

"But she's here now," his father pointed out.

Beth obviously hadn't thought this through.

She'd just wanted to get away from the ranch and the awkward tension with Wilder for a little while, and a quick shopping trip into town seemed the perfect excuse. But she didn't have Cody's stroller—and even if she did, she wasn't sure it would navigate the snow-covered sidewalks—and it was awkward to wear his baby carrier over her coat and it didn't fit under. Which left her with no recourse but to carry him in his car seat.

At least when she got inside the store, she was able to sit his car seat in the cart while she did her shopping. She only needed a few things, but after paying for her groceries, she was faced with the logistical problem of having to cart the baby, his diaper bag and three bags of groceries out to her vehicle.

She might have asked Natalie for help, if the woman she'd met on her first trip into town had been working, but she hadn't seen her anywhere in the store. Thankfully today's clerk—identified as Nina by another customer—anticipated her dilemma and called a stock boy to carry Beth's purchases out to her car.

After all of that, she decided she deserved a treat and headed over to Daisy's Donuts, the reputed mecca of everything sweet and delicious in Rust Creek Falls. An examination of the offerings in the display case required several minutes of careful study, leading Beth to conclude that the reputation had not been exaggerated.

An opinion that was further bolstered by her first bite of chocolate silk pie.

"Hey, stranger."

Beth glanced up as Natalie Crawford slid into the seat across from her. She lifted a hand to wave, unable to offer a verbal reply because her mouth was full.

Natalie eyed the plate in front of her. "Mmm…is that Eva's chocolate silk pie?"

Beth nodded and swallowed. "Do you want me to ask for another fork?"

The other woman shook her head regretfully. "Don't think I'm not tempted, but I'm actually here to pick up a Neapolitan cake for my mom's birthday and if I let myself indulge in two desserts today, I'll never squeeze into my favorite jeans tomorrow."

"Your call," Beth said, as she dipped her fork into her pie again.

"So what brings you into town today?" Natalie asked.

"Cabin fever," she said.

"We all suffer from a bit of that during the winter," the other woman said sympathetically.

"And since I needed an excuse to go out, I decided to pick up a few groceries to make chicken and dumplings for dinner."

"You're going to spoil Max and Wilder with all your fancy cooking," Natalie warned.

"It's the least I can do," Beth said. "And I don't really do anything else."

"I would imagine this little guy keeps you plenty busy," Natalie said, glancing at the baby in his carrier on the bench seat beside his aunt. Then she smiled. "He's watching you move that fork from your plate to your mouth and wondering why you're not sharing with him."

"Because it's a little too sweet and rich for a baby who only recently started eating cereal," Beth said, directing her explanation to Cody. But she dipped the fork into the whipped cream on top of the pie, then touched the tines to his lips so that he could have a tiny taste.

He rubbed his lips together to sample the cream, then his eyes grew wide and his feet kicked.

"I think he likes it," Natalie said.

"Apparently he's got a sweet tooth like his aunt," Beth noted.

"Or maybe two of them," the other woman said. "When did he get those?"

"Just yesterday."

"New teeth for the New Year. Speaking of which… I didn't see you at the party at Maverick Manor."

"Because I wasn't there," Beth admitted.

"Surely Max invited you?"

"He did," she confirmed. "But I opted to stay home with Cody."

"Just with Cody?" Natalie teased.

"What do you mean?"

"Wilder skipped out early, causing much speculation about where he was going and who he was going to be with," Natalie confided. "Because everyone's waiting to see if Max's matchmaker goes six-for-six, and a lot of the local girls are hoping to be the sixth lucky bride."

"Is that what passes for entertainment in Rust Creek Falls?" Beth wondered, feigning only mild interest.

"Well, we've got to do something," the other woman said. "We don't even have a movie theater in town."

She smiled at that, remembering a similar discussion she'd had with Wilder on the same topic.

"In that case, I'd put my money on Max," Beth said. "He doesn't strike me as a man who ever gives up before he gets what he wants."

"And Wilder seems equally stubborn."

"Could be," she acknowledged.

"But if you were going to throw your hat in the ring…" Natalie let her words trail off suggestively.

"Me?" Beth immediately shook her head. "I'm only here because of Cody."

"That's too bad," Natalie said, sounding disappointed.

Maybe she thought so, but Beth knew it was for the best.

By three o'clock that afternoon, Wilder was rethinking his choices. Because a trip into town to do some shopping with Beth and Cody had to be better than freezing his ass off in single-digit temperatures trying to rebuild a fence.

"We should sue Ferrell for damages," he grumbled.

Though it wasn't the cost of the materials that annoyed him so much as the inconvenience of having to make the repair—and the shirking of responsibility by the idiot driver who'd crashed through the fence.

"Good luck proving it was him," Xander said.

"I heard he took his truck to a body shop in Kalispell for repairs," Knox chimed in. "Claimed someone hit his vehicle while it was parked."

"With a two-by-four?" Wilder asked facetiously, rubbing his hands on his thighs in an effort to restore some circulation to his numb digits. "Because you can bet whoever does the repair finds splinters of wood while banging out the dents."

Yeah, he definitely should have chosen to go into town with Beth—except that he hadn't been invited.

And what was that about?

They'd had the "morning after" talk she insisted on, and he'd agreed with everything she'd said—even if he didn't really agree that the night they'd spent together had been a mistake.

So why would she be mad at him?

He was tempted to ask his brothers for their take on the situation, but that would require telling them what had happened with Beth on New Year's Eve. And though he'd never shied away from talking about his past successes with the ladies, he didn't want Beth to become the object of their crude jokes.

Unless he's met a woman who could actually mean something.

As Xander's words from the night of the party echoed in his head, Wilder found himself wondering if his brother wasn't right.

Chapter Fourteen

Late the next morning, Beth was checking her email while she waited for a fresh pot of coffee to finish brewing. She scrolled through the usual ads for sales and the junk that had managed to sneak through her spam filter. There was a note from her friend Elysia, thanking Beth for the books that she'd given to Elysia's daughter for Christmas. Attached to the message was a picture of the nine-year-old on the sofa, still in her pajamas, with an open book in her hand. The photo was captioned: "And there were still presents to be opened!"

Beth smiled, pleased that her gift had been well received. After sending a quick reply, she resumed skimming through her inbox. Her heart jolted when, a little further down on the screen, she recognized Leighton's email address with a subject line that read "Wayward Sister Checking In."

She clicked on the message.

Beth—

I bet you were starting to wonder if you'd ever hear from me again. And no doubt you're pissed about my disappearing act. I know I promised to explain, but I'm not sure I can except to say that I was living a life I never thought I wanted, and it just got to be too much. And that I'm sorry.

In case you haven't figured it out by now (although I'm sure you have), I took Cody to his dad in Montana. (And I am at least 90% certain that Wilder Crawford is his dad.)

I wish I could say I took him there because I felt guilty that I'd deprived Wilder of the opportunity to know his son, and maybe I did. The truth is, I'm not sure what I was thinking in the last few days leading up to the holiday, what compelled me to pack him up and take him so far away and then leave him behind.

Yeah, Wilder's probably pissed at me, too. And I'm going to have to face up to that when I go back to Rust Creek Falls to get Cody. You don't need to worry—he's not the type of guy to take out his anger on a woman. In fact, he's a pretty good guy, and if he decides he wants Cody to visit sometime, I wouldn't mind. It might be good for him to spend time outdoors, maybe learn to ride a horse and stuff like that.

But I'm getting way ahead of myself now—those things can be figured out later. I just wanted to let you know that we'll be home soon and then we can celebrate Christmas together the way we planned.

XO
L

Reading her sister's words, Beth's initial response was relief, then happiness and hope, followed by frustration, anger and guilt. And while she could blame Leighton's actions for most of those conflicting feelings, the guilt was entirely her own.

"Do you want some of this?"

"What?" She glanced up to see Wilder holding the carafe of freshly brewed coffee over her mug. "Oh, um, yes. Please."

He filled the cup she held out, then returned the pot to the warmer. "Are you okay?"

"Yeah. Fine." But she set the mug down again without taking a sip. "I got an email from Leighton."

The surprise on Wilder's face mirrored her own response—as did the shadow of guilt that quickly followed. "You did? When?"

"Just now."

"What does it say?"

She looked at the message again. "That she's sorry for leaving the way she did and—" She cut herself off with a shake of her head. "Why don't you read it yourself?"

He took the cell from her hand and dropped his gaze to the screen.

She watched him as he scanned her sister's words, noting the flex of a muscle as he tightened his jaw—the only outward indication of any emotion, though she couldn't begin to decipher what that emotion was.

Then he handed the phone back to her. "So she's on her way back here to get Cody," he noted. "And apparently she expects me to just hand him over to her, despite the way she abandoned him."

"She is his mother," Beth pointed out.

"She abandoned him," he said again, his tone implacable.

"So...what are you planning to do?"

He swallowed a mouthful of coffee as he considered his response.

"I'll apply for custody," he decided. "I'll call Maggie right now and make an appointment to get the paperwork started."

She remembered him mentioning that he'd borrowed the crib from Maggie and Jesse, but she hadn't known the woman was a lawyer. "You don't even know for sure that you're his father," Beth reminded him gently.

"Do you really doubt it?" he challenged.

No, she didn't. Not anymore. But if she admitted as much, she might as well go back to Dallas, leaving her nephew with his dad. And maybe that was what she should do.

"I thought we agreed that no decisions would be made until we had the results of the DNA test."

"Well, if Leighton's on her way back, it doesn't really matter what you think," he pointed out. "It's between me and her and has nothing to do with you."

Though the words felt like a physical blow, she knew Wilder hadn't meant to be cruel. He was only speaking the truth as he saw it.

What really hurt was that he was right.

Any and all issues concerning Cody were for the little boy's parents to figure out.

It didn't matter that she'd dropped everything to drive halfway across the country. It didn't matter that she'd been the one helping Wilder care for Cody these past eight days. None of that mattered because he wasn't her child.

She was only a supporting player in this drama her sister had planned, and it was time for her to exit stage right.

Wilder knew his unthinking remark had hurt Beth. And as he watched her walk out of the room, he acknowledged that he might have chosen his words more carefully. Or maybe he'd wanted to put some distance between them. Because it had become increasingly evident to Wilder over the past several days that his feelings about the situation with Cody were being clouded by his feelings for Cody's aunt.

And if he was smart, he would stay where he was and maintain the distance.

Instead, he followed her path up the stairs and found her in the guest room, stuffing clothes into a duffel bag.

"What are you doing?"

"I assume that's a rhetorical question," she said, as she struggled with the zipper.

"Why are you packing, Beth?"

"Because I think it would be best for everyone if I was gone before my sister got here."

"Even for your nephew?" he challenged.

"You've proven you're more than capable of taking care of Cody."

"While I appreciate the vote of confidence, I'd argue that part of taking care of him is ensuring that he feels comfortable and secure," he said. "And I'm not sure that being abandoned by his aunt—barely more than a week after being abandoned by his mother—would do much in that regard."

"I would never abandon him," Beth said fiercely.

"You came here with the intention of taking him back to Dallas, and now you're preparing to leave without him—what would you call it?"

"Getting out of the way so that what happened between us won't be an obstacle to Cody's parents getting back together," she told him.

His brows drew together then. "Is that what you want?"

"I want what's best for Cody," she said, refusing to look at him.

"Me and Leighton together would *not* be best for Cody. And I can assure you, there is absolutely zero chance of that ever happening, anyway."

She swallowed. "Please don't say that. Don't close the door on—"

"Zero," he said again, his tone gentle but firm. "Because for me and Leighton to get back together, we would have had to be together in the first place."

She frowned at that. "You're saying you weren't together?"

"We had some good times and we had sex," he acknowledged bluntly.

"Oh."

"I'm not proud of it, but I'm not going to lie and pretend it was more than it was."

"I'm in no position to judge," she acknowledged. "I fell into bed with you, too, with no expectations of happily-ever-after…or even a kiss the morning after."

His gaze slid away. "I left your bed because I heard you talking to Cody over the baby monitor, saying you needed to get some sleep."

"How very considerate of you," she noted, her tone just a little bit cool.

"And maybe I didn't want to deal with my father's questions, if he found me leaving your room in the early hours of morning."

"Or my questions," she guessed.

"*You* told *me* it was a mistake," he reminded her.

"Because it was," she said again.

"So why are you giving me grief about it now?"

"Because I wanted you to say that it wasn't."

She looked as surprised by the blurted revelation as he felt.

"Beth," he began, then faltered.

She closed her eyes and sighed. "Sorry. Forget I said that."

"I'm not sure I even understand what you said," he admitted. "Are you saying that it *wasn't* a mistake?"

"No, it was," she said. "Of course, it was. I mean, you have a history with my sister—even if it was brief and apparently insignificant. And what happened between us… it was just two lonely people finding comfort together."

"Comfort?" he echoed, torn between insult and amusement. "When your body was shuddering with the aftereffects of multiple orgasms and you were panting my name, that was because you were feeling…comforted?"

Beth glanced away, her cheeks flushed with color. "It

doesn't matter," she decided. "We agreed it shouldn't have happened."

"Did we?" he asked.

But before she could answer, he lowered his mouth to hers.

There was no hesitation in his kiss this time. This was no tentative exploration but an insistent demand.

And she responded. She couldn't help herself. The whole time she'd been packing, she'd been recounting all the reasons that getting tangled up with Wilder was a bad idea. But somehow, with his mouth moving over hers, those reasons didn't matter. Nothing mattered but the way she felt when she was in his arms.

Her lips parted to allow him to deepen the kiss; their tongues danced in a slow and seductive rhythm that made her heart pound and her body yearn. And oh, how she yearned to experience the thrill and satisfaction of his lovemaking again.

Except that what they'd shared wasn't lovemaking but sex—a purely physical coupling with no emotional attachment required or desired. And Beth wasn't very good at keeping her emotions detached. Her feelings for Wilder were already stronger and deeper than she was willing to acknowledge.

She eased her lips from his, reluctant but determined. "Didn't we agree that what happened before was a mistake?"

"We agreed that *you said* it was a mistake," he said. "But I think you're trying to convince yourself of that so it won't happen again."

"Of course, it won't happen again."

"Because you're not attracted to me?" he challenged.

Before she could respond to that, he lifted a hand to tuck a stray hair behind her ear, skimming his fingertip over the shell of her ear, making her tremble. He smiled, letting her know that her physical reaction had not gone unnoticed, so that if she tried to claim she wasn't attracted to him, he'd know she was lying.

"Because it wouldn't be smart," she said instead.

"Attraction is rarely based on logic," he said. "And I'm very definitely attracted to you, Beth."

She swallowed. "You are?"

"After the night we spent together, how can you even ask that question?"

"We had sex—once," she reminded him. "We didn't spend the night together."

"And that's my fault," he acknowledged. "I snuck out of your bed because I wanted to stay. Because I wanted more."

"You wanted more?" she asked, doubt and hope warring inside her.

"But I don't know that I'm capable of anything more," he confided. "And you're the kind of woman who deserves a lot more. You deserve to be loved—and I don't do love. I don't know that I can."

She sighed. "So where does that leave us?"

"I don't know. But I'd like to try to figure it out."

"This really is complicated, isn't it?"

He nodded. "And likely to get even more complicated when Leighton shows up."

"That's why I think I should go," she told him.

"Even if I want you to stay?" And then, before she could reply to that, he played his trump card: "Even if Cody wants you to stay?"

She huffed out a breath. "You fight dirty."

"I fight to win," he said, unapologetic.

"Leighton will fight back," she warned.

"Are you worried that you'll get caught in the crossfire?"

She shook her head. "I can take care of myself."

"I don't doubt it," he said sincerely. "You're one of the strongest women I've ever known."

She was taken aback by his matter-of-fact tone. "You really think so?"

"I do," he confirmed. "You are fierce and formidable."

"I think you've got me mixed up with someone else."

He shook his head. "*You* are an amazing woman, Beth Ames."

And the way he said it, the sincerity in his voice, almost made her believe it.

But if he truly believed it, why couldn't he love her? Was he truly incapable of falling in love, as he believed? Or was she not worthy of his love? And why was she even thinking about love after one night with a man she'd known for barely more than a week?

"You're just trying to sweet-talk me into staying so you won't have to do the middle-of-the-night feedings," she said, in an attempt to ease the seriousness of the moment.

"If you stay, I'll happily do the middle-of-the-night feedings," he promised.

"Okay," she finally relented. "I'll stay."

Beth was folding a load of laundry as she listened to Wilder read to Cody. Hearing the simple story of *Goodnight Moon* in the cowboy's deep voice, watching him point out the list of items in the great green room, warmed something deep inside her.

The ring of her cell came between "goodnight kittens" and "goodnight mittens," and though she didn't recognize the number, she connected the call immediately so the ringing wouldn't disturb the story.

"Hello?"

"Is this Lisbeth Ames?"

It wasn't until she heard the male voice and registered a

quick stab of disappointment that she realized she'd been hoping it might be her sister calling.

"Yes," she acknowledged, bracing herself for a sales pitch.

"Are you related to Leighton Ames?" the caller asked, surprising her again.

"Who is this?" she demanded.

"This is Sheriff Burke from Clearwater County," he said. "I'm afraid I've got some bad news."

"Clearwater County?" she echoed, preferring to latch onto that detail rather than contemplate the possibility of "bad news." "I'm sorry—I don't even know where that is."

"It's in Idaho, ma'am," he said patiently, as if giving her a moment to catch up. "I'm calling because there's been an accident and—"

"What kind of accident?" she interjected, suddenly chilled to the bone recalling that it had been the sheriff who showed up at the door when her parents were killed. "Has something happened to my sister?"

"Her car spun out on Harbinger Road and slid down an embankment."

"Ohmygod. Was she hurt? Is she at the hospital?"

"I'm sorry, Ms. Ames, but your sister suffered traumatic injuries in the crash and—" He paused to clear his throat. "She didn't make it."

"I don't understand, Sheriff. What do you mean?" she asked, her brain refusing to acknowledge and accept the meaning of his words.

If he was trying to tell her that her sister hadn't yet made it back to the Ambling A, she knew that already, because she was here and Leighton clearly wasn't.

"She emailed to tell me that she was on her way to Rust Creek Falls, to pick up Cody," Beth said, eager for him to understand how important it was that Leighton keep her promise. "He's only four and a half months old and he misses her like crazy."

"I'm sorry," the sheriff said again, sounding weary.

"Don't say you're sorry," Beth snapped at him. "Tell me when she's going to be here."

"Beth." She started at the sound of Wilder's voice, gentle but firm. "Give me the phone."

She shook her head, her fingers instinctively tightening on the device, desperately maintaining her grasp on this tenuous connection to the man who was talking to her about Leighton, wanting him to explain why her sister was late.

"Cody's ready for his nap," Wilder said. "Why don't you put him down while I talk to the sheriff?"

It sounded like a reasonable request. It made sense to her. Unlike the gibberish spouted by the sheriff.

And then Wilder cleverly shifted the sleepy baby into her arms, forcing her to relinquish her grip on the phone.

She started out of the room while he took over the call, introducing himself as a family friend.

As Beth carried her nephew up the stairs, the sheriff's words continued to echo in her head, but they still didn't make any sense to her.

Accident...injuries...sorry.

She was supposed to put Cody in his crib, so that he could sleep, but for some reason, she couldn't let him go. Instead, she lowered herself into the rocking chair and snuggled him close.

The baby rubbed his face against her shoulder—a telltale indicator that he was fighting sleep. She touched her lips to the top of his head as she rocked him gently, and his eyes drifted shut.

A few minutes later, she heard the slow, steady rhythm of Wilder's footsteps on the stairs. Then he appeared in the doorway, where he remained for a long moment as if uncertain what to say or do, before crossing the room and gently removing the sleeping baby from her arms.

When Cody was settled in his crib, Wilder returned to crouch by the rocking chair.

"Hey," he said.

She couldn't respond. Her throat was too tight for any words to squeeze through. He lifted his hands to cup her face, his thumbs brushing away tears she hadn't realized she was crying.

He straightened up again, lifting her from the chair as he did so, then taking the seat and settling her in his lap, cuddling her as she'd cuddled Cody.

She wanted to protest that she was too big to be held like a baby, but it felt good to be in his arms. As the strength and warmth of his embrace penetrated the ice that had encased her body, she began to tremble.

He tightened his hold as silent tears continued to spill down her cheeks. But he didn't say anything, because what was there to say?

"I want to wake up and discover it was only a bad dream, that there was no phone call from the sheriff of—" she sighed "—where did he say he was from?"

"Clearwater County."

"Do you think it's possible they made a mistake?" she asked, grasping for any explanation other than the one she knew in her heart to be true. "Maybe Leighton's car was stolen and—"

"She identified herself to the paramedics when they first arrived on scene," Wilder said. "And the sheriff confirmed that she had a constellation tattoo."

"But Leighton doesn't have a tattoo," Beth said.

"Actually, she does," he told her, a reminder that he'd been intimately acquainted with her sister's naked body. "The Leo constellation, in the middle of her back, between her shoulder blades."

"Oh." Leo was her sister's Zodiac sign. "So it really was her? She really is…gone?"

He nodded. "I'm sorry, Beth."

She was sorry, too. And sad and angry and filled with so many more emotions that she couldn't begin to identify.

But somehow she felt empty, too.

Her sister was gone.

Not on a whim.

Not for a while.

Forever.

"I need to make arrangements," she realized. "But I have no idea where to begin, what she'd want."

She was silent for a minute, trying to focus through the grief to think. "Her friends are in Dallas. Our parents are buried there."

And suddenly the answer was obvious: "I have to go home."

Chapter Fifteen

Wilder must have told his family about the call from the sheriff and Beth's plan to return to Texas to arrange her sister's funeral, because the next morning, when she was packing her car, they were all there.

She had tears in her eyes as she said goodbye to Wilder's brothers and sisters-in-law, present and future. She tried to return Avery's jacket, but the expectant mom told her to hold onto it for the journey home, since she wouldn't be able to wear it for the next few months anyway.

Everyone took turns hugging her, expressing their condolences, and promising to see her again soon. Obviously they were assuming she'd bring Cody back to visit. Or maybe she'd be the one coming back to visit Cody, if Wilder followed through on his plan to apply for legal custody of the baby after he had the results of the DNA test.

Over the past ten days, he'd proven that he was more than capable of being the father Cody needed. Equally important, at least from her perspective, was the support of his family. And Beth knew her nephew would be lucky to be part of the close-knit and loving Crawford family.

But she couldn't think about that now. She'd barely processed losing her sister—she couldn't bear to consider that her nephew might be taken from her, too.

It had been a long time since she'd been part of a family. Since the death of their parents almost ten years earlier, Beth and Leighton had only had one another to rely on. Though she'd hoped that reality would bring them closer, there remained a distance that she hadn't been able to breach. And now she never would.

She wished her sister had called instead of emailing. She would have liked to have spoken to her one last time. To tell her that she loved her, no matter what.

"Damn, it's quiet in here," Max remarked, when he entered the house at the end of the day.

Wilder nodded. "I thought the same thing when I came in."

"And there's nothing cooking in the oven for dinner, is there?"

"Not unless you put something in there. And if you did, you forgot to turn on the heat."

Max shook his head. "You want to go to the Ace to grab a burger?"

"Not really," Wilder admitted.

"You have to eat."

"I'm not feeling very sociable," he said. Truthfully, he wasn't feeling very hungry, either.

"Want to tell me what you are feeling?" Max prompted.

"Really? You want me to talk about my feelings?" Wilder asked skeptically.

His father shrugged. "I know I'm probably not your first choice of confidant, but I'm the only one left here."

And it was a testament to how raw his emotions were that Wilder found himself opening up. "I'm mad at her," he admitted.

"Who? Beth?"

"Leighton."

"Well, there's no point in being angry with a dead woman," Max said bluntly.

"I know," he acknowledged. "And yet—I can't deny that's how I feel."

"Why are you mad at her?"

"Where to begin?"

"At the beginning?" his father suggested.

He sighed. "Okay, I'm mad that she never even reached out to tell me that she was pregnant."

"Understandable," Max agreed.

"And then, after not telling me that she was pregnant and not telling me she had a baby, she just drops him at my door and expects me to take care of him."

"That's one way to look at it," his father allowed. "Another is that she trusted you to take care of him."

Wilder just shook his head. "I don't think I'll ever understand how a woman who supposedly loves her child could walk away from him."

There was a long silence as his father considered his response—or maybe he, too, was thinking of another woman who'd done the same thing.

"Are we still talking about Leighton?" Max asked.

"Of course," Wilder said.

Because he and his brothers had learned a long time ago that asking questions about their mother only resulted in upsetting their father.

"Not every woman is cut out to be a mother," Max said now.

"So why would she assume that I could do any better at parenting? And if she needed a break, why didn't she leave Cody with his aunt? Anyone with eyes can see how much she dotes on the little guy."

"You have enough siblings to know that those relationships are never simple," his father pointed out.

"It just doesn't make any sense to me," Wilder told him.

"Is that all?"

"What do you mean?"

"I think you need to consider why you're as outraged

on Beth's behalf as you are about everything else," Max suggested.

"And why do you think that is?" he asked, because it was apparent his father had already arrived at his own conclusions.

So he was more than a little surprised when Max shook his head and said, "That's something you need to figure out for yourself."

When Beth got back to Dallas, she drove straight to the funeral home. After she'd signed the paperwork and paid the bill—which pretty much depleted her savings account—she automatically turned her vehicle in the direction of her condo.

Only as she was getting Cody ready for bed did it occur to her that he might have been more comfortable in his crib at home rather than the portable playpen he slept in when he stayed with her. But she couldn't go to her sister's apartment. Not tonight. Not knowing that Leighton was never coming home again.

She blinked back the tears that burned her eyes as she snuggled with Cody on the sofa in the living room. She didn't know if he sensed her tension or if he'd spent too many hours in his car seat over the past two days, but he seemed as wired as she felt. Though it was well past his bedtime, his eyes remained stubbornly open and fixed on her.

"I don't know what to say to you," she admitted. "How to explain what I don't understand myself. But what I can tell you, with absolute certainty, is that your mama loved you. She might have been uncertain about a lot of things, but there's no doubt she loved you with her whole heart."

Cody couldn't possibly make any sense of what she was saying, but perhaps he understood that she needed him as much as he needed her. He laid his head on her shoulder, rubbing his cheek against her shirt as he snuggled in. He exhaled a shuddery sigh, his breath warm against her throat.

By the time she finally got him settled and crawled into her own bed, she was completely drained—physically and emotionally—but sleep eluded her. She couldn't help wondering what she might have done differently so that her sister might have made different choices along the line. Or even just one different choice so that she wouldn't have been behind the wheel on that icy patch of an unfamiliar road so far away from home.

Logically, she knew it wasn't her fault. Leighton had always made her own choices, and quite often risky ones. But now, because of her choices, Cody was going to grow up without his mother.

She would have to talk to Wilder about his plans, but since receiving the call from the sheriff, she'd been focused on doing what she needed to do for her sister. There would be plenty of time, after Leighton was finally laid to rest, to worry about custody of her nephew.

But she already knew in her heart that she wouldn't fight Wilder if he decided that he wanted to raise Cody on the Ambling A. Not just because that was a fight she knew she wouldn't win, but because she knew that Cody needed a father—and Wilder deserved the opportunity to raise his son.

Ranching was both exhausting and satisfying, and it wasn't often that the activity in Max's mind overruled the weariness of his body. But tonight, he couldn't stop thinking about the conversation he'd had with Wilder, the questions his son had asked about his mother—without admitting that he was asking about Sheila.

Max rarely let himself question the choices he'd made

in his life, but he had doubts now and they were keeping him awake when he really needed to sleep.

Had he done his kids a disservice by letting them believe their mother had chosen to walk away from them, choosing her lover over her family?

He'd been so hurt to learn of her affair. Furious with Sheila, devastated by her betrayal, he'd lashed out at her. She'd chosen someone else over him, and all he could think about was hurting her the way she'd hurt him.

And Logan, Hunter, Xander, Finn, Knox and Wilder had all been casualties in the battle between the two people who should have put their children's needs above all else.

Love truly was a double-edged sword, and his children had been cut deeply. Thankfully, time—and love—had healed their wounds. Of course, Max liked to think that his decision to bring them to Rust Creek Falls for a fresh start had played a part, too. And for his five oldest sons, it had.

But Wilder was still guarding his heart. Not that anyone who didn't know him as well as his father would see it. To the rest of the world, he was just another cowboy blessed with effortless charm and a cocky grin. Only Max knew how much hurt hid behind his smile and why he didn't let anyone get too close.

Watching his youngest son with his son had given Max hope that Wilder's shields were starting to come down. No matter how much he tried to hold back, he couldn't resist responding to the child's sweetness and innocence.

The child's aunt had made a connection with the reluctant daddy, too. And not the kind of superficial connection that Wilder was famous for, but something real and deep and meaningful. But now Beth was gone, and Cody with her, and Wilder's defenses weren't just back in place but actively being reinforced.

Which left Max with no choice. He was going to have

to tell him the truth. He was going to have to fess up to all his sons.

But he had to start with Wilder.

Wilder stumbled into the kitchen on a mission for one thing: coffee. He'd slept like crap for the past two nights—and no, he wasn't blind to the fact that was the same number of nights that Beth and Cody had been gone.

Not surprisingly, his father was there before him, sitting at the table with a steaming mug of coffee in his hands. Max waited until Wilder had poured himself a mug and taken a long swallow before he spoke.

"We need to talk."

"Can it wait?" Wilder asked. "I promised to ride out with Logan today. He thinks there've been coyotes prowling around the northern boundary."

"No, it can't wait," his father said. "It's already waited too long."

Wilder's brows rose in response to the cryptic comment. "Okay…so what is it that you think we need to talk about?"

"I'm worried about you," Max said. "That you've closed yourself off from the possibility of finding love."

"Seriously? That's what you want to talk about right now? Didn't we discuss enough touchy-feely stuff the other day?"

"This is important," his father insisted.

"I know my brothers all falling in love has created some kind of wedding fever, but just because I'm not in a hurry to follow in their footsteps doesn't mean I've closed myself off," he said.

"This has nothing to do with your brothers," Max told him. "Don't get me wrong—I'm overjoyed with the recent and future additions to our family, but right now I'm focused on you."

"Well, you don't need to focus on me," he said. "I'm fine. I'm happy. Life is good."

"So why did you let Beth take Cody away just when you were finally starting to connect with him?"

Wilder frowned. "I let Beth take Cody because she was going home to bury her sister—Cody's mother—and that little boy is the only family she has left."

"That little boy is your family, too."

"Did the DNA results come when I wasn't here?"

"I don't need a piece of paper to know Cody's your son," his father insisted.

"Well, I promised Beth that no decisions would be made about Cody's future until we had the results. So if we're done here, I'm going to—"

"We're not done." Max scrubbed his hands over his face and sighed wearily. "Not even close."

Wilder refilled his mug, because something in his dad's demeanor warned him that he was going to need it.

"I know Cody's situation struck a nerve with you because you think he was abandoned the same way you were abandoned."

"The coincidence is hard to ignore," he acknowledged.

"Except that your mother didn't abandon you."

Wilder wished the caffeine would kick-start his tired body and sluggish brain so that he could keep up with his father's thought processes. "One day she was there and the next day she was gone—what would you call it?"

"She didn't leave you and your brothers…she left me."

"She left *all of us*."

Max shook his head. "She planned to find a place of her own and then she was going to move out and take you kids with her."

Wilder swallowed another mouthful of coffee. "And yet that never happened."

"No," his father agreed. "I asked her not to go. I didn't

understand why she was so unhappy in our marriage, but I offered to go to marriage counseling. I promised to change.

"But she knew me better than I knew myself," Max acknowledged. "She called my bluff. We had one session with a couples' therapist and it was a complete waste of time."

"I can only imagine," Wilder said dryly.

"I was the same man she claimed to have fallen in love with, so I didn't understand what had changed, why she'd fallen out of love with me.

"I blamed her. She'd grown up out East, living a life of wealth and privilege. And while we were well enough off, she didn't know how hard I needed to work to ensure the ranch remained successful." His father stared into the bottom of his empty coffee mug. "But it was my fault. I wasn't a very good husband. I was so busy working the ranch, I didn't think about the fact that she was alone in the house taking care of six kids. I only cared that she was there for me when I came in at the end of the day.

"When your four oldest brothers went off to school, she started taking you and Knox into town for a story time program at the library. She said it would help you both develop social skills and make friends, but it was Sheila who met someone.

"Every week, after story time, she'd stop by the little café next door. That's where she met him. He was the owner of the café, and they became friends—at least that's what she told me. But over time, their friendship grew into love."

Wilder didn't know how to respond to any of this. He could only imagine how distraught Max had been to discover that his wife was in love with another man.

"And she told me that she couldn't stay married to me when she was in love with someone else."

In his father's words, Wilder heard not just bitterness

and anger but the heartache that remained after so many years. Because while no one would ever deny that Maximilian Crawford could be a real son of a bitch, there was also no doubting that he'd deeply and sincerely loved his wife.

"So I told her she was free to go," his dad confided now. "But no way in hell was she taking my sons."

"And she chose her lover over her family," Wilder concluded.

But Max shook his head. "She said that she loved him, but she would never love anyone more than her children."

"But she left," he said again.

"She left," his father confirmed. "Because I told her to get out. I sent her away."

"Why?"

Max pushed away from the table to refill his mug of coffee. "Because I loved her and she didn't love me back. Because I was selfish and angry and hurt. Because I wanted to hurt her the way she'd hurt me."

"Why didn't you ever tell us this before?" he asked, when his father was seated at the table again.

"Because I was afraid, if you boys knew the truth…"

"If we knew the truth *what*?" Wilder pressed.

"I was afraid you'd blame me," Max acknowledged. "And you should—because it was my fault. Even when I sent her away, I knew I was acting out of anger and spite and that I'd probably regret the things I said and did. But I always thought there'd be a chance to make things right."

"Then she died," Wilder said. Not that he remembered anything from that time, but he'd been told about her sudden passing soon after the divorce papers were signed.

His father nodded. "Then she died—and it was too late to undo what I'd done. And what was the point in telling you the truth then?"

"What was the point?" he asked incredulously. "Maybe

the point was that we'd know the truth rather than thinking she didn't want us."

"You're right," his dad agreed. "But it was hard enough, living with my own guilt. I couldn't bear having to live with my sons' anger and hate."

"You should have told us," Wilder said.

Max nodded again. "I've had plenty of time to think about the choices I made," he confided. "To regret the things I said and did. It was my fault she left. My fault you grew up without a mom." He looked up then, pinning Wilder with his gaze. "My fault you haven't let yourself open your heart because you don't trust a woman to stick around."

"I know you like to think you can control everything, Dad," Wilder said dryly, "but not even you can make me fall in love or not fall in love."

Max's expression wasn't unsympathetic as he shook his head. "And you're so determined to keep your heart closed off, you can't even see that you've already fallen."

Chapter Sixteen

Wilder stood on the porch and watched the white van disappear down the driveway. Only when it was gone from sight did he turn his attention to the envelope with the purple logo of the DNA Testing Center in the upper left corner.

This was it: the moment of truth.

When he opened the flap and read the results, he would know for certain that he was Cody's father—or that he wasn't. There would be no more questions or uncertainty.

He'd been waiting for this moment for twelve days, anxious and impatient for the knowledge he finally held in his hand.

So why was he suddenly so apprehensive?

Was he afraid that the results would confirm he was the little boy's father?

Certainly, when Hunter had first read Leighton's note aloud, Wilder had been blindsided by her accusation. He hadn't wanted to believe it, because if it was true, his life would change in ways he wasn't ready for it to change.

But somehow, over the span of less than two weeks with Cody, he'd realized that he was ready for it to change. Maybe, as Beth suggested, he was even ready to embrace fatherhood not as an obligation but an opportunity.

And now he didn't want that opportunity to be taken away. He didn't want to discover that there was no biological link between him and the little boy who'd already taken hold of his heart.

He was still angry with Leighton for abandoning her child. And now that she was gone, he'd never get answers to all the questions he had. But if it turned out that Cody was his child, too, he would forever be grateful to her for giving him the chance to be the little boy's father.

But what about Beth? What would the paternity results mean for her relationship with her nephew?

She would always be Cody's aunt, but as she'd pointed out to Wilder on her first day at the Ambling A, her life was in Dallas. And if he was Cody's father, he'd want to raise him here, in Rust Creek Falls.

But maybe—

He shook his head, dismissing the thought before it had a chance to fully form. There was no point in speculating about possibilities or imagining happy endings that he knew weren't in his future. Because she was a woman who deserved a lot more than he was capable of giving. She deserved love, and he didn't do love.

Except that he did love Cody. And the way his mind and heart had been preoccupied with missing Beth, he suspected that he was starting to fall for her, too.

Starting? A voice mocked inside his head.

He ignored the voice and tore open the flap of the envelope.

His fingers trembled as he pulled out the single sheet of paper.

"DNA Test Result" was printed in bold letters at the top. Beneath it was a chart with columns of numbers that didn't mean anything to him. He scrolled further down and finally found what he was looking for: Probability of Paternity.

He didn't realize he was crying until the numbers blurred in front of his eyes.

Blinking away the tears, he refolded the page and slid it back into the envelope.

* * *

The whole time that Beth was in Rust Creek Falls, she'd looked forward to the day that she could take Cody home. At no time had she imagined that it would be for her sister's funeral.

Four days after that fateful call from the sheriff of Clearwater County, her head and her heart were still reeling from the tragic and premature death of her sister. But as much as she grieved for Leighton, she grieved even more for Leighton's baby.

But she pushed those heavy thoughts to the back of her mind for another day. Today was about Leighton, and Beth was trying to focus on celebrating her sister's life rather than mourning her death. Thinking about what would happen next—

No, she couldn't do it.

One day at a time.

That was her new motto, and today was all she could handle right now. Or maybe more than she could handle. But she would get through it, because she had no other option.

You're one of the strongest women I've ever known... fierce and formidable.

Though she'd doubted the veracity of Wilder's words when he'd spoken them to her, she called on them to sustain her now. Because she knew she was going to need every ounce of that purported strength today.

Though Cody was too young to understand what was happening, she took him to the funeral home for the early visitation. She believed it was important for him to be there, to have a last chance to say goodbye. He'd held up pretty well. It was Beth who'd cried like a baby when she put Cody's Christmas gift to his mom—the still-wrapped "Mommy" ornament—in Leighton's hand inside the coffin.

But then she'd pulled herself together, dabbed some

concealer on the dark circles under her eyes, swiped some mascara over her lashes and slicked some gloss on her lips. Not because she cared how she looked, but because she could hear the echo of her sister's voice telling her that she should care how she looked, and she knew Leighton would appreciate that she'd made the effort.

After the first visitation was over, Beth took Cody back to her condo. Moira Owen—her neighbor across the hall—had offered to watch him for the afternoon, and she was grateful for the help. Though Moira had no kids of her own, her job as an auditor for a multinational corporation meant she was a stickler for details, and Beth knew her neighbor would ensure that the baby was fed and played with and read to and put down for a nap precisely on schedule.

As for the details of her own life, she'd already been in contact with her principal, and Rebecca had told her to take whatever time she needed to get Cody settled. Beth appreciated the offer and understanding, but she wanted to get back to the comfort of her own routines as soon as possible. She needed to be busy so she wouldn't dwell on the loss of her sister—or think about Wilder.

In the three days since she'd left Rust Creek Falls, she hadn't heard a single word from him. Well, aside from the OK he'd sent in reply to her text message telling him that she and Cody had arrived safely in Dallas.

It had now been thirteen days since the cheek swabs were sent off to the lab, and she expected that he'd have the results by now. But if he did, he hadn't shared them with her.

One day at a time, she reminded herself, as she returned to the funeral home to greet those who'd come to remember her sister. Several gathered in groups, sharing stories and memories and offering comfort to one another. Beth didn't know most of them—more proof that she'd existed on the periphery of Leighton's life. And though she would always regret that they hadn't been closer, she was pleased to know that her sister had so many people in her life who cared about her.

Glancing at the clock, she felt a niggle of unease as she tried to remember if she'd given Moira directions on how to prepare Cody's cereal. Maybe she could slip out to make a quick call…

The rest of the thought faded away when he walked through the door.

Wilder.

Her heart skipped a beat, then raced.

She'd wondered if he might show up. After all, he'd had a close and personal relationship with her sister—at least for a while. On the other hand, seventeen hundred miles seemed a long way to travel to say a final goodbye to a woman he hadn't seen in more than a year.

But maybe there was another reason he'd decided to make the trip. Maybe he did get the results of the DNA test and had confirmed that Cody was his child. And maybe, when he returned to Montana again, he intended to take his son with him.

That was something she definitely couldn't think about right now or she'd completely lose it.

"Hey," he said.

"Hi." She stood there awkwardly, not knowing whether to offer her hand or initiate a hug.

He made the decision for her, wrapping his arms around her and drawing her close. And during that all too brief moment, she felt such a sense of peace she wished she could stay in his arms forever.

But of course she couldn't. So she eased away and said, "It was nice of you to come all this way to pay your respects."

"I didn't come only for Leighton," he said. "I came for you, too."

His admission had her fighting against a fresh surge of emotion. "Why?"

"Because I didn't want you to be alone today."

Her eyes filled with tears then, but she refused to let them fall. "Thank you," she said, sincerely touched.

"How are you holding up?"

"I'm doing okay," she said.

"Of course, you are. Because who would keep everything together if you fell apart?" he mused.

"Believe me, I've had my moments."

She turned automatically to shake hands and exchange a few words with another visitor she didn't know, before shifting her attention back to Wilder.

"You got the test results," she guessed.

"Let's talk about that later," he suggested.

She nodded, because he was right—this wasn't the time or the place. And really, didn't she already know what the results were? The only question now was what Wilder intended to do, and that was definitely better left until later.

"Cody was here earlier," she said, certain he had to be wondering about the baby's whereabouts. "But I didn't think he needed to make the trip to the cemetery, so he's with my neighbor now. Plus, you know how cranky he gets if he misses a nap."

"Yeah." Wilder smiled. "I do know."

"But he's sleeping almost through the night now," she said.

"Are *you*?" he asked gently.

She just shook her head as the minister took his place at the podium. Wilder linked their hands and guided her to the front row, while the other mourners took seats around them.

She hadn't realized how much she dreaded having to

get through the service on her own until he was there and she was no longer alone.

Afterward, they rode together to the cemetery, then Wilder took her back to the funeral home where she'd left her vehicle.

"Do you want to come back to my place?" she asked, and immediately felt hot color rush into her cheeks. "I didn't mean that to sound like I was propositioning you."

"I didn't interpret it as a proposition," he said, then winked. "Unfortunately."

"I only meant that I'm sure you want to see Cody," she explained.

"I do," he confirmed. "But I'll come by in a couple hours, if that's okay. I've got a few things I need to do first."

"I'll see you in a couple hours then."

Beth had to buzz him into the building, so when the knock finally sounded on her door, she expected to find Wilder on the other side. Instead, she found Santa.

Though she couldn't have imagined anything would make her smile today, she felt her lips curve as she stood back to allow him entry. "You're a long way from the North Pole."

Her visitor responded with a hearty: "Ho! Ho! Ho!"

She lifted a brow. "And isn't Santa usually on holidays this time of year?"

"Usually," he agreed. "But Cody was out of town on Christmas Eve, so I had to take all his presents back to the North Pole with me. And then yesterday, Tracker—the elf who keeps track of all the good little girls and boys—told me that I could find Cody here."

"Tracker?" she echoed, amused by his elaborate narrative.

"Just go with it," he urged in a stage whisper.

"Well, Tracker was right," Beth confirmed. "Cody is here."

She led "Santa" to the living room, where the baby was propped up by a pillow on the floor, gnawing on the paw of the teddy bear that was one of the gifts she'd given to him at the Ambling A.

"Ho! Ho! Ho! Merry Christmas in January," Santa said.

Cody's eyes grew wide and wary as he looked at the stranger in the red suit, then his lower lip began to quiver.

"I should have reminded you that he slept through his visit with Saint Nick when I took him to the mall," Beth said. "So this is the first time he's actually seen Santa."

And if the terrified look in his eyes was any indication, Cody wasn't too impressed.

Sensing that a meltdown was imminent, Santa immediately pulled off his wig and beard, revealing his true identity to the little boy. "Hey, buddy."

Cody's lip stopped quivering and he offered a tentative smile, showing off his two teeth.

Wilder dropped his bag of presents onto the floor and picked up the baby. "I can't believe how much I missed this little guy," he confided to Beth.

"He missed you, too."

"How about you?" he asked. "Did you miss me?"

She was reluctant to answer the question. She didn't want to admit how very much she'd missed him, how much her heart ached whenever she thought about him—which was pretty much constantly. "Maybe," she said instead. "A little."

"Just a little, huh?" He sounded disappointed. "I missed you a lot from the moment you were gone—and then a little bit more each day."

She was surprised by his admission. "You did?"

He nodded. "As the youngest of six brothers raised by a single dad, I sometimes struggle to find the right words to express how I'm feeling," he confided to her now. "At other times, I struggle to even acknowledge that I have feelings.

"But I can't deny the way I feel about you any longer. I don't want to deny my feelings. I want a life with you, Beth. I want you and me and Cody to be together. A family."

It was what she wanted, too. More than anything. But she was afraid to trust that his feelings—and her own—were real. "We've only known each other a couple of weeks," she reminded him. "And our whole relationship, if it could even be called a relationship, revolved around Cody."

"Not our whole relationship," he said pointedly.

She knew he was referring to New Year's Eve—the night they'd enjoyed a very small and intimate celebration together—and she felt her cheeks flush with color. But as fabulous as that night had been, and as much as she might want to repeat it—over and over again—he was the one who'd told her that he didn't do relationships, that he wasn't capable of falling in love.

So this apparent turnaround was a little too sudden and abrupt to be believable. No matter how much she wanted to believe. Which led her to another, more logical conclusion. "I can appreciate that you're probably reeling from the DNA results," she said. "And now you're looking for someone to take care of your son, and I'm the obvious choice because—"

Wilder shook his head, cutting her off. "You have some serious insecurities, don't you?" he asked, seeming sincerely baffled by her speculation.

She shrugged. "Leighton was the beautiful one, the fun one," she said, though she doubted he needed the reminder. "I was always the other one."

"Leighton was beautiful and fun, and we had some good times together," he acknowledged. "But I was never in love with your sister."

She blinked, not sure she understood what he was saying.

"You, Lisbeth, are just as beautiful and just as much fun. You are also warm and kind, generous and loving, and I am head over heels in love with you."

For a long minute, she could only stare at him, stunned by his declaration. "You love me?"

"I love you, Lisbeth Ames," he confirmed.

"I didn't even think you *liked* me all that much."

He smiled. "I had some reservations at first, as I know you did about me, too."

She couldn't deny that was true.

"But over the past couple of weeks, everything changed. *You* changed everything for me," he told her. "And I can't imagine my life without you and Cody in it. Because, as it turns out, I've fallen head over heels for the little guy, too."

"I'm still waiting for you to confirm that you got the DNA results," she told him.

"I got them. And when I finally had the envelope in hand, I knew that whatever was written on the page didn't matter as much as what was in my heart." He looked at the baby in his arms. "And in my heart, Cody was already mine. The lab report only confirmed it."

She smiled then, her heart overflowing with happiness for her nephew and his daddy.

"You know, now would be a good time to tell me that you love me, too…if you do," Wilder said.

She lifted her gaze to his, so he would see in her eyes the truth that filled her heart. "I do love you, Wilder Crawford."

He kissed her then, long and slow and sweet.

And just when Beth had decided that she would be happy to go on kissing him forever, he eased his mouth from hers and said, "Now it's time for Cody's second first Christmas."

"Second first Christmas?" she asked, amused.

"Well, I didn't have any presents for him when you celebrated his first Christmas, so I brought these," he said, dumping the contents of the bag onto the floor.

She looked at the assortment of presents—small ones and big ones, hard ones and squishy ones—then at the man in the Santa suit. "Did you buy out The Toy Box?" she asked, referring to the local specialty store.

He grinned. "Not entirely."

"And you said I went overboard."

He shrugged, unrepentant. "I think I'm entitled to go a little overboard for my son's first Christmas."

"I think so, too," she agreed.

They both knelt on the floor to help Cody open his gifts. There were wooden puzzles and more books, a cuddly octopus learning toy, a ball that flashed colored lights, a miniature piano, a set of maracas, a drum, a xylophone and a tambourine.

"Are you trying to turn him into a one-baby band?" Beth teased.

"I read that there's a strong correlation between music and brain development," he explained.

"Was that in the book?" she asked, echoing the same question he'd once asked her.

"There isn't one book that's the authority on everything," he said, echoing her response. "And every baby is different."

"But most parents would probably agree that they're more interested in boxes and bows than presents at this age," she said, noting how intently Cody was focused on the shiny green bow in his hand.

"There's one more," Wilder said, setting the last small square box on the floor in front of her. "For you."

"For me?" Her heart pounded inside her chest as she tore off the paper to reveal a velvet jeweler's box. With unsteady hands, she opened the lid to reveal a dazzling diamond solitaire.

She lifted her stunned gaze from the ring to find Wilder watching her. His expression was intent, serious—and just a little bit uncertain.

He cleared his throat. "Maybe it's too soon," he allowed. "But—"

"No," she quickly interjected, shaking her head.

"No?" he echoed.

His bleak tone and grim expression immediately alerted her to his misinterpretation of her response.

"No, it's not too soon," she hastened to clarify. "But you can't just hand a woman a ring—you have to ask the question."

"Oh." He released an audible sigh of relief. "Okay, I can do that," he said. "Beth Ames, will you—"

"Yes," she said, interjecting again.

He chuckled softly and slid the ring on her finger. "A perfect fit—just like you and me and Cody."

Epilogue

Five months later

"I now pronounce you husband and wife." The minister nodded to the groom. "You may kiss your bride."

Wilder didn't need to be told twice. He lowered his head and touched his mouth to Beth's, lingering for just a moment—sealing their vows, promising his heart.

Then they turned to face their guests, and the bride lifted her skirt just enough to show off the cowboy boots she'd donned beneath her wedding gown. There were chuckles mixed in with the applause then, and the happy couple joined hands to exit along the aisle of their makeshift outdoor chapel—pausing first at the front row of chairs so the groom could take his now ten-month-old son from the boy's grandfather.

As Beth and Wilder mingled with their guests, she couldn't help but reflect on how much had changed in her life in just six months. And although she still missed her sister every day, she took comfort in knowing that Leighton lived on in her little boy, who demonstrated more and more each day that he had his mother's happy disposition and his father's effortless charm.

Those traits had been on full display as he enchanted the guests who'd come to the Ambling A for the wedding of his biological father to his maternal aunt. And there were a lot of guests. In addition to Wilder's immediate family and all the distant Rust Creek Falls Crawford relatives, there were Daltons, Traubs, Stocktons, Joneses and O'Reillys. Beth had heard more names today than she could ever be expected to remember, but she was happy to be starting a life and raising Cody in this close-knit community—even if it meant a wedding reception far bigger than she'd ever anticipated.

Thankfully the whole day had been planned with meticulous attention to detail by Vivienne Dalton, who continued to circulate to ensure that everything went according to plan. Her only failing was an inability to corral Hunter's seven-year-old daughter. Wren kept returning to the chapel to practice walking down the aisle and tossing flower petals, in preparation for her very important role as flower girl when her daddy finally married Merry in only a few more weeks.

After a delicious meal—interrupted by countless toasts to the happy couple—the bride and groom shared their first dance. As the song drew to a close, the rest of the guests were invited to join them, and Beth was pleased to see each of Wilder's brothers on the floor with their partners. Even Finn and Avery were dancing, having enlisted Max to keep an eye on their beautiful three-month-old daughter, Mabel.

Of course, the proud grandpa was happy to have his arms full of babies. And Wren, finally satisfied that she'd had sufficient practice being a flower girl, was helping mind her younger cousins.

When the bride and groom took a reprieve from dancing and returned to their table with Cody, Beth found an obviously old but beautiful jewel-encrusted book beside her bouquet.

"What's this?" she asked, as Cody reached out to touch the sparkly stones on the cover.

"My brothers believe it's Josiah Abernathy's diary," Wilder said, and proceeded to give her a brief history of the book and the writer's forbidden love affair with a mysterious woman.

"But why is it here?" she wondered.

"They've been passing it around for months, claiming it carries a love spell or something like that. I guess they've decided it's our turn to experience its powers."

"All true," Merry confirmed, as she joined them. "But there's more—a note hidden inside the cover confirmed the mystery writer as Josiah Abernathy and his girlfriend as Winona Cobbs.

"Even more shocking," she continued, as the rest of Wilder's siblings and their spouses gathered around, "is that their baby girl wasn't stillborn, as she believed. Beatrix was taken away and given to another family to raise."

A revelation that led to much speculation about whether it might be possible to find Beatrix after so much time had passed.

"This is all very fascinating," Wilder said, speaking quietly so that only his bride could hear him. "But what I really want to know is when we can steal away from this party."

"You're not having a good time?" she asked, surprised.

"The wedding was great," he acknowledged. "But now, Mrs. Crawford, I'm more than ready to start the honeymoon."

She tipped her head back to smile at him. "I like the sound of that, Mr. Crawford."

As if on cue, their wedding planner stepped up beside them to ask, "What are you still doing here when the honeymoon suite at Maverick Manor is waiting for you?"

"We're on our way," Wilder said. "We just wanted to thank you for giving us the perfect day."

"Well, I did have a little help from Mother Nature," Vivienne said, gesturing to the sun setting against a cloudless sky. "But I'm happy to take credit for all the rest."

"If only you'd had as much success as a matchmaker," Logan said to her.

"I think I did pretty well helping you and your brothers find your perfect matches."

"What are you talking about?" Xander asked. "We found our own matches."

Vivienne smiled. "Did you?"

The brothers exchanged puzzled glances.

"I might not have introduced Logan and Sarah, but they met at my office," she pointed out. "And Xander and Lily only got together because I'd set up a date between Knox and Lily, then Knox rushed to marry Genevieve because he didn't want any part of Max's scheme. I also knew Finn and Avery would be perfect together, even if I didn't know they'd already found one another, and it was because they were getting married that Hunter decided to hire a nanny and fell in love with Merry."

Wilder nodded his agreement. "It looks like you did have a hand in five out of six matches," he said to Vivienne.

"I might have found someone for you, too," she told him. "Except that you managed to find your perfect match without any help."

"Actually, *I* found *him*," Beth said, making her husband smile.

"Five out of six is an impressive stat," Finn acknowledged. "But still short of Max's target."

"And nothing less than one hundred percent is ever good enough for Maximilian Crawford," Knox remarked.

"I think I could make a case for six out of seven," the wedding planner–slash–matchmaker said, nodding toward the dance floor where the groom's father was slow dancing with the woman Wilder recognized from New Year's Eve.

"Who's that?" Beth asked, because she hadn't been at the party at Maverick Manor.

"Estelle, my former boss," Vivienne told them.

"I thought she moved to Phoenix," Lily remarked.

"And then she came back. She said she enjoyed the

more temperate climate, but planning funerals was as depressing as hell."

"Dad seems completely smitten with her," Logan remarked, apparently baffled that such a tiny woman could have captivated the larger-than-life cattleman.

"She's got a personality equal to his own," Vivienne assured him. "And Max is so happy with the way things worked out for everyone that he's agreed to honor the terms of our original contract. As a result, we'll be able to fix the roof at Sawmill Station *and* invest more money in the Thunder Canyon operation. Plus, with the way business is booming, I'm thinking of hiring extra help in Rust Creek Falls, too."

"What kind of experience is needed to work in the wedding planning business?" Beth wondered, her curiosity piqued.

"Are you looking for a job?" Vivienne asked hopefully.

"I am," the bride confirmed. "And there are no teaching positions currently available at the local elementary school."

"Do you believe in happy endings?"

Beth looked up at her new husband, and the love that filled her heart to overflowing shone through her eyes. "I do now."

Vivienne smiled. "That's a good start."

Cody apparently thought so, too, because he clapped his hands together.

Wilder's chuckle drew the little boy's attention to him. Then Cody reached his arms up toward his daddy and said his first word: "Da-da."

And Beth thought that was the perfect ending to a perfect day—and a very happy beginning for the start of their life together as a family.

* * * * *

COMING SOON!

We really hope you enjoyed reading this book.
If you're looking for more romance
be sure to head to the shops when
new books are available on

Thursday 20th November

To see which titles are coming soon, please visit

millsandboon.co.uk/nextmonth